The End of Baseball

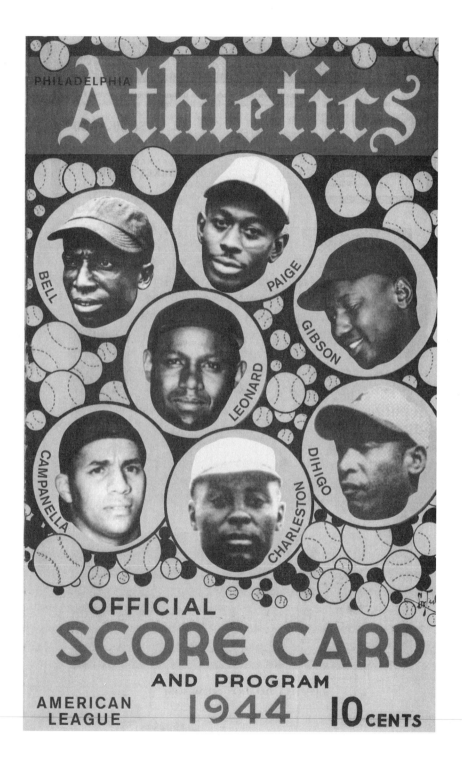

PHILADELPHIA

Athletics

BELL · PAIGE · GIBSON · LEONARD · CAMPANELLA · CHARLESTON · DIHIGO

OFFICIAL
SCORE CARD
AND PROGRAM

AMERICAN LEAGUE · 1944 · 10 CENTS

The End of Baseball

A NOVEL

Peter Schilling Jr.

Ivan R. Dee   Chicago   2008

THE END OF BASEBALL. Copyright © 2008 by Peter Schilling Jr. All rights reserved, including the right to reproduce this book or portions thereof in any form. For information, address: Ivan R. Dee, Publisher, 1332 North Halsted Street, Chicago 60622. Manufactured in the United States of America and printed on acid-free paper.

www.ivanrdee.com

Library of Congress Cataloging-in-Publication Data:
Schilling, Peter, 1968–
    The end of baseball : a novel / Peter Schilling Jr.
        p. cm.
    ISBN-13: 978-1-56663-782-4 (cloth : alk. paper)
    ISBN-10: 1-56663-782-1 (cloth : alk. paper)
    1. Veeck, Bill—Fiction. 2. Baseball team owners—United States—Fiction. 3. Philadelphia Athletics (Baseball team)—Fiction. 4. Baseball stories. I. Title.
    PS3619.C37E63 2008
    813'.6—dc22
                                                                2007045781

For Janice

not because I think I should, but *because I want to*

(with apologies to Bill and Mary Frances)

Contents

1   Deep in the Heart of Texas   3

2   Seventh Game in Santo Domingo   23

3   From the Oval Office to the Stork Club   40

4   Surrounded by Swamps   55

5   Office of the Commissioner   81

6   Winning a Bet with God   91

7   Two Opening Days   99

8   Gotham   120

9   The Unraveling   133

10 Arsenal of Democracy   153

11 Unveiling the Secret Weapon   171

12 Tormented in St. Louis   191

13 Wheel of Fortune   203

14 Sam, Wheeling and Dealing   233

15 Satchel vs. Josh   251

16 Port Chicago   275

17 Fan Appreciation Day   289

18 Season's End   306

19 Gone   335

The End of Baseball

Deep in the Heart of Texas

"It's around here somewhere," Bill Veeck said. He was driving, his arm leaning out the open window with his sport shirt wide open, happy for the sunlight and dry air. "When Josh swings that lumber," he said, again to no one, for he knew that his friend Sam Dailey had stopped listening long ago, "you're going to see some fireworks. The greatest ballplayer in history, Negro or otherwise." Though he was behind the wheel, Veeck wasn't paying attention to the silver mirages shellacking the road, the heat undulating on the horizon, the sun-scorched countryside, or the abandoned farmhouse with a *V for Victory* sign on its cracked front window. It was late November 1943, and he was trying to see into the near future, trying his damnedest to imagine the coming storm and reassure his friend that it wouldn't blow their house down. "Look, Sam, after they hit the diamond, after all those Josh Gibson home runs, and after we steamroll our way to the pennant, no one will care that they're Negroes. It's all baseball, Sam. That's what'll count."

The car hit a pothole and Veeck grimaced. He wore an artificial leg just below the right knee and was doing his best to ignore the pain, a difficult task as the apple-green Packard's shot springs and the lousy roads meant every rut sent shock waves from his soles to his molars. A man of tics, about every five minutes he would shake a cigarette from the pack and light it against the one in his mouth. A case of warm beer rattled on the front seat between the two men, and Veeck would methodically slurp from a bottle, then stick a cigarette in his mouth, inhale with all his might, and bellow out smoke in great blasts. A smile brightened his face, a grin as wide as the open collars he wore in defiance against a world of ties. Still sporting his Marine-issue buzz cut, which brought out the blond in his thinning red hair,

Veeck had the look of a blue-collar man: a face weathered from constant sun, aging him beyond his thirty years, and a voice scratched from having to shout over the clatter of the El trains of his hometown Chicago. Bill Veeck Jr. was the youngest man ever to own a major league baseball team.

The Packard roared over hills, drifted dangerously over the loose gravel, killing rattlesnakes sunning themselves on the road, and coiling dust in its wake.

"Slow down," Sam begged, grasping the door. He was pale as lard, his stomach burning from indigestion, and looked like he was steaming in his suit and tie. As they raced through the Texas countryside, Sam tried to keep his nausea at bay, gulping air. "God, Bill, they'll love us in St. Louis," he croaked sarcastically. "You think people will want to see a ball game with the National Guard hanging around?"

"National Guard—?"

"Yes, National Guard. You don't think people are going get a bit angry about this whole thing? People fight at ball games over a blown call. We're going to need police, firemen, probably the Guard to keep order. At first I thought, okay, this is another circus act. Fun and games. And here I am, going along with this, this . . . I don't even know what you call it, driving all over hell's half-acre to look for phantoms." Sam's stomach turned, and he gasped again, but held his hand up to tell Veeck to keep his mouth shut. After a moment, he continued. "Let me ask you this: Do you really think the fans can handle Negroes playing ball with whites? On the same field? Oh, not just in Philadelphia. In St. Louis. New York, Detroit—Bill, Negroes burned down half the city this year! And we don't know the character of these players. It's not the drinking or the womanizing that bothers me," Sam said, though both bothered him a great deal. "What if they're violent? What if they're gamblers? Landis won't tolerate Negroes, but he'll wreck everything if there's gambling." Sam stopped. From the corner of his eye he could see Bill had quit listening and was looking a bit pained himself. *Good*, Sam thought. I can't be the only one living in reality. "Integration," he added, hoping his last jab would hit Bill where it hurt. "I just hope you know that this great experiment of yours doesn't set integration—in baseball and everywhere else—*back* a few years." With those last words dangling between them, they both stared out into the middle distance.

It had started with that phone call in late November. Around two in the morning, and Sam figured his father was finally dead. But the noise coming out of the receiver told him right off it was Bill. There were no introductions, no "I'm back from the war!", nothing about the injury, the lost leg, no "How are you?" or "How's business?" Through the jumble Sam heard, "Philadelphia Athletics!" He heard the price, heard the job offer, and then heard the click. Within two weeks he and Bill Veeck owned the American League franchise known on paper as the Professional Base Ball Club of Philadelphia.

Back in the day they called Sam Dailey a Cornell man, though you'd be hard pressed even then to find anyone who really knew what that meant. It could have referred to his habit of trying to maintain a look of serious commercial importance at all times: the days were few when Sam wasn't attired in a sharp jacket, crisp white shirt, conservative tie. Perhaps it referred to the crew cut he had trimmed once a week, or the black horn-rimmed glasses. The whole works framed by a squared jaw, topping a portly frame. Mostly, being a Cornell man meant that he'd mention Cornell at least once a day.

Veeck had waited all his life for this opportunity. William Veeck Jr. had grown up in the dusty corridors of Wrigley Field, where his father, the stoic William Veeck Sr. had served as president of the Chicago Cubs in the 1920s and 1930s. The senior Veeck taught his son everything about baseball, and while young Bill eschewed the suits and ties of his father, he kept the lessons close to his heart. The elder Mr. Veeck was an innovator, a man who understood that you needed to build a winning team *and* provide some fun. He proposed interleague games, started Ladies' Day, and was the first to broadcast games on the radio. "Bill," he once told his son while they counted the day's receipts, "take a good look at that money. It looks exactly the same. You can't tell who put it into your box office. It's the same color, the same size, and the same shape. Don't forget that."

Veeck didn't forget. As a teenager he knocked around the stands, sanding down the seats to keep them smooth from splinters, and sold hot dogs in the bleachers. He listened to the tired men and women who endured the depression and came to watch the games after work—or in lieu of work, when no jobs could be found. Nothing pleased him more than listening to the strategies of the fans wasting their afternoons in the cheap seats. These people spent their time and money on the Cubs when money was scarce and those hours could be used to raise a few dimes just to feed your family. He never forgot that, either.

The elder Veeck died when Bill Jr. was in college. After a few years working with the Cubs, from the ballpark to the front office, the son decided the time was right to run his own team. He rounded up a group of skeptical investors—all prominent friends of his father—who felt obliged to usher the son onto the path to his first failure. After one of his squirrelly pitch sessions, with Veeck gesticulating wildly and unable to sit still even for a moment, they wondered aloud how this nut could be William Veeck's son. It was as if a banana had sprouted from the branch of an apple tree. But they figured that since this was a certain fiasco, Veeck would get his needed kick in the pants and get drummed right out of the sport. So Veeck bought the Milwaukee Brewers, a sorry minor league team that hadn't operated in the black since before the depression. He cleaned up rickety Borchert Field, made a variety of shrewd trades, and in the course of two seasons took that wormy franchise from last place to a pennant winner. More than a million fans turned up, a better attendance than any team in America with the exception of the Yankees and the Cardinals—and his was a minor league club. His investors nearly had coronaries from the news, but the money made them happy.

A few months after Pearl Harbor, Veeck, bored with three seasons of first-place finishes and sellout crowds, joined the Marines and sold his share of the Brewers. He was shipped to Guadalcanal, where the recoil from a 50mm gun shattered his ankle. Infection set in. He spent fourteen of his eighteen months of service in military hospitals. Finally they took his leg off and discharged him. When he hit the shore, hobbling on his new crutches, he didn't wait a day to start looking to buy a team on the cheap, which meant a last-place club with few prospects.

Veeck had, by his own admission, barely "five hundred clams" coming out of the war, and an Arizona ranch he could mortgage. The Philadelphia Athletics were suddenly available. Connie Mack, owner and manager of the A's, was planning on retiring and handing over the plow to his sons, Earl, Connie Jr., and Roy. But they began fighting, lawyers were called, and a disgusted Mack sold Veeck the Athletics against his sons' wishes. The boys howled and, just as suddenly, Mack regretted his decision. Veeck, desperate for a team, his financing on slippery footing, most of it coming in the form of loans from dubious sources, agreed that if he failed to show a profit by year's end (it could be but a penny), the Mack family had the right to buy the team back. And would.

Sam worried about the conditions of the sale, worried about the difficulty of repairing Philadelphia's Shibe Park, about raising this sorry club from last place . . . until Veeck mentioned Negroes. That trumped everything. It even trumped the war.

When Sam asked Veeck how in the living daylights he was going to sign a Negro ballplayer against Judge Landis's wishes, not to mention against decades of tradition, Veeck didn't even hesitate. Get this, Veeck said: For a smokescreen, he had rounded up a bunch of Negro investors and bought the Philadelphia Stars, a Negro League club, and every black player signed would be a member of the Stars on paper. They would hold *two* spring training camps: one for the A's—the white players he was going to release (and where he had invited hundreds of press to help complete the deception)—and one in Cartwheel, Florida, for the real team, no press allowed. On April 1, a couple of weeks before the season opened, Veeck would hand over the contracts to Commissioner Landis for approval, flanked by dozens of sympathetic newspapermen. At the same time he would release all the white players (who were, to a man, lousy, since the best players were fighting in Europe and the Pacific) and emerge with, as he triumphantly bellowed to Sam, an unbeatable team. It seemed to Sam that he was the only one who knew how impossible this plan was. The press didn't want to be on Landis's bad side. And why couldn't the commissioner kick them out of baseball, even if the season was about to begin? Veeck just waved those concerns away, even though they also buzzed like hornets in his head every minute of every day.

In the meantime, for appearance's sake, Veeck would hold press conferences as if nothing had changed, would use printed letterhead with his name and the A's and their white elephant logo, another for the Stars, and would make a big deal out of the value of the Negro Leagues in the World War II market. From the very start he claimed he would run the A's as Connie Mack would have, business as usual. Initially he met with many of the other owners, arguing that they should consider buying Negro League teams, or at least host his club to help raise some badly needed funds for everyone. They believed him; the press believed him; the players and the public believed him.

So it was that Bill Veeck and Sam Dailey found themselves in the middle of Whoknowswhere, Texas, on a scorching day in late 1943. They were in search of a prize, and this time the prize was a man: Josh Gibson. Veeck ached to see Gibson's artillery in the majors—the homers rising out of Shibe Park, doubles and triples and just plain mashed baseballs. For the last two weeks Veeck had been regaling Sam with tales of Josh Gibson's fabulous exploits. Their scouts told him that Josh had just come off his finest season in 1943: 41 homers and a .449 batting average with the Negro League Homestead Grays, who had been playing in Washington, D.C., that year. One of the greatest catchers in any league. Why, Josh could throw out the fastest base runners, call the best pitches, hit for power and for average. Veeck couldn't stop shouting about the guy: Josh's arms were like railroad ties! Great eyes, sees better than Ted Williams! Should've been in the majors years ago . . . that's the beauty of the thing! We'll unleash this guy and all the rest just when they aren't expecting it!

But his ballplayers were proving hard to find. With the arrival of winter, Negro Leaguers followed the heat, moving from Philadelphia to New Orleans, down to Monterrey, Mexico, back up to Oklahoma and rural Texas—wherever they could play for decent, or not so decent, wages. Veeck hired Oscar Charleston, possibly the greatest baseball player, black or white, in history, and Fay Young, the *Chicago Defender*'s great black sportswriter, to hunt down ballplayers. Both men had an eye for talent. There were only two players you didn't need a scout to tell you were the cream: the first was Satchel Paige, the other was Josh Gibson.

Sam read the press clippings from the Negro papers and was as baffled by their yellow journalism as Bill's utter faith in their reportage. When he wasn't sufficiently terrorized by the thought of Negroes invading baseball in general, Sam's baseball mind took over, and he wondered just how good men like Gibson really were. Like most white baseball men of the time, he tried to imagine what kind of pitching Gibson faced. You could find bushel basketsful of minor league hit-men who clobbered dozens of homers in a week against farm boys without any movement to their fastballs. Sam would admit that Gibson's legend was far-reaching—they'd been driving for days, following rumors from Birmingham to New Orleans and now the most lonely sections of Texas, burning through the combined gas-ration coupons of Veeck, Sam, and all their friends and families. But rumors were only rumors. And to make matters worse, some weren't good: one coach in Baton Rouge had fired Josh for reasons he wouldn't go into, and in fact wouldn't even open the door to answer the question. Then there was the teammate in Oatmeal, Nebraska, who, over a dinner that consisted mostly of beer and whiskey, reported that Josh had also spent part of last year in a sanatorium, and was once found naked in an alley mumbling to himself, "Why won't you talk to me, DiMaggio?" A fellow ballplayer in Lubbock said he went crazy. In Mobile they'd even heard he was dead.

None of this bothered Veeck. He took a long pull on his cigarette and said, "Leo Rothberg's heading to Santo Domingo tomorrow to look for Satch. We'll have Fay in Newark and Pittsburgh to look for talent there. He's got some ideas. And Oscar's racing around the South. How about this for our press conference: *The greatest aggregate of talent in baseball history!*" From the corner of his eye he could see Sam's discomfort. He shook his head and chuckled. "Would you loosen your tie? And take off your jacket. You're making *me* feel sick."

Sam loosened his tie, which only made him appear more uncomfortable. Staring out the window at the few ramshackle homes they'd pass, he wondered how anyone could live in such utter desolation. They were going to find ballplayers here? When he met Oscar Charleston, the brute seemed inarticulate, maybe violent if provoked. Sam didn't trust instinct, but his was rankled. And it seemed strange all this hunting they had to do: you look for the white boys on the sandlots, in the minors, sometimes even in colleges. These Negroes were scattered about like gypsies, their talent nothing more than whispered legend. Sam didn't truly believe that Fay Young or Oscar Charleston, Negroes both, would be fair judges. He was tired of the chase and tired of hearing about Josh Gibson. He could only blame himself for being in this predicament: he hated to rock the boat, yet always jumped in the dinghy with the crackpot at the oars. "Bill," he said at last, noticing now that there weren't even shacks to break up the sunburned fields, "what if we took just *one*? Just Satchel. I mean, a whole team of Negroes, for God's sake! While you're at it, why not a whole team of Jews?"

Veeck took a swig of beer, and then said, "Which white players are worth keeping, Sam?" Sam scowled and folded his arms. Veeck chuckled. "Sam, I'm not looking to sign Negroes. I'm looking to sign *the best.* The best happen to all be Negroes. It's the same old troubles, Sam: had we not fielded a winner in Milwaukee, we'd have lost the team for lack of profit. That goes double for the A's. We're so deep in the red we might as well be on Mars. Don't forget: promotions only go so far. Field the best players and you make money. Lots of money. So what if they're white, Negro, Jewish, Arab, or Eskimo? And these men can play, Sam. They'll give us the pennant and keep us in the black. In a big way."

"We're black in a big way, all right," Sam huffed. "Josh Gibson. Drunk. Insane. Dead, maybe. What a prize."

"You take the churchgoers, I'll go with the lushes. That would leave me with Babe Ruth, Rogers Hornsby, Grover Cleveland Alexander. That would leave you with the . . . Lutheran Softball League." Veeck laughed and lit another cigarette off the one he was smoking. "Sam, these players, they're going to have their plaques in the Hall of Fame, nearly every one . . . and we'll get them for peanuts." The car hit another pothole, almost sending Sam into the dashboard. Veeck ignored Sam's groan, and continued: "It's like war: you sit in a trench with a Jew, an Italian, a Negro, and pretty soon you realize that, hey, this guy can do the job just like anyone else. That's what people'll say when they see the A's. When we're ten games up at the All-Star break, no one's going to notice the color of their skin. And the turnstiles will be spinning."

"You forget: the army doesn't put Negroes in the trenches. I wasn't even there and I know that."

"Okay, so they don't," Veeck said, tired of talk of the war. "But we will." He nodded ahead. "Keep an eye out for the park. It has to be here somewhere."

Sam wished Veeck would listen to reason. He stared out the window at land that couldn't be used for grazing, building, anything at all but maybe roasting German prisoners of war.

Sam Dailey was a serious man. Truth was, you wouldn't find anyone who'd emphasize that point more than Sam himself. His was a family of lawyers and doctors and a bunch of opinionated businessmen whom Sam secretly loathed but respected with all his heart because they were family and made a great deal of money. From a young age he had been groomed for professional success. At Cornell Sam threw himself into the study of law, hoping to impress his family and the world around him. He graduated in '38 and moved to Milwaukee to endure the profession he felt was his destiny.

But Sam harbored secret dreams that nagged him nearly every night, dating to his youth. When he was seven his father took him to a White Sox game, and he was hooked from the first pitch. Ever since then, Sam had dreamed of becoming a ballplayer. Like most people, he didn't have nearly enough talent to make this happen, even in high school. Unlike most people, watching the game only made him want to be a part of the sport, to breathe it as ballplayers did. As he grew older, Sam threw himself into his work, hoping the demands of study and then business would help him suppress these desires. They did— but only during the day. At night, visions of a baseball life surged beneath his consciousness, pulling at his plans like an undertow.

His fortunes changed one March afternoon before the war, in Milwaukee. Sam was pining away, staring out the window of his office in the direction of Chicago. He wished it were April and that he was in Comiskey Park drinking beer next to a woman. Instead he was stuck in his office, gazing at the dull, battleship-grey skies. Lake Michigan was flat and without character. The air was damp, the snow was dingy and crusted to the ground. These are the miserable days when the promise of baseball is as profound—and, in Milwaukee, unrequited—as the promise of love. His secretary buzzed him and he jumped with surprise. "What?" he yelled. Bill Veeck was in the waiting room. "Who?" Some promoter. Works for the Brewers. Against his better judgment, Sam told her to send him in.

Veeck never entered a room when he could storm in, and knowing that Sam Dailey, Esq., wasn't expecting him, he smacked the doors open and burst through in one swift move. Veeck never sat, and Sam didn't have the opportunity to offer him a seat. But it was, Sam recalled, as if the sun were suddenly bright in that office. This nut was going to revitalize the Brewers, and he was hunting for investors and a permanent lawyer for the team. Would Sam invest, and how about being their lawyer? Sam was intrigued. He was one of the few who actually paid any attention to the hardscrabble Brewers, showing up at nearly every game, most of which were blowouts that rarely favored the home team. Veeck didn't know this, nor did he mention that Sam was his third choice, after he had been unceremoniously tossed out of two other law firms. As Veeck explained it, a little paint on the park, a few shrewd deals, and the Brewers—they of the rickety wooden stadium and last-place finishes for the past dozen years (not to mention being on the verge of bankruptcy and never having made a profit)—would rise up from the ashes like the phoenix with its tail on fire. Of course, Sam would have to work pro bono at first, but think of the possibilities! Being a kindhearted soul and enjoying this performance enormously, Sam gave this huckster fifteen minutes of his time. At first Sam listened with amusement. This guy was crazy, anyone could see that. He wants me not only to work for free but to throw away money besides? On the Brewers? It was too incredible. But as Veeck spoke, Sam felt his shoulders relax and his head grow light. His whole body tingled as if under the influence of morphine. Alarmed at this reaction, Sam ended the conversation and promised to purchase a pair of season tickets. He pushed Veeck out, then leaned against the closed door, out of breath. Baseball would be good for Milwaukee, Sam reasoned, and went back to work.

He didn't sleep that night. The next day, baggy-eyed and weary, he doubled his labors, trying to shake Bill Veeck and that ridiculous ballclub from his mind. Every fifteen minutes he'd take out his bank book and examine the figures. He liked those numbers. If he ever got married it'd be a good start, put his kid through college someday. Tapping the corner of the book on his desk, he looked around the office. It seemed cramped, the windows dirty, the view tedious. His clients paid well, but could he have found a more unimaginative group? Wills without controversy, business arrangements between such honest men that a handshake would have sufficed. Maybe he should study a different type of law, something with more spark, more verve. Satisfied with this compromise, he took half a day off. On his way home he drove by the ballpark. Every day that week Sam took long walks over lunch and lost his appetite.

Sam Dailey invested every dime he had in the Milwaukee Brewers and became their sole legal representative. He shifted his clients to his partner, mortgaged his home, and then proceeded to curse himself for this sudden recklessness. And still he couldn't sleep. But come the dawn, he raced to the ballpark, happy again. Every day was a growing joy.

When Bill quit the game and joined the Marines, Sam's heart just about broke. Without Veeck, it wouldn't be the same . . . too much like business, he thought, and he sold his part in the club and hung out another shingle. But each and every day he prayed that Bill would survive and come back to buy another team. So when Veeck called from San Diego, Sam barely listened. All he heard was "Collect call from Bill Veeck" and then "Philadelphia Athletics." He felt ten years younger. Sam had tons of money to throw at the team, having emerged from Milwaukee considerably richer than Veeck, who squandered wealth as fast as he raised it. As usual, they gathered the investors through a series of half-lies and outrageous promises. Then again, Milwaukee had proved that Veeck could deliver the moon if promised.

But after Bill explained his crackpot integration plan, Sam just about lost his mind. He fought Veeck, cajoled him, and did his very best to reason with him.

That morning in Texas, the heat inside the car seemed to rise as they bickered. "Tell me this," Sam asked. "Who can we possibly get to manage the Black A's?"

Veeck beamed. "You'll love this: Mickey Cochrane!"

Sam blinked. Slow, horrible blinks of utter disbelief. "Cochrane?" Sam said in a whisper, as if to speak it any louder would bring a curse upon them. "Bill, how many nervous breakdowns has he had? Cochrane hasn't been in baseball for years."

"You're wrong. Mickey's been coaching the navy team at Great Lakes for the last two seasons. It's surefire: Philly loves him. The triumphant return of the greatest catcher in Athletics history!" In his excitement he lost control of the car and swerved in the dust. "Think of the possibilities! We can have a 'Welcome Back Night,' a reunion of the old winners, maybe even have the old guy catch an inning or two—"

"You know his only son just died in the war?"

Veeck paused from taking a sip of beer. "No, I didn't know that." He shrugged and took a gulp. "If he doesn't want to do it, he doesn't have to. But if I remember Cochrane, he'd do anything to win. Including hiring Negroes. Can *you* think of anyone better?"

Sam couldn't, but that didn't mean he didn't want to throttle Veeck. He stared out the window, watching wind play with the weeds, the whole time turning new crises over and over in his head. Suddenly he was broken from his musings and leaned up in his seat. "Where'd those kids come from?" he said. A hundred feet from the road, tearing across the plain, a dozen children were running at full gallop, and more were on bicycles, pedaling furiously.

"That's it," Veeck said. He nodded to a group of automobiles clustered around what looked like a slapdash ball field a couple of acres away. At a pair of ruts that functioned for a road, he shot off to the right and the Packard bumped through the grass.

In the distance was a chicken-wire backstop surrounded by wooden bleachers. As they lurched toward the field, Veeck and Sam could see a derrick bobbing up and down past right field and a willow tree off to the left. Crowds filled the stands and leaned on the fences, perhaps five hundred or more. These were the people of the small towns and ranches, plus a few of the lonely oilmen who maintained the single pumps that squeezed out the drops that paid their meager salaries. Farmers and ranchers, and children brushed with the dust and dirt of the plains, gaped and cheered.

They pulled up next to a dingy blue school bus marked ETHIOPIAN COLORED ALL-STARS 1943.

"All-Stars?" Sam asked.

"Not anymore. Maybe once they could've had Satchel and his entourage, but today, with the war . . ."

"You really think he'll be here?" Sam asked.

"All I know is what our scout told us in Houston."

They climbed out and Sam readjusted his tie and slapped the dust off his sleeves. Veeck grimaced as he moved out of the car, fumbling with a pair of metal crutches before he found his balance and hobbled to the backstop with Sam.

The local boys were on the field, white kids dressed in flannels and with the name of a merchant stitched in cursive across the breast. Looking for Josh, Veeck glanced over at the visitors' dugout and sighed. It was what he'd hoped he wouldn't see: the Ethiopians were barefoot, dressed in grass skirts, faces painted chalky white.

The Ethiopians sucked down their pride every day. They rode a broken bus all night, sick from diesel fumes and muscles sore from sleeping on the road. Before each game they donned the skirts and played ball. Travel restrictions and the lack of able-bodied men made fielding nine decent players that much more difficult. And because of this, people didn't shell out the money like they used to. To bring in the crowds—almost entirely white—they'd decked themselves out in the grass skirts that went down to their knees but offered no protection from a bounced ball or a hard slide on gravel. Their legs and feet were scarred from play, and sweat made the face paint run into their eyes. But they played, these old men and nobodies, thankful to the last that they could make ends meet at baseball. Many held a lingering fear, not so much of the dangers of the South but of the creeping horror that comes to a person addicted to a sport: as soon as the body wore out, they'd be right back in the thick of migrant farming, dangerous factory jobs, and whatever demeaning work that was their due. Glory, or whatever functioned in its place, was soon to fade. Anonymity would choke them the rest of their days.

Sam wedged himself in among the crowd of major league scouts hanging on the backstop. Eager to prove Bill wrong, he was hoping to discover good white players who could take the field for the A's next summer.

On the mound stood the object of the scouts' collective affections: a corn-fed teenager hurling fastballs that kept the eyes of these men wide and dry. The kid looked good. Perhaps this was proof that there was more white talent out there than Bill would admit. As Veeck hobbled to the Ethiopians' dugout, Sam began scribbling notes, and a farmer standing by noticed. He swelled his chest, craned his neck to get Sam's attention, and with that, tilted his thumb at the pitcher. He crowed, "That's my son. Ted Rogarth, the Rocket, they call 'im. Just sixteen if he's a day. Goin' to the show soon as the war's up. Struck out . . ." He turned to a dirty little kid crouched by the dugout and shouted, "Piper! How many he got?"

Looking over his scorecard, the child mouthed 'One . . . two . . .' and yelled, "Sixteen, pa!"

"Sixteen in eight. So who you scoutin' for? 'Cause let me tell you, this boy a' mine—"

"The Philadelphia A's," Sam said, and produced a card. He watched the kid and ignored the farmer's continued stream of accolades. This is what we should be looking for, Sam thought.

The kid—who was built as solidly as the oil derricks behind him—spit a long arc of tobacco juice, nodded at the sign from his catcher, and threw a fastball right by the batter, who swung at air. The ball hit the catcher's mitt with a nasty pop, and the boy dropped his glove and shook his hand in pain.

"Oh, fer the love of—!" the farmer called. "You gotta start holdin' those!" He smirked at Sam. "But that's seventeen!"

At the dugout, Veeck ambled down the concrete steps and nodded at the batboy leaning against the fence. The poor child was also dressed in a skirt and didn't look happy about it. Veeck wondered how much he got to eat in any given day.

The Ethiopians' owner-manager, a potbellied sourpuss named Thurber, paced back and forth, stewing over his troubles and wishing just once he'd get on the lucky side of life. Judging from the crowd, he'd rake in some decent dough, maybe $200. But his All-Stars were behind, 1-0, and losing still hurt. When he saw Veeck, it was all he could take after a day of abuses. He shouted, "Players only! Get out of here!"

"Just a second," Veeck said, grinning. "I'm a scout. I'm looking for Josh Gibson."

The other players stared at him with wide eyes. "Who you with?" one asked.

"The Philly Stars."

The players jumped up from the bench, gathered around Veeck and began murmuring. "No kidding," Thurber said, shaking Veeck's hand furiously. He introduced himself and said, "Need a second baseman? A pitcher? Wilcox! Stanley! C'mere." Wilcox and Stanley pushed through the crowd and stood by Veeck. Thurber said, "These two are real firecrackers! You caught us on an off day, man!" He lowered his voice. "Maybe you need a coach? Been in the game onup twenty years."

Veeck cleared his throat. "Thanks, but just Josh for now. Is he here?"

"Sure, I understand," Thurber said, crestfallen. The rest of the men nodded in unison and slowly sat back down. "He's . . . resting. Out beneath that old willow tree. His woman Grace is with him." Veeck nodded thanks. As he turned to go, Thurber said, "Be sure to watch the last inning. You'll see some fine playing."

As he hobbled up the steps, one of the players said, "Mister, you get Josh, you won't be sorry."

Veeck called for Sam, and the two of them made their way to the willow tree in the distance. As they approached, they could see a large man lying on the sand in the shade, dressed in flannels, his head leaning against the tree, arms stretched out. A woman sat next to him, her blue dress fanned out in front of her, caressing his head and whispering a song. When she noticed they were coming his way, she stopped singing and scrambled up.

"What do you want?" she said, rolling up her sleeves as if she was going to deck one of them. "I don't care if you the law or not, Josh spent last night in jail and ain't done nothing since."

Sam took a step back, but Veeck just smiled, leaned on his left crutch, and extended a hand. She met this with folded arms. "You must be Grace," he said, and introduced himself and Sam. "We want Josh to play ball for us. For the Philadelphia Stars."

"You got a contract?" she asked, eyeing Sam. He looked like a revenuer. "All this way just to sign Josh?"

"For the great Josh Gibson, I'd drive to China. And, yes, I have a contract." He turned to Sam, who pulled it from his pocket. "We'll even pay you a signing bonus. Right now. In *cash*."

Almost everyone Veeck and Sam had talked to in the last couple of weeks warned them about Grace Fournier, suggesting she'd been the one to blame for Josh's troubles, others that she was what kept him alive. Veeck saw a beautiful woman, pale-skinned, and with wavy dark hair that looked as if she'd spent all morning perfecting it. But she also draped herself in piles of costume jewelry and too much makeup, and with her unsteady hands and endless fidgeting she had a sad, desperate appearance.

"Just a couple hundred would get us out of Texas and back to Pittsburgh," she said with a blank stare, as if she were trying to see all the way back home. "Poor Joshy got lured to New Orleans, but things went kerplow and we've been driftin' around with these jerks in their mumbo-jumbo outfits." She chewed her lip in thought as if trying to sum Veeck and Sam up. "How much you gonna pay?"

Veeck told her, and then nodded to Sam, who pulled five hundred-dollar bills out of his billfold. "Oh, Mary!" she cried, and that was that. Grace spun around, ran back to Josh, dropped to her knees and shook him. "Josh, honey! C'mon up now! Some men here want us to play baseball!" She shook him over and over, and yelled back to them, "Just give us a moment!"

Finally, Josh woke. He groaned, rubbed his eyes, and smacked his tongue around his mouth. He tried to shake the dizziness from his head and slowly lifted himself up to a lean. Even sitting, he looked huge. He exhaled blasts of air that sounded almost as if they were from the nostrils of an angry bull. Leaning on his massive forearms, he looked up, and his face, almost childlike with its soft features, seemed perched on a body not its own. He'd been dozing on the ground to get away from the heat and sunlight, and the willow floor was dark and cool by contrast. Irritable from being woken, he demanded a drink. "Bourbon!" He spat out the word.

"Don't have bourbon, hon. Get up!"

Grace struggled to lift Josh, but he shook her off. "Leave me alone!"

"Get up, honey!" she said, then slapped his face, hard. "This fellow here wants to sign you to play in Philly!"

That slap brought him around. He looked as if he were ready to slap her back, but quickly caught Veeck and Sam from the corner of his eye and checked himself. "Okay, Philadelphia," he said, with a shrug. "Who? For *who*?" He sat on his hams like he was behind the plate, then took a deep breath. "You want me to do what?"

Veeck leaned on his crutches. "To play ball for us." He smiled. "In Philadelphia. You're our star attraction."

Josh licked his lips. He gazed down at his hands, twisted like old roots. The hands of a catcher. After a moment of reflection, he shook his head. "Ah, I don't know."

"What don't you know, Josh?" Veeck asked.

Grace scowled. "C'mon, hon. He'll *pay* us! Cash!"

He leaned back against the tree trunk. As he uncoiled himself and stood, he let out more gusts of air. "No sir. All I want now is a bottle. And . . . well, never mind." His drew his lips tight. "Josh Gibson's long gone."

"We have a training camp, Josh." Veeck gestured to Sam. Sam rolled his eyes and handed Veeck the contract. "I'm willing to pay you because you're a legend. You don't even have to play. Money's good—why don't you at least look at it?"

Grace reached over, grabbed the contract, and thrust it under Josh's nose. "Baby—look at me when I'm talkin' to you!—that's right, you gonna read this!" She grabbed his chin. He jerked his head away. "Josh Gibson, we're gonna be on top of the world, 'member? 'Member your promise?" He cleared his throat and nodded almost imperceptibly. "What'd you promise?" she asked.

Josh didn't answer but snatched the contract from her. His hand seemed almost as wide as the paper itself. He kept clearing his throat as he read, a phlegmy, crouplike sound. Finally he handed the contract back. "Shit," he mumbled.

Grace gestured to Veeck again. "Hand me that case." Veeck noticed what looked like a long Fuller Brush case leaning against the tree. He nodded to Sam, who ran over, took it, and handed it to her. She laid it on the ground and popped it open. Inside were four beautiful blond ash baseball bats. They were thick-handled, heavy Louisville Sluggers, shining against the black velvet that held them. "Here, babe," she said, pulling one out. "Hold that."

Next to his name on the bat was branded a compass design, with a prominent "W." Josh took the bat. He flexed and unflexed his palms around the handle. Josh's eyes thinned. "West," he said, holding the bat high. Then he scowled and shook his head. He nodded at the case. "Give me North." She found the bat with the prominent "N" on the scorched compass. Josh gave her West, then wrapped his hands around the handle of North. He closed his eyes. Veeck closed his as well. In the distance was a noise: a rumble, the sound of maybe a couple of hundred people mumbling. The rattle of a foul against the chicken wire.

Josh held out the bat in his hand and nodded again at the case. "Now East." She reached for a bat. "Not South, East!" Grace grabbed another bat, replaced North in the case, and Josh was satisfied. He grinned sideways and squeezed her arm, then stood. Planting himself, he took a couple of short, powerful swings. He looked over at Veeck. "Sure about this?"

Veeck opened his eyes and said, "Absolutely."

Josh nodded. He spit in his palms and pushed by the three of them, through the canopy of branches. With his short stride, he surprised them with his speed. They moved swiftly across the parched lot, Veeck moving with a thrilled swiftness in spite of his crutches. At the dugout, Grace kept after Josh, but Sam and Veeck stopped and stood by the bleachers. They could hear Josh mumble to the coach, and when Thurber hesitated, Josh barked, "C'mon fatty, pencil me in!"

While Thurber ran out to the umpire, Josh barreled to the edge of the batter's box and checked his bat, weighing it in his hand. Heat and a hangover gave him sweaty palms, so he grabbed a handful of dirt to dry them. Then he rolled up his sleeves and began to take his short, sharp cuts, stumbling now and then, but always righting himself before he fell over.

"This ought to be good," Veeck said, and then he let out a yell. Sam crossed his arms and waited.

Seeing Josh, the crowd turned ugly. Somehow, in the past ten minutes, the Ethiopians had touched the young fireballer, loading the bases. Although there were two outs, the way those Negroes had manhandled their ace in this last inning left the crowd hungry for blood. Savage whispers popped between the fans. Animal-eyed and desperate for victory, they sat up, craning their necks and smiling wildly. No eating, drinking, or chitchat anymore. As if sensing that Gibson was a player to reckon with, they lit into him mercilessly. Old men, women of all ages, pink-faced teenage girls and their boyfriends, young children, men back from the war, farmers and laborers, even a banker began to call out and wave handkerchiefs. Soon they were shouting racial slurs, edged with sex and violence.

"Gosh, Bill," Sam said, wiping the sweat from his brow.

Veeck was pale. He clapped his hands feebly. "That's right Josh, just ignore it."

They didn't have to tell Josh. Years of abuse had hardened him as it had every other player on the team. He dug in the box, drew his bat back over his shoulder, and waited. At the plate, the catcher spouted his own invectives. The pitcher, Rogarth, spit another rope of tobacco juice out the side of his mouth and made a production of shaking off the catcher's signs. He glanced at the runner on first, turned back, and kicked and fired a pitch at Josh's head. Despite their loathing, human instinct gripped the crowd and they gasped. Josh dropped just in time, and it was luck alone that the ball didn't crack into his skull.

The ump cried, "Strike one!"

The Ethiopians shot off the bench, stunned at the call. Josh hissed through his teeth and dug in again. The crowd roared with approval, and now Josh's manhood was called into question.

Rogarth looked relieved at the call. His face relaxed to a confident smirk, and then he ignored the runners, reared back and threw. The pitch, unbelievably fast, seemed to shrink on its way to the plate. But Josh saw it as if it were floating through water. It was high, near his head, and again he fell back.

"Strike!" the ump cried.

"Again?" Veeck howled. Even Sam began to complain.

Josh stuck his tongue between his lips and turned to the ump, who wouldn't meet his gaze. He stepped back in. Rogarth threw another pitch, low, but Josh fouled it down the right-field line, a bullet. Josh stepped out of the box, stretched, then suddenly realized the pitcher wasn't going to wait for him to step back in and ready himself. He jumped back in, and the pitcher fired a curveball.

Josh creamed it. There was no outfield fence for the ball to tower over. It flew out over the prairie as if it had been fired from the bow of a battleship. Each and every man, woman, and child, on the field and in the stands, fell silent watching Josh's shot sail into the distance, until it rang off of a distant derrick.

The ump stared down, pointed at the dirt, and said, "Stepped outta the box, batter's out. Game over!"

The crowd roared and the Ethiopians cried out in disbelief. Josh turned to look at the ump, but he had walked away and exited the field. Josh stared at his bat, looked at the crowd cheering its team, and let the air out of his chest. Clutching his bat at the top, he walked right off the field and straight to his car.

The local boys jumped into each other's arms as if they'd just won the pennant, slapping Rogarth on the shoulders as if he were to be congratulated for serving up the longest home run in the area's history. The Ethiopian base runners walked slowly back to the dugout as the fans threw popcorn and cups of beer on them.

Veeck and Sam stared at the emptying field. "I don't think I've ever seen a ball knocked so far," Sam said. "I . . . I've never seen anything like it."

"He's knocked a ball out of Griffith Stadium, you know."

Now Sam really looked pale. "Griffith?"

"You'll see lots more, Sam. Maybe he'll even knock one out of Yankee Stadium."

It was late in the day, the shadows were long, and the sun was hiding behind a haze. Dust flew about as the crowds drove away, leaving only the faithful to clamor after their heroes. The Ethiopians scrambled back into real clothes inside their bus. While Thurber and his second baseman went off to collect, Veeck met Josh and Grace by Gibson's old jalopy, which he'd driven himself.

"So, slugger," Veeck said, holding out a pen, contract in the other hand. "You knock 'em like that up north, I won't be sorry."

"Well, I warned you," Josh said. "I'm old bones." He took the contract and scratched his name at the bottom. "The Philly Stars you say?"

"Sure," Veeck said. Grace took Josh's bonus, which she shoved deep into her brassiere.

"When?" Josh asked. "Where?"

"First, Florida. Training." Veeck said. "Town called Cartwheel. Middle of February. Give or take a few days, we don't mind."

"Yeah," Josh said. "Okay." He slammed the door shut and, with Grace behind the wheel, raced off. They were headed to Dallas, to meet a gentleman who they both knew could give them the fix they needed to get through the week, and then it was a train north to Pittsburgh.

The players gathered around Veeck, wishing him good luck, shaking his hand. Had he seen that play at second? Or my base hit off that wicked curve? Each one tried to get Veeck's attention, and all the while he nodded eagerly and handed out business cards. Deep down, everyone knew nothing would come of it. Thurber returned, and they said their goodbyes. Then Bill Veeck and Sam Dailey got back in their Packard and drove to Houston, arguing the whole way.

◇ **2** ◇

Seventh Game in Santo Domingo

Ciudad Trujillo, Santo Domingo, December 10, 1943. Had you found yourself with one of the rare tickets to that day's game, you would have had to maneuver through the crowded dirt streets, pushed past teenage soldiers, ignored the bullhorned orders ringing through the alleys, and stepped over the occasional trickle of blood in the gutter to get to Trujillo Stadium. The ballpark, named for the nation's not-so-benevolent dictator, was nothing more than a band-box of concrete and steel, whitewashed and covered with red and black political posters. El Presidente, as Trujillo liked to be known—though the notion of being popularly elected never crossed his mind—had built the stadium as a gesture of his everlasting goodwill to his exploited people: he knew they loved baseball, and he under-stood the ancient Roman practice of bread and circuses. Healthy competition never hurt anyone and, as a bonus, kept the population focused on its labors, not its politics.

That afternoon, nervous crowds filled the stands, anticipating the championship game ahead, a tough contest between Trujillo's own Los Dragones team and the upstart Orientales.

Leo Rothberg sat a few rows behind home plate, scribbling into a leather notebook with a gold mechanical pencil he kept moistening on his tongue. He was not to be missed in Trujillo Stadium, in his suit of blue-grey silk and a silver-tipped cane resting against his thigh. His belly was filled with that morning's breakfast of eggs Benedict and champagne, his pencil cost more than the week's wages of everyone around him, and his corpulent body wrapped the bench. As he fin-ished writing, Leo looked up and squinted against the brutal sun, surveyed the park, and smiled. Fifty thousand souls squeezed onto every bleacher, shoulder to shoulder. Leo's Italian wingtips stuck to the beer-soaked concrete floor. Around him people shouted, cajoled, pushed and shoved; they argued, passed food in front of him, waved money back and forth in an attempt to wager; men begged the very few young women to pull their tops off and show their breasts. Everyone taunted the soldiers encircling the field, just kids themselves and barefoot, their rifles hanging clumsily over their shoulders. The tension in the air was heavier than the penetrating humidity. Despite all this—or perhaps because of it—Rothberg felt right at home.

If there was a horse race anywhere in North America, Leo Rothberg could handicap it in a minute. Of boxers he could study the swing, the jab, the bound muscle, and the look in the eye behind the swollen brow and know, first, whether the man could win or lose, or, second, whether he could be trusted to throw the match. Rothberg calculated the odds for hockey, football, cockfighting even, and startled an opponent once with his ability to predict the outcome of the Olympic Games in Berlin, in which Rothberg staggered away with more than $200,000 and indigestion from copious amounts of lager and sausage that would last him almost two weeks. Above all, however, Rothberg knew baseball, for the simple fact that he had been smitten by the sport ever since he was a plump eight-year-old.

Successful as a young man, Rothberg tried his whole adult life to purchase a major league baseball team. The Commissioner of Baseball had other ideas. So Rothberg took the next best route by running Negro League teams, dreaming that, someday, someone would integrate baseball. When Veeck—a friend from back in Chicago—called at midnight not two weeks ago, a subtle smile broke across Rothberg's face. In the midst of a tight poker game with the mayor of Cleveland, he folded a good hand and excused himself from present company. Then he retreated to the couch, tucked the phone under his ear, and pulled out his notebook, filled with the names of the best players in America. "I do know where Satchel is, Bill," Rothberg said. "I'll be in Ciudad within two weeks."

Two weeks later, Leo's attention turned back to the field, where a small table had been set up, and a bathing beauty cut a deck of cards. Since there was only one stadium on the island, home-field advantage had to be determined from a draw of cards. For this last game of the Island Championship, the Orientales drew the high card.

As the game drew near, chanting began. It started, as chanting does, from one row of people, then grew in pitch, until the whole stadium rumbled with a new cry: "Maestro!"

Rothberg raised an eyebrow and gently tapped his neighbor with his cane. "Maestro? Satchel Paige?"

The man just smiled. "No, no, señor. Martín Dihigo!"

"Marteen Deego," Rothberg repeated, craning his neck to see. "Who's he?"

The man furrowed his brow. His wife shuddered in excitement and fanned herself quickly. "¿Cuál?" the man said. "Cuando empieza el día, ¿se tiene que preguntar?, '¿Dónde está el sol?'"

Rothberg sat back, bemused. "I *know* what the sun looks like my good man," he said, but made no further inquiries.

Tall and lanky, Leroy "Satchel" Paige looked stretched out, as if a normal-sized man had fallen into a taffy-pulling machine. His droopy gaze, slouch, and easygoing manner made him appear somewhat sleepy. With his sticks-and-kindling arms, he didn't appear to possess the upper-body strength to roll the ball to the plate, much less hurl it at speeds approaching a hundred miles per hour. Because of his abilities, and thanks to a zeppelin-sized ego, Satchel Paige knew his worth down to the very dime and could name his price wherever he played. He made more money than any of his white counterparts in the major leagues and spent it almost as quickly as he earned it.

Pursuit of the high life sent him to Santo Domingo. Last summer a well-dressed man watched Satchel pitch in one of his many barnstorming contests. When Satch returned to his apartment, sitting atop four cases of the finest Dominican rum was Dr. Aybar, who introduced himself as an agent for Rafael Trujillo, president of Santo Domingo. Aybar sat so high up his feet dangled off the ground, and he bumped his heels against the wooden cases. Please, would Mr. Paige consider $75,000 to play three months of Island baseball? "Satch'll have to do some thinkin'," Paige said, but inside he thought: Is the sky blue? Before you knew it, the contract was wet with his signature. The good doctor then gave Satch an additional 125 Gs to sign four more players—and whatever was left over was Satchel's to keep. What could go wrong?

At first, nothing. For $25,000 each, Satchel took three of the nation's finest with him: Buck Leonard at first base, Ray Dandridge at third, and Cool Papa Bell in center.

With that trio—and his close pal Gentry "Jeep" Jessup rounding out the quartet for $10K, leaving Satch a healthy forty grand on top of it all—Los Dragones couldn't lose. And at first the island proved to be bountiful. Starstruck tavern owners fed them drinks at no expense and were proud to do it. Children flocked to them on the street. Women adored them, flirting openly, even stealing a kiss now and then, which Buck and Cool, devoted husbands, found troubling. Satchel took advantage of all of this and had a new "wife" every single day. They slept in the finest hotels, ate in the best restaurants, and for a little while they could forget that a "Whites Only" standard existed anywhere in the world. They were heroes.

But after a spell things began to grow itchy. El Presidente wasn't exactly a beloved political figure. Satchel quickly realized that Trujillo was a bloodthirsty dictator who hoped that baseball might force the islanders to forget that the country was crumbling around them. But his opponents one-upped him: they bought their own teams and stocked them with the finest talent in the Caribbean. You couldn't thumb your nose at Trujillo on the street, but rooting for the Orientales over the Dragones would suffice. So when Satchel and company weren't exactly running away with the pennant, Trujillo grew irritable. He had the Americans followed. Suddenly they weren't allowed to drink—el Presidente thought alcohol kept them from winning. No more carousing. Satchel had to sit in his hotel room, dandied up in his double-breasted suit—cinnamon red with a canary yellow tie, which wrapped his thin frame the way florist's paper hugs a rose— while the guards stood watch outside his door and below his terrace. Buck's letters to his wife were seized at the post office. One evening Cool came up from the hotel restaurant after a tough loss and found a generalissimo standing on his balcony. The general pulled his pistol, fired into the air and screamed, "El Presidente doesn't lose!"

It should've been a snap, Satch thought that day in Trujillo Stadium. Him throwing those bee-balls against a bunch of banana pickers, Buck and Ray pounding drives across the fences, and Cool lighting up the base paths—hell, they should've cleaned up. In fact the Dragones won the first three of a seven-game series, and it looked like they were in the cake. But then the Orientales took game four in twelve innings, shut out the gringos in game five, and clobbered Los Dragones, 12-2, in game six.

So here we are, Satch thought. He stretched his long legs and sat back on the rickety chair in the dugout of Trujillo Stadium, trying to ignore the taunts and shouts from the bleachers above. The stadium seemed to shake and swell with the tremendous energy of the crowd. He couldn't wait to leave.

"Maestro," he said, and spit on the floor. "Old Satch is better than that goddam Maestro."

Jeep Jessup stood by the water jug with his arms crossed and his lips tight. "Satch, you gotta answer me," he said. Ray Dandridge and Buck Leonard took their seats next to Satchel. Cool Papa Bell waited at the edge of the dugout, bat over his shoulder, studying the pitcher and trying not to think about their troubles.

Satchel crossed his arms. "You niggers giving me the sizzles. Shut up and get ready to play. No one's going to get shot or go to jail or nothing." He spat again. At the end of the dugout Dr. Aybar, Presidente Trujillo's liaison to the team, wrung his hands and gaped at Satch. "Maestro, my ass," Satchel grumbled. He'd already swallowed about a dozen antacid tablets and wished he'd had some beer to take the paste off his tongue.

Jeep was red-eyed, as if he'd been crying, and kept gaping at Satch with the urgency of a poor man waiting on a loan. He was the opposite of Satchel in every way, which may have explained why Satch liked having him around. Jeep was a simple man: plain faced, tall but not lanky, a hard worker who lacked any extraordinary talent. Consistent practice made him very good—his arm was a rifle, but often one without a sight. If his nickname wasn't Jeep he'd simply go by "that fellow who pitched after Satch." Wherever Satch played, so too did Jessup. Usually you'd find him relieving, which was fine with Jeep. He knew his place and was satisfied with it. He believed in Satch the way some people believe in the stock market. Satch meant fun, Satch meant girls, and, above all, Satch meant money.

Right then, however, Satch meant trouble, and Jeep wasn't too pleased about that.

"But Satch," Jeep moaned, "Dr. Aybar said—"

"Fuck Aybar," Satch said, with his usual slow drawl. Why didn't no one pay attention to old Satch? They got to just slow it down easy, you ask him. Look at 'em out there . . . all those soldiers with their damn guns. The language barrier, the unfamiliar surroundings, the growing indifference of the fans, and the fact that he was on an island and couldn't drive off—all these things troubled him. Examining his fingernails, he said, "Settle down. Old Satch ain't gonna lose."

"Listen Satchel," Buck Leonard said, quiet but determined. "Gentry's concerned for all of us. I'd say that it appears as if you're only looking out for Satchel Paige."

"With Satch at the helm, boat's sailing fine."

"You're not even warming up, old man," Cool said. "They killed us yesterday."

"Cool, you oughta know better," Satch said. "My arm's wound up good. And what's yesterday got to do with it? I'm pitchin' today."

"Satchel," Buck said. "You lost your share of games this season. Get yourself onto that bullpen mound and warm up, before we haul your ass down there."

Satch laughed. "What the hell you speakin' on, Buck? Just leave me be and take care of yourself." Then he turned to Ray, who was tying a red bandanna around his neck for luck. "You got anything to add to that?"

Ray shrugged, then shook his head. A trumpet blared, and the soldiers raised their rifles and fired into the air, scaring Jeep. With that began the game that no one, Islanders or Americans, would ever forget.

Leaving the on-deck circle, Cool took a couple of short stabs with his bat as he strolled to the plate. The umpire raised his arm and cried, "Play ball!"

Cool was dismayed: in his life he hadn't ever seen anything like Santo Domingo. All those poor kids, he thought as he walked to the batter's box, soldierin' their childhoods away. Those kids too young to carry rifles. But, he reminded himself, they'd shoot me dead for lookin' at 'em cross-eyed. He took a few more cuts and slapped his bat.

The umpire grunted with impatience and said, "¡Ponte allí y batea!" Cool nodded and stepped in.

Cool waited for the pitch. Though forty-one, he'd lost only a fraction of his speed, and that day he felt limber, as if he could outrun rabbits. Tall and graceful, Cool had a catlike appearance, with high cheekbones and a beautiful smile. He was what they would call "a gentleman," sporting a carnation in the lapel of his postgame suit and leaping to open doors for ladies in his path. Even though he was the oldest of the bunch, he had the "youth" as Satch called it, those eternal good looks.

The pitcher was a young southpaw, fatigued from having pitched just two days before, the shutout that Jeep wept at and called "a thing of beauty." Today his pitches were fast, with quick, jittery movements. Cool outsmarted him, taking a called strike two inside where he wanted it, then bunting the same on the next pitch—risky as a two-strike foul bunt is an out. But with a clean pop the ball skidded down the third-base line, curving inward toward the mound. They should have just fielded the ball and held Cool, but the third baseman, overconfident, grabbed it bare-handed and fired to first.

Cool Papa Bell ran so fast his legs seemed to blur. Silver stopwatch in hand, Rothberg timed the run to first and a cold sweat broke out. "Still faster than any man alive," he thought. "Even Owens couldn't catch him." Cool had already hit first base when the third basemen picked up the ball and threw. As it shot across the diamond, Cool made the turn for second. Amazed, the crowd roared. The first baseman caught the ball, readied to throw, but saw that his second baseman wasn't at the bag yet and his throw would have gone sailing into the outfield. Cool stood on second, barely winded, for a bunt double.

Ray Dandridge walked to the plate, holding the business end of his bat. His compact body appeared as if every ounce of fat had been worked off him over the years at hard labor, his skin weathered from the sun. Always sporting the red bandanna, he seemed to have stepped off the engine of a locomotive before heading to the diamond. As usual he wore a look of what some thought was constant, profound sorrow, perhaps the gaze of a holy man in deep meditation. Often his cohorts would take bets on who could make him laugh. Ray wasn't particularly sad, or angry, but when he did smile it broke like the sun through a week's worth of clouds.

Ray paused at the edge of the box. Then, after considering his bat, he dug in, his stance open, body curled out, and waited. The pitcher checked Cool, who had barely a lead at second. Finally he turned back, nodded to the catcher, and threw. Ray didn't swing, and Cool stole third, so fast the catcher didn't even bother to throw.

Hungry for more bases, Cool took a few steps off third. El Presidente sat up in his chair, beaming, waving his fist in triumph, egging the people on, many of whom loathed the man but couldn't help but roar at great baseball. Cool became a hornet, buzzing off the bag, hopping back and forth, jerking as if to run, halting, and dancing in place. The pitcher could see Cool from the corner of his eye. The young hurler knew that Ray devoured fastballs, so he'd have to try to hit the corners. But the corners meant the catcher would have to lean away from the plate, making a steal of home easier. The pitcher's obvious unease drove the masses to a greater frenzy, braying and banging drums in the bleachers. Twice the pitcher threw back to third, to the sound of boos, but it didn't keep Cool from taking another big lead. Finally the hurler reared back, kicked, and threw a curve. Cool bolted for home. The pitch came in, low and inside. Ray held up. The catcher palmed the ball in his mitt, turned perfectly to make the tag into nothingness. Cool swept a good two feet around the plate on the infield side, graceful as a landing swan, slapping the first-base edge of home.

Instead of a burst of noise, instead of the deafening clamor, the crowd leapt to its feet and began to murmur "Cool!," stretching out his name so that it sounded like a friendly boo. Cool tipped his cap as he made his way to the dugout and children threw candied fruit in honor of his run.

Satch yelled, "That's what ol' Satchel's talkin' about! Cat, you keep runnin' like that, we goin' down in history!"

"This is only the first inning," Buck said. As if by those words, the Orientales pitcher settled down and sent the next three batters, Ray and Buck included, back to the dugout with strikeouts.

The first Orientales batter was the pride of Venezuela, a slugger of great repute, brought down from the shadows of Pico El Águila, a man whose massive fists and forearms made bats look like toothpicks in his hands. He dispensed with the usual tics, stepped in, and glared at the pitcher.

Satch rolled his eyes in disgust. He stood straight and reared back to throw. Stretched to the extreme, his right hand almost touched the dirt, and his left foot shot out as high as his head. As he threw he fell forward like an axe, and if you could see that bee-ball pierce the air you had the best eyes in North America.

There was a muted pop of ball and leather. The ump remained crouched, waiting. Both Satch and the catcher froze. The batter held his bat cocked and ready. Finally, the ump threw up his arms and shouted, "¿A qué estás esperando? ¡Lanza!"

"Pitch?" Satch shouted in disbelief. The catcher turned to the ump. The baseball sat in the palm of his mitt.

The ump jerked his head in disbelief and cried, "Strike!"

The people in the stands exploded with disapproval, and the batter began to curse and kick at the dirt. Bottles, boxes, shoes, and flowers rained onto the field. The soldiers fired into the air, only to receive more debris. The loudspeakers blared, "¡Orden! ¡Orden! Si no ponemos orden, terminamos el partido." Since no one wanted to see the Dragones win by forfeit, the pummeling stopped and the game resumed amidst the garbage. After that, Satch had no trouble striking out the giant in two more pitches.

Batter number two knocked a shot down the third-base line. Scurrying like a crab to the line, Ray scooped up the ball in a mitt so large it looked as if he could catch pumpkins, then arched it to Buck in the nick of time.

But even after two quick outs, with brilliant pitching and fielding, the crowd ignored Satch and began to cry, "Maestro!"

Satchel stepped off the mound, yanked up his trousers, and pulled at his belt. He took a deep breath, and then a smile broke across his face.

The third batter was a lout with a thick rug attached to his chin that gave him the look of a jungle monster lured to the stadium with fresh blood. He dug in, cursed and pointed his bat at the mound, grabbed at his crotch, spit, and made such a production that Satch just laughed. He reared up and fired a pitch right into the batter's thigh. "You lucky," he shouted to the poor fellow limping to first. "Ol' Satch let up on it a hair!"

Now every man, woman, and child rose, the murmurs turned to shouts, and the Maestro, Martín Dihigo, stepped across the grass to the box. In the stands, Leo Rothberg leaned forward and gripped his cane tightly. He wiped his brow and suddenly knew exactly what the man next to him was talking about. "That's Dihigo!" he whispered, and began to scribble furiously in his pad.

Above the chants, women screamed and threw roses in adoration. Some cried with pleasure. Like DiMaggio, Dihigo was graceful, lanky as the Clipper. A big man, but lean, he seemed as if he'd been chiseled from marble and appeared taller than his six feet three inches. Dihigo, he of a gaudy batting average, who'd knocked a dozen homers in the first six games, stepped in gracefully, took a pair of beautiful swings, and waited.

Satch didn't care. He turned and shouted, "Everybody down!"

The players gaped at one another while the shortstop, fluent in both languages, spread the word. Jeep shuddered. Dr. Aybar genuflected. Cool Papa Bell pulled off his glove, dropped it at his feet, sat down on the soft grass, and smiled. He turned to the kids in the stands and said, "Pay attention, now, little amigos."

Buck ran to the mound and Ray joined them. The Dragones manager just wiped his brow and stood at the edge of the dugout.

"Satchel!" Buck said. "These shenanigans'll murder us!"

"Bucky, we been playin' too tight. Besides, this'll knock 'em down a peg."

"I'm not removing my glove," Buck said. He looked at Ray, who nodded in agreement.

"Mutiny, huh? Well, I tell you what: you sit, or I sit." Satch stepped off the mound. "We can always put Jeep on."

Buck looked into the dugout at Jeep, who was chewing on his thumbnail like it was all he'd eaten in days. Buck grumbled to himself and reluctantly pulled off his glove as he walked back to first. Ray shrugged and ran back to third, tossed his glove on the ground, and plopped down as well. The rest of the team followed.

Pandemonium ensued. Everyone shouted and yelled, banged sticks and threw paper. The umpire wouldn't have it—he didn't like the Americans fouling up the Island games with their antics. "¡Basta! ¡No puedes hacer ésto!"

"No?" Satch yelled and waved his mitt at Trujillo. "Ask the boss, you got a problem."

Trujillo knew better than to force the team to stand. Everyone— including his own eight-year-old daughter beside him—shouted for the game to continue without defenders. He gave a stern nod. The ump retreated to his position behind the catcher. Dihigo showed no reaction to these theatrics. He stepped in, pulled the bat back, and waited.

Satchel leaned forward on the mound and gave Dihigo the evil eye. "Here's the whipsey-dipsey-do for your collection," he yelled as he began his motion. His curveball came whizzing in just like he said it would. Dihigo didn't even try. Strike one.

The monster at first base, still aching from the plunk, broke for second. The catcher didn't move—there wasn't anyone at the base with a glove on. "Next," Satchel cried, "you'll be getting a taste of Satchel Paige–brand hesitation pitch!" He stretched his arm down as far as it would go, his leg kicked high, then his whole body spun around and he . . . stopped. His arm halted for a split second before the throw, which came in like a bullet.

Dihigo's timing was nearly perfect. The ball shot off his bat, a line drive deep into left field that kicked up sod barely a foot outside the line for a foul. The runner jogged back to second, and the left fielder sat back down after scrambling up to get the ball. Satch announced a wobbly ball, which Dihigo also fouled, driven to right. Then Satch reared up, proclaimed a midnight creeper was on its way, and the change-up came right on in. Another foul, straight backward. Now Dihigo's timing was perfect: had he hit the ball with the sweetest part of the bat, it would have gone into play.

Satch was dripping with sweat and clenching his jaw. The coach paced the dugout, and Aybar adjusted his tie. Jeep buried his face in his hands. Cool kept his eyes focused on Dihigo, waiting.

Satchel Paige pulled his cap down tight around his head. Martín Dihigo flexed his hands over the bat, stepped out, and then stepped back in. Satch moseyed up to the rubber and, without announcing his pitch, reared back and fired.

Dihigo smashed the fastball deep into center field. It arced high in the sky, vanishing in the white light of the sun. The players leapt to their feet, groping for their gloves, while the runner bolted around third, heading for home. Satch threw his hat to the ground. Cool Papa Bell didn't rise, instead merely squinting into the sky, following the ball, his right hand shielding the light from his eyes as best he could. For a moment the ball seemed to stop in front of the sun. Without taking his eyes off it, Cool pulled off his hat, as if to salute Dihigo. He didn't move, didn't stand. The ball broke, descended, and fell with a plop into Cool's cap.

The crowd nearly rioted. Dihigo came to a halt between first and second, shaking his head. Guns popped into the air as the Dragones raced back into the dugout.

Dr. Aybar met Satchel in the dugout. His eyes were wet, and he had sweat through his sports jacket. "Please," he said, in broken English, "no more tricks. You must win."

"Stop worryin'," Satch said, waving off Aybar. The doctor motioned to a pair of guards, who elbowed one another and then stepped into the dugout. Aybar whispered to the men and nodded down to Jeep. They marched over and ordered him to stand.

Jeep gulped. "What's going on?"

"Please," Dr. Aybar said. "You will please accompany these gentlemen to your hotel."

"Back to the hotel?" Buck said. "Whatever for? We might need him!"

As the guards hauled Jeep out, Aybar nodded. "Please. No more tricks. You must win."

Buck said, "But what if—"

Aybar wiped his brow with a bright yellow handkerchief. "El Presidente doesn't lose. Please, you must win. Or Mr. Jessup will be . . . indisposed."

One of the guards pointed his rifle at Ray, winked, and went "pow!"

Buck turned to Satchel and said, "That's what your little joke gets us."

"Game's going our way," Satch said. "No need to fret." He pulled a bottle of antacids from his coat and swallowed a handful.

As the game wore on, Satch kept the Orientales' bats cool, and when they connected, Ray and Buck sucked up the grounders with ease. But the rooters would have none of this, and, hungry for an upset, cheered the Orientales, and especially Dihigo. In the fourth, the Orientales shortstop pulled a muscle, and the coach sent another player to center to take over for Dihigo, who'd earlier robbed both Ray and Buck of a pair of doubles. Dihigo moved to short and was as agile as anyone they had ever seen, turning double plays on a dime, firing to first perfectly. Ray shook his head, and Buck said, quiet with admiration, "That fellow's All-Star everywhere. Never seen anything like it."

With the sun beating down behind the stands, sending dark shadows across the field, the eighth inning ticked by, and in the top of the ninth the score remained a miserly 1-0. Within in a span of five minutes, the Dragones managed to fan twice (the batters looking blind as moles), and then, just as quickly, loaded the bases for Buck Leonard on a bloop hit and two four-pitch walks. Dihigo, taking this in calmly, finally raised his arms and shouted, "¡Interrupción!" and then walked casually from his spot at short to the mound. The manager joined them for a brief conference. Finally the pitcher shrugged and surrendered the ball. From the stands, Rothberg watched with a growing, wide-eyed interest. To his surprise, in came a young man, racing to shortstop. Dihigo was now pitching.

Leo Rothberg wanted to shout from happiness. His notebook was crammed to the margins with every manner of scribble, exclamation, and even a few drawings. If Veeck's successful, he thought, every other team in the league's going to want to sign this talent. Calculations rang in his head: two grand for a second-stringer like the Orientales shortstop, six for that slim right fielder from the mountains, and Fort Knox couldn't contain the gold for a lad of Dihigo's promise.

El Maestro began to warm up while the stadium rocked and bellowed, belching noise from lungs, feet, hands, tubas, trumpets, even seatbacks. Dihigo eyed Buck, who'd been on fire the whole series. Without breaking a sweat, he finished the slugger in five pitches, the last a curveball with such a severe break that Buck missed it by two feet. And then, as if he'd just tossed underhanded to a bunch of schoolkids, Dihigo strolled back to the dugout. The crowd—all 45,000—cried out his name.

Following that, Satchel, deep in his own groove, struck out the first two batters in the bottom of the ninth, raising his total to nineteen. In spite of this, the crowd kept after Dihigo. With the bases empty, two outs, and the top of the order at the plate, Satch looked ready to seal the victory. But as the crowds kept singing "Maestro!", Satchel put his hands on his hips and thinned his eyes.

He walked the next man on six pitches. Then he clubbed the next batter in the butt. The next in the order stepped up and pointed his bat at the pitcher. Satch let out a nasty laugh, taunting the dummy, and walked him in four straight. By now everyone from the seven-year-old kid yelling in the bleachers to the men on the field knew what was going on. Martín Dihigo, waiting in the on-deck circle, set aside one of the three bats he was holding, and stepped to the plate.

Ray and Buck went into a tense crouch. Cool adjusted his cap to keep the sun out of his eyes, and readied himself. Satchel Paige stepped onto the rubber, ignored Dihigo, reared back, and fired. He sent in an agonizing curve that broke clear across the plate.

Dihigo swung and powered a ferocious line drive. Satchel watched the ball, rising with a certain majesty, as it flew over the bleachers and clear on out of the stadium.

The victory tore the crowd from its seats and onto the field. Alarmed, the soldiers fired their rifles into the air, but it would have taken an A-bomb to stop them. El Presidente fled. Dr. Aybar ran out of the dugout, never to be seen again.

The Americans ran for their lives, through the dusty catacombs of the stadium toward a rear exit they hoped wouldn't be blocked. On the way, Satchel shouted, "Wait!" and squeezed into the locker room. In a moment he popped back out carrying a paper sack.

"What's that?" Cool shouted.

"Ten grand," Satch said.

"That's what we stopped for!?" Buck shouted. "What about Jeep?"

"You think a sweet word's gonna set Jeepy free? This'll save that boy."

The players ran beneath the girders, rumbling and swaying from the riots above, each man flinching at the sound of gunfire. As they raced outside, Cool led, jumping behind a schoolbus that was lying on its side. He tried to peek into the vehicle, to see if there were any children inside, and when he crouched down again his face was a stunned mask. A dog lay dead on the sidewalk, and men and women, hysterical with fear or agitated with the sizzle of revolt, raced by, ignoring them. A pair of trucks came screeching to a halt a block away, filled with teenage soldiers, armed and ready for bloodshed. In the distance the island's lone gunship was firing into the city, a rumble like thunder.

Satch had curled into a ball. Buck leaned forward and shouted, "Listen, I think our best bet is in the church across the street. We'll hide in the basement until nightfall, maybe we can even make a telephone call there—"

"You gotta be crazy," Satch said. "We gonna hide out in a church?"

"Got a better idea?" Buck said. Satch fell silent, clutching his bag of money and wishing it really would bring Jeep back. Buck nodded toward the church, and they bolted.

A limousine cut them off. Leo Rothberg opened the rear door and leaned out, grinning. "Gentlemen," he said, "I'm here to rescue you." He nodded toward the front. "You'll find Mr. Jessup with my driver." He waved impatiently. "Please get in! This humidity's murder!"

The men crowded in, and there, in the front, sat a bewildered Jeep Jessup. "Jeepy!" Satch crowed, nearly choking in his relief. "How're you sitting, boy?"

Jeep turned to the back seat with a weary smile. "I didn't think I'd make it," he said. "But we got a boat. Or a plane, right Mr. Rothberg?"

As the car sped off, Rothberg leaned back and said, "A plane, Jessup, a plane." Bumping along, the limo followed a truck of soldiers while the players watched the chaos and ducked at the sound of the gunfire. Rothberg calmly thumbed through his notes, nostrils flaring, licking his lips in glee, barely moving as the car swayed to avoid a body. "Gentlemen," he said. "I have an offer for you." He explained, as Veeck had to Josh, that he wanted to sign them to contracts with Veeck's Philadelphia Stars, in the Negro Leagues. As they pulled up to the docks, he pointed out the window at a seaplane. "There she is, gentlemen. *The Lady Luck*! We'll sign the contracts on board. This way, please."

The players almost fell over themselves rushing to the gangplank. Their pilot, a young rowdy chewing on an unlit cigar, threw open the doors and shook his head as they boarded. Everything about the sky was the opposite of the chaos below it—as clear and peaceful as the city was cloudy with fire and tumult.

Once aboard, the pilot made for the cockpit and fired up the engines. Sirens were approaching. Jeep was bawling while Ray just stared, stone-faced, out the window. Cool closed his eyes, trying to calm himself. Buck prayed quietly, while Satchel kept chattering with Rothberg. Suddenly Jeep cried, "Mother of God, Satch! Soldiers!"

All but Rothberg leapt to the windows and watched as a truckload of soldiers came to a stop at the end of the pier. The soldiers scurried out and pointed frantically at the airplane.

"Hurry!" Buck yelled to the pilot.

Rothberg kept poring over his notes as if nothing in the world were going on.

"Get down!" Jeep shouted.

The soldiers fired at the plane. Bullets shredded the fuselage, and a grenade exploded with a splash just a few feet from Ray's window. "Hold on!" the pilot yelled. They held on. Trying to find room to climb in that crowded marina, the pilot turned the plane so that it was parallel to the shore, an even more inviting target. He gunned the engines, and everyone but Leo, who was seated, fell back. The plane sped over the water straight on toward a yacht crossing the harbor. "Everyone hang on!" the pilot screamed.

More bullets ripped into the plane's side, shattering one of the portholes. "Fucking Jesus!" the pilot cried, and pulled back on the throttle with all his considerable might, lifting the machine out of the water, inches above a yacht's topmast. They buzzed away, and the players crawled to the portholes and watched the soldiers grow small. With the busted window and the low pressure, the plane flew low, barely a hundred feet over the ocean.

Satchel said, "Fellows, we got trouble."

Rothberg had fallen to the floor, filling the aisle. He was clutching his chest. Blood welled up through his fingers. "That was unexpected," Rothberg said.

"Mr. Rothberg, we'll get you home," Buck said, propping his head up with a jacket.

Rothberg shook his head. "No, I—" He closed his eyes for a long moment and gestured for everyone to draw closer. He mumbled, "Forgive me, Bill, for what I'm about to say. But circumstances . . ." Clearing his throat, he said, "Gentlemen, I'm not delusional. In these last moments I've decided—" He shuddered, and went right to the point. "You're going to play in the major leagues."

The plane hit some turbulence, and Buck almost fell onto Leo. Once righted and steady, he said, "Sure, Mr. Rothberg, sure."

"Don't patronize me," Rothberg said. "You're going to the *white* major leagues." He coughed. "The Philadelphia Athletics to be precise. Now please pay attention, I have to give you instructions."

Leo's eyes clamped shut, and blood gurgled in his mouth. He turned and spit, and the color drained from his face in an instant. "You are landing in Miami," he said, "going to the Ponce de Leon Hotel. Reservations under my name. Ah!" He gripped Satchel's arm, his eyes suddenly wide from the pain. "Damn my luck this time. Listen: board the Mohawk Lines Bus in the morning, go to Cartwheel, Florida. Mr. Sam Dailey will meet you." He fumbled in his jacket and pulled out the leather notebook, which fell from his weakened hand. "Take that notepad," he whispered, not loud enough to hear. Before Leo Rothberg could add "Don't tell a soul," he died.

They didn't need to touch him to know this. The men stepped away from the body. They took their seats, the wind whistling through the broken window, blowing their baggy uniforms about. The pilot continued to hover close to the water, and the sun was low, almost to the horizon, making the sea gold. Each man withdrew inside himself, Leo's death and his bewildering message heavy on their minds. No one spoke.

It felt like a long flight back. They landed at a pier in Miami. The pilot screamed when he saw the body, and, already having broken his parole flying out of the country, fled. "That's a good idea," Ray said at last.

"What?"

"Cops," he said. "They see this dead white man, and we'll be cooked."

"He's right," Buck said. "Satch, give us that bag of money to get us to this Cartwheel place."

"Nigger! You crazy? Ol' Satch isn't . . ."

"Shut up, boy!" Buck said. "We all in trouble. Together."

The players squeezed in around Satch. Even Jeep looked ready to throttle him. Satchel squinted and handed Buck the bag. "You boys owe me. Satch ain't gonna forget."

"Neither will we, Satch, neither will we," Buck said. He handed each player a wad of money. "We go separately to Cartwheel. The place sounds remote. We've had enough trouble without having to wrestle with the Miami police."

As they rushed to get off the plane, Ray said, "You really think Leo meant the big leagues?" Ray said.

Buck didn't stop to answer. "We'll find out," he said.

At the foot of the gangplank, Cool turned. "What about Rothberg? We can't just leave him there."

No one heard him, and in a moment they were gone, scattered throughout the docks. Cool genuflected quickly and ran on.

Inside the plane, Leo Rothberg's body swayed to the gentle rhythm of the sea, his silver-tipped cane rolling against his temple. His leather notebook lay sprawled open by his chest, soaking up blood.

3

From the Oval Office
to the Stork Club

Veeck was perched high atop one of the girders above the stands in left field, fiddling with some wires, holding a wrench in one hand, smoking, and carrying a beer in his coverall pocket. "Try it now!" he yelled, and the cigarette tumbled from his mouth.

One of his operatives below waved a green flag to another, who waved another green flag back, then flipped a switch. Handel's *Messiah* blared throughout the park, echoing loudly off the hard snow and confusing residents for blocks around. Veeck pulled a pair of binoculars to his eyes and surveyed the stands. Beneath all the new loudspeakers he had his future hot dog vendors, bouncing to keep warm, testing the noise. They all held up white flags to indicate the sound was coming through, loud and clear. He scurried down the ladder, and even though he had weaned himself from his crutches, still reached for them, shrugged, then hobbled to the scoring booth high above home plate.

"Watch this," said Milton Wiggs, the official scorer, his breath hanging in the cold air. He pressed a green button and a roaring whoop bellowed from the loudspeakers. "Milt Jr. threw that together," he said, with pride. "That's for a base hit. Now get this . . ." He nodded at a red button. "You do the honors, Mr. Veeck." With that came the screech of elephants, so loud a coal truck nearly crashed on the street outside.

"Nice," Veeck said, slapping Milton on the shoulder. "That oughta fry the Yanks when they come to town. Keep it up, Milt."

"Johnny!" Veeck shouted in the hallways, slapping a young plumber on the back. "Really get to hammering. Make some noise

over the music. Let the folks outside know we're up to something."
The kid, who'd been trying to reroute cold pipes into places that
seemed impossible, nodded, and then eagerly accepted a slug from
Veeck's flask. Taking it back, Veeck took a sip himself, tucked the
flask into a little door in his artificial leg and hobbled off, through
the crowds of men repairing lights, scraping paint, and generally
tearing Shibe Park apart. A local jazz band, Joe Tennis and his 40
Love Orchestra, blared through the loudspeakers from a bar down
the street, forcing the men to shout over one another, or, on occasion,
to bang their hammers in unison as if in some musical extravaganza.
Beneath the stands, Veeck wandered the narrow hallways to admire
the guts of the park, the ganglia of electrical and sound wires, the
pipes, the low ceilings that would make old Satchel have to bend his
scrawny frame. He made his way into the dugout, where a blast of
February wind welcomed him. "Should have brought my cane,"
Veeck thought. Then again, he'd have to get used to worse. The
weather was murder on his stump, but there were guys in poorer
shape than him—like Evan, one of his electricians. Lost an arm in
Sicily, has seven kids, Jesus. Veeck paused at that thought to muse on
Eleanor, his wife, and his sons, all holed up in his Arizona ranch.
Three people he was thoroughly ignoring. Once that Oval Office is
done, he thought, we'll have a time, the whole family, living in the
ballpark. What could be better?

Veeck took a seat on the bench and admired some graffiti carved
into the wood that read *Connie the Misr*. The dugout seemed forlorn
without hard sunlight, bats in the rack, or a lineup on the wall. The
cold seemed to conduct right into his butt, so he lit a cigarette, admired his stadium for a moment, and headed to the Oval Office to
get some work done there.

Shibe Park sat like a strange little castle in the center of Goosetown, the working-class section of Philadelphia, the perfect spot in
Veeck's mind. There was a hard crust of cruel snow covering the infield, carving small grooves into the dirt and pulling the edges of the
grass away from the mound. But in two months it would be a deep
green, worn away by the spikes of his ballclub, by Josh and Cool and
Buck and everyone else.

Shibe was made, like the factories in town, of steel and concrete.
Its façade was a mishmash of competing styles with its hard brick
and mortar and terra-cotta, and whitewashed planks separating by

five feet the sidewalk from right field (where some fans, during games, would swear they could feel the heat of a game roll off like rain from a roof). The front was proudly described, in all Athletics literature, as a "testament to the French Renaissance style," an odd pairing for a baseball park: you would buy your tickets, get your bags of peanuts, and listen to the men in striped suits hawk programs beneath arches, vaultings, and Ionic columns, and, Veeck's favorite, the towering three-story dome that shot out the front like a fat stalk of white asparagus. This stalk was home to the Oval Office: an office and apartment and tavern all in one, named for the president's place of business despite being a perfectly round room. It looked out on Lehigh Avenue on one side and the diamond on the other. Connie Mack, the previous owner, had used the place for an inner sanctum and nothing else, where no one was allowed, no fooling at all. Veeck was going to open the place right up after every game, and it wouldn't shut down until the last beat reporter had either fallen asleep on the divan or stumbled home blitzed.

The racket of improvement and jazz carried for blocks around and brought crowds and reporters nearly every day. The *Philadelphia Inquirer* had already run two articles on the crazy Mr. Veeck, thrilling write-ups about his success in Milwaukee and the coming improvements at Shibe. Veeck had hired an old German to offer hot sausages and cold beer to the boys of the press. "Can't be too cold for a beer," Veeck would say, toasting the writers, who, to a man, always toasted back and appreciated the extra shot of whiskey he'd give them. Veeck landed on radio, on the front and sports pages, in print ads and local magazines. He'd secured the grand marshal spot in the St. Patrick's Day parade. One day he was an honorary library commissioner, on another an honorary bus driver. The streets around the stadium were already festooned with colored bunting, banners of the team mascot—the white elephant, raging with a bat in its trunk—and Veeck had put armed guards in front of the box office to give the whole works an added gravity. A tin sign read TICKETS ON SALE MARCH 1. "If you wait just a little bit," Veeck said with a wink to one of the guards, "they get hungry. We'll be nearly sold out by Opening Day."

Veeck hired painters and plumbers, electricians and carpenters, but he also painted and plumbed, drew current and cut planks himself. Later that morning he went to work painting the Oval Office, a project that was solely his own. Dot Lawrey, a rough old broad who had been working with Veeck since his days in Milwaukee, sat amidst boxes and tarps in her office, shouting into two phones at once and now and again up to Veeck. Her desk sat at the foot of a wide set of stairs that rose up in marble to Veeck's office. "Philadelphia Athletics?" she said. "Hold please. Philadelphia—I know you're waiting, and you'll keep on waiting, and I don't care which bank—loan's not due . . . what? We'll send you two seats in the box section. Philadelphia Athletics? Mr. Veeck is not taking calls. Philadelphia Athletics—?"

At the sound of a cough, she looked up from her calls. There stood a dapper man in a platinum-colored suit, hand-painted tie, two-tone shoes, and matching hat in hand. He opened his mouth to speak, but she put her hand over the phone and shouted up the flight of stairs behind her to the open door, "Burley here to see you!"

"Send him up, Dot!"

She jerked her head toward the door of Mr. Veeck's office. Dan Burley was the reporter for the *Amsterdam News*, the leading Negro paper in New York City. He was a renaissance man in his own mind, a tinkler on the piano who sat in with Bird, whose daily sports column, "Confidentially Yours," was read by every Harlemite with an eye for good writing. He removed his hat and tiptoed swiftly to the door, careful not to step in any paint splotches. Burley was hungry for a story, but never so much as to ruin his shoes.

Burley shook his head with disapproval as he walked into the Oval Office. It was a riot. The place stank of paint, and canvas tarps were thrown about. Boxes were stacked dangerously high, chairs were piled on top of one another, and paint-speckled papers lay scattered about every surface. A brand new Murphy bed had been installed against the northern curve of the room, next to the door to what looked like a washroom. Standing on a stepstool was a man busy rolling paint up to the ceiling, dressed in a T-shirt, paint-smeared khakis, and sneakers, with a cigarette that bobbed as he spoke. "Be with you in just a sec, Dan," he said.

"Mr. Burley," he corrected, scowling. "And you are . . .?"

Veeck laughed—this was happening all the time lately. "I'm the guy you came to talk to."

Burley gaped. This Veeck—"old Veeck" as he enjoyed calling him to others—appeared five years younger than Burley, who prided himself on his youthful appearance.

Veeck descended the ladder clumsily, walked over, and offered his hand. They shook, and Veeck said, "Excuse me," lifted up the tarp, and pulled out a pair of old kitchen chairs. "Sorry about the mess. Still getting things straight." He crossed one leg over the other, pulled up his trousers, opened the door in his wooden leg, and pulled out the flask. "Nip?"

Burley prided himself on handling his liquor. "Why not?" he said, and took a sip. Bourbon. Decent stuff, too. Licking his lips, he asked, "How'd you lose your leg?"

"Sold it to buy the team. Listen, I appreciate your coming up here, it's great to see you in person. Most of the New York boys talk over the phone. Even you fellows from the Negro press. And I've got a great story for you: this year the Stars are going to be the greatest Negro club in baseball history. We've got scouts all over the country. We'll barnstorm . . . and get this—twenty times this year I'm going to pit them against the A's. Exhibition games. If it takes off, the owners are going to go nuts for the money, so I'm thinking the Stars'll have a whole schedule of white opponents. Why, we might even . . ."

"Mr. Veeck—"

"Call me Bill, Dan."

"Well, you can call me Mr. Burley." He gave Veeck a brief smile and said, "I know you've got Wells."

A cold chill hit Veeck as quickly as a flashbulb pop. But he didn't change his expression. "Wells? Willie Wells? Of course I do! Listen, I've got Wells, Satchel, Josh Gibson, Dandridge—"

Burley accepted the offer of another tug from the flask, cleared his throat, and pulled out a pad of paper. He began flipping through what looked like neat, copious notes. "May I read something to you, Mr. Veeck?"

Veeck nodded and lit another cigarette.

Burley glanced down at his scribblings. "I've got people in every corner of the baseball world—ahem, the *colored* baseball world—and none of them were aware of your plan. I mean, rumors burst forth every spring, but every road was a dead end. Until," he smiled, "I received a call from Mr. Willie Wells."

Veeck looked as if Burley had told him something funny. "A call from Willie?"

Burley smiled right back. "I don't like to dance, Okay, Mr. Veeck? Wells called me and he sang like a jailbird trying to get free. The Philadelphia Athletics—*not* the Philadelphia Stars—have Willie Wells' contract." He held up a hand at Veeck's protestations. "You can imagine my surprise, Mr. Veeck. In fact it was so overwhelming that at first I figured Willie was drunk. I hung up on him. But you know what got to me? It's this: Willie will brag, like all athletes, but he won't lie. He won't lie, Mr. Veeck. I called him back." Burley closed his pad, leaned back in his chair, and nodded at Veeck for another bite off the flask, which Veeck provided. "You can deny it all you want, but my editor has the front page cleared tomorrow, with Pearl Harbor–size headlines and ample room for my story underneath." He held out his hands to indicate the front page. "*Bill Veeck to Integrate Athletics.* Dull, but it gets the point across. The thrill is in the prose."

Veeck didn't answer right away. He should have known: there's loyalty, then there's loyalty, and rare is the occasion when that loyalty falls on the side of an owner, or a Negro for a white man. "Sorry, but you're wrong, Dan. The Athletics are training in Kent, Ohio, you know that as well as I do . . ."

"Willie's in Cartwheel, Florida."

"Absolutely. Training for the Stars. As much as I'd love Willie— and boy, would I!—you and I both know the commissioner won't allow it. I've got Wells for the Stars, but that's it."

"Well, Bill, you can answer truthfully or not. Either way, that's my story."

Veeck nodded, lit a cigarette, then realized his last was only half smoked. He exhaled a good-sized cloud and said, "Listen, Dan, I'd give my eye teeth and my other leg if I could have Willie for the A's. They're the worst team I've ever seen. But there's a war on. I can show you the contracts."

Burley chanced a lie. "Willie already told me you signed him to both. I think we know which one supersedes the other."

Veeck thought on that for a moment. Oscar Charleston swore to him that Willie gave his word not to tell. It always floored Veeck when someone broke a promise. "Like you said, Willie was drunk."

"And like I said, Willie doesn't lie. Besides, he leaks the truth with a few under his belt. The burden of proof is on your shoulders, at least as far as this court is concerned. I have it that Wells is opening the door." Burley leaned forward, "Listen, Bill, I need your help to make this story come alive. I need the meat. Let's work together."

Veeck sat up sharply. "You print that story and I'll sue your paper for libel."

Burley smiled. "That just tells me I've got under your skin." He stood to go.

Veeck knew he should have just thrown Burley out, but his penchant for trying to charm his way out of trouble overruled him. "Wait a minute!" he said, wearily. "Sit down! Do you know what's going on here?"

"I do. What's going on here is, even in these times, the story of the century."

"Be reasonable, Dan. Other than the scoop, why do want to run this?"

Burley was tired of being called "Dan" but suppressed his urge to correct Veeck. "Bill, if I have to tell you why I want this story, you wouldn't understand anyway. But I think we both know. As a Negro and as a journalist, this is *the* story. The story of a lifetime."

Veeck just nodded. He took a drag of his cigarette and hobbled over to the window. Right then he wished walking wasn't such a sketchy exercise. He stared out the window, down at the wet streets, and shuddered. His plans had been simple, and perhaps that's why they could simply unravel. A story broken in the *Amsterdam News* wouldn't do anything but open the commissioner's eyes and shut him down for good. After rolling in the clover of the Negro Leagues and seeing his roster stocked with such talent, the alternative struck him as dead wood. He squinted and turned to Burley. "You're wrong about Wells."

Burley had sat for a moment but now stood again. "For a moment I thought you'd be square with me, but—"

"Sit down! You're wrong about Wells . . . but right about everything else."

That stopped him. "Meaning what? Satchel?"

"Satchel, yes. And Wells."

"Both?"

Veeck sighed and lit a cigarette. "All of them. The whole team. Every single player."

"The whole team?" Burley's eyes rose with surprise, and then, just as quickly, he shook his head. "You had me for a second. Like I said before, very few people pull my leg." He put his hat back on. "Call me if you want to make a statement."

"Dot!" Veeck shouted. To Burley, he said, wearily, "Hold on a moment." When she entered, he said, "Show Mr. Burley the contracts." Dot returned with a stack of papers, all in triplicate. She handed them to Veeck with a quizzical look. Veeck held them out to Burley and said, "I think you'll find these interesting."

Burley raised an eyebrow. Veeck nodded, and Burley looked over the contracts. Each one bore the logo of the white elephant beneath which PHILADELPHIA ATHLETICS was printed in Old English type. It was a standard white major league contract, in fine print, larger typewritten numbers in the blank spaces for the names and dates and salaries. At the bottom were the signatures: Satchel Paige, Willie Wells, Ray Dandridge, Cool Papa Bell. Burley read the names quietly, as if murmuring a prayer. "Verdell Mathis, one of my favorites. Bonnie Serrell, that's an odd one . . . Gene Benson, Philly boy, good choice . . ." Perspiration collected on his brow. He never perspired.

Veeck pointed a thumb at the door. "If you break that story, it's all over, Dan. Wait a few weeks and I can give you a great piece."

Burley looked up from the contracts. "Why a few weeks?"

"Because we haven't signed them all yet. And we're still vulnerable. By April first it will be too late for Landis to do anything—spring training will be under way, and there's no possible way for us to sign replacements. With the barrage of press I'll get, and the urgency of the season, the commissioner couldn't shut us down without trouble."

Burley just laughed. "You really think I can hold this?" he shouted. Catching himself, he said more quietly, "Do you think I can go back to my editor, who I had to beg for hours to give me the front page in the first place, and say, 'Sorry, nothing's happening after all?' What do you think he'd do? Well, I'll tell you what *I'd* do, Bill: I'd assume Mr. Dan Burley got paid to shut up, and since I had the space anyway, I'd get someone *else* to write the piece, based just on rumor."

Veeck couldn't believe what he was hearing. "You mean you'd print that story even if it destroyed my team? Even if it wrecked integration?"

Burley smiled and patted Veeck on the shoulder. "You can't frighten me, Bill. When I run this, there's nothing the commissioner can do." He placed his hat on his head, tipped it back to a jaunty angle, and said, "I thank you, sir."

At that moment, Dot shouted from downstairs. "Commissioner Landis just called!"

"Mary, Mother of—put him through!"

"No!" Dot shouted. "I mean it was his secretary and she hung up already. Bill, she said that he wants you at the airport in a half an hour."

"What? Come up here!"

Dot ran as best she could up the stairs. "That's right," she said, panting, and began reading from her notes in the margins of the comics page. "The secretary said that he said that you should take the next Mid-Continent to Indianapolis, then catch another to Chicago, and meet Judge Landis at his office at eight tonight. That's what she said he said."

"Tonight?" Burley said. "He's not serious?"

She nodded at the contracts. "She said that the commissioner said that he wants you to bring those."

Veeck looked pale. "Dot," he said in almost a whisper. "First, call our boys in the press. Call Gordon, call Smith, call Wickham, and, oh for God's sake, call Daniel—God, how I hate Daniel—and see if they can spread the word."

"I already did. Call them, I mean."

"Good girl, now—"

She shook her head. "Bill, they won't touch it."

"What do you mean they won't touch it?"

"Gordon said he was busy. Smith's secretary said he wasn't taking any calls, and when I told her to tell him 'Code Pepper,' she did and then said he still wasn't taking any calls. Wickham wasn't there, even though he's usually always there. Daniel hung up on me."

For once Veeck was speechless. He cleared his throat. "I see. Well, Dot, go find my blue suit then." He winced. "Remind me not to forget the tie." With that, he summoned up a wan smile. "Well, friend, it was good while it lasted. Couldn't keep it to yourself, I guess."

"What do you mean?"

"I mean we're fried," Veeck said loudly. He began to undress as Dot raced in with a box that held Veeck's only suit. The thing looked as if it had never seen the sun. Veeck sniffed himself, pulled a pair of trousers from the box, and slipped them on over his boxer shorts. "Suits," he grunted with disgust. As he buttoned up the stiff white shirt, he said, "Landis knows and he's not happy. You must have let this story leak."

"These rumors have been flying for ages."

"I don't know what we're arguing about, it's over either way. The judge doesn't request one's presence for tea. So now there's no Satchel, no Willie, nothing but the dregs. Nothing but . . ." and he had to tail off to clear his throat. He began to shout. "So unless you want to follow some former plumber who can't hit .200, you're back to writing about the Black Yankees!" With that, Veeck jerked the tie up to his throat and almost stumbled onto Burley as he walked by.

Burley stood in the doorway, angry and bewildered. "You can't keep me from writing my story," he shouted.

"So write the story, Dan," Veeck said, and hobbled through the door.

Fine, Burley thought, time to run with the story and bury this guy. He raced down the stairs and turned to Dot. "Let me have the phone." She handed him the receiver. He called his editor at the *News*. When the operator put him through, a harsh voice exploded, "Burley, what the hell!?"

"Quiet, Jack. He wouldn't bite, so—"

"Wouldn't bite is right! This story's finished, and *you're* finished."

"Pardon?"

"Who the hell gave you this information? There's no integration. Nothing. But here's a story for you: the commissioner has banned the Negro Leagues from playing in any white stadiums this year. *Including* Yankee Stadium and Griffith. No Negro Leagues in major league stadiums! Says it agitates the press during this 'crucial time in history.' So now the Black Yankees, the Grays, they haven't got a place to play! Nice work pal! You've ruined us all!"

"But—"

"Half our advertisers threatened to quit!" he shouted. "Not one or two, *half!*"

"But I'm—"

"You're fired!"

Burley couldn't believe what he was hearing. "Fired? Why?"

"Because you're poison." He hung up.

Burley dropped the receiver to the floor. As he bent to pick it up, he somehow managed to kick it a few feet and pull the whole phone off the desk. Dot shrieked. "Shut up!" he cried. Pulling the whole machine together, he took the spaghetti-like cords in a bundle, tucked the receiver under his ear, and began frantically yelling into the phone. "Jack? Jack?" But there was nothing, and he knew there would be nothing.

Christ almighty, it was like he'd been hit with a Joe Louis left hook. He dropped the whole mess of a phone on the desk and collapsed into a chair and stared at the calendar on the wall, at the picture of the poor guy throwing a hand grenade, waiting urgently for anyone to toss some spare cash into a war bond. Burley's lips were dry, his eyes burned. What just happened? He let out a pathetic laugh, which sounded like he was readying to spit. He hadn't just lost his job . . . Christ, he was Dan Burley, had the best column in New York, had . . .

That certain something hit him, that feeling when reality washes over and drives away all rationalization. He was through. The Negro Leagues were through. Jesus, he thought, how many times had he said he felt lucky that the Negro Leagues had no one with as much power as the commissioner: usually he laughed that his white counterparts cowered in Landis's presence. Apparently the judge could reach into Burley's world as well. At least he knew Wells was telling the truth. . . .

Dot looked like she was about to cry. He watched her wring her hands and stare out at the grey skies over Shibe.

Then a thought crept into Burley's head. "Dot, I'm going to use the phone again," he explained, quietly. He was beginning to get a headache, and this call would only make it worse. If there was one human being on earth Dan Burley hated in life, it was the man he needed that night.

The line was busy. Burley kept trying, patiently, until, ten minutes later, the operator said she had a connection. She plugged him through.

"Hello, Sparks. That's right, Dan Burley. Oh, about a year. No, I haven't been avoiding you. Listen, remember that favor? That's the right, *the favor*. Well, I'm cashing it in. No, I don't need money. What? Well, that's a lot of money, but what I really need is this. You've got a pen and paper? Good . . ." And he explained.

Dot stared at him with wet eyes and not a little resentment. He ignored her. Tipping his hat by way of a goodbye, Dan Burley stepped out, walked down the stairs and out into the cold, light rain that had been coming down for the last hour. Bad weather for a flight, Dan thought. He wondered if he'd see a sunny day again.

In New York, Sparks Thompson delicately hung up the receiver and wiped his brow. He was typically red-faced, but now he appeared positively beet-complexioned. "Holly!" he bellowed. "Holly!"

A man named Holly, thin and agitated, looking as if he were ready to kill someone at a moment's notice, strode in. "Okay, okay. Whatcha want, Sparks?"

Sparks told him. Now Holly looked perturbed. "That's a tall order, chief."

"So get on it!"

Holly hopped a cab into New York's cheap merchandise district. The skies were overcast and pink from the city lights. He made his way up three flights of steps in the heart of a cold-water tenement, a flat used by the lowest of the world's businessmen. He knocked on the door of a ratty little office without windows and let himself in. There he found Chick Weathers, one of Broadway's thousands of two-bit publicity agents. Holly walked around the tiny desk, stood over Chick, and dropped two envelopes in front of him. "This one," Holly growled, holding up the envelope with a "1" on the front, "goes to the maitre d'. The other you'll open and read to him as soon as you're seated."

Chick was visibly shaken. "This one to the maitre d'," he repeated, to make certain he had it right, "and this I'll open and read." A nervous grin spread across his face. "Wow. I could really get to the big time by meeting . . ."

Holly slapped him. The blow knocked Chick backward in his chair. Holly hauled Chick up from his seat, slammed him on the desk, pulled out a revolver, and dug it into his temple. "You're going to sit with the big man because Sparks wants it, understand. It's not about Chick, get me?" He cocked the hammer and twisted the gun into Chick's skin. "Fuck this up and I'll get real joy in wallpapering this joint with your brains. Okay?" Chick nodded. Holly looked for a moment like killing him right now might just be fun. But then he composed himself, stood, and uncocked the pistol. Flush with excitement and out of breath, Holly said, "Now let's go."

Holly dropped Chick off at the Stork Club. The line out front was two blocks long and four people thick. Chick hopped out and pushed up to the doorman. He slapped Chick's chest with a meaty hand and shouted, "End of the line!"

"A letter from Sparks," Chick squeaked.

The doorman thought for a moment, then nodded toward the door. No one who valued life threw that name around recklessly. With one hand he held back the crowd, now roaring at the sight of the open door. Chick scooted in.

Inside, the club was packed, abuzz with an angry swarm of stars and the men and women who pursued the stars. Chick saw Chaplin arguing with a woman, and in another corner someone who looked like Bogart, hovering over a drink. Press agents, talent agents, publicity agents leagues above Chick stood around chatting, eager to get to the one place Chick was going to be in a moment's time. His heart pounded like it was trying to cover the sound of the music, and his stomach felt filled with raw eggs. As he stood in front of the maitre d', he lost his nerve.

"What is it?" the maitre d' hissed, the light shining off the quarter-inch part cleaved down the center of slicked-back hair. The man looked like the Stork itself. Finally he gestured to the bouncer, and nodded severely at Chick.

"Wait! Wait!" Chick said, and threw the "1" envelope at him. The maitre d' laughed as he read it. Then he looked Chick up and down and sighed. "You're lucky. I can take you right now."

At this, the maitre d' led him across the room. Suddenly the standing crowd seemed to sense where Chick was going. They began to follow him.

"Jesus, kid, WW?"

Chick was sweating now, feeling sick. His brain seemed to be floating and ready to spill out his mouth. All he could do was nod and blink.

"Holy fuckaloo," one fellow said, grabbing at Chick's lapels. "Listen, kid, I got a hundred for you, just to mention a name, 'kay? Claudia Wannamaker, she's a gorgeous girl, tell him I'm willing to change the name."

"I got two hundred for you, kid, just tell him I got the next Alan Ladd!"

"Two fifty! The hottest young thing since—"

"Don't listen to them, kid, five hundred for Claudia. *Claudia Wannamaker*. Wan-uh-maker. Tits out to here, already got talkin' parts on Broadway. This'll make her. Give ya a grand!"

The crowd thinned as he was led into the Club Room, and to a guarded corner. He knew instinctively that this was Table 50. His eyes focused ahead, and he heard the tap-tapping of a typewriter. It was quieter at this booth, like the muted sound that surrounds an operating table. The light was a touch brighter, and there were men standing, looking as if they were shielding the president. The maitre d' stopped. Chick stopped.

"You have *two* minutes." He stood aside. There was a chair at the edge of the table. "Well, sit down!"

Chick sat down slowly and gaped in amazement.

Walter Winchell was typing furiously, machinelike and without break, his hat tipped back on his head. He wore glasses, his eyes hidden behind the reflection of the typewriter in the lens. A cigarette burned in an ashtray next to him, surrounding him with a ghostly grey smoke, as if he were burning souls. Chick guessed that he was writing tomorrow's column. His eyes widened at the paper in the machine. Tomorrow, there would be fifty million people staring at those words. *Fifty million.*

"Mr. Winchell?" he croaked.

Winchell kept typing, stopping only when the machine's loud ding forced him to change lines with a quick swipe of his right hand.

"Mr. Winchell?"

One of Winchell's close pals, sitting across from him like a wax figure, fat, sweating, his neck bulging from the collar of a hundred-dollar shirt, laughed. "The oracle doesn't speak," he cackled. "State your case and fly away, little moth."

Chick's hands shook as he opened the envelope and read the contents aloud.

Walter, he read, *I have an item: a man named Bill Veeck has purchased the Philadelphia Athletics baseball team. This season, he is going to field a team made up entirely of Negro ballplayers. They will play in the major leagues. Tonight Mr. Veeck is meeting with the Commissioner of Baseball, Judge Kenesaw Mountain Landis, who will attempt to keep Mr. Veeck from this goal. He will be successful without your intervention. First, you must have an intimate conversation with R., pass this news along, and convince him to speak with Mr. Landis personally. You may use any means necessary (and we both know what I mean) to convince R. to speak out, first to Mr. Landis, and then to the press. You must include this information in tomorrow's column, at the very top. I leave it to you to determine whether or not it merits notice on your radio program.*

Upon confirmation, I will regard the situation between yourself and Ms. Kitty Temple to be concluded, and will also consider your debts paid in full.

Regards,
Sparks.

At first Chick couldn't believe his eyes. Baseball? Negroes? Christ, if he'd known, he wouldn't have read it, wasted Mr. Winchell's time. Then his temple ached where the tip of Holly's gun had burrowed in. He reread it for good measure. When he was finished, he summoned up his courage and said, "Sir, my name's—"

He was brought out of his chair by a force so powerful he thought for a moment he'd been hit by an automobile. A single hand, large and strong as a vice, dug into the scruff of Chick's neck, and his feet barely touched the ground as he was hauled across the length of the bar to the doors leading outside. "Time's up!" he heard, and was literally spun out the door, where he fell at the edge of the curb, face down. The people in the line barely gave Chick a glance. He looked at the bouncer and the big red doors behind him, eyed the crowd, and then, with blood pounding in his brain, he vomited on the curb.

Finished, he stood, adjusted his tie, ran a comb through his hair, and spit. Mustering up a little dignity, Chick began walking home. He knew he would never set foot in the Stork Club again.

4

Surrounded by Swamps

Cartwheel, Florida, was an old World War I training base, used by the army to test tear gas on the unlucky soldiers being sent to the trenches, usually local Seminoles. As isolated as it was, most everyone agreed you'd have to be crazy to do any business there. It was a strange, almost perfectly oval island that rose up, high and dry from the swamps, as if it were man-made, which in fact it might have been, by the Army Corps of Engineers, by an old tribe of Seminoles in the late nineteenth century, or by pirates—it all depended on whom you asked. The place could not be found on any map. The locals didn't even know it existed. There was one road to Cartwheel, which had flooded just after Prohibition and had vanished altogether. Rowing there in a skiff proved eminently difficult—one had to maneuver the labyrinth of cypress tree knobs, thick roots that stuck up out of the muck like the ends of baseball bats, so abundant you couldn't move. Veeck hired a crew of Seminoles to cut a couple of paths to the island, one from the east and one from the west, and without one of these Indians as a guide to ferry you to the island, you'd be hopelessly lost, your cries for help echoing across the waters. Cartwheel was certainly no place for a major league baseball team. It was as feasible as training on the Sargasso Sea.

Rothberg had originally used it as a joint to manufacture and distribute gin during Prohibition, and tipped Veeck off to its possibilities. Leo never paid for the place—it was thoroughly abandoned by the early 1920s—but Veeck went through the proper channels and bought it from the government for a dollar and fifty years tax-free, just to get the damn thing off their hands. The place boasted four soggy playing fields, a weedy but solid thousand-meter track, an officers' mess and barracks with their windows intact. Belts of fog surrounded the area like a wall. Veeck, Sam, and a trusted staff of four spent a month cleaning it up. By the first of February, Cartwheel was ready for spring training.

While Veeck bolted to Philadelphia to tie up the thousands of loose ends, Sam remained behind to oversee the Florida operation. Why, he didn't know: Sam was the numbers man, the business face of the club . . . why did they need him in Cartwheel? Bill said something about a "presence" in Florida, and this being Sam's opportunity to bond with the team. Sam didn't want to bond. He was content to sit in offices and bleachers and box seats, and own the team. Installed in a stuffy little office, Sam tried to make the best of it in this dump: he hung his law degree prominently on the wall behind him, had a medicine cabinet as crowded as a New York tenement with antacids, laxatives, painkillers, and remedies for every malady known to have afflicted him over the years, a large mahogany desk that he'd found on the base and spent hours restoring, and, to Veeck's surprise and delight, a calendar with a little fleshy cheesecake from an auto parts store. Sam saw a calendar like that once in the Brewers' locker room and figured it couldn't hurt to show the players he was one of the guys.

Sam loathed Cartwheel. It smelled like the Milwaukee city dump. The humidity was so thick it was like being inside the mouth of a dog. That first night alone he couldn't help but lie awake, listening; around midnight the swamp would begin groaning and blurping and chattering. That generator would begin its lonely dirge—why did they need it in the night? Above, the trees were rustling, as if a large snake were about to drop on the roof. Now and again there was a heavy splash, like a body being dumped from a rowboat. The maintenance staff knocked off early and played cards in the kitchen, but the cook—a raggedy old guy who looked like he was on the verge of death—liked to wander the grounds making noise with his throat.

The next evening Sam decided to sit up and read until he couldn't help but fall dead asleep. Every now and then he would remove his thick, horn-rimmed glasses and lay them on the desk in front of him. He'd rub his sockets so hard it was as if he were trying to polish the eyeballs. Around midnight he was busy poring over a few of the reports from Leo—notes from his trips through the islands, mailed just before his death. They bothered him: Sam couldn't believe half of what he read. He guessed he'd have to meet these people face to face, though mostly he disliked seeing Rothberg's handwriting—the notes of a dead man, a man killed scouting. That only spooked him all the more.

So when Sam reached over for a pen, looked up and saw Oscar Charleston filling the door frame, his screams echoed across the swamps.

"The hell's the matter with you, you never seen a nigger before?" Oscar grumbled. He was irritable—the driver of his skiff had appeared inebriated, there were no lights in Cartwheel to welcome him, and Sam's screaming was the last thing he wanted to hear.

As Sam rummaged for the small bottle of whiskey he kept in his desk drawer, he said, "Do you realize the time?"

A beat-up cigar poked out of Oscar's mouth. He pushed his brown derby back on his head but didn't speak. By his feet sat a little red carpetbag, and a baseball bat with a glove hooked around the handle leaned against the frame, just like a sandlot kid might have. For the last few months he'd been traipsing all over the South, looking for new talent, and now he was in Florida and eager to whip these kids into shape as a coach. With his jacket, vest, and hat, he looked like a cop. His pantlegs were soaked to the knees.

"Where do you want me?" Oscar barked.

"The coaches' barracks are upstairs. Mickey should be here tomorrow. We . . . we didn't know when to expect you."

"Where are the players' barracks?"

Sam cleared his throat. "Why?" When he didn't get an answer, he nodded behind Oscar. "Outside and across the clearing. You'll see a bright white 'A' on the side. For the rostered players. I guess you can stay there."

With that, Oscar picked up his bag, bat, and glove, and walked away. Sam stared at the empty frame for a good minute, sipped the remainder of his shot, and went back to reading.

Oscar made his way through the dark to the building, where the "A" stood out clearly, even in the ashy glow of the half-moon. He switched on the lights and stood for a moment to let his eyes adjust. The place was spotless: long rows of cots, each with its own chest at the foot of the bed, just like when he was in the army. He took a deep whiff—the place even smelled like the Philippines. Oscar carefully transferred his clothes into a chest, undressed and hung his wet pants and socks on the end of his bed, and leaned his equipment there. Then he uncorked a small wooden flask of port wine with his name burned into it, took one swig, and belched. He turned out the lights, climbed back into bed, and went to sleep.

Charleston was *just* too old to play baseball, on the far end of his forties, but in Veeck's mind the ideal coach. A onetime center fielder, in his day he was routinely considered the greatest Negro ballplayer on earth. The Negro press said it, coaches repeated it, white scouts shuddered at his towering home runs and awesome speed and later, privately, shook his hand. Oscar never repeated any of their claims. Whenever he coached, he chose to bully and badger and beat the fundamentals of the sport into his charges, to lead by example, just as he was led in the army. When Veeck called him to scout and coach, Oscar was wary. It wasn't the first time a white man had offered the Promised Land. But when this guy's checks cleared, and when Veeck somehow finagled gas rations out of nowhere to get Oscar to every corner of the land, and when Bill wired money to sign these prospects, Charleston found himself waking every day before sunrise, angry that the fucking day only had twenty-four hours and his weak body needed food and sleep. He had a whole country to see, men to sign. Good men, who would play in places he'd been denied his whole life. Over time he began to wonder why *he* wasn't running the team, but he pushed that thought away: there wouldn't be any room for quarreling. Like the army, the A's would have to work as a unit, especially from the top. They were going to have to fight for every goddam win. That first evening in Cartwheel, as Oscar drifted off to sleep, he thought that any failure wouldn't be for lack of coaching on his part. He'd kill a man before he'd let him fuck this thing up.

Mickey Cochrane and two others arrived by flatboat the next day. Veeck had worked his magic on Cochrane and found it wasn't difficult to get him back into the game. After being signed on, Mickey quickly brought in two of his friends, Mack Filson and Red Hourly, a pitching instructor of certain genius and a hitting coach he knew to be fiercely loyal. Then he spent the next few weeks studying his notes on managing—culled from his years as skipper of the Detroit Tigers. Lantern-jawed, with a bulbous nose and jug ears, Cochrane landed on the silent shores of Cartwheel, slit-eyed, looking very much like an explorer seeking El Dorado in the jungles.

Sam walked Mickey around the grounds while his coaches settled in, and they found Oscar sitting in the mess hall laboring over a pile of notes, already in his white uniform with its cobalt blue "A" on the left breast. Sam introduced them. Oscar pulled his cigar from his mouth and removed his baseball cap.

"Mr. Cochrane," he said. "I suppose that you and I ought to check out the grounds, see where we're going to put everyone, start a plan for training . . ."

"Thank you, but we have already seen the grounds, Mr. Charleston. I am still unsure as to your capacity on my staff, but you will be kept abreast of strategies and changes and all else. I have had copies made of notebooks: I am certain that Mr. Filson, my pitching coach, will loan you his when he is through with it."

Oscar cleared his throat. "I see. Yes, sir, I mean. When can I meet the rest of your staff?"

"You may go and meet them now—they are inspecting the grounds themselves."

"You're not gonna introduce me?"

"Over dinner, then. If you would pardon me," Mickey said, and he and Sam left Oscar standing there, notes in hand, unlit cigar twisting in his mouth.

Mickey and his coaches moved in above Sam's office, in the coaches' barracks, leaving Oscar alone in the players' unit. This suited Oscar just fine. He would turn out the lights and stargaze for a minute or two and then head off to sleep. He was going to watch Cochrane like a hawk. The guy troubled him: for weeks before, rumors flew that Cochrane was unhinged. Cartwheel didn't bother Oscar: the swamp was less of a trial than it had been in the jungles of the Philippines, fighting the remaining insurgents. But it clearly took Cochrane some getting used to. Oscar would deliberately wake in the middle of the night and check out the manager's window—every night, no matter what the time, Mickey's lights were on. In the mornings his eyes were hollowed and red.

Bill Veeck's secret would not hold. From Willie Wells's loose lips to the sudden disappearance of the players that Charleston and Fay Young scouted, the rumors flew like the seeds of a dandelion on a spring day. And they landed everywhere. Was it true that the Philadelphia Athletics were hiring Negro ballplayers? Or that this crazy man, this Veeck, was building another Kansas City Monarchs, a super-team of Negro Leaguers to barnstorm and play against whites? If you'd ever swung a bat in the Negro Leagues, you were already fine-tuned to any word or whisper concerning the dawn of a new club. Tales of Satch and Josh alone brought men from the far corners of the baseball underground—adding Buck Leonard, Willie Wells, and Ray Dandridge was like nothing they'd heard before, as if the Knights of the Round Table had come together for one last go. Add to that the nagging hope that maybe it was true that baseball would finally be integrated. It didn't matter, as the rumors were enough to uproot a man from his settled life and get to Florida by thumb, train, bicycle, or foot.

Ten days later, when Sam and Mickey and Oscar had expected about a hundred men to show, they found nearly a thousand Negro ballplayers crowding the shores of Cartwheel. They had come in the Seminole skiffs five at a time (and a buck apiece) for hours on end, camping on the shores when there was no room in the abandoned barracks Veeck had set aside for his players.

Most of the thousand came on their own accord. Fueled by these tales of baseball, men left the cotton fields of the South, others abandoned their factory jobs up north. Did it matter that the whispered tales in the parking lots of the munitions plants seemed like nothing more than fable? It did not. They knew they could not turn to the newspapers, for the Negro press was mum—the few that had heard the truth understood the need for secrecy or knew that integration had been hinted at numerous times before. The Pittsburgh Pirates had even held a secret tryout for Negroes years before, and then abandoned any idea of bringing blacks to the major leagues when the owner got cold feet. And whenever a reporter got too close, Veeck could usually outmaneuver his curiosity by pointing to the Stars and saying that these players were going to play for the Negro League club. White journalists had no problem believing Veeck, and the black journalists were simply too jaded. Nothing, surely, would come of this for the Negro.

But the promise of a paid job playing baseball was too much for most men with a talent for bat and ball—it would kill a man to know that he had ignored the call, no matter how slippery and elusive the glory. Both the impossible dream of the big leagues and the promise of a tryout for a Negro League team were sufficient to make a ballplayer drop everything and use any means to get to Cartwheel. A couple of guys deserted the army, were caught, court-martialed, and sentenced to years of hard labor. The stories knew no boundaries: segregationists heard the call too. One ballplayer was run down by a car, his legs smashed, his career over. Another was propped up dead on the mound at the colored ballfield in Birmingham with rope burns around his neck.

"Where did they all come from?" Mickey said, as he walked the Cartwheel grounds with Oscar. The players were camped on the outskirts of this swampy island, hungry, filthy, looking more like refugees than baseball players. "I thought we had them all picked out," he grumbled. "It does not make any sense."

"Makes perfect sense. This is the biggest thing to happen to us since, hell . . ." Oscar grunted, "since the Emancipation, maybe." He added this last point wearily, for he was tired of Cochrane's endless complaints. Scanning the faces for players he might have known from days past, he added, "Don't forget: these boys're going to bring us a pennant. This is the cream of baseball here. Some of it is, anyway."

Cochrane pointed his pipe at a man collapsed in a heap by a cold fire pit. "That one is not going to do much more than drink, in my estimation. Some of the others are clearly unhealthy, or they are out of their minds, or they are also inebriates. Besides, it is far too early to speculate about our chances at the flag, Mr. Charleston, so I would appreciate your keeping those comments to yourself. No need to feed them a false sense of hope."

Mickey and Oscar walked briskly past rows and rows of men tossing beat-up baseballs they had brought with them, amateurs and semi-professionals trying to impress the coaches. "Utmost secrecy," Cochrane groused. "This does not look like utmost secrecy to me. I certainly hope Mr. Veeck knows what he is doing."

Buck, Cool, and Ray arrived together, still a bit shell-shocked from their affair in Santo Domingo, and when they saw the scores of ratty ballplayers they nearly told their boat captain to turn the thing around. But when their skiff hit the shore, the throng gathered, cheering and waving. "Well, we can't let 'em down, right?" Buck said, and before he could utter another word, the crowd lifted Buck onto their shoulders and carried him and Ray and Cool to the "A" diamond, where Mickey was leading a batting clinic with Oscar in tow.

"That was quite an entrance," Cochrane said, looking less than impressed. "Mr. Leonard. Mr. Bell. Mr. Dandridge. Please suit up, grab a bat, and hit the field. I will be happy to move you up on the tryout list as soon as you get dressed."

"Thank you, sir," Buck said. "We're more than happy to get started. But tryout suggests we're having to prove ourselves, and Mr. Veeck said—"

"Of course, you try out!" Cochrane said. "I have never seen any of you play this game, and we cannot have a major league team made up of men who may or may not have the skills—"

Oscar was about to begin barking, but Sam stepped in, pulled Mickey aside and whispered in his ear. The crowd surrounding the diamond was murmuring its complaints, men shaking their heads, others slapping the end of their bats in their palms, like a cop with a grudge. Cochrane breathed deeply at Sam's words, and said, "Well. Mr. Leonard, if you would do me the great favor of returning, at your leisure, and taking some practice with the rest of this squad, it would be greatly appreciated. And you, Mr. Bell, and you as well, Mr. Dandridge."

"Of course, sir," Buck said. "We'll see you with our spikes on." With that, Sam led them away to their barracks.

Willie Wells sneaked in well past midnight, having shelled out his last dollar to get passage to Cartwheel. He arrived with nothing more than a bag with his clothes, his hickory bat and glove, and an eagerness to take the field and really cut this place up.

Within a week Cochrane had whittled the thousand players down by half. After another week he was down to one hundred, not including the core group of fifteen players that had been specifically scouted for the team, that Mr. Veeck demanded be included on the final roster. Cochrane consulted his coaches; he consulted Sam; he did not consult Oscar Charleston.

In the early hours, before dawn, Cochrane would wake from his light sleep—or roll out of bed from no sleep at all—and make his way to the showers. As he walked, nightmares still clung to him. About what? About the telegram, that nervous delivery boy who was eager to escape the bad news? *We regret to inform you that Gordon Cochrane's plane was shot down in the battle of Midway . . .* Why did he remember, to the exact detail, the color of that boy's bow tie? Light purple, lavender you would call it. Why lavender?

When he finally fell asleep there were flames. A plane, the ocean. It made him sick. He woke with what he assumed was the smell of brimstone in his nostrils. Cochrane would shower, shave meticulously, then walk to the mess hall to make coffee for the entire club. He enjoyed that. The smell of the coffee, the rich sound of the scoop in the grounds, and the feel of the water over his fingers and even its mineral taste, which he'd drink in great gulps under the tap before filling the urn. Good water. Mr. Veeck did a fine job, there. After that, he would walk the grounds, listening to the swamp and the sound of the birds entreating the sun to rise again.

Cochrane woke his players at six every morning. Rattling a billy club around the lid of a garbage can, lights booming on, he would race through the barracks, shouting. "Up! You have ten minutes to hit chow, thirty to hit 'A' diamond! Anyone late is off the team, no matter what Mr. Veeck promised you!" He rode them ruthlessly, every man, not cutting one of the hundred until the very end. Whoever didn't make it might be a good backup come the season, injuries and slumps being a part of the sport. Cochrane drilled them on baserunning, stealing, bunting, turning the double play. Training they lacked he worked into their arms, legs, and brains in a matter of weeks. They would jog the soggy perimeter of Cartwheel, burn their palms climbing ropes up the trees thick with Spanish moss, gasp through calisthenics, Cochrane shouting all the way. Push-ups and sit-ups. Squats. Run like a duck around the bases, good for your hams! When someone would complain, Cochrane, red-faced, would shove his pipe in his back pocket, drop and do fifty himself, leap back up, and bark at them some more. They would throw and throw and throw, to one another, from first to third and back, from the outfield to the cutoff man, from the cutoff man home. Each meal took ten minutes, then it was back to work, an hour drilling them on signals, no physical work so they would digest. After dinner, Cochrane gave lectures, reminding them of how to act, how to think like a major leaguer. And to shortstop Willie Wells the promise of a fine every time he fought. "You are in the major leagues, Mr. Wells, and a representative of your race. You will *not* fight. Every infraction will result in $500 from your pay." Cochrane knew that Wells was making vows against him, privately, but he didn't care. The money would keep him in line.

"God willing," he said later to his coaches Mack Filson and Red Hourly, "I will make men of these boys. Just like Detroit, just like '34, when I was given a bunch of talented loafers that just needed a kick in the pants. You remember that, Mr. Filson?"

"Oh God, sir, I sure do. . . . You licked 'em, all right, Mickey. And with my arms, mmm, hmm . . ." When speaking of his pitchers, Mack wore a child's look of pleasure. "Mickey, my arms, my arms are sweet as can be. And Satchel comin', well, mmm, hmm . . ." he couldn't even finish his sentence.

Cochrane didn't appreciate Satchel's absence. "We shall see about Mr. Paige. We shall just have to see."

"Big mistake, you ask me," Red grunted. He was trying to teach his players how to hit, and he swore he'd never seen such undisciplined batters. "They stand funny, swing funny, which makes sense, since they talk and smell funny," he said, which made both Cochrane and Filson furrow their brows, as Red's bowlegged stance, guttural voice, and lack of interest in bathing and endless tobacco chewing meant that he too stood, talked, and smelled funny. "If it weren't for you, Mickey . . ."

"Mr. Hourly, keep an even keel. Do not allow your prejudices to cloud your judgment."

"Yeah, well, my 'prejudices' are what make me a good coach, you ask me."

"They do not. There is a time for focused anger, Mr. Hourly. I have a hundred men to whittle down to fifty, then fifty to whittle down to twenty-five, and those twenty-five to whip into shape. Your prejudice will blind you, but your anger, if used correctly, will make a team of these boys."

One morning Artie Wilson eased himself to the edge of the "A" diamond, taking in batting practice. Like most of the thousand, he had not been invited to Cartwheel, but following the rumor that Oscar Charleston himself was seeking out great Negro players, the talented shortstop had hitchhiked from Springville, Alabama, dead broke and hungry, in the hope of making the team. When he arrived, Artie was starstruck—there were his heroes, from Buck to Ray to Cool Papa Bell, Charleston, and the shortstop Willie Wells, a crab of a man who scampered so fast that he could field balls shot from a bazooka, and who feared no opponent, white or black (and especially the whites he played while barnstorming). Artie played in a state of constant terror, worried about making the team and pissing off his heroes. To make matters worse, Wilson was a shortstop and Willie Wells was a shortstop.

One evening, after a particularly brutal day in which half of the hundred were sent packing, Buck Leonard was out on his "constitutional" and noticed Artie sucking up grounders in a small practice. He'd seen this kid before, hitting, but now . . . "Son!" he yelled, beckoning Artie over. Artie ran to Buck's side, wide-eyed and heart pounding. "Son," Buck said, rubbing the kid's shoulder. "Don't know why they didn't take you in the fifty. But I think you're better than the others. You've got a decent swing and can use that glove. You want to make this club? Show up for batting practice tomorrow."

"They'll let me hit with them?"

Buck laughed. "They sure won't. But you got *days* left, that's it. Then you vanish, son, unless you know people up in Philly who'll keep you around. So here's what you do: get up there tomorrow and *fight* for a spot, son, *make* them pitch to you. You don't fight here, well, you wouldn't make it with the white boys anyway."

So the next day Artie woke at dawn, as usual, and practiced his swings. At the first sign of another person, Artie recruited him to play catch. By the time the men were on the field, he made his way to the "A" diamond and waited and watched. Finally, during batting practice, when Buck stepped up to take his cuts, Artie bolted from the sidelines and ran to the plate in front of him.

"What you doing, boy?" Buck shouted.

"Cuttin' in, like you told me." Artie stepped to the plate, pulled his bat back and nodded at Dave Barnhill, the fireballing pitcher. "Give me your best throws, none of this batting practice stuff." When Barnhill hesitated, he said, "C'mon! This is your chance to show off too!"

Oscar yelled, "You! Get out! You got no place in there!"

"Quiet, Mr. Charleston!" Cochrane bellowed, admiring the youngster's brash behavior. "Let him hit. Go ahead, Mr.—"

"Wilson, sir. Artie Wilson."

Dave Barnhill stood a mere seven inches over five feet and threw with such force he fell over at times. He hurled his twenty pitches as if the life of his mother hung in the balance: fireballs and outrageous curves, one of them dropping with such force and depth that Mack clapped his hands and cried out, "Kamikaze!"

Artie hit only four of them. He thought he was through. But Cochrane was smiling. "Mr. Wilson!" Cochrane yelled, waving his arms. Artie ran up. "How old are you?"

"Twenty-two, sir."

"I see." Cochrane lit his pipe. "You have been engaging in constant practice?"

"Every day, sir."

"True, Mr. Filson?"

"How should I know?" Mack said, beaming. He had been watching Artie himself and had even written a report on the kid for later in the year, if they needed to bring someone up. "He's up *earlier* than everyone else. Dawn every day."

"And you play—"

"Shortstop, Mr. Cochrane, sir."

"Take the field, Mr. Wilson. At shortstop."

Don't cry, Artie told himself. *Don't cry*. "Thank you, sir!" he said, breathlessly, and ran out to the field.

"Mr. Wells, I want you to take second base today," Cochrane shouted. Wells, standing at short, gaped. Cochrane didn't flinch. "Take second base!"

Wells turned to Oscar, who scowled and said, "Willie! You heard the man! Move!"

Wells took second but fielded poorly, making a few blunders on purpose. He lobbed a throw to Artie and mumbled, "Ready for some pain, motherfucker?"

Artie didn't answer him. Jesus, Lord, he'd displaced the great Willie Wells. Everyone was going to hate him now.

"Pivot, Mr. Wells!" Cochrane shouted as Wells muffed another double-play attempt. "Go easy on the toss!"

Oscar yelled from his spot at the third-base line, "Wells can't pivot 'cause he's a fucking shortstop. He ain't used to it."

"Come here, Mr. Charleston, please." Oscar walked up, taking his time. "Mr. Wells," Cochrane said in a low voice, "is now our starting second baseman, primarily due to his bat. From what Mr. Filson tells me, Mr. Wilson will be our shortstop. Why didn't you tell me about him earlier?"

"Because we *got* a shortstop. Willie's been playin' shortstop his whole goddam career. And it's in the contract."

"Wells has a contract to play where I tell him to play. His arm is growing weaker, Mr. Charleston!" Cochrane said, louder. By now the players had stopped and were watching the discussion. "Have you seen his throws? *I* could beat them out, and I was slow in my prime! Mr. Wilson is taking over short, Mr. Wells is at second, and Mr. Butts can back up both." Then, in a lower voice, he added, "Do I make myself clear?"

"Clear as cake," Oscar said.

That backbreaking afternoon they played a game Oscar called Spikes High, in which he would knock a hard grounder at second while another player slid, feet first, spikes up. Whoever was covering second—and in practice this was every infielder—had to field the ball, touch the bag, and either jump out of the way of the razors or take them in the thigh. Artie caught some spikes from Bonnie Serrell right in the calf. Limping away, he sat down on the weathered bench, feeling lucky it didn't break the skin. Oscar approached Artie and handed him the water bucket. He grinned and Artie grinned back. Then Oscar turned, made sure no one was looking, spit, and said, "Don't make any fucking mistakes, nigger, because if you do, I'll rip you apart." Then he walked away.

The next humid afternoon, Buck Leonard played catch with Ray Dandridge on a dry patch at the edge of the island. Neither spoke, enjoying the heat and the feel of the glove and the ball. They appreciated all the fresh baseballs Veeck provided: as many as they wanted, bright white with tight red stitches, firm in the hands. Every day they wore fresh flannels. There was good food and plenty of it. And hard work. Both men sensed that they were of the same mind: this was how it should be. Neither spoke.

From a distance, the belching roar of an outboard motor drifted in from the swamp. "Do you hear that?" Buck said, and Ray nodded. They walked to the shore. The sound drew closer until finally a small skiff emerged from the fog, carrying Josh Gibson and Grace Fournier.

Buck beamed. "This is a good day, Ray."

"Damn right," Ray whispered, then turned and ran to gather the rest of the players.

The skiff eased in with a soft bump against the sand, and an angry-looking Seminole hopped out and pulled the boat onto the shore. He mumbled to Josh.

"Five bucks!" Grace shouted. "You said—"

"Quiet!" Josh shouted, and paid the man. Then he stepped out and fell flat on his face.

Buck ran and helped him up, but Josh shoved him away. "Leave me alone, nigger!" he cried, wiping mud off his face. Then the dawn of recognition broke across Josh's face, and he smiled. "Well, if it ain't that old motherfucker, Buck Leonard."

Buck embraced him. "Great to see you too, Josh."

As they crossed the field and over to the diamonds, a crowd of players gathered around them. In the distance one of the many men waiting his turn to bat far off at the "C" diamond elbowed his neighbor. "Goddam," he said. "Look at that."

"She's nice, all right."

"Not her, you idiot. Next to her. That's Josh Gibson!"

"Jesus." He shouted to the rest of the men tossing baseballs. "Gibson, boys! Let's go!"

"Where the hell are you going?" cried Red, managing the "C" team.

One fellow ran by and said, "Red, that's Gibson!" Soon the whole field of men had run off to join the growing knot of people surrounding Josh. Red just sighed. "Great. Another right out of the jungle."

Josh Gibson moved silently, his brow furrowed. He carried the black leather case and a cardboard valise in either hand, and licked his lips constantly.

As they approached the "A" diamond, Cochrane folded his arms. "What is going on, here?" he asked.

Roy Campanella said, "Gosh, Mr. Cochrane—" and his eyes glowed as Josh approached "—this here's Josh Gibson!" Campy ran up to introduce himself and shake Josh's hand. "Sir, I'm your backup catcher. Boy, it's a pleasure to meet you."

Josh huffed. "Calm down, son." He grumbled deep in his chest, and frowned. "Where's my room? I need to eat."

"Mr. Gibson," Cochrane said, entering the circle of men surrounding the catcher. "Breakfast was an hour ago, and lunch will be served no earlier than eleven." He looked Gibson up and down. "If you would be so kind as to take batting practice, I would appreciate it. I have heard a great deal about your hitting." He winced at the smell of alcohol drifting off Josh. "I am certain you are eager to begin."

"Let him hit!" Serrell shouted. At this the men began to chant, "Let him hit!"

Josh, aching from the drink and the boat ride, nodded. Maybe if he knocked a few he could retreat to his room and have a shot, maybe something to eat, some of the jerky in Grace's bag. He sure was hungry. So he set the case down on the dirt and cleared his throat. Then he flipped open the locks.

The crowd craned its collective necks trying to see inside the case. Josh's eyes thinned as he ran his fingers over each bat, finally choosing South. Clutching it, he held the bat up for everyone to see. He cocked his head, as if listening for a note that would tell him if it was in tune. His jaws tensed and his eyes thinned, and for a moment he seemed far away. Then he smiled and pointed it at Grace. "Give it the good luck, baby."

Grace smiled, keeping her eyes locked on Josh. She took the end of the bat in her long slender fingers, gripped it tight, and kissed the end.

"Son of a bitch," Serrell said, wiping his brow.

Josh looked around, stone-faced, and addressed the pitchers. "Who do I want?" He nodded at Hilton Smith. "Okay now, Hilton," he said. Winking at Barnhill, he mumbled, "Impo." At Verdell Mathis, he smiled. "Verdell. Say, where's Satch?"

Verdell grinned, exposing his silver teeth. "Nigger's not here yet."

Josh grunted. "Figures. Know what? I need some new blood."

"That's me!" George Jefferson stepped out of the crowd, beaming. "I heard all about Josh Gibson. Let's see what you got."

The crowd broke and teams took the field. Mack stood as ump. Even Sam emerged from his office hideaway, hoping to see more of what he'd witnessed in Texas. Campy crouched behind the plate, and

Cochrane waited behind the backstop with Oscar. "Mr. Charleston," he whispered. "What do *you* think of Mr. Gibson?"

Oscar looked surprised. "Well, since you're asking, only yours truly was better. But Jefferson, you know, I scouted that boy myself. This oughta be something."

Josh dug in. Jefferson stepped up to the rubber, crouched, and took his time thinking of what to pitch this behemoth. He shook off a couple of signs, nodded, and stood.

"Don't hold nothin' back!" Josh yelled.

Jefferson didn't. The ball came in and Josh watched it sail by.

"Ouch," Mack said, grinning. "That's a strike, and a nice one."

Josh looked stung. "Big zone you got," he mumbled.

Jefferson went into his windup and challenged Josh with a fastball, chest high. Josh swung late and missed, spinning around on his heels. "Damn this swamp light!" he said, chopping his bat a couple of times from frustration. "I can't hardly see." With that he rolled his shoulders and stepped back in.

"Get 'im, Josh!" someone cried. Josh pointed his bat in the direction of the shout and said, "Thanks, friend."

Jefferson threw a fastball outside that Josh lunged at, missing by a foot. Someone coughed. Gibson began to sweat through his shirt.

"The humidity," he said, pulling at his shirt.

"You will get used to it, Mr. Gibson," Cochrane said.

"Listen to that," Serrell mumbled to Barnhill on the sidelines. "Old Cock riding Josh!"

Josh didn't even foul off one of the next seven pitches. After a moment, Jefferson sighed and threw a change-up at Josh, who almost fell over at the force of his swing. Finally Campy signaled a fastball, and Jefferson readied to throw.

Josh shook himself and waited. The pitch came in, he saw it perfectly and hammered it deep into the swamp. "There we go!" Cool cried, and everyone cheered. Josh bowed, and then hit his bat on the plate. "More!"

Jefferson shook his head. "Sorry. I'm . . . tired. We're done."

Josh broke into a slight smile, as if it were all he could muster in that heat. The crowd cheered him. "Knocked the pitcher out quick, didn't I?" he crowed.

Cochrane clapped his hands. "Everyone back to practice, please! Mr. Gibson, you may take your bags to Barracks 'A.' I wasn't expecting a lady, Miss—"

"Fournier," Grace said, curtseying. She nodded at Sam, who had joined the group and seemed to be sweating onto his glasses. "Mr. Dailey," she said. "Haven't seen you since that day in Texas."

"Mr. Dailey," Cochrane said, "do we have a home for Miss Fournier?"

"We stay together, Cap'n," Josh said. "Got it in my contract. She goes where I goes."

Cochrane was about to correct him when Sam said, "Campy, why don't you take them to Bill's apartment, next to mine. I doubt we'll see much of him."

"With pleasure!" Campy said, grabbing Gibson's bags.

Once settled in their room, Josh eyed Campy. "So you're Roy Campanella, the pride of Philly," he said affectionately. "What'd you think, baby?"

Grace smiled, seductively. "Nice. Handsome. You got a smile on you, kid, melt a woman's heart. And your fat's in the right places, like Josh, here." She squinted at him. "You're light, too. Ma white?"

"No, ma'am. My father's an Italian."

Josh found that funny. He sat on the bed, shaking with the laugh. "So, boy, you decide to be a wop or a nigger?"

Campy cleared his throat. "I didn't get to make that decision. Otherwise I'd be in the majors."

"Listen," Josh said, sitting up. "I've heard of you, you know that?" He gestured at Grace, who knew to produce a bottle. "It's true. I 'member hearing about this Roy C., throws like—bazookas?— and hits like he done sold his soul to ol' Scratch." Josh took a swig from the bottle and said, "You sell your soul, boy?"

This bothered Campy's Catholic sensibilities. He cleared his throat. "Oh, please, sir."

"Take it easy, boy! How about a drink? Sit down, take a swig and we'll talk strategy." He patted the bed next to him, then leaned back next to Grace. "The great Biz Mackie taught me all I know. And I'd be glad to teach you—"

"Yes, sir," Campy interrupted. "But—"

"But you're nervous about the Cap'n," Josh whispered, suddenly changing thoughts. He glanced at the bottle. "I see. The old son of a bitch'll ride you, right? Well, listen. Don't you have a slug after all. You're a good kid. Been catching five years?"

"Eight."

"Eight! How old 'r' you?"

"Twenty-three."

"God. You hear that, Grace?"

"You oughta drink to that," she said.

Josh smiled and took another pull of the whiskey. "That's why I love her," he whispered and tapped at his temple. "Of one mind! Anyway, Campy, eight years, you know how it gets. Catchers, we get beat up. The game, it hurts us especially. Grinds your hams into sausage, cuts out your knees, replaces 'em with splintery wood. And my hands—" he held up his hands. "Damn it, boy, you know I can't sleep sometimes for the pain." He shook the bottle. "Sometimes this is the only tonic in the world."

"I hurt as well, sir. That's me all over too."

Josh looked at Campy and could hardly believe what he saw. Gibson's eyes were wet. "So you understand," he said, sniffing. "Heck, then, what I was thinkin' earlier is true right now. You're my . . ." he snapped his fingers three times. "Shit, Grace, what was I sayin' earlier?"

"It was 'protégé,' baby. French, 'member?"

"Exactly. You're my *protégé*. Got that from the crossword puzzle! It means sort of like my own kin. You know, I watch over you. Kid, I'm going to make *you* the next Josh Gibson. You like that?"

"I would, sir." Then Campy's voice grew stern. "But first, sir, I want to see the real Josh Gibson." He crossed his arms. "The one that doesn't need me to ask the pitcher to lighten one up just so's he can hit it."

Josh licked his lips and blinked. "Just so's he can . . .?" He leaned back against Grace, whose face had crunched into a scowl. "You oughtn't a told that boy to lay off. I ain't swung a bat in hell knows how long." He held up the bottle. "And let me tell you, sometimes this is better than a pair of twenty-dollar eyeglasses." He nodded at Campy. "Kid, you keep your nose to yourself. You been playin' for a long time, but Josh has been playing longer. And better. You want me to show you a thing or two, you ease up, nigger."

Grace eyed Campy. "You got a lot of nerve, little boy."

Campy said, "That's fine, ma'am. I'm just worried, is all. Just want to make sure he's the best there is. We got a lot ridin' on you. The whole world does."

Josh nodded to the door. "Don't want to hear it. Now get out. We'll have fun if you won't."

Campy stared at the door for a moment after Josh closed it behind him. He looked at his hands, already busted up from his eight years of Negro League service. Then he looked up at the door, jaw tensed. "Yeah," he said. "I'm going to *make* you play like Ruth if it's the last thing I do."

As the days progressed, Cochrane would not let up, even as the club showed definite signs of improvement. The players began to grumble out loud. It wasn't the hard work that bothered them: Cochrane forbade drinking and gambling. He made them haul their uniforms to the laundry and rake the infield. "Exactly what I did when I was in the low minors!" He taped up an edict that the players would begin washing dishes—but the protests of every player, including Josh and Campy, forced Sam to remove it and let the kitchen staff do the cleaning.

Campy followed Josh everywhere, "like a goddam sheepdog," Oscar noted. The elder catcher instructed Campy on the finer points of his art, the strategy of the game, even the facts of life.

"So you see," Josh said, stretching out on his bed one night. "Two raw eggs and a dash of hot sauce—only from Louisiana mind you—will ease up a hangover. And go ahead and fart in your crouch. Anything to keep the batter off guard."

Campy was shocked: he didn't realize he could learn so much from this man. The game seemed to be in Josh's every breath, infectious like a generous disease, Josh watching the field, thinking, seeing plays before they happened. And after a few days his eyesight appeared to have returned: he was clobbering the ball everywhere, driving hits into gaps and blasting homers into the deepest parts of the swamp.

When he was sober, that is. In the last seven days, twice Josh failed to show. His absence was gaping. On those days Campy barked at his pitchers, riding them unmercifully. At night he would retreat to Josh's room to instruct him on any developments in his pitching staff, get some pointers, and see how blasted the big man was. Sometimes Campy would bring along his best friend, Gene Benson, their starting left fielder and a fellow Philadelphian. On those days Benson would get in Josh's face and they would all argue. Sometimes, when Josh was ripped, he would tell fabulous stories of knocking homers out of Yankee Stadium, of how Dizzy Dean used to sing his praises, of this feat and that feat. As he got rolling, tears would come to his eyes, and he'd punch Campy lightly on the arm and say, "Sometimes, kid, you make me feel like I could just about give the hooch up, really focus. Be the best again. Show the world. I'm gettin' old, you know—not much time left in the old chassis."

On their way back to the barracks after one of these evenings, Campy said to Benson, "Wouldn't that be grand, if we can get him to knock off—"

"Roy," Benson said, "The Josh ain't just a drunk."

"How's that?"

Benson made a motion as if jabbing himself in the arm with a needle. "The cat's got a line of 'em down both arms. Girl too."

Campy scowled. "Gene, you always see the worst in people."

"I'm a realist, Roy. Big man's got it bad. And that shit he was feedin' us? Yankee Stadium? Fuck almighty, Babe Ruth never hit a home run outta the king park."

"Josh is better than Ruth."

"Nada," Benson said, and they argued the point through most of the evening.

Cochrane tried to pretend that running this club didn't bother him, but as the days wore on he began to grow gaunt; he barely ate. Oscar noticed that some of his pipe stems had been bitten in two. During meals Cochrane smoked and watched his men eat, talk among themselves, and give him what he thought were sullen looks. Charleston invited Mickey to sit with him over meals, and when that failed, sat next to his manager on his own. Cochrane wouldn't utter a word to him, just pushing his food around and scribbling in a notepad.

Over lunch one day in mid-March, Mickey Cochrane made his final decisions, and the entire team was set. His roster was written on a scrap of paper he carried with him at all times, grown soft from constant fingering. There they were: Buck Leonard at first, Willie Wells holding down second, excelling despite his attitude. Artie Wilson and Ray Dandridge at short and third, respectively. In the outfield, speedy Cool Papa Bell in right, the incredible Monte Irvin in center, Gene Benson—still rough, but a star in the making—in left.

Sam Jethroe platooning when Mr. Bell's knees would give out on him. Roy Campanella and maybe Josh Gibson behind the plate.

Thank the Lord for Mack Filson, Cochrane thought. His coach's enthusiasm was infectious. "We got an arsenal, Mr. Cochrane, an arsenal, let me tell you," he would repeat. Their pitching staff consisted of Hilton Smith, with a sore arm; Dave Barnhill, "short, but a cannon, kind of like those PT boats that knock off destroyers!"; George Jefferson—who was going to be hard to keep in line, the man looked as if he were aching to fight someone, anyone; and Satchel Paige as the starters. *Perhaps.* If Cochrane had his way, this Paige fellow wouldn't pitch at all. Satch and Jeep Jessup had yet to show after all these weeks, and Veeck said the chances were good they wouldn't get him until Opening Day. *It was in his contract*, Veeck reminded Cochrane. Contracts, contracts, contracts, Cochrane thought to himself. They will be the death of this club.

Turning back to his notes, he had six relievers: Barney Morris, Verdell Mathis—who probably should start, Gready McKinnis, Bill Byrd (and here Cochrane smirked because he liked the presence of a spitballer), big Carranza Howard, and this Jeep Jessup. Then there was the fun part: the backups, men plucked from the mass who looked as if they'd been given a pot of gold: Bob Harvey and Lester Lockett in the outfield, good players, solid bats. Archie Ware at first, Pee Wee Butts and foulmouthed Bonnie Serrell in the midfield. And that, he thought, folding the paper, was the Philadelphia Athletics.

He tried to take a reasoned inventory of the trouble: of course they were the first Negro players in history, and he would have to constantly push those fears aside just to focus on the baseball. Whenever he desired a moment of pure fear about the future, he would go to Sam's office and simply listen. So he chose to worry about what he could control, or thought he could control: after all these days they were still undisciplined, making the mistakes of double-A players. No one knew how to back up a base, how to cover first, how to get in position to field a bunt. They could hit, but you never trusted hitting in the spring, especially when their own hurlers were all they'd seen. And this concern also addressed the pitching: how would these men, this team of rookies, fare in the big leagues, against big league hitters? How would they handle the attention?

In spite of it all, he thought, lighting a new pipe, this team might just amount to something. There was a bit of the old soldier coming back to his bones, the feeling that, for the first time since his son's death, the world didn't seem drained of the life it once had. The magical calculus of baseball, the symmetry, the sounds so familiar to him that had been lost or forgotten on the day the kid in the lavender tie came to end his life, all this was slowly growing back in him, like green grass reemerging in April. Anger still pulsed through him, but it was tempered now with that old feeling again, the feeling that maybe, maybe he'd make something of this crew. If they could survive the season.

Wells paused from filing his spikes down to glare at Cochrane. "Crazy fucker," he said. "Lookit him talkin' to himself. Sits all alone. Don't think anyone likes him."

Serrell snorted. "Damn right, Willie. That white son of a bitch doesn't know what he's doing. Why the fuck did I ever leave Mexico for this? Treat you like a man down there. Inmates here."

"Quiet the both of you," Buck said. "Don't you understand, we gotta interest in Mickey? A business interest. This is no time to start . . ."

"No time to start!" Serrell shouted, and then quickly lowered his voice. "It's *exactly* the time to start, you ask me! What, we should wait until the season's over and that crackpot has us in last place? That boy's got mental problems," he said. "What? He have two, three breakdowns with the Tigers? They kicked the guy off the team he brought a pennant to, sent him to an institution, he was that crazy!"

"Really?" Pee Wee Butts asked. He could see from the look on Buck's face that what Serrell said was true.

Serrell continued. "Campy tells me the guy lost his kid a year ago, at Midway. This is Campy tellin' me, and you know that boy loves Cock like he's a father. And look what he's doin' to us! Shit, Buck, he's got you swinging funny, even got Cool to work on his jump. Fastest man alive, Old Cock's sayin' he's got some problem with his lead. Shit." Serrell slunk down in his seat and grumbled, "All I know is, I have a manager, and his name is Oscar Charleston." Wells cursed in agreement.

That day Cochrane posted the final lineup and walked the grounds. Around two o'clock, with the sun still igniting the sky and the humidity thick, he rode Serrell unmercifully. Serrell was tired, a bit hungover from some hooch he'd bought from a Seminole. He didn't run out a bunt. Cochrane yelled at him to move, and Serrell said, "Fuck off."

"What was that, Mr. Serrell?" Cochrane shouted, running to Serrell. "You would have it much rougher on the front lines in Germany than anything I could throw at you! Now go back, bunt, and run it out!"

"Fuck that," Serrell mumbled, walking back.

Cochrane shouted, "So is this how niggers play baseball?"

Everyone ceased. Serrell looked like he'd swallowed a red-hot coal, he was so angry. "What did you say?"

Cochrane eyed the group, now gathered around him, eyes hot. "Do you know what it means to be in the major leagues, Mr. Serrell?"

Serrell didn't answer. Cochrane turned and shouted, "Do you know, Mr. Charleston?" Oscar didn't speak. Cochrane glared at the circle of men. "We have been here four weeks, and I still see mistakes that rookies make in the low minors." He marched over and stuck his face in Serrell's. "Let me ask you this: what do you think people will be saying when you fail?" He spun around and faced the crowd. "*I* know what people will be asking. They will be asking: what are you doing playing a white man's game? You will hear it in St. Louis, Mr. Serrell. When you step up to bat with that lousy stance of yours, and your slow-footed jog to first, you will not hear, 'Serrell did not run it out!' No, you'll hear something else, like 'that nigger is lazy.' Smith!" He reared on Hilton Smith. "When you fail to back up third, and watch the ball sail away from Dandridge on a bad hop, as happened yesterday, what are you going to hear among the boos?" Smith didn't answer, thinking the question rhetorical. "Answer me!"

"Something I heard a million times before."

"That's right!" Cochrane was gasping for breath. He shouted, "Only thing is, you forgot something. You forgot about all those colored faces. Those *Negro* faces. Because when you lose, when things get rough, all those colored faces are going to be just as mean and ornery as the white faces. They might not call you nigger. They might not blame your race. But you will hear things you never thought you would hear before. Because this is the big leagues. You will get it from every side, from your own press and ours. You will hear it on the radio and see it in the newsreels. When they catch you gambling, when they catch you drunk, every reporter in America—Negro *and* white—is going to write, 'That is what the coloreds do.' Or they will say you are a disgrace to your people. Because no one wants you here! Not the players. Not the folks in the stands. And they will be looking for reasons to cut you loose. So unless you grab that pennant with both hands and tear it away from your competitors—" He gasped. Cochrane picked up a baseball and hurled it at Serrell. "From now on, Mr. Serrell, when I say you run out a bunt, you damn well better run it out!"

When no one moved for a moment, he shouted, "Get to work!" Slowly they moved back to their positions and finished their practice.

Later that evening, Red eased up to Oscar Charleston and tugged on his sleeve as he watched Artie Wilson take some cuts. "What?" Oscar shouted in surprise. "Oh, whatcha want?"

"Mickey wants to see you," he said.

"Mr. Cochrane," Oscar said through a painful sigh. He turned to Artie, who was trying out a new batting stance, and barked, "Don't stop practicing because I'm gone."

Cochrane was smoking a pipe in his office, a plain little room that looked out on the swamp. He put a finger on a speck of dust and ground it away as Oscar stepped in. Cochrane stood and offered his hand and they shook. "Sit down, Mr. Charleston," he said, and took a few puffs. "What were you going to do out there today? When I insulted Mr. Serrell?"

Oscar returned Cochrane's hard stare and said, "I don't know. I understand what you was trying to say, but I just don't know about it. That's all."

"You would not be confused if you had faith in my leadership. But then, that is the problem."

"The problem?"

"Yes. I do not believe that you trust me."

"Well," Oscar stammered, surprised. "I mean, I think you're making some mistakes."

"You have a right to your opinion. But I am in charge of this team. Do you understand that?"

Oscar's jaw tightened. "Yes, sir. I always have."

"The gambling is over."

"Pardon?"

"You heard me. The gambling is over. I know that you are send-ing players to me to discuss strategy during the eight o'clock hour, to distract me so that you and a few others can play craps. Gambling has always been a problem in baseball, and to be frank, I expected it here, as many of these players have worked for known gamblers. Craps does not surprise me. You, however, surprise me. It is one thing not to have faith, it is another thing entirely to lie."

Although Cochrane was right—Oscar was allowing the players to gamble and even drink—this was the last straw. "I don't care if I surprise you or not!" Oscar said, with a quiet anger. "Simple game a' cards, tossing some dice, and you act like they're throwing games. And you know what else, I can't tell you anything. I'm the best god-dam player in history, and one of the best baseball minds—hell, sportswriters in New York even said that once—and you don't listen at all. I believe in workin' these boys to death, just like you do—harder even!—but then you gotta let 'em blow off steam in the night. But do you care? Hell no. Goddam it all, Mickey, I could look up and point out the sky is blue and you'd tell me to clamp it. Just 'Do this, Mr. Charleston, do that.' But I got eyes, and I see that you got these boys all cramped up the way you're teaching them, fucking with their heads, keeping them from being ballplayers!"

"Watch your language! You of all people should know how del-icate this situation is. If the commissioner finds gambling, this whole club will be shut down."

"Not down here. These men need to unwind. Why you treating them like babies?"

"Are you finished?"

"Hell no," he said, still with a lowered voice. Oscar shouted only on the ballfield. "I've been playing ball and managing since when you were a pup, and I seem to be the only one to see that you got the best damn team ever assembled out there. Problem is, you got them wantin' to cut your throat. And that's trouble." Trying to be reasonable, Oscar took a deep breath and said, "Listen, Mickey, you and me, we ought to stick together, pick each other's brains. Let me handle the veterans. I've seen 'em, I know what makes 'em tick. You with those kids, hell, you got a good touch, you—"

"I will run this team, thank you very much," Cochrane said. His foot was tapping like a piston at full throttle. "From today forth, you will function as a bench coach. Nothing more. Mr. Dailey is in complete agreement. I cannot fire you, but from henceforth I will not heed your advice, and I would appreciate it if you would keep any comments to yourself."

"Those are *my* boys out there, you know. Running the show isn't just being called 'manager.' Men gotta *believe* you're in charge."

"Thank you, Mr. Charleston. Goodbye."

"Mr. Veeck know about this?"

"Goodbye, Mr. Charleston."

The following morning Cochrane walked toward center field. As he approached, the banter ceased, and the men threw in a hot silence. "Nigger boys ain't do no gambling, suh," Serrell mimicked behind Cochrane's back. He ignored it and walked on, past the outfield, to a grove of trees by the water. You can take this team to the pennant, he told himself. Gordon would be proud. Cochrane nodded and lit his pipe, clenching down on it. Blinking, as if trying to clear his eyes, he wished he hadn't promised his wife back home that he would quit drinking. A scotch would surely help relax him, but a promise was a promise. With his team practicing behind him, Mickey Cochrane rubbed his temple, sucked on his pipe, and stared out at the swamp. His head throbbed and he tried to concentrate on a pair of blue jays, screeching and fighting in a tree.

◇ **5** ◇

Office of the Commissioner

That evening after his meeting with Dan Burley, Bill Veeck caught a flight to Indianapolis, hopped another to Chicago, and at the airport hailed a taxi and raced to the commissioner's office. Even though he was two hours early and famished, he did not stop to eat. He did not stop to get a room and did not take a swig from the flask in his leg, though he wanted one badly. He pushed into the lobby of the building and double-checked that Judge Landis's office was still on the third floor. As usual, Veeck avoided the elevators to exercise his legs and practice climbing stairs. He didn't stop to take a breather until at the very top, then took one long gulp of air and pushed open the door to the hallway. When he found the judge's office, he paused, took another deep breath, and entered the waiting room. The secretary took his name and motioned him to take a seat. Veeck would wait, even though the commissioner wouldn't see him until the appointed time—still an hour and twenty minutes away—because waiting was precisely what Landis expected. His secretary was a beautiful young woman, but this was no place to entertain lurid dreams. Besides, Veeck told himself, I'm a married man. She was as stern-faced as her position demanded and asked Veeck in a clipped voice for the contracts, which he handed to her. With that she vanished into the commissioner's office and delivered the documents. She didn't say a word until it was time for his appointment.

While waiting, Veeck took a seat and sank into the low-lying chair so that his knees seemed up to his chin. Landis was going to eat him alive. He wondered what the judge would say to him. Officially, Landis had never once stated that Negroes weren't welcome in the big leagues. What could he do? Veeck almost laughed out loud at that thought. He could do plenty.

Veeck thumbed through dull legal journals lying on the coffee table. All these months, he thought, right down the drain. Poor Leo, shot to pieces by Trujillo's thugs. Had he died for nothing? Veeck was unused to these feelings: typically, he'd faced down the worst and always managed to talk himself into a frenzied determination to succeed. But this was Landis. And the judge intimidated even Veeck's daddy, from 'way back. To himself, Veeck tried to imagine parrying with Landis, trying to convince him like he'd convinced everyone else. It was no use. He felt trapped. The room was like a coffin, boxed in mahogany, its large windows—which he guessed looked out on Grant Park and Lake Michigan—obstructed with heavy mahogany blinds. Small lamps with thick green glass shades barely lit the place. It seemed like he was inside the judge's head. Twenty minutes later he'd filled a large ashtray and had run out of cigarettes with an hour to go. He fidgeted away the rest of the time.

Finally, and with no noticeable warning, the secretary stood, marched over to Veeck, and said, "The commissioner will see you now."

"Well, Hail Mary and all that," Veeck mumbled, in an attempt to lighten the mood, if only to himself. She led him in.

The judge's chamber was the same as the waiting room—mahogany paneled, with forty-watt bulbs feebly lighting the room and shades drawn against the view. But there were also books, on shelves that ran from floor to ceiling, circling the entire room.

As Veeck approached, Judge Kenesaw Mountain Landis did not stand. Sitting in a leather chair and across the desk from the commissioner was J. G. Taylor Spink, editor-in-chief of the *Sporting News*, the most powerful baseball publication in the country. Spink leaned forward as if to stand, but Landis gave him a sharp nod, and he sat back down. The judge cleared his throat and gestured to a chair. Veeck sat.

"Good to see you, Mr. Veeck," the commissioner said. There was a ponderousness to his speech, as if he were pausing to allow the grandeur of each sentence to settle on the accused. A short man, he missed having the height of his benches in court. Landis's head was tremendous, huge in contrast to his diminutive frame. With his large forehead and solid brow, he wore a stern visage, framed by great wisps of hair that rolled over his scalp like clouds circling the mountain he was named for.

Judge Landis was a traditionalist. To his supporters this meant that he held the old values close to his heart. To his detractors it meant that he was a racist who didn't cotton to blacks fouling up the purity of the sport, but who had the wherewithal to keep these opinions to himself.

Landis asked, "How are things working out for you in Philadelphia?"

"Fine, sir," Veeck said.

"Mr. Spink believes you have a good season ahead of you."

Veeck looked over at Spink. Owl-faced and rigid with self-importance, Spink rode high from his pulpit at the *Sporting News*, protecting baseball from all that was unholy, or, in Veeck's mind, fun. Spink had railed on Veeck in his days at Milwaukee, the editor constantly reminding his readers that baseball was above such antics as parades, clowns, fireworks . . . pretty much every promotion Veeck could conjure up. All this was fine with Veeck, who always relished an enemy, especially one so easy to make light of. But Veeck didn't take solace from Spink at this moment. He needed friends, and Spink was hardly that. Right then, however, he simply nodded and said, "I certainly hope so, Tom."

Landis cleared his throat. "Your father would be proud you purchased a team as distinguished as the Philadelphia Athletics," he said. "The senior Mr. Veeck was a close friend of mine, as you're aware. Helped put me into this position, yet he never asked a favor. Not once. I feel I owe him a great debt."

"He thought highly of you, sir. He wouldn't have expected any favors."

Landis smiled. "Of course he wouldn't. Your father had a great deal of respect for baseball. And for this office."

Veeck shifted in his seat. "Yes, sir."

"Unfortunately, I understand that Mr. Mack is bitter about his sale of the Athletics. I warned him, told him that he better think over his decision carefully. But he sold it, and we approved the sale. Furthermore I understand that there's a contingency about showing a profit in the first year, is that correct?"

"Yes, sir," Veeck said, shifting again. "Connie—er, Mr. Mack—felt it was in the best interests of the club. I don't think I'll have a problem—"

"*Very good.* As you are aware, this office is a friend of the owners. The mayor of Philadelphia, for instance, used to give Mr. Mack a great deal of trouble, usually regarding Shibe Park. Almost had it condemned once."

"You'll be glad to know I'm renovating—"

"The mayor was a stickler for code. Every nail in its right place, every girder rust free. Are the hot dogs at the right temperature?" Landis looked pained. "Ever since *The Jungle* ruined free trade, you have to be especially careful with meat. These little things can give an owner terrible headaches. Nickels and dimes, Mr. Veeck, nickels and dimes. The difference between profit and loss."

"Yes, sir."

Landis paused to breathe deeply through his nose. "Mr. Veeck, it was this office that persuaded the Philadelphia police to offer security to the Athletics and the Phillies as part of their normal routine. This used to come from Pinkerton, and out of the pockets of the owners. Not anymore."

"Thank you, sir."

"No thanks are required. I believe that it is in the best interests of baseball to see to it that players and owners are happy and able to do business with the least amount of trouble, especially while we're a nation at war. This office helps ensure that you have hot dogs during rationing. We do our best to see to it that your men are properly treated by the draft board and not singled out. That you have no trouble finding a train to taxi your team from city to city. That your players act in a manner that is proper. And one that doesn't disturb the general populace. During these troubled times, when baseball is so important, we make absolutely certain that the city and the state don't give you problems. No one wants trouble at a ballpark."

Disturb the general populace? Veeck wondered, but kept it to himself. "I appreciate your efforts, sir."

Landis patted the stack of contracts to his right. "I have to congratulate you on your wise decision."

Veeck sat up. "Really?"

"Mickey Cochrane will do a fabulous job leading your club. Mr. Spink and I cannot imagine a better man to whip your boys into shape."

Veeck sat back. "That he will, sir."

Spink cleared his throat. "That Cochrane's lost his son in the war won't go unnoticed, Bill. His sacrifice will inspire thousands of our readers. I'll personally see to it that he gets a whole page in our Opening Day issue."

Morbid, Veeck thought, but said, "Thank you, Tom."

"Here you are," Landis said, handing the contracts to Veeck. APPROVED was stamped on each one. "As you are aware, major league contracts are a touchy business, especially during wartime. Often it is the case that promises are made that cannot be kept. Should you have any problems, please don't hesitate to contact my office."

Veeck looked down at the contracts and noticed that they *weren't* the ones he'd brought with him. In fact they were for the white players, simply renewals of last year's. "Sir, the contracts I brought in—"

"Mr. Veeck," Landis said, over Veeck, "I believe that you were misinformed earlier when you purchased the A's. It is this office's decision that an owner cannot own *both* a major league and a Negro League club. After you sell the Stars, you should make a handsome profit. However, I'm afraid that you will not be able to rent Shibe to them anymore, due to my recent edict to ban the Negro Leagues from playing baseball in major league parks."

Veeck was speechless. Finally, he mumbled, "Did you even look at the contracts I brought in?"

"If I may answer that, Judge," Spink said, and began at the nod. "Bill, the rules of major league baseball specifically prohibit any player from signing a major league contract within a year of playing against Negro League teams or barnstorming units. The *Sporting News* has learned that every single member of your team—your *other* team—violated that rule."

"But that's because they *are* Negro Leaguers. Where else were they going to play?"

The commissioner cleared his throat. "Mr. Veeck, it is a conflict of interest to own a team in both the major leagues and the Negro Leagues. That is the rule. We must do our best to preserve the integrity of the sport."

"Commissioner," Veeck said, his voice rising, "I've read every one of the laws and bylaws, and I didn't see that mentioned anywhere. Besides, I'll gladly dump the Stars if you approve the right contracts. The contracts of my Negro players."

"Bill," Spink said, "the commissioner's office is regulated to act 'in the best interests of the sport.' *That* is in the bylaws, and no court would go against it. Especially during wartime. Negroes? Bill," Spink caught himself beginning to shout, "there can be no question about the damage your . . . experiment will do to the sport. It would be the end of baseball. Riots. Attendance falling—and it's already as low as it has been in years. Besides," Spink leaned in, "look at them! James Bell, born 1903? He's forty-one years old, for God's sake."

Bell! Veeck thought, you lie to me about your age but print the truth on a contract? "So what," he said, loudly. "Or is the *News* going to rail against one-armed men? And I didn't see anything against the Reds hiring Lisenbee. How old is he? Fifty?"

They began to shout at each other when the judge banged a gavel he kept for such occasions. "Sit down, Mr. Veeck! And Mr. Spink, I'm surprised at you. Now," he raised his gavel in the direction of the door, "Mr. Veeck, I'll expect no trouble from you, just as I wouldn't have from your father. You have my decision. Thank you for your visit." He smiled patronizingly. "Be sure to call me if you have trouble of any kind."

Veeck stood. "Judge Landis—" He stopped abruptly. What good would it do? But he had to say something, if only for his men. "Mr. Landis, these are the finest ballplayers in America, Negro or otherwise. They've got family off fighting. Shouldn't they be given the same chance as everyone else?"

"Good evening, Mr. Veeck," Landis said, and began to scribble away at a document in front of him. The meeting was over.

Spink walked Veeck to the door. "Don't bother asking for help from your friends in the newsroom. The judge and I have put a lid on this, understand?" Spink lowered his voice. "Of course, there's a number of *other* newspapers that might find this interesting, like the Communists and, what is it, the *Pittsburgh Courier*? Yes, those colored papers always print stories like that, true or not." Veeck turned to go, but Spink took his arm. "Let me tell you a little secret: this isn't Milwaukee, Bill. This is the major leagues. The commissioner didn't like what you did with the Brewers, and we don't like what we're hearing about Philly. Understand this: you *will not* make a travesty of this sport. You *will* treat it with respect. The *Sporting News* will see to it."

"You make it sound like I bought a prison."

Spink held open the door for Veeck. "You're lucky, Bill. He gave you a gift. Thanks to your father, he didn't kick you out forever."

As Veeck stepped out of the office, the secretary set the phone down abruptly. She looked flushed.

He gave her a thin smile. "Drink?"

"Of course not," she said, and pushed by him into the judge's chamber.

Veeck made his way across the room, opened the door, walked down the hall, and moved slowly down the stairs, gripping the railing like an old man afraid of heights. Outside it was Chicago in all its February misery. In his rush to get out of Philadelphia, Veeck had forgotten his winter jacket. He turned the collar of his suit up against the damp wind, which blasted in from the lake. Michigan Avenue hissed with the sound of cars on the wet pavement. The sky above the lake was black, without stars, and the water below looked just as dark and ruthless. He had a difficult time walking with the wind and the icy sidewalks, and as he slipped along his wooden leg abused his stump, rubbing it raw. At that moment he felt sorry for himself, and he hated nothing in the world so much as feeling sorry. Pausing for a moment in front of the Allerton Hotel, he decided to forgo the swank—in a month he wouldn't have two dimes to rub together. He hailed a taxi. In the back seat he remembered some of the run-down joints in his old neighborhood near Wrigley Field, cheap but comfortable, where the rookies would hole up. Maybe some of the regulars would still be haunting the pubs, men and women who used to sit in the bleachers with him.

The taxi hustled him to Wrigley and deposited him on the corner of Addison and Sheffield. Like all ballparks, it looked drained of life in February. Veeck had to give Phil Wrigley credit: the old man kept the sidewalks clean of trash and snow even now. He looked up at the flagpole that he put up himself, with the green and red lights at top, the green boasting a Cubs win to the El passengers, the red lamenting a loss. He missed those days.

As he watched the clouds roll by, he thought about the meeting. Landis was right, his daddy held the commissioner's office in the highest regard. Landis saved baseball, daddy used to say. His old man wouldn't have pulled such a stunt without clearing it with the judge first. Veeck should have thought of that: now not only did he not have a moneymaking team, he'd have to break the news to those poor men, send them packing without so much as a cap for their memories. He'd given them false hopes. Did he think he could bully Landis into approving his club? He should have kept everything clean and above board. As the cars sizzled by on the damp streets, he made his way to Falstaff's bar, looking for something to cool the heat of his humiliation.

"What's the matter, pal?" the bartender asked as Veeck pulled himself up on a stool. "Your eyes are damp."

"The wind," Veeck said. He knew he was in trouble because he wasn't in any mood to talk. Instead he ordered a beer and a pack of smokes. Drops of rain clung like dew to his red hair. He noticed before entering that all the taverns around Wrigley were empty of customers. But Falstaff's still had the coldest beer in town, Veeck thought as he gulped it down, and he wondered if they still had those burgers with the grilled onions and pumpernickel buns. They did. After eating, he turned up his collar, decided he'd had enough of the cold, and made a beeline for the York Hotel.

The place was just as he remembered it—nothing too fancy, clean enough, a good place to sleep if you didn't mind the roar of the El, which he didn't. Up in his room he checked the telephone and noticed it had a long cord, so he pulled it as far as he could, into the bathroom, all the way to the edge of the vanity. Then he sat on the edge of the tub and began to run the water until it was scalding hot. When it was almost full, he kicked off his shoes, rolled up his pant leg, and, heaving a loud sigh, unfastened the artificial leg. Sure enough, there was fresh and dried blood all over the stump. He leaned a bit, dropped his stump into the water, and grit his teeth against the sting and the heat. After a moment it was heaven. Veeck sighed, patted his chest, and cursed—his smokes were in his coat pocket on the bed. To hell with it, he thought, and leaned over and grabbed the phone.

"Person to person to Eleanor Veeck, Scottsdale, Arizona," he said. The phone buzzed. He drummed his fingers on his warming thigh.

A voice rough with sleep said, "Hello?"

"Eleanor. It's Bill."

"Bill who?"

"Stop fooling around. Thought I'd call, say hello."

"What do you want?"

"Rough day. Just want to talk. You're my wife, remember?"

"Considering it's been a month since we last spoke, I kind of forgot. What do you want to talk about?"

"Tell me what you and the kids did today."

He heard the click of her lighter and the sound of smoking. "If you were here, you'd know, right?"

"I suppose that's true," he said, rubbing his chin. "Given any thought to moving up to Philly?"

She laughed, but not a good laugh. "And live like we did in Milwaukee? Bill, we see more of you holing up out here at the ranch. Why don't you ever call during the day?"

"Because I'm trying to run a ball club. Things are crazy. Besides, you could have called me, you know."

"I did. And I know Dot doesn't forget to give messages."

Veeck felt the back of his neck itch with shame. "Okay. You're right, what can I say? So I'm a louse. I just had it rough, and I wanted to give you a ring."

Eleanor paused. "You should do it more often. And not for me. For the kids."

"Can I talk to them?"

"Of course not. Bill Jr. has school tomorrow, and I have to get up with him."

"Are they doing well?"

"Actually, yes. Bill Jr.'s doing better than last term." He heard her exhale. "Sunday you going to be around?"

"Sure."

"At your office in Philly?"

"Oh, absolutely. Building a winning club is a seven-day affair."

"How could I forget. Listen, Bill, I'll have them give you a call on Sunday. Maybe." There was a pause. "Think the kids would like Philly?"

"They'd love it! El, you should see Shibe. I'm getting it cleaned up, and if they make it for Opening Day we could—"

"Yeah, we'll see," she said abruptly. "Take care of yourself, Bill."

"Okay, Eleanor. Sleep tight."

She hung up. He laid the receiver down and swished the water around with his stub, then reached over and pulled the plug. Every twenty minutes he had to refill the tub to keep the water hot. He called the front desk and asked the night clerk if he could run him an errand for five bucks. About twenty minutes later the kid knocked and he shouted, "Avanti!" Nothing. "Come in!" The kid gave a startled gape at Veeck's half-leg.

"Taxes, kid," Veeck said. "It's rough." He paid him the money to buy a case of cold beer and a carton of cigarettes.

Fifteen minutes later the kid kicked the door open, struggling with the smokes and the beer, which he set on the toilet seat by the tub. "Fine job," Veeck said. He pulled a bottle opener from his pocket, popped a beer, and guzzled half of it. Then he lit a cigarette. Briefly satiated, he nodded at the kid and pulled the fiver from his pocket. "Beer?" he asked.

The kid shook his head. "On duty."

"Well, why don't you keep me company for a while? Can't be too busy. You like baseball?"

"Sorry," the kid said. "Got to watch the desk and study."

"Illinois?"

"Northwestern."

"Nice," Veeck said. He admired kids in school. "How'd you keep out of the draft?" The kid shrugged, embarrassed. "Forget it. What are you studying?"

"Chemistry. Advanced biology. Physics."

"Not all at once, I hope?" Veeck laughed. The kid just shook his head. "Tell you what," he said, as he pulled another five spot from his pocket. "I'm bored as hell. Lend me whatever book you're not reading and I'll give you this. When you need the book back, come back up with another, and I'll give you another fiver. Deal?"

It was a deal. Chemistry was first, which suited Veeck just fine. On his way out, the kid tuned the radio in the bedroom to a decent station, then slunk downstairs to cram for tomorrow's classes. Veeck sat on the edge of the tub, smoking and drinking beer after beer, sweating in the steam, and reading textbooks. Now and then he'd set the book down, drain and refill the tub, and just listen. Pipes groaned, the ceilings resonated with heavy footsteps, and he could hear the elevator rattle down the hall. The El shook the hotel with every pass. Wind rattled the windowpane. For whatever reason, he wondered what Josh Gibson was doing at that moment. Maybe he was drunk. He hoped so—the guy was going to need a lot to drink when he got the news. Veeck lit another cigarette, cracked open the next textbook, and read through the night.

◇ **6** ◇

Winning a Bet with God

The next morning Veeck woke with a copy of the night clerk's physics textbook open on his chest. As he pushed it off and kicked his leg out of the tangled sheets—which had cigarette burns in them—beer bottles clanged about the bed. A yellow light dribbled in past the curtains, a dim glow that portended another cold and miserable day. The troubles of last evening flooded his brain then, as did his nightmares: if he found his lost leg, everything would be fine. But whenever he found the leg, the flesh fell off in his hands in sticky blue gobs, until he was down to bone, which was black with mold.

He remembered calling Eleanor last night, felt her in his head and the melancholy residue that always toyed with his emotions after talking with her. Boy, he hoped he hadn't irritated her or promised her something he'd now forgotten, but he guessed he probably did both. Sitting up, he noticed that his leg was off—hopefully it was on the floor next to him. Veeck pushed himself to the foot of the bed and looked around the room. His leg was on the dresser, upside-down, the foot in the air like some kind of Dadaist table lamp. That's right, there was a drunken bet with God. First, balancing that damn wood stump on the dresser, then leaning precariously on the good leg, he looked up and shouted that if he could make it to the bed without falling, he'd get his team back. Just you watch!

He couldn't remember if he'd won the bet.

This time Veeck left God out of it, stood, and hopped to the dresser without falling. Maybe that was a good sign. He strapped on the prosthesis and made for the shower, his brain already in overdrive, already trying to wiggle out of the straitjacket he'd been put in. For a moment he could drown out the world under the hot water and blast out the hangover with the steam. Everyone is down in Cartwheel having a great time, he thought, without a clue that the house of cards has fallen. There were no phones, so he would have to fly down to Florida to deliver the news in person. Maybe, he thought, he'd sell the A's and keep the Stars. Maybe he'd sue the commissioner, take his case to the Supreme Court with the money he didn't have. Maybe he'd ignore the commissioner's ruling and get drummed out of the sport with only his silly daydream to remember the season by. Maybe he should eat and have some breakfast and look at things realistically for a change.

After showering, and dressed only in pants, Veeck sat on his bed and stared at the telephone. Now that his contracts weren't worth his old bathwater, he wondered if there was any way he could convince another owner to buy one of his players—at the very least he owed Josh Gibson one try. Maybe Branch Rickey or Horace Stoneham would integrate . . . they'd been in the game a long time, and each had an eye for untapped talent . . . maybe they'd have some sway with the judge. If he told them the whole story, from Texas to Cartwheel to Santo Domingo, well, maybe he'd impress them enough that they'd be the first to drop the hammer. Then again, all these notions were about as plausible as signing FDR to pitch.

He called the front desk and promised the grump who answered a sawbuck if he'd bring up a pot of coffee and six fried eggs over easy. Sure enough, he could see through the break in the curtains that it was pouring rain. Maybe that's why Landis kept his shades drawn, to keep out the endless grey.

Veeck took a deep breath and picked up the phone to call Branch Rickey, legendary general manager of the Brooklyn Dodgers. Although Veeck wasn't looking forward to one of Rickey's sermons, he knew that the Mahatma, of all the front-office folk, would be up at this early hour, and might be open to fighting the commissioner.

As always, Rickey answered the phone on the fourth ring. "Mr. Veeck?"

"Morning, Branch. Before we . . . wait. How'd you know it was me?"

"Who else is awake this time of day and ready for business? You're a smart man, one who doesn't wait for the answers to come crawling to him. Above all, who else knows the value of his players like you do? But I have to air my grievances as well. This decision of yours comes at quite a price, quite a price. Costly in terms of sacrifice. In terms of morale. In terms of politics, even, for there will be no end of troubles this season. Costly in terms of actual dollars. In troubled times . . ."

Veeck rolled his eyes. The old bastard could squeeze a buck from a peanut shell, then sell the husk to you for another quarter. Since he seemed to know what was going on, either Spink or the judge had tipped him off, which meant trouble. Any advantage for Rickey meant a hard sell. Veeck didn't like Branch because he was the only man in the sport who could outwit him. Well, he thought, his lips tight with determination, it wasn't going to happen this time. He didn't have any leverage—after all, the contracts had been voided, the men were free to sign with whomever and at whatever price—but he'd be damned if he was going to let Rickey pay these men cents on the dollar, as if they were mere rookies without seasoning.

"Listen, Branch," he said, "have your secretary type up the sermon and mail it to me, would you? I want to get the fleecing over as soon as possible and call Stoneham, who'll be up if he didn't close New York last night, and it being Friday I doubt he did. So these players, well, you know the score. . . ."

"Of course, of course," Rickey said with a huff. "Between us, I have to admit that it was a necessary step, and I applaud you."

"Excellent. Let's get down to business, shall we?"

Rickey didn't like to be interrupted and huffed again before saying, "While I know that some of your players are outstanding, you have to understand that here, in Brooklyn, there will be difficulties. Preparing these men will cost money! It will cost time! Many of my players are Southern born and bred and won't stand to work with Negroes! Why, the effort I am going to have to make, the expenses!" Veeck let a guffaw slip out, halting Branch, who quickly returned to the subject. "But, as you said, we should talk business. Now, I have to tell you that youth is the cornerstone of the Brooklyn Dodgers Baseball Club. We're not interested in quick pennants. Still, I couldn't help but notice that first baseman of yours. Buck Leonard. My scouts have given me nothing but good reports. Has a wife who's educated. He's a churchgoer. Drinks, but in moderation. A leader. Now, I have this list of players I can read to you, and you tell me who sounds good, and we'll chat. Then you tell me who you want on my staff, and we'll work from there."

"What is this? One of your staff? You act like I can make a trade."

"Of course. Unless you're interested in keeping your team entirely Negro, which I assure you is a terrible mistake. Do you want to send a message that colored men should be separate from whites?" Rickey paused. "Unless you're interested in straight cash?"

Cash? Veeck thought. *He's being generous, watch it.* "You mean a scouting fee, right? Otherwise, I have no rights to them."

Rickey sighed. He did that a lot. "Bill, I don't know what you're talking about. If you're going to be that way—"

"I'm not being *any* way. I can't trade with you, and you know that."

"For God's sake, why not?"

"Branch, you tell me: how am I going to trade?"

Silence. "Then what is a fair price to you?"

"To me? This isn't about me. All I'm saying is that you'll pay them the same that I would have, and if you try to pull the wool over any of their eyes, I'll tell them to sign with Stoneham just out of spite. . . ."

"What are you talking about?" Over the phone it sounded like Rickey knocked something over. "Stoneham? He hasn't got anyone worth trading!"

"Listen, Branch—"

"*You* listen, young man, I've been in this business since before you were born, and while I appreciate innovation, I do not cotton to disrespect. You've made a mockery of this game, which I'm willing to overlook, but you will not make a mockery of me. The Dodgers need a hard-hitting first baseman like Leonard."

Now it was Veeck's turn to shout. "Branch, I won't let these men be taken advantage of! Of all the low-down tricks you could pull, if you want me to sell these guys like they're meat and not talk about paying them a fair price, I'll—" By now Veeck was standing, and as he flailed about in his anger he caught a glance of a crowd gathered down on the sidewalk, pushing and shoving to get at a pair of newsboys hawking *Extra!* editions of the *Sun*, the *Tribune*, and the *Daily Times*. He stopped talking. There was a sharp knock at his door.

"You have no right to shout like that!" Rickey roared on. "Of course I have to honor their contracts! I alone understand the value of your players, and you will not, from the Browns, the Yankees, and especially not Stoneham . . ."

"Branch," Veeck said quietly, "you're saying you want me to trade one of my Negro players. One of *my* Negro players? You mean my contracts are valid?"

"Are you insane? Of course they're valid. Now, if you're going to listen to reason . . ."

"Bye, Papa," Veeck said, and hung up. He went to the door and found an agitated young bellhop with his breakfast.

"Jeezis, mister, what's the matter with you? You some kinda celebrity?"

"What do you mean?"

"What do I mean?" the boy said, gulping like he'd swallowed a golf ball. "You got half the reporters in the whole world waiting in the lobby for you! By God, I never seen this place so packed! You even got the nigger press waitin'. What you do anyhow? Kill someone?"

Veeck shoved a ten-dollar bill in the kid's hands and shooed him away. He pulled on his shirt and stuffed the tails into his pants, tried to slip on his shoes while standing but fell promptly on his ass, then stood up, red-faced, slapped his hair against his head, and ran right out the door and to the elevator. The elevator man smiled and nodded, and Veeck handed him a ten-spot not to stop until they reached the main floor.

When the doors opened to the lobby, Veeck stepped out to a cry of "There he is!" and a crowd of reporters, nearly a hundred strong, raced toward him. Flashbulbs popped and questions rang out all at once. Veeck heard *Winchell! Roosevelt! Integration! Cochrane! Where are you— What are you— Who are you—?* Veeck pushed his way to the front desk amidst the shouting and yelled to the manager, "Got a newspaper?"

The manager, irritable at the noise, threw the paper at Veeck. He unfolded it, and there was the biggest headline he'd seen since Pearl Harbor:

ATHLETICS SIGN NEGROES
First Colored Team in Major League History

At first Veeck didn't understand. As he scanned the front page, it slowly became clear: Walter Winchell broke the story on last night's radio program, which praised both Veeck and Judge Kenesaw Mountain Landis for their foresight in bringing Negroes in to play baseball. Winchell even read a telegram from one Mr. Franklin

Delano Roosevelt, President of the United States, also congratulating the wise commissioner on his wise decision to approve the contracts of the Philadelphia Athletics, every one, and avoid making an issue of the subject of integration during these trying times. Baseball, that most American of sports, was proving itself again to be at the forefront of democracy. Roosevelt's telegram was reprinted in its entirety. Checkmate, Winchell.

Veeck roared with laughter—only Winchell had the kind of pull to nag the president into badgering Landis to approve the real contracts. It made him wonder what the commander-in-chief owed WW. It wasn't who you know, Veeck thought with a chuckle, but what favors you're owed. But then he paused and wondered: who could have told Winchell?

Breaking from his reverie, Veeck slapped the desk. "Open the bar!"

The manager stared at him a good hard second. "It's nine in the morning."

"Thanks for the news," Veeck said, and stuffed a wad of dough into the manager's paw. "Now—open the bar!"

Veeck stormed into the dank hotel bar, followed by a raging current of thirsty reporters shouting among themselves and waiting for the right moment to bellow out their questions. Veeck watched over the reporters lining up for free beer and a shot and tried to pick out clues as to what they were saying. There was nothing but cacophony, muttering about whether Veeck would wreck baseball, the usual garbage. He waited to pump them for clues after they'd had their free drinks and asked their questions. After about two minutes, he dragged a wooden crate of beer behind the bar, stood on top, then slapped his palms on the bar and shouted, "Are we all soaked? Good. Fire when ready, Gridley!"

"Thank you, sir," shouted a slim fellow in a mouse-colored coat. "Now, if I may—"

"And you are . . .?"

"Well, I'm Bob Gridley from the *Des Moines Register* . . ." Gridley scowled at the laughter. "Okay, Mr. Veeck: I want it straight from you—who exactly are these Negroes you plan to field this spring? None of my readers know these boys."

"Delighted," Veeck yelled, "excellent start!" and then proceeded to regale the men with stories of his great players: *his* Satchel Paige, *his* Josh Gibson, *his* Buck Leonard.

"Forty-year-old rookies?" asked an old reporter with dark eyes so watery they shined like coal.

"Why not? Better a forty-year-old genius than a one-armed man!" And so it went: Veeck charming the pants off them, gesticulating like a rubber windmill, rocking back and forth as he talked, smoking, drinking, while the men scribbled their notes. Political cartoonists were already portraying Veeck as an Abraham Lincoln with a wooden leg on their cocktail napkins. He was going to be a war hero with democracy on his mind. Veeck played to the Movietone cameras whirring in the back, grinned from ear to ear for the photographers, and made every soul in the room zing to the image of parades, clowns, and, best of all, the pennant of the American League flying over Shibe Park that autumn.

"Mr. Veeck! Is it true you'll watch the games from a dirigible painted like a white elephant?"

Veeck chuckled. "Stop it now—you'll make me sound like I'm not the one with the great ideas. But why not? Unless there's some sort of air space restriction—we won't get in the way of the war effort!"

"Mr. Veeck," interrupted a loudmouth, "The Communist Party of America applauds your effort!"

There was a great deal of consternation at this. "Are you associated with the Communist party?"

"No! We are in no way affiliated with—"

"Aren't some of your players Communist?"

"You didn't know my players five minutes ago . . . how can—"

A solemn and undrinking reporter from the *Boston Globe* asked, "Tell the truth Mr. Veeck, is Mr. Dailey really going to run the team, or is he going to take his cues from you on the sly?"

"On the sly?" Veeck polished off a shot. "Mr. Dailey and I run this club together. But we both want our ideas coming from all directions. From the fans. From the press. During games I'll be in the stands, consorting with the folks who come out to watch the game. And after every game, members of the press corps are invited to drinks and eats in the Oval Office! It's my personal belief that there's a real mine of information out there . . ." he trailed off. No one spoke, not even the usual murmurs. The reporters were now gaping at him. ". . . that the fans in the cheap seats . . . that the beat reporters . . . all right, is there something I should know?"

Dan Daniel of the *New York World-Telegram* shouldered up to Veeck. "Bill," he said, in his oily voice, "you can't sit in the stands. You can't have anyone over for drinks, my friend. You've been suspended from baseball." Veeck was about to speak, but Dan cut him off. "*Indefinitely.*"

"Banned . . .?"

"Bill," came a shout at the back of the room. "It means that bastard judge isn't going to let you into your own park. Hell, you can't go into any park in the majors. The whole damn season!"

When Veeck didn't do anything but scowl in confusion, Daniel added, "For consorting with gamblers, Bill. Leo Rothberg has been associated with your organization, and there's reports that you bribed dictators who may or may not be a part of the Axis powers. Until they prove otherwise, you aren't a part of the Philadelphia Athletics. You aren't a part of baseball. You're *persona non grata.*"

Smoke trickled out of Veeck's nose while he pondered this. It might have been easier to take from the mouth of anyone but that snob. "I see," he said at last. "Well . . . for once I'm at a loss for words." He cleared his throat by way of a laugh. "Gentlemen, thanks for your questions, but if you'll excuse me, I have plenty of work to do. Season begins in less than two months."

Veeck pushed out, followed closely by the crowd, still shouting questions about Walter Winchell and his influence on Roosevelt, whether the Communists had helped the A's scout, and whether Veeck was going to sign the boxer Joe Louis to play as well. The elevator operator managed to get the door closed with only Veeck inside. As they rode up to his floor, the op turned to Veeck and said, "Some day, huh?"

"You said it."

They rode up in silence for a couple of more floors before he asked, "Say . . . you got Ray D.? Ray Dandridge at third?"

Veeck smiled. "I got him."

"Shit," the man said, flashing a golden grin. "You gonna take that pennant like it was a pie sittin' in a window."

"Yeah," Veeck said, laughing in disbelief. "It'll be just that easy."

◇ **7** ◇

Two Opening Days

On the morning of April 14, Artie Wilson hid behind the heavy curtains of the tall, second-story window of the Dunbar Hotel in Washington, D.C. As far as he could see, fans had lined up outside for a glimpse of the Athletics. As far as he could tell, they were mostly black, but not a few white fans were speckled in the crowd, shouting—what? From up there, behind the heavy glass, he couldn't tell. A cheer might be a hate-filled slur, might be a rousing call of support, or could be a cry for a lynching. He could spend hours trying to analyze these people. Though he tried to keep his presence there a secret, whenever he peeked past the curtains someone would point, and what seemed like a hundred heads would look up to him. It was no better inside his room, where the phone rang all day, where to keep the peace he'd finally taken it off the hook. He stopped opening his letters when a woman wrote him to say she had named her newborn Artie. He checked the alarm clock on the dresser. Here it was, just after seven in the morning, and already there were hundreds, maybe thousands, of people on the street, just hoping for a look. White folks, probably hoping to kill him. Black folks, resting all their hope on his shoulders. Didn't they have jobs?

Three days earlier the team had abandoned Cartwheel and climbed aboard the Orange Blossom Special from Miami to Washington. Veeck had hired out a pair of the finest club cars, hoping to avoid confronting the integration question on this first train ride. Artie shied away to the observation deck while the rest of the men played cards. As their train clattered through the small towns of Georgia, it seemed as if every quiet intersection was filled with men and women—blacks and whites who would never get a chance to see a major league team. At one stop there was simply one lone observer, dressed in the white robes of the Klan, standing with arms crossed. Mostly, though, it was all the same: folks jumping and waving and holding up babies while their older children ran alongside the speeding train. All he could bring himself to do was wave feebly to each of them.

"They're proud of you, Artie," Buck said, having followed him onto the deck. "We're leading the way, clearing a path," he said. "Don't forget that."

That was the trouble: Artie couldn't forget it. As Opening Day drew nearer, he couldn't sleep and lost his appetite. When they reached D.C. it grew worse, and his late-night pacing kept Bonnie, his roommate, awake. To keep from bothering Serrell, he took his bat and went down to the bathroom in the lobby to practice his swing, working so hard and so long that he tore off the calluses on his hand. In the middle of the night he threw up his dinner. Early in the morning he tried to read, tried to think about baserunning, checked on the crowds (still there), and then called his mother, who said she was so proud of him, the whole church was having an Artie Wilson Day. He ate a half-bottle of antacid tablets. Later, at ten in the morning, those crowds were still there: blacks and whites, all those people hoping he would carry them into a future that was—

"Artie!" Serrell shouted. "Get away from the goddam window! Might be a sniper out there, fuckin' idiot." Artie stepped back, amazed that his heart could race even more. Suddenly there was a bang on the door. Artie yelped. Oscar burst in, clapping his hands.

"This is it! Let's move it! Down to the lobby, let's go!"

Down the hall, Campy pounded on Josh's door. "I shoulda stayed with him last night, Gene," he whined. In his right hand he held a pot of coffee. Gene Benson stood behind him, arms crossed, shaking his head. A bellhop with drowsy eyes stood next to the two of them, uninterested. Campy took a deep breath and yelled, "Josh! C'mon! We're ready to go." He turned to the bellhop. "Okay."

The kid unlocked the door and Campy stepped in while Benson shoved a buck in the bellhop's hand and said, "Dangle."

The room reeked of booze and sweat. Josh and Grace lay sprawled across the bed, both naked, a sheet tangled around them.

"They dead?" Benson asked.

"Shut your mouth and open that window," Campy said, rushing over to the bed. With the light of day now streaming in, both

Grace and Josh began to shift, complaining and throwing their arms over their eyes. Campy ran to the bathroom and filled the ice bucket with water. He walked over to Josh, lifted his arm up, and dumped the water on him.

"Son of a—what the hell was that about!" Josh roared. Grace shouted and dived under the covers.

"Gene—grab his right arm!"

Benson looked at Josh like he was an alligator about to snap.

"The heck, Gene, grab him!" Campy yelled. They heaved and pulled Josh out of bed, surprised to find that it was only his lungs and arms that held any spark. He wasn't anything more than dead weight. They dragged him to the tub and dumped him in. "Coffee!" Campy shouted. Benson grabbed the pot. "Josh! Open!" Campy worked Josh's mouth until it spread open, no wider than a teaspout, and dribbled coffee down his throat.

Josh began to spit. "Hot!" he cried.

Campy tried to feed him more. Josh struggled. Campy slapped him hard a couple of times.

"Shit, Roy, you look like you takin' special pleasure in that."

"Quiet! We got to get him out there."

"Yeah," Benson said, sarcastically. "*Our Ruth*. Stand aside, I'll run some of the cold on him."

"When you're done with that, check on Gracie."

"Whore's fine, but if she kicks off, 's probably best for Old Fat, here." Benson saw that Josh's eyes were shiny, like a dog's. Damn, he thought, the boy's fried and good. Then the slugger groaned, took a deep breath, and tried to stand. When Campy reached down, Josh slapped him away, then pushed himself up, swaying as he did.

Campy looked like he was going to cry. "Camp, don't worry," Benson said. "We'll get him there."

The nation's capital was alive with baseball. Crowds from all over the East Coast, and especially Philadelphia, made the trip in droves: by car, by train, by hoboing. Those who couldn't get tickets were jazzed just to be in the general vicinity of the Athletics—many of the crowds outside their hotel watched the team come and go without having seen them play. Those Philadelphians who had to stay home crowded around the radios to listen to announcer By Saam drawl out the action. Every corner of the city was alive with the promise of integrated ball—for the first time the whole crazy quilt that was Washington, D.C., could celebrate Opening Day, and the streets were mad with anxiety and anticipation. Baseball elbowed its way into the subways, filled the stuffy air of the tenements and the narrow width of alleys as children replayed last year's World Series among the garbage cans and parked cars. In D.C., as in the rest of the country, the grip of cold had loosened, the cherry trees were in bloom, and the gutters were filled with water and the alluvium of winter, like forest streams in the heart of the city. These were the signs of spring. Above all else, to the city dweller, spring meant baseball.

For as long as they existed, the Washington Senators had opened the baseball season. It was a happy coincidence that the Athletics were slated to begin their season in the capital, so that "Veeck's Great Experiment," as the *Washington Post* called it, could have a nationwide opening. Newspapers from Portland, Oregon, to Portland, Maine, had sent reporters, and magazines from *Time* to *Look* to *Life* had the players and coaches lining up for interviews and staged photographs all morning. The *Ladies' Home Journal* and *Redbook* sent their writers to interview the wives and girlfriends and ask pertinent questions such as "What is Mickey Cochrane's favorite cake?" (*Not* German chocolate.) The Negro presses were on hand, the *Daily Worker* sent its crew, and newsreel operatives wandered the fields, poking their cameras in everyone's face, from Josh to Buck to the batboy and even one of the men whose job was to roll out the tarp in the event of rain. And of course J. G. Taylor Spink had weighed in, days earlier, and his *Sporting News* was just hitting the stands that very day. "With their old men, draft dodgers, and agitators," Spink wondered, "will the Philadelphia Athletics bring about the end of baseball as we know it?"

Veeck couldn't sit in Griffith, not out in the open, anyway. Instead he slipped a janitor a sawbuck and sat in the cramped little box behind the scoreboard in right center field. Sam Dailey spent the better part of an hour in the executive men's restroom by Griffith's office, adjusting and readjusting his tie and practicing exactly what he would say to FDR, whom he'd be sitting next to, as was his privilege as the owner of the Athletics. "Back at Cornell," Sam whispered, and then elaborated on what he thought of MacArthur, the New Deal, this year's election. Should he offer to buy the president a soda?

Should he keep score? He remembered the words spitting from the mouths of the fans in Texas, the hateful cries of people infuriated by the mere presence of Josh Gibson. His stomach burned. This was going to be a hell of a long day.

Half an hour before game time, down in the visitors' locker room, the men were preparing. Artie taped his hands and lied about his calluses. "I always tape up my palms before a big game; my palms sweat." Artie's hands were bleeding, and when he tore the tape off it was going to be a mess and hurt like a motherfucker. Cool dressed early, berating himself, his age, and his leg for keeping him from playing today. Buck and Ray kept to themselves, quietly going through their pregame rituals, lacing their gloves, checking their bats, and, for Ray, swishing his hat around as if it needed airing out, for luck.

Out in the dugout, Josh and Grace admired the green grass of the infield. She rubbed Josh's shoulder. The slugger had sobered up considerably. Grace had arrived around noon, dressed to the nines, having tooted up a half shot to keep her head clear, and looked as if she'd hadn't been konked out at all. When Wells saw her he cursed and scowled: she looked as though she was hoping to fuck the whole team.

Josh was staring out at the field like a bird dog eyeing its prey. He said, quietly, "Damn this old stadium! I sure hit 'em hard here, didn't I, girl?" Grace nodded. Josh stood and made a show of swinging all four bats and talking up his game. "I got every direction in my hand, and I'll blast 'em to the four corners of the earth!" he shouted. Grace laughed and applauded. Josh smiled feebly. He was sick inside, utterly sick to his stomach with nerves. Last night's bender hadn't helped, even though it was one of his tried-and-true remedies—a deathly hangover usually distracted him from worry and helped him focus on his game. That morning everything was heavier, harder, farther. His body felt old, touched with aches and fatigues. Griffith Stadium seemed strange, the field stretched to ridiculous distances. The fences that he had once blasted home runs over had moved to Baltimore. This was game one. All those many years and all those wonderful seasons, filled with home runs and fat averages and incredible plays, they were prologue. Shadow and smoke, they were—now there were record books, and every at bat, strikeout, and single were carved into history. Now when he stoked sixty big bombs the world would shudder, and not just Homestead, Pennsylvania, and Black

Bottom and East St. Louis. He looked at his hands. If only my body can keep up, I'll knock this game on its ear.

He turned to the bench. "Say Willie!"

"What?" The last thing Wells wanted was to talk to that lush. He filed his spikes down to stilettos, hungry for any one of these white boys to try to act tough on him. Screw old Cock and his fines. But then he remembered the rent, and the drink . . .

"Do you remember, Willie, my home run 'gainst you back in . . . August! August '41. That long shot. Sailed right over center."

"That's a long way, baby," Grace purred.

"I didn't throw the fucking pitch," Willie said. After a moment, though, he added, "You think you can cream a few today, big man? Like you used to?"

Josh just nodded, either not hearing or ignoring Wells's comment on his weight. "And I'll show everyone a trick or two behind the plate."

Grace tickled him. "Do that, and we'll celebrate fine tonight."

Jethroe ran to the dugout. "Everyone back in the locker room. There's a message from Mick." Wells rolled his eyes but followed the rest of them back. Josh kissed Grace goodbye, and she made her way up to the stands.

Back in the clubhouse, Cochrane was beaming, his one leg up on a chair, leaning forward, looking like a fellow about to give directions to a lost traveler. "Listen up, men," he said, clapping his hands. "You all know the trouble Mr. Veeck is in, and he appreciates all the letters and goodwill. And I know you are all excited to see other Negroes up in the stands, and all the ones outside the hotel, and how they must admire you. I do not believe that I have seen so many people since the days of Ruth. Be proud of yourselves. You deserve it.

"Thing is, though, I do not want you to think about any of that during the game. Men, let me confess something: I have never witnessed a better collection of ballplayers in my life, better even than either of my Tiger pennant winners, better even—and I never thought I would say it—than any of the Athletics clubs *I* was on. Probably the best team since the '29 Yanks or the '37 Grays, and I would bet even Josh and Buck will back that up." Buck nodded and Josh whistled. "Gentlemen, remember that you are not playing for Philadelphia, for the boys overseas, or Mr. Veeck, for that matter. Play for yourselves. Play for the Athletics. When you do that, you play for everyone."

Cochrane stood up straight. He suddenly looked as if he were at a loss for words, and said quietly, "So good luck!"

Oscar clapped and said, "You heard him—now let's fight!"

As the team filed out of the locker room, Cochrane shouted to Josh. "Mr. Gibson," he said. "I just wanted to let you know, catcher to catcher, that I'm especially excited to see your talents blossom. And you know that you're Mr. Veeck's personal favorite. Do me a favor . . ."

"Yes, sir?"

Cochrane smiled. "Tear this league apart, Mr. Gibson. Tear it apart."

As the team burst into the dugout, fans from across the stadium saw them and roared like a thousand airplanes. The A's could hear individual words popping through the din: now and then "nigger" and taunts of "coon" and "go home" broke through, vicious shouts that seemed to come from children, women, men, maybe that red-faced priest; ladies declaring their undying love (and their hotel room numbers); the cry "Kill!" alarmed Artie, until he saw the mousy fellow, a bespectacled black man in a polka-dot tie who followed that instruction with "Kill the Senators, boys! Don't give 'em an inch!" Dozens of photographers, gathered by the dugout, began shooting pictures, their flashbulbs popping—a sound not unlike a gunshot. By now there wasn't an empty seat in the place, and not a soul kept his mouth shut. Campy, unable to control himself, ran out and waved, and the crowd above the dugout went crazy. "Get back in here!" Wells said, though he was laughing. "Don't you go stealing our thunder!"

Then Cochrane was fuming because, to no one's surprise, Satch hadn't yet shown. He began shouting at Oscar. "You told me he was here! On Opening Day and . . . Good Lord!" He picked up the phone to the bullpen and, when he had an answer, yelled, "Get Smith warmed up!"

"Satch'll be here!" Oscar shouted over the din.

Cochrane yelled, "You sit down and keep quiet." He pulled out his lineup card, due in minutes, and scratched away at it. "Satch is *not* pitching today." He didn't notice that Lockett had vanished down the hall, running at Oscar's command.

To the sound of drums, a battalion of soldiers marched into center field, guns over their shoulders, a flag waving above them. The PA rang out with welcomes to the soldiers, announcements about war bond and blood drives, and then it was time to introduce the teams. A cop strolled over to the dugout and motioned to Cochrane. He stepped out, to where Sam was waiting, and they argued as the trainers were being introduced. Then they separated, Cochrane's face red as a beet, his jaw clenched. He scratched at the lineup card again and shoved it deep into his pocket.

The PA announcer began to call the roster, beginning with the A's and starting with the bench players. Their names echoed across six city blocks and over the crowds gathered outside the stadium. As the regulars came forth, first Artie, then Ray, Buck, and the rest, the crowd exploded into a sustained cheer that seemed to grow louder with each name. Half the city'll be hoarse tomorrow, Artie thought. Now and again, buried deep within the noise were dozens of fierce epithets, invectives that Artie seemed to hear acutely, and he would scan the crowds, searching in vain for the source of such hate. He would focus on a white face, such as the stout woman yelling herself into a frenzy, only to discover she was maniacal in her adoration of Willie Wells, and kept blowing kisses. Certainly the shouts of "nigger" weren't coming from children, right? Or the old ladies and men?

When it was all said and done, and the Senators had been announced to far fewer cheers (and catcalls for that matter), the crowd hushed for the ceremonial first pitch. Roosevelt, surrounded by a phalanx of advisers, flanked by both Sam and Clark Griffith, struggled to stand and gripped Sam's arm for support. Baseball in hand, the president steadied himself, and then threw the ball with all his might to Rick Ferrell, the Senators' catcher. He nodded at the applause, thanked Ferrell for returning the ball as a souvenir, and then sat down. Sam wiped his brow, pleased to have been Roosevelt's living crutch. As he turned to look at home plate, he caught the eye of Commissioner Landis, who remained standing, his arms crossed, as if he were staring down a condemned man. Their eyes locked for a moment, and Sam's mouth seemed to go instantly dry. He gulped, and turned away.

When *The Star-Spangled Banner* came to a close, the crowd went right back at it, some fans leaning over the fences, reaching out to try and touch the players. Artie, his hands now bleeding through the tape, sick from nervousness and the fact that he hadn't really eaten in two days, waited in the on-deck circle. He heard Cool say, "Well, dears, this is the day we all been waitin' for. Every at bat, every swing, in every paper and on every station. And ain't it sweet."

Artie tried to smile at that. For weeks he'd thought of this moment, but the sound of the crowd, the sheer size of the stadium, not to mention seeing the Senators out on the field—it was like being dropped headfirst into the middle of a turbulent sea. He tried to tell himself that it was nothing too big, just a game, just get a hit and everyone'll be happy. His throat was dry. He'd forgotten to go to the can before the game. He watched the pitcher, Johnny Niggeling, taking his warm-up throws, the fielders tossing the ball around, just like they did in the Negro Leagues. The umpires strutted around, surveying the diamond and trying to look important. Artie paced in front of the dugout, and each step was heavy. He reached down and grabbed a bat from the row stretched out in front of the dugout. It felt funny, as if it wasn't his. He looked it over—it was his, all right. The wood felt warped, heavier. He should've put more tar on the bat, it felt like it would fly out of his hand the minute he swung.

Artie's every move was captured on film. Crowds of photographers crouched behind home plate, Hearst's newsreel men squinting behind their handheld cameras, his image going out to the whole world tomorrow. The first Negro to play in the major leagues.

The ump gestured Artie to come to the plate. By the box he adjusted himself, pulled at his shirt, and stepped in. He dug in, kicking dirt around. "This ain't a sandbox," the catcher grumbled. Artie ignored him. The ump lifted his arms and shouted, "Play ball!"

Artie was nervous, but not nervous enough to take a fastball in the temple. He fell back in the dirt, and the catcher had to leap for the pitch. The crowd blew Artie some raspberries, booed and cackled, cheered and hollered, and the game had begun.

Artie Wilson watched two good curveballs shoot in for strikes, then lunged at a pitch a good ten inches out of the zone. It went that quick. As he sat down in the dugout, Wells spit and said, disgustedly, "I'd taken that first one in the back. Been on first you'd done that."

Ray walked, and Buck disappointed the throng by getting on first with a bloop single, a fluttering fly ball that dropped just in front of the Senators' left fielder. It was a letdown from the towering home runs the crowd expected with every at bat. With A's at first and second, though, the fans were on their feet at the announcement of the great Josh Gibson. They were nearly delirious, pointing to the oak behind the center-field fence, 420 feet in straightaway center. "Hit it there, Joshy!" someone cried, and every fan of the old Homestead

Grays—his old club—was hoping for more of the fireworks he used to provide on a daily basis.

Josh squinted in the bright sun. He cut a couple of short swings with West while the defense stretched to the perimeter of the diamond in anticipation. When he stepped to the plate, he looked hungry, like a starving man who's finally found it in him to kill for food. With the first toss, Josh swung and missed, almost falling over in the process. He righted himself, shook his head, and stared at his bat like it had deceived him. Next pitch, Josh swung early at a fastball, missing by a good three feet. He stepped out of the box, grabbed a handful of dirt, rubbed it in his palms and on the back of his neck. The crowd was roaring, calling his name, yelling for him to knock it into the Potomac. While the pitcher fretted over the signs, Josh cocked his bat back over his shoulder. This was it, slugger, he told himself. This is the ringing of the Liberty Bell, Josh Gibson's in the big leagues. He dug in. The kid threw a hanging curve right over the sweet part of the plate. Josh swung and knocked a soft grounder to the shortstop Sullivan, who scooped it up and lobbed to the second baseman, who pivoted and threw to first for an easy double play. Josh, knees killing him, wasn't halfway down the line when the throw came to first. Where did that pain come from? he wondered. I ain't young any more, but still. . . . Josh hobbled back as the crowd applauded politely.

Then, as if for no apparent reason, they began to cheer.

"Here we go!" Oscar said, pointing to center field.

Satchel Paige walked from the bullpen with an exaggerated shuffle, his head hanging down from his thin frame like a sunflower in August. Veeck wanted a show of it, and make a show Satch did. At the mound he spit and shook his lean frame.

Cochrane picked up the bullpen phone and shouted, "Mack, was Satch here the whole time?"

"No, sir, Mr. Cochrane. But, Mickey, listen, this is Satchel Paige, with that golden arm," he said, voice quivering in delight. "Besides, Mr. Veeck said you were under contract to pitch Satch today, so I sent him. Ain't warmed up, he—"

Cochrane threw the receiver down. Oscar sat on the bench, wearing a tight smile.

Satch was the thinnest thing out there, and the white reporters—most of whom had never seen him pitch—couldn't help but marvel at the thought of this stick hurling anything but lobs. As the batter stepped in, Satch scowled. "Game ends here," he crowed.

From that moment on, not a soul in the stadium could believe what unfolded: it took Satch exactly ten pitches to get out of that inning, a mind-bending combination of bee-balls, off-speeds, curves, sliders, a hesitation pitch that the opposing manager argued was illegal, and then, to the last batter, three straight heaters that zipped by without even a swing. The Senators could have used straws to hit, they were so outmatched.

At first Satchel's antics made Cochrane appear as if he were going to chomp his pipestem in two. But the pitching silenced everybody. As Satch settled down on the bench, Cochrane strolled by and was about to recite the admonishing speech he'd repeated in his head the whole inning when—a surprise to himself—he simply mumbled, "Well . . . that was some pitching, Mr. Paige."

Things changed dramatically in the next inning. As if sending his fans a love letter, Monte Irvin shot the first pitch on a clothesline into the left-field bleachers for a home run. Next, Sam Jethroe, holding down right field for Cool, took a walk in five pitches. As soon as he reached first, he rolled up his pants leg, a lesson from Cool. "I'm gonna steal is what that means," he told the first baseman. Cochrane signaled to first to keep Jethroe there. The Senators catcher had a good arm, and Cochrane hadn't seen Jethroe steal a base once during spring training. But Oscar scratched his chin, giving Jethroe the green light. On the next pitch he bolted, and when the catcher fumbled the ball, Jethroe stood on second without even a throw to keep him company.

Cochrane slapped at his chest and adjusted his cap furiously, the signal for Sam to stay put. This time Jethroe didn't even bother to check. "Okay, sloth," Sam yelled. "That curve of yours fooled no one but your own fella. Third's a shorter throw. Toss that heat, see what you got."

The catcher didn't even signal to Niggeling, who wound up while Jethroe bolted. The fastball came in. Willie Wells clobbered it for a home run down the short left-field line.

"Motherfucker thinks I'm gonna sit on a called fastball, he's crazy," Wells mumbled as he jogged the bases.

Eleven men touched home that inning. Cochrane benched Jethroe for insubordination, replacing him with a terrified Lester

Lockett, who made two errors later in the game. In spite of that, nothing could stop the A's. Working a no-hitter into the sixth, Satchel surrendered a blooper after two outs, then just one more hit in the eighth. He struck out seventeen, tying the major league record. The A's surprised even themselves with the manner in which they mowed down the Senators; as easy, Cool said, as pouring coffee into a saucer. Everyone but Wilson, Lockett, and Josh Gibson knocked in hits, and Monte Irvin clocked three homers and a triple. When Satchel grew bored, he walked the side, then struck out the side. That stunt didn't amuse the commissioner. "He does that again," Landis stated, "he'll get fined a thousand dollars for every walk." Upon hearing the threat, Satch repeated the act the very next inning. The commissioner fined him three thousand dollars.

In the locker room, reporters crowded around Satchel, his arm worked over by his personal trainer, Jewbaby Floyd, a lanky black man who wasn't the least bit Jewish. They asked Satch: Why do you move so slow? "With the hurry-ups," Satch answered, "you get ruint. Slow down, you last longer." How'd you manage to pitch so well? "Simple: keep the ball away from the bat." And so on, for an hour. When asked where he was staying, Satch said, "At my new wife's house," a statement that piqued the interest of his current wife, and later, her lawyer. The press had picked up on the feud simmering between Paige and Cochrane, and when pressed, the pitcher just said, "Been too busy with the old Satch regimen to show up early. But Mr. Cochrane knows Satch is for real. He's the best manager you could ever hope to find." Of the commissioner's fine he said, "Landis and Satch're on the same page. That three grand is going straight to the War Bond drive, so Mr. Satchel Paige is happy to pay." This was news to the commissioner's office, which of course complied. Later, with Jeep and Jewbaby at his side, a couple of ladies in the backseat, Satch drove off, followed by his own paparazzi.

After the game Artie dressed quickly, hoping to avoid reporters and well-intentioned teammates offering suggestions on how to hit. His palms were killing him, bloody and looking as if they'd been scraped with broken concrete. But Buck hunted him down and told him that he and Ray were taking the rookie out to a nightclub to see the best comedian in America. "Wrap that hand up, son, and dress yourself in some nice threads," Buck said. "If only my wife were here, we'd have an even classier time. You ought to find a good woman like I did. Nothing keeps you out of trouble like a good woman."

Artie was enthralled. He needed a break, and this sounded like the perfect thing. After a good dinner, they made a beeline for the Howard Theatre. Artie couldn't believe the place—it was the swankiest joint he'd ever seen, one of the best black nightclubs in the country. He was as rural as you could find: didn't go to movies, didn't read the magazines. "I've never seen such a sharp group a' Negroes," Artie whispered to Buck. Men and women dressed in silks, in tuxedos, in their suits and ties, doctors, lawyers, the cream of Washington, D.C. He looked down at his own suit, which, he noticed for the first time, was a couple of sizes too small. Drinks cost a fortune. Ray picked up the tab. Should he pick up the next? It would look bad to check his wallet now. How much money did he have? Man, was everyone sweating like he was? They bought more drinks, which went right to Artie's head. Was he laughing too loud? Sure are some girls here, pure class, probably offended by a rube like me. . . .

The whole time Buck kept giggling in anticipation of the act. After the opening set, Pigmeat Markham was announced, the "Grand Comedian of the Age," and Buck hooted and applauded along with the rest of the crowd. Markham was, in Artie's mind, quite simply the ugliest performer he'd ever seen, with a face that looked as if it had been pressed flat by a vice. Before Markham could get to telling jokes, he announced: "Ladies and gentlemen, we got pioneers in the audience! Pioneers! Everybody! Please give a warm welcome to Buck Leonard, Ray Dandridge, and Artie Wilson of the Philadelphia Athletics!" Suddenly the spotlights turned on the ballplayers, who stood slowly, nodding and waving to a standing ovation. Artie looked like he was going to vomit all over the table. "History was made today!" Pigmeat yelled.

After the game Campy had dressed quickly and followed Josh and Grace, watching to make sure they made it to the hotel and out of trouble. He sneaked up the stairs while they jumped in an elevator. For two hours he waited outside their room, in the silence and dusky gloom of the hall, noticing a few giggles coming from behind the door every now and then. After an hour, there was only silence. Campy sat on the floor, going over that day's game, over what he knew of tomorrow's pitcher. What he wanted more than anything was a big plate of his mother's spaghetti, a tumbler of red wine, and a night of peace and quiet.

Around eight that evening he knocked softly on their door. Nothing. Sighing, he took off to enjoy the night himself. He was catching tomorrow, so he figured Josh could have his fun and a few belts, no sense in sending the guy into the DTs.

Having beaten the Senators 8-1 the following day and then suffered a rainout, the A's hopped a train back to Philadelphia. In the club car Bonnie Serrell surprised everyone by shouting, "Son of a bitch!" as he hurled the latest copy of the *Sporting News* to the floor. Dave Barnhill sat next to Serrell. He casually picked up the paper and read J. G. Taylor Spink's column, which was the fuel that had tendered Serrell's fire:

> *The spectacular catches, the four home runs, the thirteen runs batted in, a perfect 1.000 batting average in two days, makes one wonder what Monte Irvin can't do. Thank God this Superman isn't fighting Hitler! All this leads us to wonder: does the draft board have Mr. Irvin's address?*

"It's the usual shit," Serrell complained. "They don't really want us niggers fightin' in the heat of battle, alongside whites. Yeah, Monte's going to put the slop on the plate, or clean out the can, but that's it."

Barnhill seethed right along with Serrell—it was as if he'd had no pleasure in the previous day's performance. He had struck out nine, giving up one run while Jeep Jessup closed out the game in the eighth and ninth for their second victory.

"You got that right," Barnhill said quietly, echoing Serrell's complaint. "Doesn't do a Negro any good to fight. I just wish we could change things."

A little drunk and very belligerent, Serrell shouted, "To hell with Uncle Sam!"

They pulled into Philadelphia late that evening. As the train came to a stop in Pennsylvania Station, mixed crowds rushed to the edge of the tracks, shouting and cajoling and carrying signs regaling the team or damning Bill Veeck. Dozens of uniformed officers shouldered the club through the tangle of people, at times using their billy clubs to hack an opening for the A's to get to their waiting bus. The going was slow, the team moving about as fast as if wading through three feet of swift water, while fans shoved scraps of paper in their faces, murmuring softly, politely. Then, from far in the distance and echoing through the cavernous station, a shrill voice yelled, "Hang the niggers!"

"Who said that?" Sam shouted. There was suddenly an abrupt, painful bark, as if someone in the vicinity of the heckler had been stabbed or hit in the kidneys. The players waited, tense, half-crouched and ready to fight, surrounded by officers with their clubs up, wide-eyed and savage.

And then there was nothing. The crowds dissipated, the clock ticked loudly above, and an announcement for the next train interrupted their brief moment of reflection. "Let's move this circus!" one of the officers commanded.

It took a good two hours to get the players to their apartments and hotel rooms, and some found whole armies of fans waiting in the streets by their buildings, armed with rakes, shovels, and other implements to protect their Athletics. Buck stared in disbelief and said, "They gonna keep watch all season?"

Philadelphia was a one-and-a-half-team town, and barely even that. You had the A's and a thing called the Phillies, a milquetoast team with a milquetoast name. The Phillies began their season in Shibe and were a photonegative to their American League counterparts, losing three lopsided games in a row. They stank, and always stank, and it was only those gluttons for punishment who rooted for them over the A's. Even the local racists—and the city had its share—couldn't bring themselves to cheer on the Phillies. Between these losers and the A's, the city had suffered without a champion for thirteen years.

The next day was perfect for baseball, all sun and little white clouds dotting a sky as blue as a newborn's eyes. The home opener was the big show, and Veeck was so nervous he'd sucked down four beers by ten that morning. Then Sam called and said that the city had decided "no beer."

"No beer?" Veeck shouted into the phone.

"That's right," Sam said. "Mayor's afraid they'll get drunk and start fighting. He said that's what caused the Detroit riots, a bunch of drunken coloreds. His words, not mine."

"No beer?" Veeck shouted again. "If these fans are anything like Milwaukee's, that alone would cause a riot."

Things grew worse. Without Veeck's knowledge, the mayor and the governor ordered police and National Guardsmen to line the streets of the parade route from City Hall to Shibe, and they looked as if they were ready to break skulls. Unlike Washington, whose mayor seemed at worst indifferent to the A's, Philadelphia's leaders, in spite of assurances to Veeck that all would be calm, went absolutely batty trying to keep the peace. Snipers walked on the roofs of buildings, and the press had a field day with the death threats the team had received. The night before, some black fans were assaulted; at midnight a house burned, though no one yet knew if it was simply a house fire or an attack. The mayor issued a stern warning to the black community to remain peaceful.

The roughly three-mile parade began at City Hall, a long march straight up Broad Street to Lehigh and over to Shibe Park. The players were to sit in the backs of convertibles Veeck had gathered from every pal and acquaintance in his arsenal. Serrell elbowed Artie and nodded at the snipers. "For us, or for them?" he said with a chuckle.

"Ought we to have bullet-proof vests?" Artie wondered.

Serrell shrugged. "Some cat wanted to kill ya, he'd blast your head. Vest won't help. Shit, them cops won't help."

Satch waved from his howdah, swaying on the back of a blameless elephant painted white and blue, all the while fanned by beauties in harem garb. The sight disgusted Barnhill, as did the clowns and the midgets in baseball uniforms, the all-white high school bands and cops on their horses and the crowds, looking very much like they were waiting on some minstrel act. Barnhill and Verdell Mathis climbed into the backseat of one of the waiting convertibles and waved flaccidly at a group of black soldiers who were waving and tossing their caps in the air.

"Look at that," Barnhill said.

"I am," Mathis said, saluting the men. "We'll give 'em something to see."

"Where do you think they'll sit?"

"Sit? You mean in the ballpark?"

"Not up close. When Uncle Sam needs cannon fodder, you can bet they get right up close. When a man wants to see a game, he's gonna hold his hat in the back row, you better believe."

Mathis shook his head. "Shut up for once, would you Dave? Christ, you can't enjoy nothing, can you?"

A group of musically inclined fans made a ruckus with their "White Elephant Band," belting out songs like they were drunks on a bender. "V for Victory" signs were draped over every car and float. Even the Communist party had a float against Jim Crow. Pulling up the rear, Veeck rode a bicycle with a sign that read "Honorary Disposed," honking a goosy-sounding horn while Sam followed with a sign of his own design that said "Puppet Owner." Sam wondered why he'd been talked into this: he was roasting in his suit, sweat dripping off his red face and making his glasses slide down and pinch his nostrils. People recoiled at the sight of this guy, and a couple of paramedics kept an eye on him, in case he fell over from a coronary.

When they reached the front entrance of Shibe, at the corner of Twenty-second and Lehigh, the players jumped out of the cars and stood in formation, bats on their shoulders, led by the team's batboys carrying a banner that read "Baseball for Democracy." The players stood at attention while drums rolled. Then Sam, his shirt soaked, jacket rumpled, glasses all over the place, bit his tongue and shook hands with Veeck, who handed him a large golden key. Then the midgets shackled Veeck. The tiny ringleader wore a bowler with OFFICE OF THE COMMISSIONER stitched on the side. Veeck tried to escape punishment by offering the "commissioner" his wooden leg, but it wouldn't go. They drove off in a bright pink paddy wagon to Veeck's apartment to install the deposed leader of the club. Veeck had managed to rent one of the Twenty-first Street houses that flanked the park on the east side, and whose third floor—and rooftop—commanded a beautiful view of Shibe from above right field. Years earlier, in 1935, Connie Mack had raised the right-field wall almost forty feet to cut off the view from the "wildcat" seats—independent bleachers installed on the tops of the homes. Veeck took the walls back down to eight feet, to let the lucky homeowners (and himself) watch baseball games. The press christened Veeck's new digs "Devil's Island," after the last stop of the great Napoleon.

At the apartment Veeck, followed by a happy contingent of reporters, climbed a set of rickety stairs to the roof, where he had fashioned together a set of wooden bleachers and a bar, which looked across the street and out over right field. "A better view than the Yankee Stadium nosebleeds!" he gloated to his entourage. While Veeck was getting safely ensconced in his exile, the A's marched through the cheering throng and into the empty stadium.

Shibe Park was famously "green" that year: the seats, girders, doors, handrails—every nook and cranny a variation, in shades the color of olives and limes, jade and emerald, brand-new jeeps and the ocean on a cloudy day. Thanks to the war, paint sales for civilians had dried up entirely, with every drop slated for the military. So Veeck had rounded up every stray can of paint that even resembled green, and slapped it, helter-skelter, on the park. To match this ruckus, he planted different variations of the finest grass in any American League park. Kentucky bluegrass in the diamond, a mixture of deep green ryes in the outfield, another mixture of prairie grasses in the foul territories. The bases were rounded, puffy things, looking like folded parachutes. Before this season the field had been an uneven, rough, worn-out patch of land surrounded by seats, and nothing more. Not now. Taking a lesson from Wrigley Field, Veeck had seen to it that Shibe practically shined, with ivy planted on its walls, flags and bunting, and even new uniforms for the players. It was a strange place: unlike most fields it was perfectly square, defined by the city block that held it, the half-circle of the infield the only round edge. Inside the players made their way through the tunnel to the outfield. They stood in center and admired the place, still empty. The sun was low in the sky, hanging just over the right-field wall, sending dark shadows into the stands but igniting the remaining dew on the field as if the stars had fallen in the night. A janitor banged the seats down and wiped them, one by one.

Cool beamed. "Well, darlings," he said. "This is home." Buck picked up a ball, tossed it up, and knocked it into the seats just to hear it carom. Then Buck slapped Ray on the shoulder, and they bolted, one by one—even Josh as best he could, his knees still aching—across the outfield and into the dugout, grabbing bats and mitts, then back out again, ready to begin practice.

In only a half-hour the place was filled beyond capacity, great arteries of people streaming to their seats and gaping as their heroes took batting practice. Trains marked "White Elephant Special" had brought fans, most of them black, from all over the country, an irony that wasn't lost on many people. Sam and Veeck communicated with walkie-talkies, issuing reports on the state of the vendors (five hadn't shown), the food (looking good), and beer (the crowds were growing ugly). Veeck suddenly beamed. "Sam, does it say we can't *sell* beer, or have beer on the premises?"

"What difference does it make? We're not giving the beer away."

"We sure are," Veeck said.

Half an hour later there came a burst of applause from the thousands who had filed in to see batting practice. "What'd you do?" Campy asked Irvin, waiting at the cage to take his cuts.

"Nothing at all." They turned and saw what the ruckus was all about: free beer with purchase of a cheese sandwich. For fifty cents you could have a cup of beer with a mangy cheese sandwich. Seventy-five cents got you a dog and a "free" brew.

The Red Sox were victimized that afternoon. For the second time in four days, Satchel took the mound. No one else could've pitched; the occasion demanded Satchel Paige. History was being made, but history wasn't going to keep him from showing off. The first batter he nailed right in the arm. Then, as the next batter waited for the pitch, Satch spun and picked off the runner he'd just plunked. The batter didn't like seeing his fellow teammate snuffed out so quickly, so he huffed and puffed, looking as if he was going to kill someone, most likely himself. Satch struck him out on three pitches. As the next batter stepped in, Satch paused. He looked around at the stands, filled to capacity with thousands of certifiable maniacs, roaring like a hundred Flying Fortresses. He turned and waved his hat to the outfield. From his perch across the street, Veeck stood and waved a green flag.

Satch burst into a grin, flashing a gold tooth. "Everybody down!" he shouted, flailing at them with his loose glove. The fielders sat, even Buck. Jewbaby ran out on cue, handed Satch a glass of Bromo Seltzer, which he gulped, then belched. Jewbaby spit on Satchel's arm and rubbed it and shook his lean frame. He ran back to the dugout while Satch just strolled around the mound. He walked up to the rubber, put his hands on his hips, and yelled at the batter: "Ready, son?"

The batter glowered at him. Satch giggled.

Three straight fastballs, ripping through the heart of the plate, and three heavy swings, right on the money if they hadn't been late.

When the umpire's fist poked the air to end the inning, Satch walked away slowly, and the crowds did their part, beating and banging seats, whipping noisemakers over their heads, and clapping until their palms stung. One guy even bawled in appreciation.

If anyone sat on the edge of their seat that game, it was only because they'd spilled something. By the fifth the A's led by a dozen. The only tension came with a fifth-inning beaning of Willie Wells, followed by a few throws to first and hard tags that caught Willie on the chin and shoulder. "Lucky shit," he mumbled to the first baseman. "We beatin' you so bad my spikes in your thigh wouldn't do nothin' but make the press mad. And cost me some money." For those words he got another throw to first and a glove on the side of the head.

"I thought they said this league was tough!" Jethroe said as they made their way back to the locker room. Josh sat on a bench in his underwear, poring over a scrap of paper. He went three for five that day, and he worked the math with a stub of a pencil: .333 for the two games he'd played. Not bad. Could be better, he told himself. Season's young. Middle of the year, they'll be scratching his name on the MVP award.

Cochrane brushed by a clot of players gloating and drinking beer. He said, "You men had better believe that it will not be this easy all the time. Do not crow after three games. It is unseemly and . . ." he wanted to add, bad luck. But he smiled, and said, "Oh, forget it, you guys were great!"

The next day would bring rain, so they would have but one game in Philadelphia; the next morning it would be the Manhattan Limited to New York, and the following day it was the Yankees. Satchel would make for New York early the next morning, flying in his private plane, as he had appointments with *Collier's*, the *Saturday Evening Post*, *Look*, all the major newspapers, and the Hearst newsreels. Maybe, he thought, he'd even pitch against the Yanks. He never claimed to need much rest.

Back at Devil's Island that night, Veeck's apartment was filled with reporters, drinking his liquor and flirting with his sexy hostesses. "Did you see it? In the stands? White and black," Veeck said to Spink, who was in town for the A's opener. "That and the fact we're in first tells me this whole thing was nothing but beautiful. Don't you agree?"

"Three games, Bill," Spink replied.

The place was a wreck—he hadn't had the time to renovate, so it wasn't anything more than a bowl with peeling wallpaper and a single bulb that blasted light over everything. No one cared—jazz ricocheted off the walls and floors from a band playing by the erratic beat of champagne corks popping at the bar. Veeck descended on the writers, shaking hands and slapping backs, carrying trays of drinks. It was quite a spread. The writers, used to the stinginess and arrogance of Connie Mack, adored Veeck, if only for the victuals. Besides that, he was good copy.

At a break in the music, Veeck stood on the makeshift stage and, holding up a champagne bottle, shouted, "Gentlemen! Here's to the 1944 American League pennant!" The reporters cheered, and Veeck drank to everyone's success.

Sam hopped up with him and took a sip of champagne from the bottle. "Mayor's already threatened to shut us down for the beer," he said quietly.

"So what? Today's all there is."

"We'll have to sue," Sam said. "And I can't do it—that's not my expertise. We'll need to find some more money . . ."

"I'll get it," Veeck said. "Look. Isn't that a pretty sight?" Veeck pointed to Spink, who was red in the face, upset that Wendell Smith of the *Pittsburgh Courier* had just proven him wrong on some minor point. Veeck and Sam guffawed, desperately wishing someone would pop Spink square in the jaw.

Sam rubbed his eyes of tears. "Tom said the A's were going to be the end of baseball as we know it," he said through a soft laugh.

They toasted again. "Then here's to the end of baseball," Veeck said.

But during the rainout, and before they could leave for New York City, Monte Irvin was drafted into the United States Army.

◇ 8 ◇

Gotham

After speaking at three luncheons that rainy afternoon (NAACP bene-fit, Elks Club, Negro Soldiers' League), Monte Irvin came home to the room he'd rented from an angry old woman who was a friend of a friend of his mother's. As usual, she left his mail on the bed. There, beneath a request for an autograph and a bill from his cleaners, lay a yellow envelope containing his future in the U.S. Army. Inside it was plain and simple: *Monford Irvin reporting for duty April 25, 1944.* It wasn't addressed to anyone else and wasn't any day but the next. Nothing but plain yellow on the back.

Irvin was gone before he could say goodbye to the rest of the team. Clad in his new army uniform, he called a press conference from the recruitment office to announce that he was proud to be fighting for democracy. "I'm just trading in a bat for a rifle," he said, and meant it. It was a remark that didn't sit well with a few of the Athletics, especially Barnhill. He would have been the first to stand up and applaud if he thought Irvin was going to fight; in fact he would have enlisted himself. But look at his uncle, Hal, an electrical engineer relegated to hauling bombs around rickety gangplanks in Port Chicago, California. Dangerous, backbreaking work, of little value to someone with a brain—or someone black. Negroes, no mat-ter how well educated, no matter how able, didn't do anything but grunt work.

On the Manhattan Limited everyone lingered between moods of anger and bewilderment. They tried to remind themselves that Irvin was but one player. A great player, yes, but he wouldn't have kept at his torrid pace all year. Besides, consider the positives: Cool's leg felt better, and they still had Sam Jethroe and Gene Benson at either corner in the outfield; they were set. Soon they would have a new out-fielder, Lloyd Davenport, who Fay Young claimed was going to make everyone forget Monte Irvin. So when the A's pulled into Penn Station around ten in the evening, they at least wore the appearance of having moved on.

"Straight to the Biltmore, gentlemen!" Sam shouted as the train slowed, his glasses nearly falling off as he did. "No stopping! We have a line of taxis waiting—I repeat: no stopping to talk, sign autographs, et cetera."

Benson laughed and slapped Campy on the knee. "If there's skirts around, I'll et cetera all I want," he said.

No one expected the crowds. This wasn't Washington or Philadelphia: this was New York City, the unsurpassed Capital of Baseball. More than ten thousand fans crushed into Penn Station: black, white, Hispanic, Jewish, men and women, young and old. Some were soldiers spending their leave to catch a glimpse of Satch and Josh. This late hour saw kids who had sneaked out of their homes, lumps under their blankets, on the lam like convicts. Cops had volunteered to man the crowds so they could get a look at the most fascinating assemblage of baseball talent since the Gas House Gang. Priests, politicians, and reporters tried to get a word in, shouting against the hurricane of noise. Citizens climbed onto trash cans and benches, young girls screamed and some threw garters. One man was desperately trying to get the players to give their testimonials to Jesus. As before, you could always catch the guttural cry of hatred in the background, some rube with nothing better to do but spout off and ruin the fun.

The sight terrified Sam. As he descended from the Pullman, he slapped at a cop standing on the platform, sweaty and pale. "Hey! You have enough manpower to cover us?"

The cop looked like he was going to faint. "Jeez, I never seed it like this before."

Normally the throng would have thrilled Veeck, giving him the green light to show off, but in view of recent events he wanted to make certain that none of his hotheads spouted any anti-draft rhetoric. This would be impossible to spin in the eyes of the press—Veeck could have trouble with drinking and women, but being unpatriotic . . . holy cow, you couldn't have enough clowns to make people forget that. And in New York the sportswriters were barracudas. With a battery of expensive Pinkerton detectives at his disposal, and the help of New York's finest, his team was going to be as cloistered as convent girls. Only Satchel, on the magazine circuit, was absent.

It took more than three hours to get the team from the train to their luggage, their luggage to the taxis, and their taxis to the Biltmore. Everything was swell in the Big Apple: Sam had little trouble finding lodging for his players, for though many hotels didn't allow blacks to register, there were a good number that did, and the Biltmore was agog at the thought of housing the team. Although the cost of a luxury hotel was killing Veeck, he knew that in some cities, like St. Louis, they'd be forced to house the players among black families, often in meager conditions. He wanted to keep his players in the silk whenever he could. Besides, the nicer the digs, the less chance they'd want to flee to the nightclubs. Veeck hired Count Basie to play in the hotel ballroom that night, Sarah Vaughan the next, and he let word out to all the local celebrities. It was the event of the season.

But someone stole Ray's luggage. "Who'd steal my bags?" Ray said, in despair. His mitt was gone and, worse, a framed photo of his two dalmatians, Daisy and Max, which he kept by his bedside.

"Daisy and Max'll be with you, whether or not you got their picture," Buck said.

Ray was despondent. "How am I going to field with a new mitt? The old one was soft, so soft. Perfect. New one'll be stone. Solid concrete. Yankee Stadium and I'll be dropping every ground ball."

That evening Sam sent a local sporting goods dealer over with four boxes of new gloves, and Ray spent two hours trying them on. He eventually found a glove that satisfied him, nearly as huge as the last, but it felt like granite in contrast. They also brought in some socks and underwear, a pair of slacks and a shirt that felt as stiff as cardboard. Ray sulked the whole evening, during dinner in their room and while unpacking the clothes that he examined constantly, holding them up to the light as if that would erase his concerns about size or comfort. He punched, pulled, stretched, and even stepped on parts of his new glove with his cleats. To no avail. I'm cooked, Ray thought.

After dinner, while Ray was chewing on the thumb of the glove, Buck pulled a cribbage board and a bottle of decent brandy from his bag. "Good thing *I* had the board, hey?" he said.

Ray watched Buck set up the game between them on the night-stand and poured a couple of fingers of the brandy for each of them into the sanitized hotel glasses. Ray eased himself over on the bed and checked the hand Buck had dealt him. Buck reached over, took the glove, and began to massage it himself.

They sat over the brandies, silently, Ray snickering with every point, since it was Buck who had taught him the game. In twenty minutes he'd built a sizable lead over his friend.

"Know who's pitching tomorrow?" Buck asked.

Ray smiled to himself. Whenever the game seemed to get out of hand, Buck would suddenly become interested in something else. But it was also true that Buck was intent on getting the word from his friend on the next day's game. In some respects Buck was jealous: Ray was a superior fielder and a good hitter, and Buck always admired those men who toiled in relative obscurity. Ray approached his defense like he approached wiring a house: there was a way to do it, you did it right, and that was it.

Buck was glad to see that Ray's attention had been turned from his luggage to cards, but as the game wore on, Buck himself was restless. Ray asked, "Still the paper?"

Buck slapped a card down. He'd been interviewed by the *Pittsburgh Post-Gazette*, by some cub reporter with a friendly face. "How do you feel, being in the majors?" he'd asked Buck.

"Great. I enjoy playing here, playing with this group of the finest ballplayers in the world. It's a privilege."

The next morning Buck opened the *Post-Gazette* to read:

How do you feel, being in the majors?

Well, ah shore feels just fine, I do. Dis place is one happy place fur me, and playin' wit dese gennulmen is a right fine honor, yes sir.

"I don't sound like that, do I? Mary says that I have a slight Southern lilt, nothing to be ashamed of."

Ray shrugged. "Best to keep your mouth shut." He loved Buck, but he sure couldn't figure his friend out sometimes. The papers always lied.

His pal was also having trouble buying a house in Philadelphia. Buck would call a realtor—any one of the dozens in the book—and as soon as he spoke it seemed like they were busy. No one returned calls. When Buck stopped into the office, a quick-thinking secretary told him that every one was booked up, here's a card, they'll get right back to you.

"Thing is, Ray," Buck said, "there's really nothing I can do. I can't force them to represent me. You have to find someone who likes you, who will listen and find you a good home." Neither he nor Mary wanted to live in the black neighborhoods of Philadelphia. Since they had some money, they wanted a nice home out of the city. Few blacks, if any, lived out there. It wasn't *who* lived there, he often said, it was *where*. Among the trees and by a brook, if possible. Only it didn't seem possible. "Maybe after they see us play," Buck sighed.

Sure, Ray understood where Buck was coming from, but Ray didn't care where he lived as long as the roof didn't leak and he could keep it clean and cozy. That could be anywhere. Well, Ray thought, actually it probably wouldn't be in any white neighborhood—folks there do all they can to kick you out. Dogs on edge all night, then *you're* on edge all night.

The dogs. He wanted that picture back, it smarted him every time he looked over at the naked end table. With a swig of brandy rolling around in his mouth, he thought his dogs might be in trouble. He had a neighbor boy looking after them. What if they were stolen?

"Your dogs will be fine, Ray," Buck said, noticing the long face. "They just took a suitcase with a photograph in it, that's all. Let's stop this game and talk about tomorrow's pitchers."

Ray smirked. Just two more hands and he'd win. But he laid his cards down and went to gather the notes Veeck's scouts had given them.

With the energy of New York City humming in his ears, Veeck woke at dawn. He shaved and showered, ate breakfast, ear cocked to the door and the phone. By seven no one had bothered him. He glanced out the window at the city, already throbbing with life. He sat down. Then he turned and looked at the phone, as if expecting it to ring. It was too quiet, he thought. Something had to give. As if by that thought, the phone rang. "Yes?" Veeck shouted into the receiver. This time it was his broadcaster, By Saam.

"Mr. Veeck, they won't let us in the booth," he drawled.

"They won't let—what do you mean?"

"Why, Mr. Veeck, I mean just what I said. Mr. Barrow of the Yankees told security to tell us that we can't use the radio booth to broadcast today's game, and that we can't use the booth to broadcast tomorrow's game, either. That includes me and my entire staff. That means that we can't broadcast. What do you think we ought to do?"

"Where are you?"

"Now I'm in the lobby, but earlier I was—"

"Forget about it. Don't do anything," Veeck said, and hung up. He called Sam, who would call the commissioner, though the chance was fat that they'd get any help there. Veeck phoned Ed Barrow, general manager of the Yankees, who, to Veeck's surprise, actually answered the phone. When Veeck tried to read the riot act, Barrow shouted him down. "League bylaws give me the right to deny you space, and the commissioner agrees! You can conduct your revolution in Philadelphia, but you won't do it in Yankee Stadium." He hung up. Although Veeck didn't know it, Barrow had gone nearly berserk when he first heard the news of integration, and over the following weeks had come to believe that the whole affair would be scuttled before the team hit New York. He had whipped himself into the belief that Veeck was a Communist, a notion made easier by the pages of Athletics coverage in the *Daily Worker*. Barrow even had to be argued out of covering up the monuments of Lou Gehrig, Babe Ruth, and Miller Huggins in center field, as if they would be witnessing a travesty. But no one, not even his advisers, could persuade him to allow the A's to broadcast from Yankee Stadium.

This flap didn't ruffle Veeck—he knew he'd have scrapes with all the stuffed shirts; it was the press that enraged him. Veeck called his pals in the local white papers, but none would bite. "You mean to say that you'll kill a good story to cover the flatfeet in the Yankees dugout?" he cried to Dan Daniel.

"Bill," Daniel said, in his dry ice manner, "this war can't last forever. A clubhouse ban could." Next Veeck confronted Phil White, at the *Philadelphia Inquirer*, who made the news even worse. "The commissioner's saying you violated wartime regulations by mentioning the weather in your last broadcast. The FCC might shut you down for good." Of course the Negro press would cover the story in full, some fairly, others with journalism so yellow it might drip lemon juice. None of which would ever sway the commissioner or Ed

Barrow in the least. There would be no broadcast back to Philadelphia from Yankee Stadium.

After wasting an hour arguing with reporters, Veeck bribed the hotel manager to let him and his radio staff up on the roof. Hauling all their equipment up the service elevator to the fourteenth floor, then up two flights of stairs to the roof, they set up shop on a pair of card tables and a steamer trunk. They had a Philco radio to catch the Yankees' coverage, from which By Saam would call the game as if he were there; Dan Burley, Sam Lacy, Wendell Smith, and Joe Bostic from the Negro papers—who had been barred from the Yankees press box under the dubious claim that they weren't from legitimate papers—helped, along with some sympathetic members of the white press. By making crowd noises behind Saam, the reporters tried to create atmosphere and drown out the sounds of the city roaring below. An electrician pal managed to "ride" the broadcast through the telephone lines, all the way back to the fans in Philadelphia.

"We got ourselves a record crowd," By Saam drawled in his Texas accent, and the reporters went as wild as a dozen men could get. At the start of the broadcast, Veeck just sighed and collapsed onto a folding chair. He'd forgotten to bring beer and was too tired to get it. If Eleanor were around, he thought, she'd have some kind words for him. But she wasn't around. And despite the fact that everyone seemed to be having fun, he was already sick of not being able to mingle in the bleachers.

Earlier that day the team was on the field for batting practice. All the rookies stood in awe of the great stadium, which seemed majestic in contrast to tiny Shibe and slapdash Griffith. Josh and Buck crossed their arms and wore expressions of great satisfaction—they'd torn up this park a number of times with the Grays.

Jethroe pointed at the Yankees. "Look at those guys," he said to Campy. "They ain't got nothing on us."

"My word, the game ain't even started yet," Campy said, frowning. Like most ballplayers, he was superstitious, and he'd never seen a team that gloated so much before a contest.

Nothing seemed to go right that day. In spite of the sun, there was a cool, damp air, the kind that seemed to settle in your joints and creep up to your brain and grow head colds. The players weren't limber. Overconfident, they didn't push themselves in batting practice, especially the youngsters.

"Run, run, you loafers!" Cochrane shouted, racing alongside a pack of Athletics jogging aimlessly in the outfield. Even Cool was tired of hearing Mickey, who'd been shouting all morning.

Around the time a local fireman stepped up to warble the anthem, Cochrane overheard Wells arguing that Oscar should run the team and Mickey felt—though he couldn't prove it—that Oscar was privately telling the players to disregard the manager's signals. By then neither man was speaking to the other, outside of a number of small, barely audible grunts, which was probably worse than if they had come to blows. Finally, as they screwed their hats back on at the close of the anthem, Oscar muttered a command to Serrell, which Cochrane overheard. "Security!" Cochrane bellowed, and a pair of doughy cops escorted Oscar from the dugout.

"You can kick me out all year long, Mick," Oscar grumbled. "But it don't mean you got respect."

Satchel Paige was their next headache. Paige had decided that he would pitch the second game of the match. It made sense: the Athletics biggest attraction in the greatest theater in the nation. But Cochrane decided that the antics were over, and Satchel wasn't going to pitch whenever he pleased: he would throw at his appointed hour, every fourth start, just like all the others. He had two other pitchers who needed their innings. So Satch figured he wasn't even going to show up. Since he wasn't going to toss even one ball, why, he might as well see the town, then fly on up to Boston, the next stop on the road trip. "No sense in stretching out on d' bench when you got a city full of young women," he said.

The Athletics dropped their two games in New York. During the first they missed a pair of cutoff throws that allowed runners to advance, then score, enough for a Yankee victory. The A's couldn't get men home, their ten hits trapped in the amber of solid defense and poor timing. Twice Artie Wilson stood at the plate with runners in scoring position; twice he struck out. Dandridge made a pair of errors with his new glove. In the fourth, Buck clobbered a solo homer into deep center field, tying the game. Josh struck out three times. Afterward he added up his totals again, went home, and broke the seal on a new bottle.

During the first contest, whenever Cochrane made a move, Wells crossed his arms and rolled his eyes. Nothing Cochrane did could keep Wells from his complaints. By Willie's way of thinking, the Old Cock didn't let them steal enough, though they made six attempts that day. Cochrane pulled the regulars early, especially older guys like him, and what for? To give Pee Wee Butts the opportunity to screw up? And look, Artie Wilson plays the full nine, despite the fact that he hasn't but one hit so far. Wells thought, Cock coulda shifted me to short, slipped Butts in to play for Artie. Hell, this Wilson kid is falling apart, he needs rest.

Someone, Oscar figured, would come and talk to him after the game was over. But the press swarmed over the players and ignored him. There was one reporter, a cub from the *Ronkonkoma Reader*, who asked Oscar how intimate he was with Satchel Paige. "Not very," he grumbled. "Okay," the cub said, and turned his attention to Jeep. *Jeep Fucking Jessup*, Oscar thought, fuming. That white boy had the opportunity to talk to Oscar Charleston and he goes for Jeep Jessup. Holy shit.

Around ten that night, Oscar put on a coat, a shirt, and a tie. Nodding at one of Veeck's Pinkertons, he walked down the hallway to the elevator, rode it down to the lobby, and made his way out the front door of the Biltmore.

Oscar was furious, boiling beneath his hatband. At the parties both nights, Cochrane had insisted that he stand off to the side with all the coaches, feeling like the chaperone at a high school dance. Walking down the street, not a soul recognized him. He lied to himself that this was exactly what he wanted, some goddam privacy, but it was, in fact, contrary to his inner feelings. Being ignored didn't suit the man.

Oscar trekked block after block, one mile then two, double that to four until he came upon a little tavern called Glynn's, near the Polo Grounds. It was nothing more than a hole in the wall, in a blue-collar neighborhood of mixed races, a joint he could feel comfortable in and wet his whistle. Glynn's was lit by gas lamps, had a couple of old paintings screwed onto the walls, and nothing but beer and some bottles of hard liquor. No food, no women.

Being summer, the regulars spoke baseball: of the A's, how they'd fare, whether or not they were the real thing, of the Yankees and the Giants and the Bums. Of Irvin's conscription, Satchel Paige, and one of the customers kept on saying just you watch, that Buck Leonard was going to show the league the what-for. "Irvin had six before he was drafted, but Buck's already got four and counting!" he chimed. They wondered whether or not the A's would challenge the Yankees for the pennant. Mickey Cochrane was mentioned. So was Ray Dandridge. Bellying up to the bar, Oscar listened for his name. As the bartender Glynn stepped up, Oscar lit his cigar and growled, "You remember John McGraw?"

"McGraw?" the bartender said as he wiped the bar in front of Oscar. "Who doesn't?"

"You know who Oscar Charleston is?" Glynn thought on that a moment. Oscar continued. "McGraw called Charleston the greatest ballplayer ever. Period. Better than Ty Cobb, better than Joe DiMaggio. The best."

"I see," Glynn said. He put another shot and a beer in front of Oscar. "On me. For the greatest ballplayer in history. Period."

That gesture toned down Oscar's animosity a notch. Glynn joined Oscar for a short one, and they drank for a while, chewing over the noble sport . . . but the guy kept having to put his two cents in, and Oscar grew tetchy. After a few drinks he realized that no one else in this hole was giving him a second thought, and the pleasant glow of the gas lamps didn't relax him. They were too bright, annoying in the way they flickered whenever someone opened the door. Everyone spoke too loud, on stupid subjects. "You know," Oscar shouted, pounding on the bar, "I been playing ball longer than any man alive. Center field, first base, better than your goddam motherfucking DiMaggio."

"Take it easy," Glynn said.

"You realize I managed some of the greatest ballplayers in history?" He was shouting now. "Hell, I even fought for this country. Philippines. Killed a man. Now I'm a bench coach. Nothing but a fucking coach for a man that couldn't manage his way out of a sandbox." He gripped his shotglass like he was trying to break it.

"Take it easy there!"

From the corner of his eye, Charleston saw one of the white patrons make a face as if to indicate Oscar was drunk. Fast as a cobra strike he turned and hurled the shotglass into the man's face. The fighting began.

Veeck heard a pounding on his door around three in the morning. He looked up from his book and roared, "Avanti!" He was getting sick of hearing about trouble and had a cold from sitting on that chilly roof. Which he'd have to do again tomorrow. As the door opened, he yelled, "What is it now, Sam?"

"Oscar," Sam said, in pajamas and out of breath, "is in jail."

"Oscar?" Veeck said, setting down the *History of the Peloponnesian War*. "What is Oscar doing in jail?"

"Fighting. It took six officers to haul him in. The bartender claims he wasn't drunk—maybe he's on junk too."

Veeck cringed. "He's not on junk, Sam. The guy's all wound up. Fighting, huh? And I thought this place was on lockdown," he said, his voice growing louder. "How much are we paying those Pinkertons?"

"I don't know, Bill. I could figure it out and let you know."

"Rhetorical, Sam, rhetorical. Any reporters?"

"No, Bill, the tooth fairy got him away on time."

"Well," Veeck said, with a look of surprise, "someone's employing sarcasm for a change." Both men stewed for a moment, and Sam leaned on the doorknob and stared down at his knuckles. Veeck lit another cigarette. "How much are we going to have to pay the guys he hurt?"

"I don't know yet. Probably a lot."

"Just fighting?"

"Isn't that enough?"

"Talk to the press?"

"I've already heard from Powers. Oscar belted a couple of white men. Powers claims he's not going to run the race angle, but you can bet the *Post* will."

"I see." Veeck popped open a beer and took a deep swig. "If Oscar gets fined, it's coming from his pocket."

"The voice of reason for a change," Sam said, shaking his head. "Dammit Bill, we can't have too many of these episodes. Just remember our deal with Connie Mack. Trouble like this comes straight from the profit. But I'm not running this team," he said, arms up in surrender, and walked out.

Veeck sat for a moment and stared at his cigarette, its smoke curling upward. He'd find money. Lots of it . . . he always did. He was in this for the money, and there was still tons of the stuff lying around in figurative buckets. Trouble, to Veeck, was merely grease to the wheels of innovation that spun twenty-four hours a day in his head. Hopefully the A's didn't win too much, too soon—cakewalks never helped anyone sell tickets.

Landis, being his usual benevolent self, suspended Oscar for ten games and fined him five hundred bucks. This troubled Wells no end, but the relief it gave Cochrane was abundant.

After the pair of defeats, the A's arrived at Penn Station around four to travel to Boston for an afternoon game to start that series. Due to wartime travel restrictions and seating priority for soldiers, the team was bumped from their 4:00 train. And again at 4:28. Then 5:02, 5:33, 6:04, 6:40. 8:25. 10:17.

"What's going on here?" Veeck shouted at the station manager. "This is a major league ball club! We have to make it to Boston!"

"Sir, are you suggesting that your team is more important than our soldiers?"

"Of course not! But I've got eyes—those cars are leaving with civilians."

"They are," he sniffed. "Your instructions were to keep your passengers intact, which is almost impossible in today's climate."

"You mean we've been waiting here for six hours because you couldn't split us up? Why didn't you say anything?" The manager didn't give him a decent answer, and when 11:00 hit and not a single member of the team had boarded, Veeck blew a gasket. "Smith!" he shouted to *New York Herald-Tribune* sportswriter Red Smith over the phone. "What do you mean you can't make a story of this?"

"What's the story?" Smith said. "The A's get bumped for our servicemen? Bill, I'm on your side—but no one said they were going to pamper you." Veeck slammed down the phone just in time to watch a car filled with civilians pull away.

Dan Burley was incredulous. Having talked himself back onto the staff of the *Amsterdam News*, he was given the plush assignment of following the A's. For Burley, following meant that he would go wherever the team went—in their hotels, in their boardinghouses, riding on the same train and in the same car. He was the only reporter with the team while it was delayed. When all seemed lost, he broke from his rule of never interfering with the story and called a pal who worked for the Harlem Ecumenical Baptist Church. In two hours they had a rickety old school bus that would ferry them to Boston.

When the old bus pulled up, a rusty thing that reeked of diesel fuel, Cochrane couldn't believe his eyes. The thing *leaned*. "This bus is falling apart!" he shouted.

Wells just smiled. "Not too hard for us, skipper. Shouldn't be for a man who toiled in those rough minor leagues."

As Cool boarded, he sniffed the diesel in the air. He tapped Buck on the shoulder and said, "Buck, old friend, don't you just love that perfume? Like old times, hey?" Buck nodded and ran his hand along the cracked leather seats. He'd take the comfort of the trains over nostalgia any day. The A's pulled out around midnight, every seat with two men apiece, cramped and crowded with all their luggage and equipment piled in every corner and aisle. It took a good hour to get out of the city. They drove through the moonlit countryside, and most of the men stared out the dirty windows and watched the fields fly by. It *was* like old times, back to being who they all were before the big show. As the crescent moon inched over spring wheat, everyone was asleep but the driver, humming to himself by the blue of the dashboard lights.

◇ **9** ◇

The Unraveling

Their bus broke down just outside Southbridge. Dawn lit up the morning fog, rolling in like two hundred ghosts over the fields. A dead raccoon lay in a pulpy heap by the road, and a bullet-riddled sign told them that Southbridge was a good eight miles away. After ten minutes of trying to get the bus going again, the players walked two miles to a service station, but the attendant, eyeing the players, claimed to be too busy fixing a scooter to help. One hour, two stations, and the promise of a hundred bucks later, they found their mechanic.

"Won't get this thing movin' 'til 'bout six in the p.m.," he said.

"Is there a bus in town we can use?" Veeck asked. "We have a ball game to play."

"Well, yer talkin' to a mechanic, not a driver."

It would be another hour before Sam could call the commissioner's office to ask for postponement and get the bad news that it wouldn't happen. Plus, failing to show on time would result in a forfeited game.

"Listen, fellows," Veeck said. "Unless we hitch, there's no way we can make it to Boston by one o'clock." The men looked miserable: unshaven, clothes rumpled, standing by puddles in the cold, foggy air. The news obviously didn't thrill them. "I leave it up to you. We can stay and wait and probably lose the game to forfeit, or thumb it up to Boston."

"If this isn't somethin' else," Serrell said. "I bet Ted Williams never put up with this shit. You gonna give us a raise for these troubles?"

"You're right, he didn't," Veeck said. "But you know the situation. There's nothing I can do about it, including giving you a raise. Tell you what—drinks are on me tonight! So what do you say?"

Buck spoke up, "Let's go, boys. There ain't a soul among us that hasn't used his thumb to get to a game." There was grousing, but it was better than waiting at the gas station. "Get these uniforms on," he added. "They might help us catch a ride with some whites. C'mon!"

With Sam fidgeting as lookout, they dressed behind the station. Veeck took off with them, thankful he'd sent the equipment ahead separately, not to mention By Saam and his radio team.

Surrounded by luggage, Sam grumbled a little prayer as he watched the Philadelphia Athletics vanish into the fog. He felt positively dead, spiritually exhausted. This was unbelievable. A major league club, and they're walking down the street hoping to hitch a ride to play the Boston Red Sox. Their supposedly great slugger, Josh, lay dead asleep on the floor of a garage. Veeck promised Sam that Josh would turn it around soon—what did he say, Gibson always began the season in a slump? Maybe, Sam thought, it was because the guy was always blitzed. He sighed. How the hell did I manage to bury myself in such trouble?

The last few weeks had left Sam hoping to God that he was in possession of a good ticker. It wasn't the dollars: he figured that he'd lose a bundle in the first year or so, funneling the profits back into the team so they would end up in the black. And it wasn't just his fears of race riots . . . no, it seemed as though horrible new fears were roaring out of nowhere, like this travel situation. Or By's being kicked out of Yankee Stadium. Or running the team this way. Bill was supposed to be the mouthpiece, the face. In many ways he still was, but Sam found himself at press conferences and public events much more often than he had planned. After all, as far as the major leagues were concerned, Veeck didn't exist. Sure, he could traipse around the Massachusetts countryside, but in league meetings it was Sam all the way. Worse, Sam was beginning to wonder if Bill knew what he was doing. As he gobbled his third candy bar of the morning, Sam thought, maybe I ought to start acting like the man who runs things. . . .

Buck was right: the uniforms helped. A pair of scatterbrained farmhands drove twelve members of the team to Fenway on the back of their pickup truck, shaking their heads the whole time and saying to each other "The goddam Philadelphia Athletics. You really the Athletics? Goddam, the Philadelphia Athletics!" Campy and Gene caught a ride from a young widow who worked as a maid for one of the wealthy white Brahmins of Boston. Veeck and Cochrane, who kept deferring their seats for their players, in the end had no trouble at all, and managed to get Mack and Red to tag along in a large red sedan driven by a pastor and his daughter. Ten of the A's didn't make it on time, hopping freights that stopped in Springfield for a few hours, and one was stuck with an old lady whose car ran out of gas in the middle of nowhere.

Half the team stumbled in about forty minutes before the game, but without a minute of batting practice. They couldn't shower— there was no running water in their locker room, with all apologies from the stadium manager, who just shrugged when Campy asked if the white teams showered. Veeck called up Tom Yawkey, the Red Sox owner, to complain about the conditions. "Why are you calling me?" Yawkey asked, and when he discovered Veeck was phoning from the locker room, promptly reminded Veeck that he couldn't be in any ballpark, and he was escorted out.

When the A's tried to play a quick game of catch, simply to work the kinks out of their arms and legs, the umpire shooed them back to the dugout. "Too late—game's about to start!" he barked. Cochrane exploded, demanding the A's get a few throws in with twenty minutes before gametime. He was ejected.

As he stomped to the locker room, Cochrane blared, "Roy! You're in charge!"

Without waiting for confirmation, Campy grabbed the scorecard, took a quick survey of who was with him, and, tongue out in concentration, filled out the lineup. As he was doing this, Satchel made for the exit. "Where are you goin'?" Roy shouted.

"To warm up. Satch got to have at least a few pitches."

"Sit down," Campy said. "Skip barred you for the next four games, and his word is mine. Got it?"

Satch pouted and said, "So what you fellas think about that?" They ignored him, hotly, still fuming from his absence in New York and the fact that he'd flown his private plane to Boston without enduring their hardships. Satch took a seat and sulked. Campy climbed up on top of a bench and called the players around. "Listen! Barn-hill's throwing, so Pee Wee, suit up and catch him."

Despite the cold and clouds, you couldn't fit more people into cozy Fenway Park with a crowbar. At first they were a polite bunch, applauding at the sight of the A's but without the same hysterics as in Washington, New York, and Philly. None of the players was familiar with the city or its stadium—Boston was one of the few towns that not only didn't have a Negro League team but didn't take to the barn-stormers either. "Where the hell's our people?" Barnhill wondered aloud, staring up at the stands. From first glance, they were filled al-most entirely with whites. Only a few blacks managed to show.

The A's managed three hits the whole afternoon and lost by a run.

When the game ended, the players waited outside the park with a small group of reporters. The mechanic had sent the rest of the club on their way around noon, and they had made it into Boston around 2:30.

Sam, by now red-faced and drenched with sweat, explained the situation. "We're not allowed in any hotel in Boston," he said. He had just spent the last two hours fighting with indifferent hotel man-agers, trying to find a place for them to lay their heads. "So we're go-ing to a place called Sunnydale Cabins, about a half-hour out. Supposed to be nice, so let's all go eat, and I'll wait here for the rest of the team."

But Boston wasn't New York; it wasn't even Birmingham, Alabama. When they first sat down to eat, it was as if they were invisible. No signs said "Whites Only," but they certainly weren't serving blacks. When a waitress gave Veeck a menu, he asked, "Are you gonna help them too?" and suddenly she wasn't talking to him, either.

"At least in Georgia you know where you can eat," Jethroe complained. For the next hour the players—hungry, tired, aching, and without showers—tried to find a place that would serve them, to no avail. By six o'clock no one had eaten, and everyone was just about ready to throttle one another. None of them had any experi-ence with Boston and couldn't find the black section of town or the restaurants that would serve them. Tired of being rejected at every greasy spoon, the players asked to head to their cabins.

A realtor would say that the Sunnydale Cabins were rustic. Each was as big as a two-car garage, and there was one bathroom for the whole team to share. There were holes in the screens and a stale smell, like old sneakers left under a radiator. Veeck, hating an unhappy ball club, and remembering his promise to them, brought in sandwiches and beer, and tried to liven things up. Satch, hoping to win back the favor of his team, asked them to gather in his cabin for a shindig. He had a car of his own and sent Sam out to buy hard liquor and cards; Sam sent the bus driver. Veeck begged Dan Burley to sing, along with Buck Leonard, who played guitar and knew all the Mills Brothers songs by heart. Most of them got drunk together, even Sam Dailey, who tossed off a bottle of red wine by himself and then fell dead asleep. Exhausted, the rest stumbled back to their cabins around midnight.

Campy spent the night on the floor of Josh's room. Benson joined him, and they plied Josh with a half-bottle of Old Grand-Dad, trying to get him to sleep.

"Wish I had my girl, my Grace, here," Josh said after taking a long pull off the bottle. "She understands. She understands."

"Understands what, Josh?" Gene said disgustedly.

Josh glared at Gene. "You hate her. But you don't know her at all." He tapped a finger on his left temple. "She knows how it's buzzing up here." He drank again, a long gulp that nearly drained the bottle. "Yeah. You boys, you boys got it lucky. Young. You're young and you got your health and a whole baseball life ahead a' you. Bastards. Sorry—not you Roy. You're a help. But John . . ."

"It's Gene, Josh," Campy said.

"Fuck you, then, Gene. See, all my good years are down that goddam toilet. All my good years. You watch, I can still see the goddam ball, but my good years, my good years . . ." He stared at his hands, and then flexed them. "My body, it's leavin' me. Hurts. I can barely pee right, without some pain. And I gotta prove that I am who I am. If I only hit ten bombs, they won't believe I ever hit sixty, do you get me?" When they didn't answer, Josh roared, "Do you get me? They gotta know I'm Ruth! Gotta see I'm better'n Ruth!"

"Take it easy, dammit all!" Gene said, standing suddenly and readying himself for battle.

But the effort to stand and shout, along with the whiskey, sent Josh tumbling back on the bed. "So tired," he mumbled. "You boys, you lucky. Got your health. You got it. You'll be . . ." And with that he fell asleep.

"Know somethin', Gene?" Campy whispered over Josh's sudden snoring, which was as loud as a ripsaw. "I don't remember the last time that boy ate. Other'n candy I mean. Good thing Mr. Veeck convinced him to keep his woman away. Think he's missing Grace too much?"

Benson, sprawled out beside him, sipping from the bottle himself, shrugged. "It ain't missing a woman: King Fat's strung out. Only way to beat this mark is to haul 'im to a hospital. Boy's flyin' high right now, even."

"It's just whiskey."

"And dope. Probably snuck into a closet at Fenway and ran the needle. This boy's fucked up."

"No sir! And even if he is, I'll watch him from here on out, every minute. Keep him from doin' what you say."

"Shit no, Roy. You cold turkey the man from heroin, he could croak."

"C'mon, Gene, you don't know what you're talking about."

Benson walked quickly across the room and began rifling through Josh's luggage, his uniform, the bat bag, and finally he found an old Bible stashed in his duffel. The Bible was hollowed out. "Son of a . . . oldest trick in the book." Benson held out four Syrettes.

"Okay, that doesn't mean nothin'."

"That's heroin, squirt. Gonna kill the Fatty you don't check him in."

"Gene, you just don't know . . ."

"Fact is, I do, Roy." He stood, flipped off the light and flopped back on his makeshift bed. "Pal of a friend of my brother's died that way. Found 'im myself, green like a hard-boiled yolk. Just *one* day free of the junk. Found 'im on the porch, stiff. The boy was *stiff*."

"When?"

"Couple years ago. 'Round Christmas."

"So maybe he froze to death." Campy reached for the bottle he'd taken to bed with him, took a hit, and handed it to Benson. "Maybe Josh *is* using that stuff. Maybe he's only got a small habit. Maybe it's just Grace got the problem. Golly, I really don't know. But I think it's just liquor that's got Josh by the tail. Gene, I'm gonna break this boy if it's the last thing I do. Off the drink. Off whatever the heck you talkin' about."

"Heroin, Roy. Don't mess with it. Let a hospital—"

"Hospital?! And ruin him in the press! Dang it, Gene, we can't have the press devour him before he makes it big."

"Ain't gonna make it big he keeps up this way."

Next day, with an entire squad of aching players (the mattresses felt like they were stuffed with old boots) and all their equipment, the Red Sox bombed Jefferson and walked away with another win. The fans didn't cheer much or call out nasty invectives, but there was an almost unholy chill about Fenway. In the seventh, someone hurled a hot dog at Cool, and when he spun around he found himself staring at a sea of blank faces. Usually there'd be a guy scowling or shouting, and another guy trying to pound the offending fan. People usually took pride in their heckling. But here . . . nothing. Children, the elderly, men and women, and even a pastor in his black shirt just stared back at him, as if to wonder what he could possibly be looking at. Cool tried to ignore them, but they were like zombies, staring blankly at the game on the field.

In baseball, whole sets of games can fall in what seems like an instant. You drop one game, then that loss becomes two, then two becomes three, then you've lost four of five, eight of ten, fifteen of seventeen, and you're eight games out of first and wondering if the whole season's slipping away. April closed with the Philadelphia Athletics already four games out of first place, and then they came home and lost a heartbreaker to the Yanks, 2-1. Barnhill pitched as well as any man could, allowing only four hits and those two runs. After the eighth inning, as Josh struck out for the fourth time that day, Campy, nursing a bruised wrist and unable to play, walked over to Josh and said, "Up."

"What's the matter? Leave me alone."

Campy yanked Josh by the collar of his uniform and almost threw him across the dugout. Buck turned to Ray and said, "You know, that boy's got some gravity in him."

Campy pulled Josh into the hallway and whispered, "Boy, what's eatin' you? You act like you're sleepwalkin'."

Josh smiled, feebly. "Listen, Roy, I'm tired. My eyes, they're deceiving me. It's like they're not mine. And the aches. Jesus, Roy, I . . . I didn't count on the pain. I always hurt durin' a season, but this year, shit, it's killing me. But listen, the day won't be a loss. Listen, after the game I'll show an old trick Biz Mackey taught me—"

"Tired?" Campy grabbed Josh's arm, twisted it, and checked the crook of his elbow. Black pustules snaked up and down his veins. "My word, Gene's right. That's what's messin' up your eyes. Or do you take it for the pain?"

Josh jerked his arm away. Campy shook his head. "Sometimes, Josh, it's easy to forget you once amounted to much of *anything*." He turned and walked back to the dugout.

Josh stole away after the game, Grace in tow, and this time Campy didn't follow him with anything but his eyes. Benson said, "Want me to . . .?" and nodded after Josh.

"No. Let him think on what I said for a while. Might do him some good."

The players dressed, a heavy melancholy descending over them like a canvas tarp. No one spoke, except to say, "Excuse me?" or "Cigarette?"—simple questions with one-word answers.

As Campy knotted his red bow tie, dressing up for a dinner at home with his family, Cochrane called him into the office. "Sit down, Roy," he said. Campy sat. "I wanted to let you know that I appreciate what you are doing for Josh. However," he added, "the fact of the matter is, well, if you cannot redeem him, it is all over. This is a professional baseball team. We go by production. We do not go by sentiment. On this issue, Mr. Veeck is in agreement, for the bottom line is also money, and an overweight catcher hitting .200 does not bring in fans of *any* color. I have an idea about what is troubling Josh—an *idea*, that is all, and it's more than just aches and pains— and I know what he means to you and to the rest of the men on this club. So," he said, "if Josh does not straighten out soon, he is gone. Permanently. Same as anyone else."

"'Course. I mean, yes, sir."

"Mr. Veeck has informed me that he has a physician who can help us as well. If you think that is necessary."

"Heck no! Let me and Gene see what we can do."

Cochrane looked down at his hands again. Gnarled, the hands of a catcher. Gibson's were the same. Campy's would be someday.

"Thank you, Roy," he said. "But take care of yourself too. We need you. Understand?"

"Oh, yes, sir!" he said.

Next day, under a clear sky and warm breezes, Satchel led the A's to victory, a squeaker decided by Ray Dandridge's first homer, a shot over the right-field wall that kicked mortar off the bricks on Veeck's apartment across Twenty-first. Taking the second game of the series gave players and fans a renewed confidence. Even better, after that last game with the Yanks, the A's were about to meet the runts of the league: first the lowly Senators for four, followed by the last-place White Sox and then the Browns, consistently the worst team in both leagues. From the players in the locker room to the last fans soaking up the sun to the tired men and women drinking in the taverns and restaurants to the folks heading home on the buses and trolleys, everyone speculated about the coming destruction of these next three teams. "A win tomorra and then ten sleepers," you might have heard on a bus. "B'leeve me, these guys'll take nine of ten. The Senators? Jeez, that's four right there!" If there was a question about anything, it was how the Browns, a Southern team made up primarily of regional players, would react to this Negro club. Black fans were thrilled at the notion of being able to see their heroes lay into these bastards from St. Louis, and some of the sportswriters—Burley included—were excited about the possibility of a symbolic blow to the Jim Crow laws. "In a small way," he boasted, "this'll be like Louis-Schmeling all over again."

But when the A's dropped three of four to Washington and found themselves swept by Chicago—blowing a six-run lead in the last game when Barnhill served a butterball in the eighth that went sky-high for a grand slam—the fans began to show their collective displeasure. Soldiers, kids, and even women in their coveralls, fresh from the munitions plants, threw whatever they could lay their hands on at the players. Coffee cups, beer cups, peanuts, old shoes, scorecards—the field was littered with trash.

The black press was sympathetic: the Senators were looking good this year, in fact they'd come in second just last year, so, it was argued, they were better than everyone expected. But, they wondered, why did Cochrane keep pulling many of his regulars? Was any pitcher but Satchel going to throw a complete game? The *Philadelphia Record* cracked wise that the A's had become "unglued." The white press had taken to calling Cochrane "Black Mike," arguing that he had lost control of his team. Some crank had gone around selling buttons with the A's logo, and underneath: "I wish my elephant was white again!"

The St. Louis Browns strutted into town fresh off a four-game winning streak. A cold front walloped Philadelphia, bringing heavy clouds and a light mist that made the A's situation that much more miserable . . . but not miserable enough to call any of the games. It was winter in May, and Veeck, eager to combat the declining attendance, handed out mittens with stitched A's logos, and served hot chocolate and coffee while the band played "White Christmas" for the crowd, which prompted more racial catcalls. That day's game started at ten, for the third-shift workers in town.

Artie Wilson was in a corner of the clubhouse, swinging his bat, searching desperately for answers to what was beginning to seem like a permanent slump. The others were going over strategy, or wondering just what kind of crap the Browns were going to give them. "Heard they got a crate of watermelons to taunt us with," Jethroe said. He cocked his bat and laughed. "What I hear, that pitcher Hollandsworth ain't got nothing but watermelons to throw us. We'll show 'em."

"We haven't shown anyone in a long time," Buck reminded him. "So you would do best to keep your mouth shut and your mind focused."

Oscar, back from his suspension, was perturbed: his club seemed bewildered and overwhelmed even in batting practice. Despite their words to the contrary, despite claiming they were going to break this team over their knees, he noticed they were short-tempered. Wells started griping at McKinnis, who was tossing batting practice. "You gotta pitch so tough?" he said, giving Gready a nasty look. In the dugout, Oscar overheard the gossip. Ray Dandridge and Buck Leonard were talking quietly next to him. Ray's dogs were fighting, and he had to put Daisy in a separate cage. Buck's wife wasn't talking to him. And when Serrell said, "Yer old lady sounds like she could use a good slap," Buck hurled him out of the dugout and onto the grass. "And if my wife were here," Buck said, "I'd be sitting on that bench watchin' her do the same." The Browns, now on the field, began to whistle. Serrell brushed himself off, stood, and gave them the finger.

When Cochrane finally stepped into the dugout, he was unshaven, looking as if he'd had maybe an hour's sleep. He tacked up the lineup, wandered up and down the dugout chewing on his pipe, barking questions. The men fidgeted, looked around, bit fingernails, and smoked. Cochrane shouted, "Is everyone awake? Then pay attention." Barnhill crossed his arms and grumbled something, so Cochrane waved a hand and said, "All right, get out there in left and toss some balls around. You guys are making me ill."

Mack Filson shuffled up to Cochrane and whispered something in his ear. Cochrane's face fell. "Tell me you are joking." Filson looked down and shook his head. "Has anyone seen Satchel? Does this have to happen *every* week?!" Jeep mumbled that Satch went out to buy some new duds. This brought anxious murmurs from all the players—they needed Satchel desperately; he was the only hurler who seemed guaranteed to win.

"Son of a bitch is probably not coming in," Jethroe complained.

"My Lord!" Cochrane said to Filson. "We have to have someone warming up." At that point the rest of the starters had been used the last three days; Smith couldn't pitch on two days rest. Cochrane rubbed his chin and said, "Okay, Oscar, come here." Somehow looking surlier than everyone else, Oscar lumbered over.

"Well," Cochrane said, arms crossed, "now is your chance to show off your managerial skills. Do you have a suggestion for which reliever might be able to start?"

Oscar was shocked to hear this, but later he decided it was further evidence of Cochrane's inability to run the team. Something was up. He shrugged. "Jessup," was all he said. Wasn't going to give that bastard the satisfaction of offering the peace pipe.

No one knows how or why Jeep Jessup remained on the Athletics roster as long as he did, except perhaps that Satch wanted him along. Satchel's absence made Jeep nervous, and when Jeep was nervous, he was one of the worst pitchers in baseball.

But Cochrane had taken a chance on asking Oscar. He wanted peace in the ranks and a victory over these Southerners, a victory to break the losing streak, hell, he just wanted to get some numbers in the win column. So he told Mack to inform Jessup to warm up, he was starting.

"Really?" Mack said. "Okay, boss, I'll get that boy's sling whipready. But—"

"What is it, Mr. Filson?"

"Why, it's nothing. Jeep Jessup, coming up!"

There was the usual overflow crowd, and this time it was mostly black faces, hungry to see their Athletics pummel the Southern boys. There were banners, horns, screaming for Wells, Cool, and Buck to "really give it to 'em!" Jethroe mopped his brow. "Damn, it's like the Civil War all over again."

To rile up the Browns, Veeck had the band play the "Battle Hymn of the Republic" right after the national anthem. Before the first player came to bat, a droopy-looking clown in a Browns uniform ran out, toy bat in hand. The ump, not in on the joke, began to bellow, which prompted a fat clown in a Browns uniform—this time with MANAGER across his back—to come out and kick dirt on the umpire's shoes.

In spite of this, the Browns were calm, collected. They watched the clown show with only a few chuckles on their side, nobody eating watermelons, nobody in blackface. The Browns just sat on the bench, without commentary, without gesturing, nothing. Their first batter stepped up to the plate blank-faced, ready to hit.

For this morning game, vendors wore pajamas and slippers, served coffee and doughnuts. The band started in on "Sleepytime." But all of Veeck's antics couldn't turn a losing game into a barrel of fun.

Jeep fell apart quickly. "What the living hell is the matter with you!" a black woman screeched to Jeep as he walked back to the dugout after finally recording three outs in the first. But it was 3-0 already.

In the A's half, Artie took a deep breath and approached the plate. "Artie!" shouted a heckler. He tried to ignore the man, who seemed hidden in the seats behind home plate. The heckler roared, "The hell you got Artie in there for? He couldn't hit the side of a whale if you dropped it on him!"

Artie reminded himself that the bat felt good in his hands. Nothing was wrong. *Today* he was breaking out of his slump, even if the tape on his hands felt too tight. Early in the season, right?

"Artie!" Came the cry from the stands behind home plate. People called his name—every player's name—all the time. But Artie hunched his shoulders and grimaced. It was loud, a shrill screech, that made his teeth ache. "Yeah, Artie!" came the cry again, and even the ump turned, squinting, looking as if he'd just sucked on a lemon.

Making his way to the plate, Artie walked right into the catcher. The crowd hooted and hollered and rained peanut shells on him as he tried to untangle himself.

He stood, brushed himself off, and stepped back into the box. The heckler continued: "That's right! Dig in, boy. The better to knock you down with!" Artie leaned back a bit. "Good boy, Artie," came a screech. "Don't let that pitcher prove you're bad luck."

He swung at a fastball a good four inches outside. The heckler shouted, "We forgive you, boy!"

"Damn," the catcher said, "That guy's so loud my ears ache."

It was like a hammer of sound. There was clanging, screeching, weird clucking, and a whistle that seemed to shoot right down his spine. Artie mumbled, "Take it easy, just noise," and stepped in.

"Oh, you look *relaxed* all right! No worries!" Now the crowd was encouraging the heckler, applauding, cheering, chortling at whoever he was. Artie felt sick. It seemed like he'd fallen down this bastard's throat, that the voice box was ringing right next to his temple. He tried to focus: Would the next pitch come inside? Junk? A fastball?

The ball hit him square in the back. As he struggled to get up, there came that whistle, only this time it came out as a tune, "Dixie," followed by the cry that seemed to punch at the sore spot: "If that's the only way you can get on base, I applaud you, boy!" At first base, Artie craned his neck trying to put a face to the noise. The heckler must have sat down, vanished in the sea of people. Artie took a deep breath. He led off, took a step or two, eager to steal, to show them his prowess on the basepaths, to make up for his blunders—

The heckler cackled, "Artie!"

The pitcher shot a throw to first and picked him off. Artie lay face down in the dirt, his right hand a good six inches from the bag. He sat up, hunched on his knees, eyes closed, and soaked in the abuse raining down from the stands. As he cut across the field, the loudmouth lit into him with special glee.

This time Artie got a good look at him. Bare-chested and wearing an old German army helmet with the spike on top, the heckler was a man of tremendous height, a giant, towering over the rest of the crowd, so loud the people around him leaned away as if heat were radiating from him. Seeing Artie, the man waved a chicken's foot attached to a string. There was a bone tied to it. "Chicken hex!" he hissed. It was like the guy was shouting from inches away. Artie almost tripped coming into the dugout. His stomach felt queasy.

Artie plopped down next to Campy. "Chicken hex? What the hell does that mean?"

"C'mon, Artie, leave it alone, it's nothin' but fun," Campy said.

In the middle of the second, Satch ran into the dugout, pulling on his uniform. "Fuckin' cops kept old Satch for a good hour, just fer speedin'!" he yelled. Seeing the score, he shouted to Cochrane, "Get Jeep outta there!" Cochrane ran out to the field, followed by Satch, jogging for the first time in world history. Jeep gratefully handed the ball to Satch, who didn't even warm up. "C'mon," he shouted at the ump. "Nothin' says Satchel Paige gotta warm up."

And he didn't. With fifteen pitches he struck out the side. As they wandered back to the dugout to start their half, Satch asked if the Browns were treating them rough.

"Nothing," Jeep said wearily. "They're just playing."

"Not these Southern boys? Watch. Ol' Satch'll rile 'em."

Satch pitched brilliantly, going so far as to nail a couple of Browns just for fun and spite. But it was as if the Browns had dug deep inside themselves to keep the A's from scoring. Normally an awful defensive team, the Browns made spectacular plays to match the A's inning for scoreless inning . . . except that St. Louis had been spotted a three-run lead.

As the game flew by, the crowd grew uglier. A group of kids from Cool's neighborhood threw pieces of hot dogs at him and said they were going to break his windows. "What's the matter with you guys?" a pastor yelled. "Can't you beat these Southern bums?" He was wearing his collar to the park for good luck, but it only made his question that much more ominous.

The heckler bugged Cool about being hurt, being an old man, being slow in the head. He shouted to the A's dugout, asking Cochrane if he was sleeping at night. The giant now held a little chalkboard and ran his fingernails across it. From his bag he pulled a rope in a hangman's knot, slipped it around his neck, and yanked it heavenward. Blue in the face, he shouted to Artie, "Here's a suggestion for ya!" In the fourth he blew up a balloon and rubbed it, then popped it in the sixth, causing Artie to jump a good foot. At one point, in the seventh, a pitch came in, the heckler yelled "Strike!," and immediately the ump cried the same.

"That was a foot outside!" Wells cried. "That guy doing your job?"

The ump tossed Wells from the game.

By the top of the eighth the fans began to file out in huge numbers. Veeck watched them go from his perch across the street, surrounded by a group of bankers he'd been wooing to keep them from calling his many loans. Veeck's visions of late-inning beer and dog sales vanished like a daydream. "Yet another defeat," one of the bankers said, slapping Veeck on the thigh and making another trip to the buffet. Veeck just chewed his lip.

In the locker room, Jethroe said, "You notice we're niggers, now?"

Wells was already drinking, sitting in front of his locker with a bottle in his hand, shirtless and sockless, looking like he was ready to tear someone's head off. "Who in the living fuck was that guy?" he finally said, referring to the heckler.

Campy laughed. "That's Pete Adelis. The 'Iron Lung of Shibe Park.' I'll tell you, boys, ol' Pete yellin' at you means you made it."

Wells walked over to Campy's locker. "I don't like you," he said. "Defendin' that mental patient doesn't help any." Glancing up and down at him, as if sizing up his duds, Wells grunted. Campy kept dressing. Then Wells turned and said, "Look at us. Greatest team I ever been on. Last place." He grunted again, then craned his neck to see if Cochrane was in earshot. He was nowhere to be seen. Wells said, "Most of all, it seems to me like the main trouble is who's running the show. That old Cock—"

Campy stood, fists clenched, but Gene told him to simmer down. "You're wrong, man." Campy said to Wells. "I'm here to tell you to keep your mouth shut. Unless of course you find it in you to say something good."

Campy struck out twice the next day. To make matters worse, the Athletics lost both games of the next day's doubleheader and were swept by the St. Louis Browns.

After the last game, on his way out the player's entrance, Ray met one of the Browns. The ballplayer, a young man named Spike, hissed, "We got you good, boy. Now we'll see you in St. Louie." He drew a finger across his throat.

Detroit was next; Cleveland followed. Four games each, and the A's won but two. Veeck watched from his bleachers in mounting disbelief. He slapped his forehead when they threw to first instead of third; dropped the cigarette from his mouth as one, two, four, then seven strikeouts would sail right by them without the bat leaving the shoulder. They missed signals and the cutoff man, and now and then they ended up two men on a bag. The White Sox had romped, the Browns bullied, the Tigers devoured, and the Indians toyed with them, all in his own park. Which, of course, he was banned from entering. While he did nothing to hide the fact he was running the club from his Devil's Island apartment, there were meetings, phone calls, everyday machinations that he wasn't privy to and that Sam didn't bother to tell him about. All the while snickering journalists were seasoning great cauldrons of steaming crow for him to eat. The kid who'd worked the Milwaukee Miracle was facing big league music and couldn't keep up. And where he thought he'd sit alone during the losses, the press joined him, briefly, just long enough to rub his nose in it. "Some team," a press photographer offered one day, as if Jethroe's dropped ball were proof positive of anything.

And now Veeck needed cash. Sam reminded him of this each and every day. Veeck had calculated sellouts—they hadn't happened. To fill the stands he'd spent money on contests, clowns, bands, balloons, maps of the Philadelphia area, tires, and a dozen free meals at local restaurants. Landis was always breathing down his neck, fining the team for its uniforms (too short in the sleeves), for the cut of its grass (too long), and it was clear that all the grief the city gave them came directly at the judge's prompting. Sam kept begging him to postpone repairs on the park, to get cheaper hot dogs, to do something, anything, to shore up their sagging bank accounts. Veeck didn't listen: he sunk money into the park, tons more than Connie Mack ever did, and yet he was in violation of every code under the sun.

And the fans! The fans were losing their itch, Veeck thought: once the silence hits, it hits hard, and you have empty seats and broadcasts going out to no one. His advertisers were already demanding discounts, which he agreed to at the end of the season. And now he had a last-place team headed for twenty games on the road. Cities with losing teams don't go see games against other losers, and he needed his half of the gate receipts in other cities as badly as he needed them at home. He had to get fans into those parks. Sure, in Detroit you had the dual promise of a first-place team and a large Negro population. Chicago, too, was the second-largest city in America. But Cleveland, holy cow. When was the last time they had a full house?

What kept Veeck from sleeping were the not-so-subtle suggestions that the A's would be better if they were white. Veeck was grinding his teeth to powder over that one. Look at Buck, look at Satch—hell, look at half the team. Check their numbers against last year's A's. It made him want to swear, and he never swore. He almost got into a fight with one of his scorecard vendors on the sidewalk—guy complained his sales were hurting because "no one wants a colored scorecard." He couldn't believe what he was hearing. And Josh! Josh only made matters worse. That guy was breaking his heart. Josh Gibson was the best ballplayer of the last decade, and no one would ever know it to look at him now. Maybe he should have left the guy to his past glories and not exposed him to the realities of the present. Maybe, maybe, maybe, he thought. The "maybes" are killing me.

The A's had an off-day before traveling to Detroit, so the *Philadelphia Record*'s Stan Keller thought it would be a good idea to take Dave Barnhill out for a meal. Keller was a reporter with an eye for controversy, and from the beginning he had paid very close attention to the personalities of the Athletics. He knew that Dave Barnhill read all the papers. He knew that Dave Barnhill did not like most of what he read. And he knew that Dave Barnhill didn't keep his opinions to himself. As usual, Barnhill arrived, dressed sharply, looking like he was out on a date. Over dinner, Keller picked a topic out of thin air: he asked Dave about a coming transit strike—the city of Philadelphia was integrating the buses, and the union didn't cotton to that, so a strike was looming. It was like a homer on the first pitch of the ball game, he thought: Barnhill sang like the proverbial canary.

Dave began quietly, trying to have a two-sided conversation, but as Barnhill's energy fed on his own words, he raged for a good twenty minutes about the commissioner, about his keeping the best from baseball before now, and even now it was a fight. But he wouldn't stop there. With nary a prompt, Barnhill got to the part that Keller liked best—the war. "So they take wops and kikes but not us niggers, is that it?" Barnhill said, sawing into his steak dinner. "See, that's how it is right now in America: when the invasion comes, it's the wops and kikes and you name it, and when the whole thing's over, why they're Italians and Jews and gentlemen of Polish descent." Keller scribbled furiously while Barnhill scraped his knife across his plate, cutting his meat into smaller and smaller bits. He wasn't eating for all the talking he was doing. "Philadelphia," he said with disgust, almost spitting out the word. He took Keller's silence for approval; it felt great finally to have the ear of a reporter. "It's an injustice that we're not allowed to drive buses, fight in major battles, do anything but wash dishes and play Stepin Fetchit. We're proof that integration works, and you ask yourself whose democracy we're fighting for? We got the invasion coming and Negroes aren't a part of it. You got all that fighting in Guadalcanal and Negroes aren't a part of it. The Arsenal of Democracy and we're not a part of it."

"You're a part of all those," Keller said.

"Cleaning toilets, spooning up potatoes, working in the boilers of the factories isn't being a part of it! I mean, if that's *all* you do. It could be beautiful. Instead we get dishpan hands and they get the medals and promotions."

Keller opened his mouth to speak, but Barnhill kept on. "Look at my uncle, loading bombs and shells out west in Port Chicago, California. By hand, from trains to ships. Dangerous, unsafe conditions, and no one cares. When he tries to improve conditions, he's an uppity and unpatriotic nigger.

"Hell, some of us are flying planes, proving to be as good a fighter as a white man. But *separated* from whites, of course. Now roll this over your mind: yesterday me and Serrell couldn't get a bite to eat at a diner in our *own* city. I read about that brother who can't get a job driving buses. Why? Because white people drive buses. This is Philadelphia? This is democracy?" He pointed his fork at Keller and leaned close, conspiratorially. Keller nodded: everything positive, always say yes, this guy's on fire. "Why not now? We gotta wait until . . . when? Now that we're in baseball, there's no telling where we can go. We can drive buses. Run for office. Live where we want, marry who we want, go where we want. That's the Constitution. You don't give this to us, well, I say we sit, simple as that, or walk. Bus drivers. War workers. Maybe even ballplayers. At home, on the seas, or even in battle. Isn't that our right in a democracy?"

"Thank you very much!" Veeck shouted, hurling the paper to the floor. Barnhill's picture was on the front page. "That was some conversation!"

Barnhill tried to ignore him and stared out the window. The morning's clouds were darkening to grey—good thing they were traveling, Barnhill thought. He sat across from Veeck in a large, overstuffed chair that a city councilman had fallen asleep drunk on just the night before. Barnhill had to admit that Veeck had a beautiful view of Shibe. Pictures of Veeck with numerous baseball players hung everywhere. Comfortable. Sometimes he wished he could live in such comfort, without troubles.

Veeck continued, "Did he put these words in your mouth?" Barnhill shook his head. "So this is all yours. Fantastic. You want to call Landis a bum for keeping Negroes from playing, I'm right there with you. But the war? I can't even make it out like you were quoted out of context, can I? Fabulous. You talked about deserting the armed forces? Endearing."

"I didn't say—"

"Listen to them," he made his way to the window of his apartment and jerked his thumb to the street. "Protesters. Unbelievable. Politics and baseball don't mix! It's unprecedented. We're losing about every other game, and you go and make 'em hate you all the more. And hate you because you're a Negro! Don't you get that? I ought to suspend you for this whole road trip, let things cool down a bit."

That riled Barnhill up. "You do and I could get the NAACP—"

"Shut up, would you! Since I can't afford that kind of publicity, you're still in. But I can hit you for other things, so watch your back. Unfortunately I can't afford not to have you pitch." He sat down and leaned in, then said, quietly, "Dave, how could you do this to us? Look at the crowd: they're going to be on fire today, and tomorrow and the day after that. But if we make this political, well, they just won't come. And if there's a transit strike like they're saying, boy, they're going to think we're responsible. And rioting . . ." Veeck ran his hand through his hair. "People come to the ballpark to relax. To forget about their problems. They don't want to hear—"

"Are you forbidding me to talk to the press?"

"Just listen for a moment—"

"I have a right to my opinion and a right—"

Veeck shouted, "You have every right in the world, but—" Barnhill stood up abruptly and turned to leave. "Where do you think you're going?"

"You're not going to bar me from anything, and your sugar won't convince me to keep my mouth shut, so is there any use in talking?"

"Fine! Maybe this'll rattle around in that head of yours: as of today I'm shopping Dave Barnhill. If I can find any other team willing to integrate, willing to ship me a decent arm, you're gone. Got it? And the NAACP hasn't got anything that can keep me from that, understand? So help me, you'll be throwing for the Browns if I have my way."

Barnhill's throat was tight. He nodded. Veeck felt like slugging him. "You haven't got anything to say now, do you? Maybe if I offered to splash it across the front pages you'd speak up." He bit his lip. "Get out of here."

For the first time this season, Veeck wasn't joining the team on the road—not yet, anyway. Sweating like nobody's business, he wondered if he'd ever have it easy. Doubtful. He ran his hand through his hair and wondered if Sam had managed to find a hotel in Detroit that would house his black team.

◇ **10** ◇

Arsenal of Democracy

If baseball were your guide and you'd been dropped square in the center of Black Bottom, the Negro section of town, you wouldn't know it was Detroit. The A's were received at the Michigan Central Station like heroes returning from war; hand-painted signs proclaiming "We welcome the A's!" were taped in storefronts and bay windows; restaurants renamed meals after each player. Barnhill's was a grilled cheese sandwich and tomato soup. He wondered if that meant anything.

While walking down Hastings Street in Detroit, Dave Barnhill ran into himself. He and his cousin Luke were heading to Lip's Barbershop, moving slowly, enjoying each other's company in silence, when they came across a stickball game in the middle of the street. It was Philadelphia against Detroit, and the kids playing the home team didn't look too happy about it.

The kid playing Barnhill was short and stout and in the process of striking out an urchin posing as Hank Greenberg, who was thin and sporting a pair of jug ears. Satchel Paige played first, a timid-looking boy whose eyes bugged out at the sight of Barnhill.

"Let me get this straight," Barnhill said to the child, no more than eleven. "You're on first and you're Satch?"

He spoke through a stutter. "Can't pitch *every* day, sir."

Barnhill and his cousin Luke laughed, and when they continued their walk the game dissolved and the kids began to follow them. Two days in town and Barnhill felt as if he'd walked ten miles in Black Bottom. As he took in the squalor, he shook his head and thought bitterly to himself, "Detroit. The fucking Arsenal of Democracy."

The citizens of Black Bottom were crammed into this neighborhood, segmented by unwritten rules as concrete as those physically on the books in St. Louis, Birmingham, New Orleans. Black Bottom had so many businesses and homes packed into its twelve blocks that it looked as if the city fathers had kindly given their black residents a half-block for every five they actually needed. Clapboard homes were piled on top of, and sandwiched between, one another. Businesses were squeezed in too: bars and barbershops and groceries, laundries and the numbers runners who holed up there. Most of the toilets were outhouses, and garbage filled the alleys. This was a sign to many white outsiders that the residents of Black Bottom preferred squalor to decent living; the city, however, refused to collect garbage more than twice a month there, and the concentrated humanity made it pile up. Barnhill was surprised by the coziness to the place, though, the human warmth that comes from everyone knowing everyone else, shouting hellos and how-are-ya's, and the laughter, the constant laughter. And he ate well at his cousin's, even if it was on a wobbly table in a small, greasy kitchen.

They had other company as well—rats and cats and dogs and seagulls on every rooftop and fence post. There was a fascinating mix of people—doctors and lawyers and professors who would love to leave the poor behind but couldn't find decent property near the city that anyone would sell to a black person. Ministers and electricians and musicians dwelt alongside the men and women who labored in the munitions factories; they, in turn, lived beside and below gangsters and whores. You had the unemployed and the unemployable. And, of course, you had children, tons of children, everywhere underfoot, scrambling for work. In spite of everything, there was always room for baseball.

With his favorite cousin Luke working in Detroit, Barnhill made it a point to visit as often as he could, and over the years the city had become a second home to him. As he and Luke walked on they passed the burned-out remnants of a house. Luke slurred, "That fella next door's lucky he only got singed. Smoke went up all the way to the sun, it seemed. Never seen smoke move so fast."

The '43 riots. Detroit had split apart, its residents—white and black—doing their best to kill and maim one another, to tear the city down brick by brick, burn down home after home, and shatter the glass of every business they could. On a sweltering June afternoon on

Belle Isle, a fight had broken out between a white man and a black teenager. No one knows what they were arguing about, but crowds of white men witnessed the skirmish and decided things were getting out of hand. They attacked the kid. Black men, thinking this was a lynching, rushed to his aid. The melee exploded from Belle Isle and into the city itself. Sailors took to beating any black they found, just as they had done to the Mexicans five years earlier in Los Angeles. Black men and women began to pummel any whites they encountered. Homes and businesses burned. A brick had hit Luke's skull, leaving him in the dirt. Another had struck his friend Teep in the throat and killed him.

A neighbor walked by and mumbled his hello. "What'd he call you?" Barnhill asked.

"Sleepy. Don't you *ever* call me Sleepy." Luke's injury had left him with a face spiderwebbed with scars, slurred speech, and a pronounced limp. "Thought I'd never walk again, so I ain't complainin'." Luke lost his job at the Willow Run Assembly Plant while he was in the hospital, and when he recovered it was cleaning out the toilets for him. They couldn't use a man that walked and talked like that. "It's a job!" Luke said, trying to sound hopeful. "That day," he added, as they walked on, "you had the National Guard all over the place. Smoke on up to the sun," he repeated.

That's why this meeting is so important, Barnhill thought, as he pulled a handful of antacids from a bag in his pocket and chewed them to mush. He and Luke were on their way to Lip's Barbershop, having convinced most of the team to meet and discuss ways to shake up the world. The Communists were going to be there. Barnhill shook his head and marveled at his own audacity—baseball players thinking they can shake up this world.

Detroit buzzed him like coffee. The city kept sleep at bay, kept him from quiet thoughts. Half his family and most of his friends had settled here in the great migrations of the depression, when work was tough in the Carolinas and it seemed as if Henry Ford was welcoming them like brothers. But that wasn't entirely true: Papa Ford paid well, but the jobs were rough and dirty . . . and dangerous. No one was offered management positions or work on the line with whites. His cousin Luke had moved up in '34 with Barnhill's Uncle Hal. Luke found a job maintaining the boilers in Willow Run while Hal, in '37, sick of the same, joined the navy. Then the war hit. They segregated the navy, and when the men took off for war they gave the good jobs to the women. White and black girls, true, but Luke never moved out of the boiler room. Or the toilets.

All the while Barnhill played clown ball in Indianapolis. Painted faces, goofy costumes, and baseball. He was trying to win fifteen games to qualify for a bonus, and in the process he managed to add the curveball to his repertoire. While Uncle Hal fought Jim Crow in the navy and Luke battled both the unions and management, Barnhill threw under the name Impo. Developing his cut fastball while Hal moved munitions out in California. Working the count while Luke got his face busted in the riot.

As they walked on, kids shouting, families waving hello from in front of a burned-down shack, he felt disgusted with himself.

Two days earlier the A's had holed up at the Book-Cadillac Hotel downtown. Barnhill's room smelled of artificial pine. Above, the ceilings were clean white. No water stains. He could go over to the tub and run hot water all night if he felt like it. Luke would give his right arm to give his kids ten minutes of this. From his room, after that first game, he could hear doors slammed, and there was laughing outside. Celebrating. One win against the first-place Tigers and everyone's daffy. Barnhill felt trapped by his visions of the outside world, heavy from the awesome gravity of normal life. He waited until midnight that day, grabbed his suitcase, and took a taxi to Luke's house, where he stayed the whole trip.

Since then it was two losses against the Tigers—one step forward and two back, the story of the season. Later that afternoon Bill Veeck held a press conference from his Devil's Island office. "The Philadelphia Athletics have just finished negotiating the purchase of the single greatest baseball player the earth has yet seen," he crowed. "Our secret weapon will be unveiled in the first game of the double-header in Cleveland on Tuesday. Ladies and gentlemen, baseball fans here and overseas, you will not be disappointed. This is a player so incredible, so amazing, you'll wonder if he's really human!" This Superman disgusted Barnhill. Satch and Josh disgusted Barnhill. Uncle Tom and Junkie Moe. As Barnhill and Luke walked the neighborhood, the crowds growing behind them, Barnhill could overhear them talking baseball. Talking about old Sambo Satch, happy to please the white folks. Talking about how these guys had to win, why weren't they winning, what they oughta do. Dump Josh. No, keep Josh. Fire Mickey. Ain't his fault, it's they can't hit. And what's the matter with you, Dave Barnhill, can't *you* win now and then?

Sometimes Barnhill hated baseball, hated the frivolity of the whole enterprise. Hated its uselessness, the men playing a boy's game, men paying good money to see a boy's game. At times the game made him feel bigger than life; there, on Hastings Street, it made him feel small. An old man hunched from years of menial labor waved at him with calloused hands—Barnhill waved back with hands calloused from pitching a ball. At work he wore a white or grey uniform with an elephant on it; Luke and his wife wore dungarees and duck-cloth, torn and greasy, and at times dappled with small dots of blood from the many minor but painful accidents on the line. Usually he dined on steak and shrimp and beer while Luke and his family had to get by in a cold-water shack, eating face meat and knuckles, thanks to rationing. And salted, boiled potatoes. Jesus.

He wished Hal were around to give him advice. Uncle Hal taught him to fight for everything, that no one was going to give him anything because he was Negro, and small to boot. "Throw with everything you have," he used to tell Dave when he was a kid, demonstrating his pitches against their barn wall in Greenville, North Carolina. Hal fell over, he threw so hard. Barnhill did the same.

"People are gonna take one look at you and say, 'That boy isn't worth anything,'" Hal told him back then. "So when you try out, bully your way in there. Make them drag you off that mound, son. Otherwise they won't give you shit."

"Don't say 'shit,'" Barnhill said. "Ma said—"

Hal laughed, but he wouldn't disagree with his sister. "Sure, son, sure."

Hal added, "Whatever you do, whether it's throwin' a ball or shoveling coal, do it the best you can, with all you got." Hal said it about picking tobacco, the nicotine seeping into his cuts and scrapes and eventually making him dizzy. Hal said it while working the railroad, fighting every day with his foreman to get paid for the work he did. Hal said it at college, while he swept up after the white boys and stole biology and chemistry books to read. Now Hal was in the navy, in Port Chicago, fighting over the conditions that he and his fellow sailors were enduring, loading bombs off trains and into ships. Dangerous work, and it seemed lucky the place hadn't blown to smithereens. Just the other day, Hal was telling Barnhill the same thing over the phone, to do the best you can. Only he was saying it about baseball.

"I oughta be fighting," Barnhill said.

"You oughta do what God told you to do. With that arm, you throw a baseball. Don't be Jonah." Barnhill knew the story, the one that Hal retold many times: Jonah ignored his talents and was swallowed by the Leviathan. "Happens all the time in this life. A man ignores God's call and gets swallowed up by a whale called Hate. Hates himself. Hates the world. Boy, you play baseball, or you'll hate everything."

It seemed like he hated everything now.

He and Luke moved along in silence, breaking only to answer questions from the kids. Barnhill never really walked alone in Detroit: from the periphery he could see the faces peeping out at him, hiding behind the drapes when he turned to gaze at them. Women would wave and, in spite of himself, he wished he could catch a date or two, but he always had business. Sure, he was dressed to kill, a sharkskin suit and sunglasses, but he didn't have the time anymore. So why did he keep dressing that way? In spite of his shades, the sun was in his eyes, reflecting off the cars and windows as if the world were on fire. The light gave him a headache. He tried to look happy, to look pleased to be the center of attention, but he was brooding and couldn't help but look sour.

Luke didn't know what to say when Barnhill was in these moods. A ballplayer and he barely likes to talk about it. Strange. "Think you'll take 'em tomorra?" he asked.

Barnhill nodded.

"How're you gonna pitch to York?"

"Down and away. Just like I did when I met him in Philly."

"That's right, Dave!" one of the kids yelled. "You can beat that son of a bitch with your cutter!"

"Where'd you learn to swear like that?" Barnhill snapped.

Four kids mumbled apologies to that, and he forgave the offender by patting his head.

Luke asked, "Who's gonna be here?"

"Everyone, I hope. Except Mickey, Roy, and Gene. And Satch. Josh, of course, is blotto. Burley's coming, but that's about it for the press."

"And the Reds." Luke looked down. When he walked he wore a look of constant frustration, as if fighting his own impediments. "You really think they'll help?"

"You enjoy the game today? From the bleachers?"

"What's the Reds gonna do about it, Davey? They ain't gonna get me a good seat. Stick with *our* press, stick with our people."

"I've tried. After the *Record* article, none of our papers will touch me."

"Stick with your own," Luke repeated. "That's what Hal would say. You talk to him lately?"

Barnhill only turned to the crowd. "Any of you kids see the game today?"

They didn't understand the question and felt ashamed to have missed it. "Listened to it," one of them said. "Go tomorrow!" called out another.

"Great." He turned back to Luke. "Hal's a union man, just like the Communists. Luke, these kids couldn't get in, even if they had money. You think that every white man and woman in the good seats bought those tickets in advance, like they claim? I don't. Look around you, Luke." He waved his arms wide. "Detroit, Michigan, the Arsenal of Democracy, as Jim Crow as Birmingham, Alabama."

"They don't lynch people here."

"Teep was lynched. They didn't use rope. But they lynched him." They walked in silence the rest of the way.

Lip's Barbershop was hopping. Barnhill and Luke came around a corner and onto Chauncery Street and met a crowd of soldiers standing in front. As they approached, someone cried out "Impo!" and Barnhill had to restrain from grimacing. God, he hated that name. But they began applauding, clearing a space for him. Luke looked as if he were enjoying himself, Dave noticed. The first good feelings that man had had in a long time. The men peppered Barnhill with questions, and another soldier opened a door for him.

The shop was closed for the day. Inside there were long tables laid out with snacks and drinks: peanuts and cake, bourbon, soda, homemade wine and beer. Roast beef sandwiches and chicken. Most of the Athletics were already there. Each man was tucking into his meal, murmuring to one another. Oscar stood in the back, cigar burning in his mouth, his derby pulled down nearly over his eyes.

Lip ran up to greet Barnhill, beaming all the way.

"Here he is, gennulmen! My God, Skinny's looking sharp! That's some suit a' clothes you got on, Skinny." Lip was dark as crude oil and fat: a man with most of his weight gathered in a two-foot ring around his waist and a massive set of chins, all this perched atop a pair of table legs. And those lips, big and wet, that he chewed constantly. But everyone agreed that Lip could cut hair and throw a spread together. He brushed at Barnhill's hair and scowled. "What is this? Big ballplayer like you got some blind man cuttin' your hair? Sideburns uneven, for God's sake. Well, come in, set down, eat. The Reds ain't here yet."

Lip's was the center of the Black Bottom universe. Nearly everyone had their hair cut at his establishment. "Anyone's who's Anyone," he was fond of saying. There the Athletics were kings. Lip set up a ham radio in the front room upstairs, which served as a blind pig for servicemen (supporting the military was the only way Lip knew to keep the cops off his back). Downstairs in the barbershop, he built two twenty-foot chalkboard scorecards, to show the progress of every game, manned by a couple of urchins whose sole ambition in life was someday to cut hair at Lip's and play on his celebrated intercity baseball team. Or, thanks to the A's, in the pros.

As soon as Barnhill and Luke settled in, Dan Burley stood and raised his hands and shouted, "Quiet everybody!" When there was silence, he smirked and said, "Allow Mr. Barnhill to have a drink so that he can enlighten us on the beauty of the Communist ideal. Mr. Barnhill?"

But before Barnhill could speak, Buck shouted: "What in God's name is this about, Dave? Christ, son, last time you threw a decent game was . . . how many days ago? Did you hear what they've been saying about you? About us? Colored and white people getting angry, Dave, in a place they go to forget their anger."

Barnhill took a deep breath and said, "To answer your question, Buck, and thanks for asking, it was about two weeks ago that I had a 'decent game,' so I'll thank you to shut your trap for just a few moments. You're not the only one who's got an interest in the team." He took a shot of bourbon and said, "Now, listen, fellows, I know I don't need to tell you what's going on in the world. We all know it.

We all see it. Problem is, unlike the rest of America, we do our jobs and then we hole up in a fancy hotel and get soused or play cards." He looked around the room, trying to look into each man's eyes, trying to shame them. "Maybe I'm saying it's *time* we get angry at the ballpark. All those people watching us, they go to work, then they come home, dog tired, and they still fight. They march. They join organizations, donate money."

Buck shouted, "Ray 'n' I've donated over—"

"Shut up, man!" Barnhill bellowed. "So help me God, Buck, I'm going to knock you into the back room you don't be quiet!" He lowered his voice and continued. "Money *isn't* enough! We've got *responsibilities* to go along with baseball." He glanced at Burley. His voice lowered. "So, Mr. Burley's right, I do have something to say. Something I'd like to say in the *Amsterdam News* or the *Pittsburgh Courier*. Something I'd like to see in print. Only I can't. Since my little talk with the *Record*, I'm not able to get anything in print . . . to anyone."

They started shouting, but Burley hopped up on a chair. "Barnhill," he yelled, "you're bad press, know that? My paper's fighting Jim Crow all the way. Problem with you is that you want to squawk inside the park! Insulting the rest of the world. And another thing: you want to bring baseball into the fight for integration? Fine, we'll talk to you ballplayers—*when you start winning*. Look, you guys are twelve games out of first. I might remind you that the Philadelphia Athletics are the face of Negro America right now. We're having more problems busting Jim Crow because the Philadelphia Athletics appear inferior. I don't like it, but that's how it is."

Serrell stood up, blinking and shaking his head with exaggeration. "The fuck you said? You're not blaming *us* for Jim Crow?"

"No, I'm not. But Mr. Barnhill wants to start yelling about communism—"

At that, everyone began shouting.

Lip banged on a cowbell and yelled, "Point a' order, point a' order! Let Skinny have his say—he's the one brought ya here!"

Barnhill downed another finger of bourbon and said, "All I'm saying is that the Negro press is acting like we're a disease just because of the way we're playing. But we still sell tickets. We're still in the papers. Only we're talkin' baseball, nothing else. People look up to us, just like the white ballplayers. Pearl Harbor hits, and everyone here wants to know what Hank Greenberg's thinking. Or Joe DiMaggio. When the city of Philadelphia first said that niggers can't drive trolleys, well, goddam I wanted the whole world to know that the Athletics weren't going to stand for it. I wanted the people who listened to us on the radio to say, those are *men* out there, men just like anyone else. Now I want them to open the paper and see *us* talking about the military, about housing, and where we can sit at a ball game. Because they *are* paying attention to us, white and black. Now, we can help out our brothers trying to drive the buses and trolleys. Can help our soldiers get the promotions and medals they deserve. We've got a real opportunity here to fight for something. If none of us played ball, we'd be fightin'. D day's coming—"

"Barnhill," Burley said, with a pained sigh. "You're focusing on the wrong thing. You get the Communists involved, you're gonna get the police, the FBI, and the commissioner breathing down your neck. He hates you already. Fans are starting to hate you. You'll start more riots. Think about it: Commies are big on strikes, on making the rabble out there act up. Embarrass the rest of us. Right now you've got to focus on winning."

Serrell's eyes bugged out. "Did you say rabble?"

But Burley didn't answer. Two white men had stepped in, quietly, and the room fell silent. "Gentlemen," one of them announced, "if I might be able to say a few words, perhaps I could help explain the situation."

Lester Rodney, sports editor for the *Daily Worker*, surveyed the room as he spoke. He wore the uniform of a sergeant, and with his wire-rimmed glasses covering his baggy eyes, he looked gruff and ready for confrontation. Behind him, eager to push through, was Nat Low, the *Worker*'s lead sportswriter. Low appeared to be the stereotype of the Greenwich Village Red—worn jacket, frayed collars, fingers stained with nicotine.

"There enough drinks for everybody?" Rodney asked. "Someone close those blinds." Rodney slapped his hands together and rubbed them. "Say, is that roast beef?"

He introduced himself and Low to the crowd. "Before we proceed," he said, munching on a sandwich, "I want you to know I'm not interested in converting anyone. And I'm not going to use the Athletics, or the game itself, to foster any propaganda. We're here to help, that's all. But," he said, looking up and around the table, "I'm also not going to shy away from who I am, or what I write for, and neither is Mr. Low. You want help, you've got it. But it's from Communists, plain and simple. Understood?"

Ray spoke up, to everyone's surprise. "I got a question: What do we need you Reds for?"

"Good question, Mr. Dandridge," Rodney said, through a mouthful of roast beef sandwich. "And, I might add, fine play today in the third inning." Rodney took a sip of beer. "First of all, we're organized. Better even than the NAACP, who, I might add, we're also working with. We have a newspaper that reaches across the country. We've marched for years to pressure baseball to integrate. Wrote letters, articles, met with executives and legislators, though of course never with your esteemed Judge Landis. You may not believe it, but we're as committed to this as you are," Rodney said. "And whether or not anyone in this room cares, our operatives—dirty Reds every one—have bought six thousand tickets for tomorrow's game. In what are considered the white sections." He paused to allow them to murmur as he thought they would. "We're giving these tickets to Negro families around Black Bottom, free of charge."

After more murmuring, he continued. "The commissioner's not going to openly oppose the A's. And frankly, I can't see Detroit pulling out the riot gear for tomorrow's game. In fact they'll probably send out every photographer between here and Chicago to show how things have improved since last summer. The problem's going to be St. Louis. And Philly. And Europe. Let's start with the first: were going to challenge Jim Crow in St. Louis. As you know, they're segregated *by law*. We've already bought ten thousand tickets for each game, given the tickets to people from all over the South: Negroes and whites, soldiers, women, children. They'll be there; we'll be there. Early. We show up first in line. If they refuse to seat us, we drop. Right there in the turnstiles, at every gate. White *and* black." He paused to take a drink. "We don't get in, no one does."

Lip began to clap furiously. "That sounds pretty damn good!"

Rodney nodded and smiled slightly. "It *is* pretty damn good. And I'm here to tell you that I'm not just interested in desegregating the ballpark." He looked around the room. "Every one of you knows a soldier. Nat and I've talked with Negro men in uniform. In London, shot to death for having the gall to pick up a rifle in battle, or looking sideways at a white woman. For fighting in Guadalcanal and saving a half-dozen other soldiers but remaining a buck private." He poked himself in the chest furiously. "I've heard it. I've seen it. Now we're asking you to take the fight to the ball field."

Buck was incredulous. "You act like we just out there on a picnic. Unless you been denied a seat on a train—even as a major league ballplayer—then you don't understand even a drop of what we've been through. Not even a drop."

Burley added, "There *will* be violence."

"Not from us," Rodney said. "We're too organized for that. Violence comes when things just spring up. Like last year's riots."

Barnhill stood up. "Rodney here is at least willing to fight with us! Damn it all, if the St. Louis strike gets ugly, and it will, holy crap it will, then we need to take a stand. If the Philadelphia transit strike gets out of hand, we need to be there."

"And what does that mean? *'Take a stand.'*"

"It means," Rodney said, "fighting in the ballpark. Talking to reporters. Dedicating home runs and wins to the Negro soldiers who aren't recognized. We have bulletins for you to read that will even help you with what to say. People skip over this news on the front page. But they listen to what Buck Leonard or Ray Dandridge say. And," Rodney continued, "eventually it might mean going on strike *yourself.* In St. Louis, if they don't let Negroes in. And Philly, if they don't let Negroes drive the trolleys."

"Madness!" Buck yelled. "You're going to wreck this team! Mr. Veeck's losing money, we can't fill Shibe . . ."

That started everyone shouting, but Lip rang his cowbell. "Point a' order!" he cried. After the din subsided, Lip added, "This does sound altogether crazy. But something's gotta do. And, you know, didn't it sound like nuts when Veeck threw you all together?"

"Sure it did," Serrell said. "That fucker stood up for us and fought. And he made money. But he hadda know that we weren't gonna sit back and take what's goin' on in the world. And we can't be responsible for how much dough he brings in."

"You gonna tell Mr. Veeck?" Buck asked.

Rodney took a deep breath. "Be reasonable, for God's sake. Of course we can't, because he will most definitely oppose a strike. Besides—"

"I won't do nothin' if Mr. Veeck isn't involved," Buck said. "It's all because a' him." Many of the players nodded and mumbled.

"What you don't unnerstand," Low interrupted, "is how big this is going to be! St. Louie'll be the fulcrum. From there, it's Jim Crow in the military. Look at Philly! Christ, you guys come to town and everyone says we don't gotta take this anymore. Whites say, golly, why'd they put up with it for so long? You say a war's on, I say so what! Any a' you know someone who died fighting?" They fell into silence. "That's right, every last one a' ya. Just like me, just like Lester here. For what? Democracy? So they export Jim Crow to the Krauts? Now that makes all kinda sense, don't it?"

"Our job is to play baseball," Buck said. "Look at the soldiers. If they fought as badly as we're playin', they'd say Negro soldiers aren't any good. If we fail, we ain't nothing but a bunch of lazy niggers. You want to distract us even more?"

Rodney looked at the ballplayers. He sighed. "Unfortunately, there's some truth in what Buck says. If you could start winning, that would make things easier. But it doesn't mean you can't participate."

"Well, this is too much!" Buck shouted. He stood and pulled on his sport coat and said, "Now we ain't winning to win, but winning for the Reds. Strikes and Communists." He slammed his hat on his head, pushed through the crowd to the door. "I'm goin' to win the fight on the diamond. Anyone else not interested in Mr. Rodney?" With that, all but Barnhill stood. Buck watched as the rest of the men crowded to the door and stepped out in a single file. Oscar paused for just a moment to stare at Barnhill, and left without speaking. Finally Buck and Ray stopped by Barnhill. "None of us going to have anything to do with you, Dave. Silence from now on."

Lip plopped down in a chair and poured himself a drink. Luke looked awful, like he was going to cry or scream or both. Rodney touched Barnhill's arm: "You don't need a whole squad to make this work. Just a few—maybe even less than five or six. Especially the catchers. You only have two catchers, and if we get both of them, we're fine."

Barnhill sighed and nodded. Rodney and Low bid goodbye to them, and Barnhill, Serrell, and cousin Luke were left to clean up with Lip.

Next afternoon Barnhill was angry. He threw hard in the bullpen before the game. "Don't burn yourself out!" Campy said, lobbing the ball back. But it seemed like every time Campy spoke, Barnhill looked more irritable. It didn't help that the crowd kept after him.

"What's black and white and red all over?" came a shout in the seats above the bullpen. "Dave Barnhill!"

Mack Filson, sitting in the bullpen with his pitchers, thought for a moment before asking reliever Bill Byrd. "I don't get it: what's the white?"

Byrd shrugged. "Beats me. The baseball?"

Barnhill saw that the Communists had been successful here: blacks and whites were seated among one another for the first time in the series. He didn't expect everyone to hold hands. And he had to admit that Rodney understood Detroit as well as Luke did; there wasn't even a ripple of protest against their forced integration, and the news and radio reporters banged the drum on the story. Hypocrites every one, he thought.

Spink was in the press box, but he had a different angle. He broke the story that one of the Athletics players *was fostering Communist tendencies, trying to ingratiate the entire league behind a Red menace, nearly as crippling as if he were a member of the Nazi party.* He added, *Negroes and old men may take solace in the Communists, but mark my words (and the standings if you prefer), when the real players return, you won't see many white elephants with black faces.*

The game began on time. Barnhill warmed up. He was a quick throw—that is, as soon as he got the ball from the catcher, he crouched, nodded at the sign, and hurled the ball in, usually with such force as to knock his hat off his brow. No waiting, just get the ball and pitch.

"Cutter's lookin' good," Campy shouted from behind the plate. He stood and walked the ball back to Barnhill while the first batter took his cuts in the on-deck circle. At the mound he stuck the ball in Barnhill's glove. "But please relax, Dave! Don't go wastin' all your heat in the first two innings."

Barnhill grumbled, "Look. Still no Negro faces here by the 'pen."

"Good golly, you ever satisfied? They fill the stands with black folks, you be complainin' that the vendors are white. Jesus."

"Life's just peaches for you, ain't it Campy?" Barnhill grunted. "All you see is sunshine and smiling faces. Makes a fellow blind."

Campy shook his head and turned to walk back to the plate. "Shut up and throw the ball. At least *I'm* still talkin' to ya."

Campy handled Barnhill that day like a circus juggler. Barnhill threw junk, threw speed, curves, shook off Campy's signs, and scowled and kicked. Campy went to the mound five times in the first three innings, just to keep his boy straight. And through eight innings the score was knotted at zero.

In the top of the ninth Barnhill grabbed his bat, ready to open the inning. Cochrane yelled, "Mr. Barnhill! Sit down. Mr. Serrell—pinch-hit."

"Wait a minute!" Barnhill shouted. "I gave up nothin' through eight, and you're taking me out?"

Cochrane shouted, "Mr. Serrell, get up there!"

Barnhill stepped in Serrell's way and growled, "Brother, don't do this."

Serrell turned to Cochrane. "Skip, let the boy finish the inning."

The umpire strode over and said sternly, "Kid, you heard Mr. Cochrane. Step aside."

Barnhill yanked his shoulder from the ump. The ump's fat face grew beet red. He pointed at Barnhill and shouted, "You're gone!"

That set Cochrane off. He broke away from the bench bellowed, "What is that all about? He didn't do anything!"

"Shaddap Cochrane!" the ump screamed. "Now you're gone!"

The crowd loved it. Any excuse to bellow and hurl what they had on them: down came a hailstorm of garbage and souvenir key chains they'd been given that day.

"If this doesn't cease," the ump cried, red-faced and flailing about, "I will forfeit this game to the Tigers!"

"Wait a minute!" Campy said. "That's against the rules. You can only forfeit to the visiting team. Those ain't—"

"Gone!" He said, jerking his thumb behind him. He pointed at Buck, Ray, and Cool, all of whom were now out of the dugout from sheer curiosity. "Gone! Gone! Gone!" He was panting from fury, swinging about. "Now anyone else? Fine!" He gasped. "Let's play ball!"

The booing continued, without anything else being showered onto the field. Oscar took over from Cochrane, sent Lockett up to bat, and had Benson drag Josh to the showers to wake him up.

Demoralized, the A's couldn't hold things together, and the Tigers took the game easily. As the A's left the field, both white and black fans stood and began to jeer and shout, "Go home!," raining bottles and food on them.

Landis suspended Barnhill for four games, ostensibly for "hitting an umpire," and fined him a grand. The rest of the men were touched for fifty dollars each.

That night Sam called Veeck, now in Cleveland. "Did you listen to NBC? Spink won't lay off."

"Figures. With a direct feed from Landis, it's no wonder. Boy, those Pinkertons certainly are worth every fat buck we feed them. Communists. Secret meetings. This is the worst."

"Bill, don't start. You want me to run things, well, Mickey begged me to let the boys have a night on the town without detectives. How could any of us have known they were going to meet with the Reds?"

"You're right, you're right." Veeck paused. "Okay. With the secret weapon, we need to make some space on the roster."

"When did this secrecy begin, anyway? Secret weapon? I'm no longer part-owner?"

"It's secret like a Christmas present. But it means cutting someone."

"I know that. I already spoke with Bob Harvey, and he figured it wasn't going to be long before . . ."

"Keep Harvey," Veeck said. "Throw Barnhill to Milwaukee."

Sam stared at the receiver. "Christ, Bill. That won't go over well with some of the fellows."

"It'll go over well with a whole lot more."

Sam was about to gripe, but caught himself. He shrugged and smiled to himself, feeling relieved. "I guess I'm just used to arguing with you. Maybe we should've done this a long time ago."

"Barnhill's a problem, but he's going to be a great pitcher someday. Maybe soon. So, listen: I'm still owed favors in Milwaukee. Today he was simply brilliant, and I wouldn't mind seeing him on the club again. I don't want to cut him loose entirely. I spoke with Oscar—"

"About what?"

"Oscar's going to break the news to Dave on the trip to Cleveland. *You* tell him, he'll quit altogether, mule that he is. Oscar doesn't like this Red stuff either, but he'll convince the kid to sign with a minor league club. Plus this way we'll integrate the minors and bring in some revenue for my old haunt."

For once, Sam thought, Bill was making his job that much easier. "Thanks, Bill. My stomach feels better already."

"Yeah, well, we need something other than booze to calm us down, right?"

Barnhill sat nursing a tall chocolate shake in the club car on the train to Cleveland. It seemed like all he could eat lately were shakes and malts and cream soups. The Athletics filled the rest of the car, still bitter from yesterday's loss. Serrell joined Barnhill for a drink. "There booze in that?" Serrell asked.

"Stomach can't handle even beer right now," Barnhill said, toasting him.

Serrell was carrying a handful of shotglasses. He poured a hit of whiskey down his throat, grimaced, and said, "Fuck, Dave, I was ready to pop you out there. Don't fight me, man. Shit pisses me off. Even if you are my pal."

Barnhill nodded. He watched Campy scrambling out the lounge car, toward the front of the train. "I wonder," Barnhill said. "I mean, look at Roy. All excited. It would be good to just play, just thinkin' about the pennant. How does he do it?"

"Do what?"

"Stay so calm. The poor guy's trying to keep Josh dry, trying to keep all us pitchers in line. But he doesn't stay awake at night like I do. He doesn't get angry like I do."

"Maybe he does. You gotta 'member he's but a kid."

"I wish I was like that when I was his age. I wish—"

"What?"

"It's like today. Sometimes I wish I could just think about who this winged wonder is that Veeck's bringin' us. That I could laugh if it was a midget. That I could just throw." He finished his shake in one final gulp.

Serrell said, "Think it'll be a Negro?"

"What?"

"The midget? Think he'd get a little nigger? That'd be the right thing to do."

Barnhill shrugged. "I don't know. I care, but I don't care." He stood up and tossed a couple of bucks on the table. "Drink a couple for me, wouldya? I'm going to bed."

Serrell nodded and stared into space. Shit, he thought, it looks like no one's talking to *me*, either. "Boy, you just can't win," he said, and ordered another round.

Unveiling the Secret Weapon

Despite a cold mist that sprayed for hours from low-lying clouds, Cleveland Municipal Stadium was already three-quarters full for batting practice. Slightly oval, the stadium had the look of a college bowl—a track circled the field, a giant slab of rock stood imposing out in deep center, with the scoreboard and two giant clocks like eyes staring out at the action. The outfield fence was chain link, to break up the tremendous distance from home. In the grass behind the fence, you could buy standing-room-only tickets for a quarter each. There the fans, both black and white, swayed like reeds waiting for the action, eye level with the outfielders.

Veeck had stormed in the week earlier, gathered every last one of the Cleveland chapter of the Order of the Pachyderm—a growing nationwide fan organization—and they wallpapered the town with signs proclaiming BASEBALL SUPERMAN! and DON'T MISS THE GREATEST DISPLAY OF BASEBALL TALENT THE WORLD HAS YET SEEN! Still suffering under the commissioner's edict, Veeck made it a point never to break the letter of the law—but the spirit he flaunted mercilessly. "I understand that Judge Landis is busy investigating rumors that I was consorting with gamblers," he demurred, even though there was no evidence that the commissioner was doing anything but sitting on his decision until the season ended, hoping he could find something, anything, that would bury Veeck. "And I'm certain that this inquiry will clear me of any charges. In the meantime I'm still a fan, and I can still promote the A's in my own way, as a private citizen, as long as I'm not in any ballpark, nor consorting with the executives of the Philadelphia Athletics Baseball Club." When asked about his relationship with Sam Dailey, Veeck shrugged. "He's one of my best pals. We think alike! You can't keep a man from seeing a friend and making a few suggestions, can you?" When asked about Devil's Island, Veeck just laughed. "I gotta watch the games somehow, right?"

So as Citizen Veeck he took up airtime, made speeches, and worked in great secrecy with both Alva Bradley, the Indians owner, and the Cleveland mayor, who gave him a key to the city, to drum up support. For the most part they worked out in the open. The judge wasn't an idiot—he knew that Veeck was behind every decision, every silly promotion and oddball entertainment. But Landis, Veeck knew, was hamstrung by law—if he wanted Veeck out, he was out . . . but if he wanted Veeck legally barred from seeing Sam, unable to sit in Devil's Island, or hold press conferences, the judge would have to give Veeck his day in court, which was the last thing the old man wanted. Half of the commissioner's power lay in his being able to wield his iron fist with the impunity that comes with secrecy and an absolute devotion on the part of the owners. No owner would challenge the commissioner, because no owner wanted to take the fight to the public courts, and in the world of baseball, Landis's rule was law. Veeck decided to take his game public. Fighting with the president and Winchell burned the judge, who was normally able to pull his strings without undue notoriety. Failing that, and unable to rein Veeck in completely, he continued to scheme privately, raging to the public through Spink, who was merciless in his every criticism.

"Were these men white," Spink wrote, "few would play in the majors. Satchel, yes, Buck Leonard, of course, but Artie Wilson? Josh Gibson? When, we wonder, will the Philadelphia Athletics abandon this misguided experiment, if not for the players (who are, generally, embarrassments), if not for the city of Philadelphia, but for the good of baseball?"

Before the first game in Cleveland, in a hallway behind the scoreboard in center, Alva Bradley balanced a tray of cocktails and nodded at the door in front of him. Veeck opened the door and ducked into a small, dark room. It was lit by a single bulb and dusty light shining in around the squares that held numbers for the fans on the other side to see. "Here it is," Bradley said, setting the tray down on a coffee table he'd had brought up for the occasion.

"Perfect," Veeck said, and it was. Bradley had done it up nice: a little rug, a cooler of beer for Veeck, a platter of cocktails for himself, and a five-pound bag of peanuts. Veeck lit a cigarette and listened. Bradley listened with him. Some organ music. The crowds beginning to come to life. The resonant crack of Artie Wilson tearing the cover off the ball in practice. The steady grind of the Gruen clock above them. "Alva, you've outdone yourself," Veeck said. He was thankful for his good fortune in Cleveland. Two weeks earlier he'd called Alva Bradley. Since the call was about money, Bradley, who'd hemorrhaged cash for the last two years, listened.

Fortunately for Veeck, Bradley was an obstinate man. A self-made millionaire who knew one thing—railroads—Bradley bullied his way into the sport thinking he'd strike it rich there as well, and have some fun doing it. But baseball success eluded him, and he hated the system. A maverick in his own mind, Bradley didn't like to be pushed around. Landis pushed the owners around. And while Bradley wouldn't challenge the commissioner publicly (that was bad business), he paid close attention to the Athletics, who had drawn much better than last year and whose road trips swelled with fans by the thousands.

"God, I hope they're both close games," Veeck said.

"Who cares?" Bradley shouted, practically rolling in his chair from glee. He raised a toast to his guest. "We're full today! First time in three years."

At one o'clock, down in the dugout, the players filed in, their ears still ringing from Cochrane's tirade that day. He didn't like the fact that he had no idea who was pitching for him, that he couldn't discipline Satchel for skipping Detroit. "Twenty-five!" he yelled in the dugout, still fuming. "Seventeen by one!" These were the numbers he cudgeled them with: twenty-five losses in the last thirty games, seventeen by one run. "Inexcusable."

Satch crossed his arms and wore a nonchalant look. "King Satch got six wins. Jeep, how many losses?"

"None, Satch," Jeep mumbled.

Scenes from the locker room: ointment, tape, eyedrops. Artie was taking medicine for a head cold and going over bunting with Buck Leonard. Campy's hands were killing him, and his shoulder was stiff. With its low concrete ceilings and damp walls, the locker room contained them like a dungeon. The batboy offered water and antacids to everyone, avoiding Wells, who'd threatened to knock the kid back to Philadelphia if he so much as looked at him. No one mentioned losing streaks, St. Louis, transit strikes, or communism. No one spoke of, or to, Dave Barnhill. No one mentioned secret weapons. Above all, no one mentioned last place.

Josh Gibson was sitting in a corner, gazing at a scorebook, muttering about the batters, what he'd tell Satch to throw them, and conversing as if Joe DiMaggio were with him.

"Roy," Benson said, nodding at Josh.

Now Josh was bobbing in place, as if asleep. "I see him," Campy said with a sigh. "Boy, I just don't get it. I was with him and Grace all night."

"Christ, gotta boil that sucker out again." Benson stormed over and ushered Josh back to the showers, to try to ply him with cold water and coffee, a remedy that was having less and less effect.

After Josh spent twenty minutes under a cold shower, he dressed and sat humming to himself, twirling his bat South in his hands.

"Do you believe you can play, Mr. Gibson?" Cochrane asked, looking at him with barely concealed disgust.

"Chief!" Josh said, shaking himself from his stupor. "Listen. You have to let me in today. I'm seeing real well, in fact, I got the goods on a few batters, now listen . . . ," and he proceeded to relate to Cochrane what he'd read about each batter in the Indians lineup that he'd culled from newspapers and the *Sporting News.*

Cochrane was impressed, as much as Campy and Benson were shocked. "Fine. Mr. Gibson is in for game two."

With the close of a mangled version of *The Star-Spangled Banner* the crowd, another mix of whites and blacks from every corner of Ohio, came to life as the Indians ran onto the field. Cleveland's wartime ace Mel Harder walked to the mound, slowly, taking his time, still not believing he was about to pitch in front of eighty thousand people. He hadn't seen it this packed since DiMaggio ended the hitting streak in '41. And he'd never seen so many Negroes in his life.

Artie stepped up, the ump bellowed, and the game was on. It was a short first half for three straight outs: Artie went down swinging, Ray grounded to first after ten pitches, then Wells popped out.

"Here we go!" Veeck shouted, pulling the binoculars to his eyes.

Trumpets rang out, and the crowd rose to their feet. A woman pointed and yelled, "My God, there it is!" Over in center, the crowds parted as a silver van roared out from an entrance ramp, tearing up grass in center and heading straight to the edge of the mound. Two armed guards hopped out of the cab, saluted the umpire, and ran to the back of the van.

"Ladies and gentlemen!" the PA rang out. "Now pitching for the Philadelphia Athletics . . ."

The guards opened the doors and jumped inside.

"From Havana, Cuba . . ."

With a heave, they rolled out the platform draped in velvet.

"Number 27, Martín Dihigo!"

Amidst the roar, Dihigo whipped off the velvet and tossed it into the van. He stood stock still, a look of pure calm on his face, his hand outstretched like a conductor gesturing to his orchestra. He towered above the guards. He towered above the other players. He seemed to tower over the entire stadium.

Bradley leaned forward, a look of disgust washing over his face. "That's it?"

Veeck beamed. "Watch, Alva. Just watch."

But the crowds weren't having it. "It's just another Negro!" came a cry, and suddenly the arena filled with a hailstorm of boos. This team of black men wasn't doing much more than losing, so what good would another do? Even the crowds of black fans, eagerly hoping for something that would pull their beloved club from the basement, wondered aloud what exactly this Cuban would bring to the A's. All hopes of a silver robot, of some sort of gorilla-man, a midget, or even a white hero like Stan Musial evaporated as this unknown stepped onto the field.

In the dugout, McKinnis nudged Hilton Smith. "Look at Satch."

Though he didn't rise from the bench, Satchel's fists had balled up so that his knuckles were white. His lower jaw stuck out. "Jeep," he said, "tell me that ain't—"

Jeep wiped his brow. "Satch, what I got to tell you anything? You can see yourself."

The van raced off, and Dihigo stepped to the mound. He either didn't hear the catcalls or didn't care. Campy tossed him the ball. Dihigo waited. The rest of the Athletics simply gaped, wondering if Veeck hadn't lost his mind.

The batter stepped in, an older player, a purist, disgusted by all the pomp and integration. "C'mon, shine," he shouted. "Let's see whatcha got."

What he "got" was the most fluid motion you could find in a pitcher. Dihigo turned, his hands gliding smoothly around and down, so that as he threw his torso was parallel with the ground. The ball sailed in, nothing but a blur of white. Without hesitation, the ump shot his arm to the right and bellowed "Steeek!" and the crowds quieted. With the next pitch, Dihigo wound up, precisely the same, and the pitch drifted in, it looked like a ball high. Then, to the batter's disbelief, it sank a good three feet at the last second, right through the heart of the plate. The ump turned, fist pumping, another "Steek!"

They called for the ump's head. A man in a rose-colored suit cried, "Take the stick off your shoulder!" Others screamed worse. Finally the last pitch, looking identical to the first, was a beautiful change-up, and the batter swung a good two feet early.

The batter returned to the Indians' dugout, flopped down on the bench, and sighed. He looked stunned. "Boys," he said, slapping his hat onto his knee. "I don't know what he is, but he ain't human. Every pitch, he looks the same. . . ." He fell into an awed silence as Dihigo dispatched the next two batters with seven beautiful pitches.

Up in the press box, Dan Burley was unimpressed. "This guy's from Nowheresville, Cuba," Burley said. "Mark my words, next inning, the Indians'll knock him clear back to Havana."

Nat Low liked the sound of that. "Twenty bucks says he lasts through the game."

Burley did a double take. "You kidding? I thought gambling was a tool of the bourgeoisie?"

"There's my twenty. Let's see the clams, capitalist."

It is one thing to cram almost eighty thousand people into an arena; it is another thing altogether to keep them in their seats. But inning after inning, gravity seemed to become heavier by ounces as Dihigo pitched with such quiet brilliance that even the most diehard Indians fan must have acknowledged its wonderment. Dihigo did not appear the least bit fatigued, and his motion never varied. Through six, the Cuban kept the Indians dazed. The crowds were equally flabbergasted—after each scoreless inning, the rumble gradually turned to polite applause, gurgling from the stands as if this was an orchestra hall. In the dugout, Satch kicked at the floor, disgusted at the applause given to a pitcher inferior to his great talents.

The applause rose to a sustained bluster when the A's stepped to the plate. A change had taken place: no one seemed to be rooting for the Indians anymore, white or black. None of the A's, however, could score; nevertheless each hit was cheered as if it were the winning homer. With every batter stranded came anguished groans.

At the close of the sixth, Satch stretched out on the bench and yawned. As the players took their seats, he said, loudly, "Well, hell, Maestro, you got a pretty good no-hitter going."

The men in that cramped dugout froze. Satchel Paige couldn't have uttered a greater blasphemy if he had tried. It is an unwritten code, perhaps the most profound of all, that *no one* should mention a no-hitter while it is in progress.

Buck stepped down from the on-deck circle and into the dugout, looking like he was choking on something. He spoke as if every word were its own sentence. "What in God's name is the matter with you?"

Satch just shrugged. "What?"

Buck stepped closer, but Cochrane jumped between them. "Take it easy!" he roared. "Everyone, sit down. Relax, Buck, get that hit you need."

The press box was an oasis of silence in the sea of murmuring people. Every reporter was busy scratching away his angle on the game, taking notes with every pitch and throw to first. In the Indians' half, as Dihigo threw another effortless screwball past the last batter of the inning, Low counted silently over his scorecard and said, "Strike three, and that's seventeen."

Up in their secret box behind the scoreboard, Alva Bradley sucked on his cigar and said, "Holy cats, Bill, I'm sorry I doubted you. You know, I should have had a pile of dames out there, half-naked and carrying signs for each inning. Like boxing, you know?"

It remained scoreless as the ninth inning began. Down in the dugout, as Cochrane watched Benson step up to the plate, he wondered if this wasn't going to be yet another defeat at the hands of poor hitting. Now he was beginning to believe Satch *had* jinxed everything. How the hell else did Cool hit a triple to open the seventh and not score? He was not going to send him home on a steal, the game was too close for that, and Wells could mind his own business. Then, as if watching some Keystone Kops movie with the action at top speed, Benson and Jethroe popped to the infield with only two pitches. Cursed. By his own player!

Dihigo stepped to the plate, having done nothing more than stare at fat pitches and strike out three times. The Indians' Harder grunted. The crowds were restless, hoping for a walk, anything to keep the inning going. The catcher made his sign. Harding nodded right away and fired.

The five reporters on the field and four photographers crouching behind home still claim they've not seen a ball shoot so fast off a bat. Dihigo stepped into the pitch, a level swing slicing over the plate, rocketing the ball deep into center field. The outfielder jumped, turned, took four long strides, and stopped abruptly, watching the ball rise out of the park. A sharp gasp exploded from the crowd, fraying into a sustained roar as the baseball zoomed up and over the bleachers and into the center field scoreboard where it smashed through the zero on the A's half, showering the score over the crowds below.

Dihigo doffed his cap at home, and as he walked to the dugout the noise from the stands hit the field like a driving rain. Martín Dihigo did not allow his fielders to participate in the Indians half as three pinch hitters swung, fouled, and stood awed at twelve different pitches, the last seeming to come in only a blur. The ump paused, stood up, and shouted, "God love ya!" and then pumped his fist for strike three. Twenty-three of twenty-seven for strikeouts. A perfect game.

Nat Low found himself twenty dollars richer. "A stunning contradiction," Burley laughed, glad to hand him the sawbuck.

Amidst the celebrations it was safe to say that no one paid any attention to Satchel Paige. He was fuming as a result. Satchel's mind was racing, his eyes thinned in concentration.

"Satch? Watcha thinkin'?" Jeep asked.

Satch walked over and picked up the dugout phone. "Get me the PA operator," he said, coolly.

Jeep Jessup listened in on the conversation, a look of shock on his face. "Satch, why'd you say you was Mr. Dailey? You didn't sound anything like him."

"PA man don't know that. Satch sound like a white boy, they jump."

"But Satch . . ."

"Jeep?" Satch said, running his fingers across his mouth. "Zip it."

Cochrane was grinning with such elation it looked as if his face would break in two. They had half an hour to prepare for the second game, and everyone had filed into the locker room, shouting, laughing, slapping one another on the back, getting worked over by the trainer. They would have a break now—the backups would come in to play the second game, let the old-timers rest, they liked to joke. As they circled Dihigo, asking him about this pitch and that, the PA announcer broke in:

"Attention! Ladies and gentlemen! The Philadelphia Athletics would like to announce that in the second game of this doubleheader, Satchel Paige will take the mound. The management is proud to announce that the Philadelphia Athletics have guaranteed a *second* no-hitter . . . or your money back!"

Up in the scoreboard, Veeck dropped his can of beer. "Alva, what the hell is that!?"

Bradley yelled, "I didn't do anything!" He picked up the phone, got his PA announcer, and gasped. "Dailey set it up!" he said.

"Sam Dailey? He wouldn't . . ." Veeck closed his eyes. "Satchel . . ."

Silence fell on the A's with the speed of a safe dropping. The batboy tugged at Campy's sleeve. "Mr. Campy, how are we gonna get another no-hitter?"

"Grace a' God, buddy, grace a' God," he said, and flopped down on the bench.

Cochrane emerged from his dark office, chewing on Sen-Sen to cover up the smell of vomit on his breath. "Well, you heard them. Keep your eyes open. Above all, try to relax." He clapped his hands. "Josh, you are behind the plate. Everyone else, ready up."

In the press box, Low turned to Burley, waving that game's lineup. "Dihigo in center, for Bell. So this guy can play center field too. Think professional jealousy will keep Satch going strong enough to blank them a second time?"

"Impossible. No one's ever called a no-hitter. Veeck's got to be the world's biggest idiot."

Low shrugged. "But if it works out, he's a genius."

In the dugout they were a sweaty, gum-and-tobacco-chewing pile of nerves. Artie grabbed his bat, turned to Cochrane, and said, "Sure you want me in, skip? Bat's been cold as ice lately, and . . ."

"Get in there, Wilson. You are my best glove man. Have faith, your bat will come around."

At the top of the first, the Indians' pitcher, Orval Grove, screwed his face up as if he'd eaten something bad. Artie stepped in, waiting.

The Indians' catcher bounced in place. "Man, this is a gone game, huh? You guys are somethin' else."

Artie ignored him. The crowd was doing its level best to make more noise than in the first game. Artie waited. The pitch came in, he swung and, shocking himself, knocked the first pitch into the gap. Artie raced into third for a stand-up triple. As he stood on base, he pounded his fists together, crying out, "Look at that, Mickey!"

Dandridge took the first pitch deep into right, a perfect sacrifice fly that scored Artie, only the third time all year. Then Wells tripled, and the riot began. Buck homered on the first pitch. Dihigo singled to center. Then Josh Gibson walked up.

Most of Cleveland didn't know much about Josh, hadn't heard of his reputation as a ballplayer, merely that he was the lush of the A's. And he didn't care at that moment. Right then his head spun and his mouth tasted dry as fresh socks. To his utter surprise, the first pitch sailed in so slow it might have been a balloon. Gibson creamed the ball. It caromed off the stone scoreboard and out of the stadium. It took him almost a full two minutes to circle the diamond, his legs hurt so much, but he would have run it a dozen times for the joy pounding through him.

Grove came out, and a greybeard named Heving came in, an old man who would've retired three years ago if it hadn't been for the war. He promptly served up a fat pitch for Benson to lob down the left-field line for a home run. By the time the inning was over they'd batted around one and a half times.

Veeck and Bradley both sat at the edge of their seats, drinks in hand, eyes wide open. Bradley was cursing, red-faced and sweaty. "Please, please, please," Veeck chanted, cigarettes burning in his mouth and his hand.

"At least maybe they'll go buy some hot dogs," Bradley whined. "That last game, no one's eating. This is good, right?"

Veeck cringed. "Are you kidding? All these runs make them careless."

Satch grumbled as he took the mound in the first, kicking at the dirt, spitting. With a sigh, he stood on the rubber, nodding at Josh's first signal. He struck out the first man, forced the second to ground out to first. For the last out he induced a long fly to center.

"Golly, Satch!" Campy shouted at him as he stepped into the dugout. "You didn't even run to cover first. You're lucky that boy was fat. C'mon, you want this no-hitter, you better run 'em out."

"Quiet, puppy, old Satch ain't doin' nothin' he doesn't need to do." He crossed his arms and stared out at the crowds. "Lookit. Folks wanderin'. Chatterin' up that goddam Maestro. Why'd you have to score so much?"

They scored more. Although Satch swung at bad pitches for an easy out, the rest of the team circled the bases like they were a part of a giant clock.

In the second inning Satch walked the first two batters to make things spicy, then unintentionally gave a free pass to the next. He stretched, wiped some sweat from his brow, scanned the diamond. Lou Boudreau, the Indians' shortstop and manager, stepped in, ready to hit. It was unlikely he'd knock it out, but he knew where to put the ball. Satch decided to psych him out. "Don't want a curve, boy," he yelled at Josh's signal. "It's time for the old Popsy-do!"

Boudreau nailed the Popsy deep into the gap in left. Benson gasped and sprinted, then dove at the warning track. The ball hit his glove, glanced off, and bounded off toward the fence.

"Jesus!" Bradley cried, spilling his drink. He grabbed the phone, yelled for the operator to connect him with the scorekeeper. "That's a fucking error, you understand? Score it a hit and I'll have your kneecaps broken!"

The bases emptied, and Boudreau ended up panting at third. As the "E" lit up on the scoreboard, the crowd groaned.

Then came the cry. No one knew from where it came, but one fan, deep in center field, began to yell, "Maestro!" The word rose to a frightening crescendo. Around him the crowd fell silent as his cry grew in intensity and seemed to infect one other, then two, then a dozen. Dihigo turned and doffed his cap. Soon the cry of "Maestro!" filled the park.

When the inning ended, the silence in the dugout was hot as a blowtorch. Satch sat by himself while Jewbaby worked on his arm. Mickey turned and looked at Charleston for a moment. Finally, Oscar nodded, and Cochrane turned to Dihigo. "Mr. Dailey tells me you could pitch both ends of a doubleheader. Is that true?"

Dihigo nodded. "I am not even . . ." he thought for a moment, searching for the right word in English—". . . fatigued."

Cochrane clapped his hands together and heaved a great sigh. "That is precisely what I needed to hear. Go warm up."

Satchel sat up, slowly and deliberately, and wrested his arm from Jewbaby. "Wait a minute. You ain't askin'—"

Cochrane spoke briefly. "Out!"

"You can't—"

Without waiting for Mickey, Oscar grabbed Satchel by the collar and hauled him down the length of the dugout, choking on his anger. Satch tried to speak but could only sputter nonsense. Oscar pushed Satchel a few feet down the hallway to the locker room, slammed the door in Satch's face, turned, and walked back.

There was a moment in the ninth inning, a moment in which the entire stadium fell into an awed bliss. Around the stadium, through section after section, the bleachers to the box seats and up into the press box, there was a stunned silence. Everyone was mesmerized by the majesty of the Maestro, at the smoothness of his delivery, as batter after batter went down, themselves struck by the sheer impossibility that a man could hurl nine innings of perfect ball, play center for three, then step in and throw as if he'd rested for days. His speed never diminished. His control was perfect. And from the looks of it, he appeared fresh and calm, like he wasn't doing much more than eating a chocolate sundae.

It was unquestionably the only 19-4 no-hit game in the history of the sport. At the final out, no one ran to Dihigo to manhandle and bully him into the air as in the last game. They jogged in simply to shake his hand, too exhausted really to celebrate. The crowds applauded—the thunder of hands striking against one another, the chatter of amazed people trying, with their neighbor, to make sense of what they had just seen.

"I don't believe it," Bradley said.

"Me, neither," Veeck said. "I feel like I'm dreaming."

The only rush was from the press box, reporters scrambling to the Athletics dugout, others clinging to the stories that were forming in their heads, whacking away at their typewriters, some reading out loud. Spink was the only writer who wasn't busy scribbling. He simply stared down at the empty field. Something wasn't right, he thought, and turned to his scorecard. Something wasn't right at all.

After losing the following day's game, the A's hit the tracks for a three-game series in Chicago before they made their way to St. Louis. Oscar Charleston sat in the club car, sipping a whiskey. He was going over strategies, pondering the fate of his club. Oscar was about to lose a great pitcher. A great one: he knew in his heart and in his brain that Dave Barnhill was a hell of a pitcher, despite losing the day before and despite all this rabble-rousing. Mouthy, yes. Maybe a cancer in the clubhouse right now. Right now—not forever. Was tossing him alone into a whites-only minor league team such a good idea? What was a good idea anymore? Hell if he knew. He stood up, left half his shot behind, and made his way to the berths.

Oscar knocked and heard the sounds of Barnhill waking from sleep—the muffled "What?", the fumbling for the light, the clump to open the door.

"Oscar?" Barnhill said, standing aside.

Oscar nodded and walked in. "Kid. Sit down for a second."

Barnhill folded his arms. "You got something to tell me, say it."

Oscar stuck his tongue in his cheek and hissed a deep breath. "Dave . . . Damn you, son. You . . ." He paused to gather his thoughts. "If I were running this thing, boy . . ."

"Get to the point, would you, Oscar?"

Oscar's jaw clenched. "Suit yourself. At Central Station you'll break from the club and take a train straightaway north to Milwaukee. Report to tomorrow's game with the Brewers." Oscar smiled sarcastically, pissed about Barnhill's attitude. "Lucky fellow. You get to be the trailblazer in the minors. Hope you have a good time."

For the last few weeks, ever since his name blew up all over the papers, Barnhill told himself that he expected something like this. Now, as the news sank in, he realized that he hadn't really expected it at all. "Milwaukee," he repeated, and sat on the bed.

Oscar cleared his throat. He had expected Barnhill to mouth off more. "Well, kid, you know, you bring it up a notch down there, we'll see you again. See, they had to make room for the Cuban." He saw that Barnhill was tearing up. "C'mon, kid, you'll do fine."

Barnhill stared at the floor. "Yeah. Guess it doesn't pay for a nigger to open his mouth."

"Well . . . you've been strugglin' too."

"Worse than Hilton?"

"I'm not the one signin' the paychecks. Neither is you." He pulled out a couple of cigars and offered one to Barnhill. "Smoke?"

"No thanks. I'd rather be alone."

"I'll leave you alone. Take one anyway."

"Thanks." He took the cigar. Oscar struck a match and Barnhill lit his smoke. "See you later, Oscar. For what it's worth, I think you're getting the shaft too."

"Okay, kid. Mow 'em down up there in Milwaukee. Stay fit and we'll see you again." After an uncomfortable silence, he nodded and closed the door.

Outside, Sam Dailey squeezed by Oscar in the hallway. "Charleston, say, did you—"

"Fuck you and fuck Veeck," Oscar said, storming away.

Pouring rain greeted them in Chicago. Barnhill slunk away without saying goodbye to anyone but Serrell. In fact, most of the club didn't fully realize he was gone until the next day's game: rumors swirled, but considering only Serrell was talking, most of the men didn't believe it.

At the hotel, Cochrane fumed. As a surprise, his wife, Mary, made the trip to Chicago to keep him company and hopefully calm his fraying nerves. She listened to his tirade while massaging his shoulders. "Barnhill!" he complained. "Mary, Mr. Veeck must have his head on backward. He was our most promising pitcher, Communist or not. Why does he insist on keeping Satchel Paige when he sends down a young man with . . ." he clenched his jaw around his pipe. Mary rubbed his neck, trying to placate him. "It makes me look as if I am not in command of this club."

"Honey, it's the same as it was in Detroit all those years ago. You need to ignore your critics. Mr. Veeck is doing what he believes to be the best."

Cochrane sighed. "All I want is a pennant. I don't care about Communists or integration. And I believe that Mr. Barnhill is more important to us than some of the others. I just wish I had been consulted. That my opinion would have been considered. That is all."

He sat on the bed next to her and stared out the window at the rain. The skies had really torn open. The smell coming in through the barely opened window reminded him of another May afternoon, just last year. Might have even been exactly a year ago. His son looked sharp in his navy uniform. That was a great day: there wasn't the usual bullheadedness between them. Gordon told tales of how he'd fly his plane at maneuvers, and Cochrane just couldn't believe it. They hopped into the "old jalopy," as Gordon called it, and headed down to Pete's for one on the house before he was shipped out. They spoke uncomfortably about dating: Gordon had dumped that kind girl who Cochrane thought was just wonderful. Then Gordon said that strange, strange thing: "Someday I might like to own a home in California."

"California?"

"Sure. I sort of fell in love with Los Angeles."

"I couldn't live in California," Cochrane said.

"Not asking you to live in California."

They dropped it. But Cochrane was sure that Gordon would forget about it. He always saw his son living in Ohio, near them. He tried to laugh it off with Mary. "How're you going to keep them down on the farm after they've seen Paree!" he sang. He didn't know what bugged him; it wasn't as if he wanted Gordon to run any of his affairs.

In the hotel room Mary noticed him staring, his mouth hung open slightly. "Mickey?" she asked.

"I wish I knew what he'd seen in California," he said, not taking his eyes away from the window.

"Gordon?"

"Is it coming to an end, Mary, like Detroit?"

"Mickey," she said, pulling him close and shushing him. "Please. Tonight, no baseball." When he kept staring, she took him by the chin and turned his head to her. "Listen to me! No baseball tonight, Mickey. Let's just sit here and listen to the rain, like we used to on the hard days. Remember?"

He did. Cochrane climbed up on the bed and leaned back against the headboard with Mary. They shut the lights off and stared at the square of grey light, droplets shimmying down the glass.

The next day it was a torrential downpour, and the game was called before eight that morning. That afternoon Mack Filson sat in his room, watching the ice melting in his rye, biding his time. He'd been brooding the last three days.

Red Hourly shook his head. "Christ, Mackie, Barnhill has a lousy record. Leave it alone. He'll be back or he won't. If he won't, it's 'cause he ain't good enough."

"Oh, no," Mack said. "That kid's arm was a diamond in the rough." He thinned his eyes and pulled the glass near, staring at the room through the smoke-colored liquid. "I hope they'll take care of him down there. . . ."

A sharp knock came to the door. Red answered it and found two men in grey suits, standing stiff as English beefeaters. "Mr. Mackinaw Filson?" one asked.

"No. Whaddya want?"

"Mr. Mackinaw Filson."

Red bristled. "Well, maybe he's not in."

Mack hurried to the door. "Okay, okay, Red, I 'preciate what you're doing. What can I help you with, gentlemen?"

Mackinaw Filson was to accompany them to the commissioner's office immediately. Red, now wishing he hadn't spoken ill to Landis's men, helped Mack on with his coat.

"Red," Mack whispered. "I don't smell like the drink, do I?"

"You're fine, pal, fine."

They hustled Mack down to a car waiting in front of the hotel, then down Michigan Avenue to the commissioner's office. Mack waited in the same lobby Veeck had seen months earlier. It's cold in here, Mack thought. He wished he had a glass of hot rum with lemon to keep his insides warm. Finally the door opened, and the taller of the two men beckoned him inside with a sharp nod.

He closed the door behind Mack. Landis stood regally behind his desk, wearing a smile that made Mack uncomfortable. The two men who drove him there waited silently in the shadows by the wall. And another man, short and squat and with a bulldog face, stood by the desk. "Mr. Filson," Landis said, "this is Mr. J. Edgar Hoover."

Hoover extended his hand. He wore a tense expression, like he was about to have a coronary. Mack nodded and took his hand. It was clammy.

"Mr. Filson," Landis said. "Sit down, please."

"Okay." He sat, smiling politely. He waited. Hoover sat. They stared. Finally, Mack cleared his throat and said, "Some game the other day, wasn't it?"

Hoover gripped the armrests of his chair and looked like he was going to leap out of it and bite Mack.

"Mackinaw—" the commissioner began.

"You have Communists," Hoover interrupted.

Mack swallowed. "Pardon?"

"You heard me. Communists. I've already got a file this thick." He indicated a good two inches with his chubby fingers. "We're going to flush them out of baseball."

"I thought the Communists were our allies?"

"Filson," Hoover said, his voice sharp. "Stop thinking and you'll live longer." He leaned in. "What we need is a mole. And you are going to be our mole."

"Mole?" Mack said. He didn't know what that was, but he didn't like the sound of it. He turned to Landis. "Sir, could I trouble you for a drink of water?"

"Don't give it to him. Now Filson—"

Landis said, "Mr. Hoover, please. You are a guest and shall act as one."

Hoover turned slowly to Landis. "I'm *not* here as a guest," he said, with a voice so firm it seemed to fill the room. "You don't have any sway over me, that homosexual Winchell doesn't hold any sway, nor does the White House for that matter. If I had my way I would shut down this game of yours to focus on the war at home and abroad." Landis licked his lips and adjusted his gavel on his desk, nodding at Hoover to continue. The FBI chief turned slowly, glared at Mack, and gave him a wicked smile. Then, with an oily voice, he added, "We're fighting the Communists, Filson. The military's doing its level best to lose this war while my men are fighting here, on the home front. Sure, you may read that the Reds are our allies and that's just how we want it." When Mack opened his mouth, Hoover raised his hand and went "shush, shush, shush" and continued. "Don't you worry about the Bundts—those Krauts are not well organized in the least. No, I'm talking about the Reds. *They* are as much a threat as the Nazis. Perhaps more." Hoover tapped his fingers on his stomach and smiled. "And that's where you come in." There was a long silence before he added, "Well? Don't you want to know how you come in?"

"You told me not to speak."

"You may answer."

"Yes, yes! I'll help," Mack said. "But, you don't understand, Dave Barnhill was sent down to Milwaukee today. He was the Red."

"Filson," Hoover said, standing suddenly and pacing behind him, "we want to build a case against these ballplayers. If they're unpatriotic in any way, we can really drive the nail in the coffin. I haven't figured out how yet, but trust me, my office will do something about it. First, though, you gather information. Build a file. And then, when they least expect it, we hit them." He clapped suddenly and Mack jumped. "Fortunately for baseball, the judge here is cooperating."

Mack wiped his brow and tried to retreat into his clothing. He was freezing, and he could hear the rain pounding on the glass. "But . . . none of these guys have done nothing."

"They're Commies, Filson. Are you a Communist?"

"No! I—I'm just the pitching coach."

"Then you can show your patriotism by helping this office."

"But I fought in the first war." Mack said, feebly. "I thought I did what I was supposed to—"

Hoover stood over Mack. "Listen. I don't care if you're Douglas MacArthur. You're going to do as we say or that's it for you. You'll never see a ball field again. You understand, Filson?"

Mack turned to the commissioner. Landis was stone-faced and seemed almost embarrassed. Mack blinked. "Never see . . . I don't . . ."

"Why, it's easy to figure out, Mack," Hoover said, pulling his chair up close. He sat down, touched Mack's knee, and then pointed a finger in his face. "You'll be gone from baseball. The major leagues *and* the minor leagues. Anyone having anything to do with the game of baseball, even college and high school, will be barred from contact with you. Judge Landis has agreed." He shrugged and gave a chuckle. "Why, Mack, of course, you could try and sneak over and teach what little you know to the Japs. I understand they love to play. And then we could catch you and shoot you for treason. That's your option."

Mack's eyes felt dry. He blinked a few times and a tear etched his face. "I don't get what you want me to do."

Hoover grinned. He reached over and wiped Mack's tear away with the ball of his thumb. He sat back and crossed his fingers on his stomach. "These Negroes are agitators. But they seem to respect you more than any white coach there. They talk to *you*. We want you to encourage them to talk. And we want you to encourage Veeck to talk."

"But . . ."

"You'll wear what we call a wire. It's like a microphone, one that you strap to your body."

"Wire?" Mack asked, though he knew very well what that meant.

"That's right. Wear a bug. Tape conversations in the locker room. In Veeck's office. On the train."

"But I'm usually out in the bullpen."

"Not before the game, you're not, and not after the game, either. On the road, you sit with them. Besides, the bullpen might just prove fruitful."

Mack looked ill. He turned to Landis. "Mr. Landis, could you do this to your fellow judges?"

"They aren't Communists, Mr. Filson. And if they were, I wouldn't hesitate."

"I can't go against my own players, my own club." He looked again to Landis. "Why are you doing this, Mr. Landis? Do you hate these men that much? 'Cause they're colored? Or is it me? I've never done anything to you."

Landis cleared his throat. "Mr. Filson, this is for the good of the sport. I think you should ask yourself, do I care more about baseball than the players I work with? Who may, or may not be, Communist agitators?"

"These boys, they just get a little upset now and again. They don't mean—"

"They mean to take over this country," Hoover interrupted. "And that makes them treasonous."

Mack fidgeted. He shifted in his chair, turned, and looked at the other two men, smoldering by the door. Not a friendly face among them. "Can I think about it?"

Hoover laughed. "Think about what? If your answer's 'no,' you're pumping gas in Gary, Indiana."

Mack's hands were shaking. "I . . ." He didn't know what to say. The men he worked with, those pitchers, his pals. You never went back on a pal. Especially someone you play ball with. "Isn't there nothing else I could do?"

Hoover slapped his hands on the armrests and made as if to stand. He said, "Well, Judge, he isn't participating. Goodbye, Mr. Filson."

"No!" Mack said, shooting up out of his chair. "*Please.* I can't live without baseball. I got nothing else. I can't even pump gas."

They laughed heartily at that. Mack shrank in his seat. Hoover grinned, stood, and slapped Mack's shoulder. "Then I guess you've made up your mind, haven't you? We'll go over what you need to do, how to put the thing on and all that. You can get started right away. In St. Louis. And relax. After a while, it gets to be fun."

Mack wasn't listening. He just nodded, quickly, and sat back down. There was a flurry of activity as Hoover opened a briefcase full of wires and began explaining.

"St. Louis," Hoover said, "is ripe with possibility. Mack, you'll be the man who shakes the tree."

Mack stared ahead. "St. Louis, sure," he said, barely audible. He looked over at Landis. "Can I have a glass of water now?" he asked, for he felt as if he were about to die of thirst.

◇ **12** ◇

Tormented in St. Louis

When their trip in St. Louis was all over, Lester Lockett remarked, "At least they didn't burn the ballpark down."

The team slept through most of the trip on the Superchief, the red-eye express that left over an hour late from Chicago. Willie Wells sat up most of the evening in the club car, boning his hickory bat and irritable that he'd squandered his paychecks and couldn't borrow a couple of bucks to buy a cheap drink. Unlike the rest of the club, Wells seemed thrilled by the rumors coming from St. Louis: that the Klan would welcome the Athletics to town with their trademark pyrotechnic and religious display. He heard about the protests, the death threats. He even got one. A letter from someone who said he "was going to wait in the stands with his sureshot Army rifle from back when he was shooting them down dead in Mexico and no one bothered him and so now he was going to shoot Willy [sic] down dead in St. Louis and that no one could stop him becuse [sic] he was *The Wanderer*." Beneath that scrawl was a stick-figure drawing of four lynchings. Wells kept that letter on him as a reminder. And a challenge.

A good two hundred fans met the club at the station, mostly soldiers and few hecklers, fewer even than New York City. The A's borrowed a fleet of automobiles to take them from the station to East St. Louis. When the caravan pulled into the parking lot of a local Baptist church, everyone filed out, Cochrane barked instructions for the next morning, and they were dispensed to their boarding homes nearby. To no one's surprise, there wasn't a hotel that would house the club, so Sam and Veeck planned for weeks to organize these homes within a one-block radius, and added another when Cochrane insisted that he and his staff room in the same area.

Next morning Cochrane had the Athletics gathered at 6:45 in front of the red clapboard house where he and the rest of the coaching staff slept. There was a goose-bump chill, slightly damp. The batboy couldn't stop yawning, slapping himself to keep warm. A bus ground to a halt in front of the house, loaned by the local church. "Men," he said, "we are beginning practice at seven because Mr. Veeck believes it is a good idea. He believes that the Browns might try to scuttle practice. He does not know how. Perhaps," he broke into a rare smile, "Mr. Veeck's chicanerous mind will be a benefit to us today."

They filed into the vehicle, Buck humming a song, the rest staring out the window, still sleepy. Campy was especially fatigued, having sat up most of the night watching Josh from the corner of his eye. He wasn't going to let the old boy fall apart. Not here. Though he was scheduled to catch that day, Campy knew that Josh could do or say things that would get all of them in trouble. The guy had been murmuring to himself on the trip down and was in a full-fledged conversation in the room before he seemed to cool down. Campy kissed his rosary and prayed for a good day.

They drove through the city streets, each man lost in his thoughts. Nearer the stadium, small pockets of people were beginning to gather. At one intersection Jethroe noticed a man in the middle of a larger crowd point to the bus. Every head in the crowd turned. A stone flew from the knot of people and banged against the side of the bus.

"Can you go faster?" Cochrane yelled.

"Sure." The driver roared the bus through the stoplight as they drove past crowds of picketers, some for the Athletics, some against. Cool noticed a number of fights among those gathered on the sidewalk.

"What is going on?" Cochrane shouted.

"The road's blocked!"

"Where's the police?" Cochrane yelled.

"Trying to clear the road," the driver said. He looked determined, like he was trying to think of some way to plow through these roustabouts. "They *never* assign enough police."

It sounded like they were in a hailstorm. Rocks, eggs, and all sorts of vegetables, rotten and soft as mud, splattered on the bus. Angry men and women pounded on the sides, shouting, "Go home, niggers!", "Commies!", and epithets of such rancor and originality it sounded as if they had worked for weeks just to come up with new ones. Cool pulled the batboy onto his lap to calm him down. Artie looked like he was going to jump out of his skin.

"I suppose they sent our bats ahead?" Oscar yelled. No one answered.

The driver leaned on the horn and moved the bus ahead two feet, then nothing more. The pounding began again when Josh yelled, "A gun!"

Everyone dropped and scrambled below the seats or ducked into the thin aisle, heads covered. They lay there for a moment, waiting. Jeep was crying. Then, slowly, from outside, there was a laugh, and soon the whole crowd erupted into derisive cheering. "Godammit Josh," Benson said, especially furious for having his sharkskin suit dirtied. "There ain't no gun!" Slowly they pulled themselves up.

"Thought I saw a pistol," he said, hands shaking.

The bus lurched ahead another two feet, and the driver laid on his horn.

Oscar jammed his bowler on his head. "How far are we from the stadium?" he asked, as he swayed to the front.

"Two blocks," the driver said. "Block'n a half."

"Fine. Stop here."

"What the hell you doin'?" Serrell asked.

"I'm not being a coward, that's what." With that Oscar jammed a cigar into his mouth and glanced around the bus. "I faced worse. But never alone. It'd look a lot better if I wasn't alone."

Sam, his face smudged and his glasses crooked from his dive under the seat, gasped, "God no, Oscar. They'll kill us."

Campy stood, pulling Josh up with him. Buck was also up quickly. Campy said, "Let's go. They're after us, Sam, not you."

Slowly they all stood, steeling themselves for the march out the front door. Cochrane pushed his way to the front and stood behind Oscar, licking his lips and saying nothing. At the sight of the team preparing to emerge, the crowds laid into the bus with even greater vigor.

"Ready?" Oscar yelled.

The driver opened his shirt. Tucked in his belt was a revolver. "Buddy, you need this?"

"Get that damn thing away! Now open the door."

With a screech, the door opened. This was the last thing the crowd expected, and a stunned silence fell on them. Oscar stepped down and walked, glaring, cigar jumping back and forth in his lips, looking like he was ready to grab someone with his thick arms and tear them limb from limb. He moved slowly but steadily into the crowd, which parted reluctantly. Sam gasped a prayer. One by one, the players stepped out, winding through the crowd like a snake on water.

An egg hit Oscar by his left ear, but he didn't flinch. Artie turned to the sound of his name, and a young girl spit in his face. They stuck their fingers in the faces of the players, shouted, threw more rotten food. Someone dumped a beer on Benson.

The police barreled through, pushing and shoving, clubs in the air. "Christ almighty!" one yelled as he approached. "You oughta have stayed in the bus."

"And miss the game?" Cochrane yelled. "You were some help, sir, some help!"

Bullhorned orders echoed over the crowd. Someone cried out "We love you!" and then there was a fight in that direction. Finally they reached Sportsman's Park and the players rushed in through a side door.

As they descended into the locker room, Cool halted. He nodded at the floor. Mack said, "Crikes. What's that?"

A line of hundreds of beat-up old black dress shoes stretched across the room. Jethroe slapped Mack on the shoulder as he walked by. "Get it? We shine shoes, us niggers. Ain't that sweet?"

As they dressed in the rank locker room, a greenish light trickled in through the pair of glass block windows, which were at ceiling height but sidewalk level. They could see the shuffling of feet, and now and then the roar of pressurized water could be heard against the wall. "They're hosing those poor folks down," Serrell said, trying to see though the glass.

They sat for a good two hours, the shadows of the melee outside flickering across the walls. Some played cards while others, like Wells, merely sat and pondered the situation and wondered if they were going to get any batting practice in. Jefferson stole up to Serrell and whispered, "Drop today?"

Serrell gulped, worried about being cracked on the head or hosed down. He wondered if the Commies had people outside, people who were taking beatings so everyone could watch a damned ball game. "Tomorrow, I think. Yeah, tomorrow."

Cool occupied the batboy in a small, windowless room, trying to teach him the fundamentals of bunting and take his mind off the fracas outside. By noon the action seemed to have waned, and they could hear the sounds of the crowds gathering in the stands above. The organist began playing "Dixie." Byrd chuckled, "So here we go. Ten gets you twenty there's gonna be something about watermelons. Or fried chicken."

"Something we've seen and heard a million times before," McKinnis said. "We win the game, it'll shut everybody up."

Serrell said, "Let's win us one for Barnhill!" No one answered that.

When the players reached the dugout, the crowd began to roar. "Not a bad reception," Campy said.

St. Louis was a baseball town akin to Philadelphia: one stadium, two teams, one with a storied past and one that was merely a door-mat. Sportsman's Park wasn't much more than a concrete and metal bandbox, barely maintained, as the prevailing wisdom in St. Louis dictated that you could put the least amount of money into the place and fans would still line up in droves. They were right—people loved the Cards. On any given night the Cardinals would pack the house. On any given night the Browns would play to empty seats. But for the first time in memory, the Browns had the thrill of being tied for second and were threatening to reach first.

Serrell stared out at the stands and said, "Damn." Despite the promises of the Communists, there wasn't a black face in the crowd, not in the stands behind home, not in the segregated right-field pavil-ion. Maybe they had the tar beaten out of them, maybe they were in jail. He didn't know what to do. Make a speech?

As Cochrane was about to walk out to hand the lineup to the ump, four midgets in blackface ran out, dressed as clowns in Athlet-ics uniforms. The crowd laughed and applauded. From the Browns dugout, one of the players whipped the body of a dead black cat onto the base path.

Artie walked to home plate, poking at the air with his bat. He rolled his shoulders and dug in. The shouting rose to a fever pitch. A banner unfurled in center: THE SOUTH SHALL RISE AGAIN. "Watch this," Artie bragged to the catcher, but then, just as he pulled the bat back, Pete Adelis, the great heckler, began banging on his helmet, scraping his blackboard.

He screeched. He cajoled. In St. Louis he could really let it go, and the crowds loved him. Even in the din, above the organ blasting "Dixie" and the heckling from the Browns dugout, Adelis's voice pierced through and jammed Artie in the ear. Artie turned just as the Lung pointed a greasy finger at him and began to scream about his inability to hit, about his lack of sleep, about his upset stomach. Adelis began to carry on about the private life of Artie Wilson, the girl who dumped him and laughed at him two weeks ago. Artie blinked a few times, stepped in, and watched the first pitch sail by for a strike. He didn't leave the box between pitches. Finally, as he had for most of the season, Artie Wilson struck out.

"There's your slugger!" Adelis roared, banging his helmet at the last strike. For the next at bat, Wells's big stick did no good. Then Leonard, hot on a thirty-eight-game hitting streak, was intentionally walked.

Cochrane threw his cap to the floor and kicked it across the dugout. "Cowards!" he shouted. "Precisely what I was afraid of!"

"Skip?" Campy said from the on-deck circle.

"They will walk Leonard every time. Gentlemen, his streak ends today. Roy," he shouted, "get up there and make them pay for it."

Campy stepped in, fouled a few off, then grounded back to the pitcher for the final out. The crowd responded as if he'd just ended the game to send the Browns to the World Series.

George Jefferson took the mound against the Browns. He glared at the first batter who kicked at the dirt. Jefferson wanted to strike, wanted someone—anyone—to try and come at him with one of those clubs. Fists or knives, he thought, I'll bring 'em down. With that in mind, he straightened up and nailed the first batter right in the thigh. The stadium erupted in boos and catcalls. The next batter stepped up, and Jefferson wasted no time. He sent a fastball thudding into the batter's shoulder blade, where it caromed off with a sickening crack. The ump and the first-base coach had to rush to the batter to avoid a confrontation. Campy ran to the mound.

"What are you doing?"

"Declarin' war."

"Well, you gotta play sometime. And you just put two guys on base. . . ."

"Gonna put two more across. Gonna hit the whole side once, then start."

Buck marched to the mound to put in his two cents. Seeing him, Jefferson swore and told the lot of them to scatter, get back to their places, they could all go to hell. Cochrane ran out with Mack. Jefferson spit at the ground, pointed his mitt at them, and said, "What the fuck do you want?" There was an argument, and then the crowds began to rain boos on the field. Jefferson called them all cowards. Cochrane yanked the ball from Jefferson's hand and told him to hit the showers, he was finished. Mack ran back to the pen, rubbed Verdell Mathis on the shoulder, and said, "Pitch?"

Mathis nodded. This was what he had hoped for—not an argument on the mound, not Jefferson sticking two guys on for him, but a chance to play in a big game, and not just when Hilton Smith was aching. He came in, took his eight warm-up throws, then struck out a man and induced a double play to get out of the inning.

Through eight innings, no one could score. A group of Marines, stationed four rows behind the A's dugout, began to chant, "Let Buck hit!" They waved and cajoled Buck to doff his cap. When he did, he received a harsh round of boos, but one Marine, a smaller man, ran up and shouted, "We ain't all cavemen down here! You kill these Browns, Buck!"

Someone tried to shut him up, and the Marines, already infuriated, blew apart, trying to knock down anyone in their path. As order was restored, Buck stepped in, and they walked him one last time.

McKinnis stepped in to replace a weary Mathis, and he shut the Browns down through ten. With one out in the bottom of the eleventh, he walked a man on seven pitches, the last a curveball that Cochrane roared should have been a strike. He was ejected. The next batter drove a double into the gap and the game was over, 1-0.

Afterward Cochrane closed the clubhouse to reporters, and the players scrambled to taxis that shuttled them back to the home of a loyal rooter for a barbecue feast. Sam, his nerves so stricken that he was shaking and sweating as if under the DTs, had Pinkertons surround the house to keep the mobs of fans and press from disturbing the club. The streets around their homes were packed with automobiles: police cars, taxis waiting on the press, cars for the detectives.

Around midnight, full of beer and chicken, Serrell and utilityman Lester Lockett sat up playing cards and joking, trying to keep each other from thinking about tomorrow. When the phone rang, Lockett almost jumped through the window, he was so surprised. It kept ringing. "You going to answer it?" Lockett shouted, "'cause I ain't talkin' to the Klan."

Serrell chewed his lip while the phone kept up its racket, then finally walked over, stared at the receiver, and picked it up. "Yes?"

"Bonnie? This is Low."

Serrell blew out a hot breath. "Nat. I thought you were going to fill the stands today. . . ."

"Temporary setback—we got caught up in that near riot with your bus this morning, and we couldn't get people in the seats. But the press came to our rescue. We won, my friend, we won."

Serrell looked heavenward for thanks. "Really?"

"President Roosevelt declared that the National Guard's coming if they don't let people—white or Negro—in with a paid ticket. If a Negro holds a ticket, even in a white section, it has to be honored. So tomorrow the park'll be jam-packed. The press is also devouring this story—Movietone, some of the big papers in the South, all the Northern rags. Especially because they walked Buck today. That's unsportsmanlike. Not the way it's done in the good ol' South."

"Thanks," Serrell said. "I'll call Dave with the news, okay?" He hung up.

Serrell rubbed his jaw. He plopped down on the bed. Though he wanted to tell his friend, wanted to keep in touch, it killed him at the same time. The thought of Barnhill all alone in Milwaukee, fighting every day, but by himself. "That Impo," he said. "Son of a bitch's probably in a argument every damn minute." He chuckled at the thought and picked up the phone. He got through to Barnhill's boardinghouse, his coach, and finally the Jackrabbit Bar and Grille, where the coach claimed he'd be. Barnhill came to the phone after a long wait. "Davey!" Serrell yelled over the noise he could hear through the phone. "It's Bonnie! How's Milwaukee?"

Barnhill sounded a bit tipsy. "It's Milwaukee, what can I say? These guys stink down here. They know it and I know it. But I don't care. I don't congregate with them, nor they me. The fans treat me like shit, and I feel nervous sitting in restaurants." Barnhill paused for a moment. "But tell me: how's St. Louis? Did Low and Rodney get the brothers in?"

"Not today. But tomorrow." He explained. Now Serrell was standing by the window, his face lit by the streetlamp, staring down at the crowds that had gathered after the party across the street. "And Mr. Veeck's puttin' the squeeze on, demanding the Browns pony up the money as if they'd had a sold-out crowd. Just 'cause they don't let people in doesn't mean they don't pay their share. Swears he's going to get the Supreme Court involved if he has to."

"If there's a buck involved, Veeck'll find a way to get it. But I guess he wasn't opposed to working with the Reds."

"Yeah. Dave, it's rough without you. But listen, don't work it too hard. You gotta get back up here, man."

"I don't know. All I can think about is the fight, you know. There's people worse off than us, that's for sure. Like Hal—"

The last thing Serrell wanted was another speech about Hal. "You listen, Dave. Play, man, like your Uncle Hal said. I 'member— that old guy told you to focus on the ball game. Those people that got it rough, man, they need you to win ball games. That's your gift to this world, boy. Work it, and come back. Then you can really do good."

Barnhill laughed. "Yeah, well, that seems like asking me to step casually to the moon, friend. You seem a long way from Milwaukee, and I feel like a long way from anything worth doing." He sighed. "I'm going. Got to get up early and do what I do best," he said.

"Dave—" Serrell said, but his friend had hung up the phone. Serrell looked at the receiver, then he turned to Lockett. "I wonder if we'll ever see that boy in a uniform again."

There were clouds in the sky and an oppressive humidity waiting for both teams. A doubleheader would be exhausting in any climate; here it was as if someone had turned up the gravity. As the A's readied for the game, Cool glanced around the clubhouse. He looked worried. They'd practiced all morning, to a growing crowd of whites and blacks, to the same cheers and tauntings that had plagued them the last two days. Cool craned his neck and caught a glimpse of Cochrane in his office, rubbing his brow. He stood, walked over, and knocked quietly. "Mickey?"

Cochrane sat up quickly. "Yes, Mr. Bell?"

"Where's Campy? And Josh?"

Cochrane took a moment before answering. "They will not be playing today."

"They won't . . . Benson too?"

"Yes, Benson too," he said impatiently. "He is not playing, I mean. Thank you, please close the door behind you."

"Mickey—?"

"You will be in center field today, Mr. Bell. Dihigo will be catching. Thank you and please close the door behind you."

"Mickey," Cool asked again. "C'mon. Where's Josh and Campy?"

Cochrane sighed. "Both men, and Gene Benson, are . . . They are in the hospital, watching Gibson." At seeing Bell's response, Cochrane held his arms up. "Relax. No one is in any danger. Mr. Gibson has . . . well, I believe you can piece it together. There was a fight. Roy has hurt his wrist. Mr. Benson has a black eye. Nothing serious. Mr. Bell, you may pass this along to the men. As I hear word, I will pass it on to you. Now, please go play baseball as best you can."

The rest of the series the crowds did not fight, they did not riot. The National Guard patrolled outside Sportsman's Park, and for the first time in history blacks and whites sat side by side . . . and yet there was nothing but a baseball game, as if desegregation happened every other week. But the A's rooters—and they were in the park in great droves, carrying signs and dressed to the hilt—could only watch in defeated silence as the A's dropped game after game. Adelis continued to grate on the team even if he was now surrounded by A's sympathizers. He went on about Lockett's relationship with a sixteen-year-old girl, and unnerved the outfielder so badly that he dropped two routine flies. "The guy's personal," Lockett whined later. "I mean, how does he get this stuff?" A group of soldiers on leave threatened Adelis, but that didn't stop him. Neither did women asking him to tone it down. Finally, after the last out of the last game, a cry came from above the A's dugout: "This is the worst team ever!"

Soon even supporters were chanting, "Go home, bums!" as Adelis led them on, swaying like a bandleader.

Lockett sat in the clubhouse, sobbing. Wells slammed his glove to the floor. "Four straight," he said. "Four goddam straight."

Cochrane said, "Take this travel time to unwind, men. Get your thoughts in order. Remember that the season is long."

"The season's long," Wells mimicked after Cochrane closed the door.

The players boarded the Superchief to head back to Philadelphia and did so late, in an empty station. No one was there to see them off except a porter who waited an extra twenty minutes before he clocked out. "You boys'll pull it out," he said, grinning.

Josh sat in his sleeping compartment and stared out at the dusky horizon, his eyes thinned in an effort to make out the shapes that flew by. There was a farmhouse, a silo, and he swore he could see some kid riding a horse. Sometimes, in the worst moments when his club was lousy, or he was in a slump, he'd notice things like farms, filling stations, men and women working anonymously, and he'd feel a tinge of regret. Right then, with the noise of these days in St. Louis still ringing in his ears like a tinnitus, he wished he could work on a farm. With animals, and that smell. Was it hay or straw? Sweet, organic, smelled like life itself, he thought. No one shouting you down for missing a hay bale or dropping a pail of milk. All this politics, all this losing . . . he'd seen it before. Not the politics, but he'd been on clubs chock-full of talent that just couldn't get it together to win on the field. Mickey was right, the season's long. And he would start hitting again. Wouldn't he?

Josh stood in the center of his compartment and stretched. He took out North and gripped the bat at the handle. He swung a few short chops. Damn this game, he thought—here I am, playing baseball, and I just want to die. Batting around .200, barely able to crouch when I'm catching. My legs feel like they're splintering apart. No one even noticed me back in St. Louis. Didn't care. That crazy man, the fat guy who scares Artie, that guy doesn't even give me the time of day. And that Gene Benson, riding me all the time. Had to pop him one. Didn't mean to hurt Campy. Seemed like all he was doing lately was hurting people.

Josh's muscles ached—by now it seemed that his aches and addictions were devouring him. For a moment he wondered if his failures weren't dragging the team down, keeping them from first. With that thought he closed his eyes. Josh stood, swaying ever so slightly, and from behind his eyelids he could sense the sunset filling the room with a pale gold light. He made a vow to himself and to the A's, a prayer of sorts: let me go into that sunset with some glory, please. Don't let me hurt my team. If I fail now . . . he paused on that thought, sat down, and pulled a worn paper bag from under his pillow. Inside was a syringe, a packet of white powder, and a spoon darkened by flame. Josh closed his eyes. "No sir," he said aloud, quietly. "If I fail now, I go away. All my years before this, gone. Forgotten." He filled the spoon with powder and pulled out his Zippo and began to melt it into liquid. "Don't make me forgotten, Lord," he asked, and then concentrated on the task at hand.

◇ **13** ◇

Wheel of Fortune

Philadelphia was in misery, and no one knew that better than Bill Veeck. He fought the growing melancholy of the Athletics' fans by working his tail off every day. At night, well into the small hours, he pored over newspapers, histories of pipe manufacturing, poetry, glib biographies of long-dead vaudevillians, city manuals, and medical journals . . . nothing could defeat his anxiety or ease him into even three hours' sleep. When he had exhausted that night's library, he emptied another bottle of beer and began to play little games, like flicking ticket stubs into the trash can and wagering that if he hit ten in a row, the A's would win the pennant.

Didn't matter, he thought, as long as we fill the stands. During the daylight hours he did his level best to help the city and his players forget St. Louis, forget his ostensibly championship-caliber ball club sitting eighteen games under the break-even mark and dead last. He could see the fatigue of lost hope in the dour faces of the customers in the greasy spoons he frequented, in the people who worked the factories and in those weary commuters on the trolley, even those he found in the churches and synagogues, schools and hospitals. Everywhere he noticed despair: the sudden frown at the sight of yesterday's score in the box on the upper left-hand corner of the front page, the quick turn to the sports section, the face stiffening as the article was read, the lips thinning in disbelief—They couldn't hold a lead again! Another one-run loss!—and then the quick collapse of the paper into an uneven fold, tucked under the arm. The Athletics were losing, and their fans were losing right along with them. The ache of war, cutting deep into every soul, seemed even more acute when the hope of a pennant turned rancid. Men were brutal; women shrill. There were prayers and even a sermon or two, candles lit at the cathedral, and the flocks questioned: where's God when you need him? Nowhere near the A's.

Veeck publicly railed against the St. Louis management, fan base, grounds crew, pets, and people of that city who may have had anything to do with making his team feel uncomfortable. St. Louis, he thought, has now become our number one enemy. And enemies, he knew, were great for business. Fortunately for him, the Browns were scheduled to come to town over the Fourth of July, the best weekend in the business yet far enough away to fire the cauldron of hatred to red hot.

Meanwhile Veeck prepared to make Shibe Park a circus. When the A's were out of town he ignored the commissioner's ban and walked right into the stadium, confident that no one of any prominence would notice (always before dawn, though, just to be safe). Only once did he have to hide in a janitor's closet for thirty-five minutes while a cop visited with a vendor. Out in the bright sunlight, he applauded at the sight of juggling vendors practicing their art on the diamond. His fake leg, at least, was beginning to feel a part of him, and he now moved nearly as swiftly as anyone. As he paced across center field, he looked up at the men installing bright whirligigs above the scoreboard, lighting up green and red and yellow for a home run. He knew a fellow in the Army Corps of Engineers who finagled the bulbs for him. "I'm lucky I've got my pals," he thought.

Even better, the city announced that in another month the blackouts would end. (At this point in the war it was assumed that the Germans were not about to bomb Philly.) This would be a welcome gesture that had nothing to do with his ballpark and everything to do with the other businesses that missed their neon signs calling customers in off the streets. With the end of the blackouts Veeck could have night games and throw together a fireworks display every weekend, a thought that almost literally made him swoon.

It was also time for "Nights." "Nothing like a Night!" he would remind Sam at every opportunity. Satchel Paige Night, Buck Leonard Night, Roy Campanella Night. Army Night, Navy Night, WAC Night—*especially* WAC night, with those gals in their lovely uniforms. Special programs, tickets with photos of their favorite players on the stub. Local merchants donating prizes for the players. A silver cup for a prize, autograph sessions before the games for the kids. Everyone loves a Night, Veeck mused.

He cashed in every favor owed to him. By now he'd burned through most of them, so he turned quietly to the pals of Al Capone, men whom he'd come to know in his days with the Cubs, who had reluctantly loaned him money for the Brewers long ago, and less than reluctantly accepted their investment back tenfold. Through them he was able to secure fifteen thousand silk stockings. "That's Ladies Day!" he said, watching the truck toss box after box onto the shipping dock. He found meat. He found chocolate. He found trinkets. With that and OTHER PROMOTIONS LIKE YOU'VE NEVER SEEN BEFORE!—as the banners, billboards, and radio ads practically screamed—Veeck was certain he could bring in the crowds in spite of everything.

He was a pest to every radio station that would have him, elbowing the war off the local programs, giving them a lighthearted break. Because of the ruckus in St. Louis, the press didn't feel the need to attack him for making a mockery of the game, but everyone wanted his take on the matter. On any matter.

Things were starting to look up, Veeck thought, as he stood by the pitcher's mound at Shibe. Barnhill's gone. And the Cuban! Well, he's the feather in my cap. Every doubleheader would be a duel between him and Satch, no doubt about it. Veeck lit a cigarette off the one he was smoking and admired the jitterbugging groundskeepers who were practicing their steps in center. To Veeck's right, a busy little man was applying the finishing touches to a giant wheel standing on a platform on the pitcher's mound. It was canary yellow, and in the center was a picture of Martín Dihigo. The wheel read in bright blue: WHERE WILL HE PLAY TODAY?

"How's this going to work?" the guy asked. His face was dotted with yellow paint.

"It's a game, Joe," Veeck said, toying with the wheel. "One lucky fan draws big, and he or she gets to take a spin on the wheel. Where it lands, that's where Dihigo plays. Except pitcher, of course— that's on fourth days. And get this! You get to have your photo taken with him, and ten pounds of chuck."

"I don't know about the photo, but I could sure use the meat."

"And look at this!" He slapped one of the slots on the wheel. "JACK OF ALL TRADES!"

"What's that mean?"

"It means," Veeck said, spinning the wheel, "that Mr. Dihigo plays *every* position!"

Later that evening, Veeck took a walk around the grounds. The staff was gone, the lights shut down. By the right-field wall he reached his right hand out and thought, you could feel the energy of the place. The moon was out, the night soft and warm. Someone was practicing a tuba in the distance, someone was listening to a radio. He unlocked a door and walked into the stands.

Veeck didn't turn on any lights, but not out of fear of discovery. He'd spent so much time preparing the park for Opening Day that he could maneuver the place in the pitch-black. Besides, he liked the dark at that moment; it allowed him to concentrate on how Shibe smelled. Like hot dog buns and dust, the confident aroma of concrete and the damp iron of plumbing. The soul-reviving scent of grass and dirt. As if in a trance, he sat down and admired the diamond.

If there was one thing he had enjoyed at Wrigley, it was looking at the field in the bright moonlight. Same here. Maybe it would be nice to shut the lights down after a night game, let the folks see how nice it was. Everything silver, almost as if the world had turned into a black-and-white movie. He lit a cigarette, which glowed like a single firefly. Just a few months ago he imagined himself the toast of this city, alone in first place, the world knocked on its ear. He wished that Eleanor were sitting next to him then, gazing up at the stars. The kids asleep on a blanket in center field. How long would it be before she just chucked it all in, handed him the papers, and walked out of his life? He'd deserve it, that was for sure.

He turned his attention back to baseball and tried to conjure up something that would get him out of the jams he was in. But winning was all he could come up with—all the bread and circuses in the world can't take a man's mind off a last-place club. Even with a season like Leonard's, it all came down to winning. Veeck sighed. He could barely see the Wheel of Fortune in the moonlight. Tomorrow I'll be back across the street at Devil's Island, my old apartment and the rickety bleachers on that tar-reeking roof. When, he wondered, would Landis let him back in? When was the judge going to own up that his A's weren't doom and destruction? Sure, they were in last place, but the bums they replaced wouldn't do much more than scrape the bottom either, and didn't have a star among them. His daddy used to say that the judge was stubborn, but when the truth hit him he'd shout to heaven to make sure the world knew it. Okay, Veeck thought, he'll come around soon. He's a baseball fan—how could you not thrill to Buck Leonard's towering home runs or Dihigo or Satchel's mind-bending throws? Sure, Veeck thought, exhaling a cloud of smoke that rose in the moonlight, he'll come around. With those notions relaxing him, Veeck went home and read, dozing off at his desk around two.

He woke abruptly an hour later. Jerking up, he shuddered, feeling as if dozens of eyes were watching him, or that he was being listened to. He sensed that some great activity was going on nearby, right over his shoulder. Odd: the city seemed more alive than usual for this time of night. He found a pack of cigarettes and lit one. Then he waited, staring out the open window, keeping the lights off.

The city *was* wide awake. The air was balmy—that toasty late-night warmth anticipating a scorching day. He stared down the street. No extra cars. No sirens. A breeze fluttered the curtains. The moon was low on the horizon. Outside, Shibe was nothing but a black pit in the center of the block.

It was the radios. An inordinate number of radios were playing, their sounds trickling through the open windows of the homes around him. Talking, not music. One or two lights on, and the whispering radio. Then he heard a phone ring next door, heard the muffled, muted garble of his neighbor talking briefly and then hanging up. Then he heard her radio come on.

Still preferring the dark, Veeck sat, sucking on his cigarette and wondering if he really wanted to hear what was happening. Finally he reached over and switched on the Philco. It glowed a soft white light. A voice mumbled into clarity.

Edward R. Murrow announced that the Allies had landed in Normandy. Veeck sat, his face turning a pale orange with every puff of the cigarette. He barely listened to Murrow's sober announcements but turned in his chair and stared out the open window. He knew quite a few men fighting in Europe, guys his age and young men too. Like old Lou Balboni, a hot dog vendor he used to know in Milwaukee. Left his post, like Veeck, to go fight, except he ended up in Britain. "Lit in London!" he wrote on a postcard with a picture of Big Ben. "You got to watch those English gals. Dark beer, awful stuff!" Veeck wondered what had become of Lou, if he was hitting that beach right now. Most of his old ballplayers from the Brewers were fighting, guys that Barnhill would never know. Hy Worley, his old third-base coach, had a couple of kids out there. Veeck sighed and felt his stomach drop. This must be killing Mickey, he thought. Every day probably kills Mickey.

He called Sam. The operator couldn't get anyone through—the lines had been tied up for more than an hour. Okay, he thought, so I never get to call you with the news.

All through the wee hours Veeck sat, in a trance, listening to Murrow and watching the moon set and the city come into shape with the dawn. Around eight and starving, he fried some eggs and drank some coffee, reading a novel about turnip farmers, trying not to worry. Later he took a trolley to a breakfast meeting with an advertiser. The trolleys were packed, filled with city employees and war workers: gals in coveralls, guys in coveralls. Most of their faces were buried in the gazettes. Some of them were pained from worry, some were pained by regret. Some suppressed guilt every day, happy they weren't fighting and feeling awful for the thought. When they saw Veeck's slight limp, some turned their faces in embarrassment. Maybe I'm crazy, Veeck thought, but in a little while these people will need some baseball. D day's games were canceled, but come tomorrow we're right back at it.

Most of the Athletics welcomed the day off. Campy and Benson recuperated from yet another beating Josh gave them at the station. "Bad hop and too much of it," Benson lamented over dinner with the Campanella family one evening. He was holding a slab of liver over a new black eye; Josh almost broke Campy's finger in the brawl.

It had begun on the train: no Josh when they pulled in, so Sam asked Campy and Benson to stop by his compartment to round him up. Josh didn't answer, so they finally busted down the flimsy door. They found him delirious, complaining that Babe Ruth was trying to kill him, that the landlady was trying to kill him, that everyone was trying to kill him. The son of a bitch Ruth didn't want Josh breaking any records, that's why he was out to get him. Campy laid a hand gently on Josh's shoulder and said, "Easy, big fella." Josh sprung at him, swinging away with a metal ashtray he was hiding behind his back. Campy ducked and went to clock him in the nose, but only succeeded in elbowing Gene in the eye. When Roy turned to help his friend, Josh jumped on Campy, choking him. Campy elbowed Josh in the gut, and as he tried to pull Josh off his back, Josh almost snapped Campy's middle finger.

The noise of the melee brought one of the porters. He pulled Josh's arms off Campy like he was merely arranging kindling on a pile, laid him out with a single blow, sighed, and told Campy and Gene he was calling the cops.

After Josh dried out in the city jail, Veeck sprung him on bail. It took barely an hour after Josh stepped out of the cab for him to get high again, and Campy and Gene found him and Grace blasted and sleeping under their bed, curled up and shaking. So Veeck installed the couple in a fourth-floor cold-water flat on the outskirts of Philadelphia. One of Capone's old doctors, an old pal of Veeck's, attended to the catcher. For the money, the good doctor would be discreet. And effective.

The doctor, a thin man with the somber, corpse-hungry look of an undertaker, worked over both Josh and Grace, who was also strung out, even worse when Josh was on the road. The doctor shot them full of Pentothal and strapped them to a pair of beds, all the while watched over by a couple of male nurses who looked as if they could pick Josh up and swing him around like a baseball bat. After a day of this, Campy was sick from the whole thing. He'd come by in the afternoon, and the nurse standing outside the door would shake his head while the screams coming from inside chilled Campy to the bone.

After three days the doctor, per Veeck's request, called Campy with the news. "I'm done," he said in a voice that rattled with phlegm. "My nursing staff will remain for five more days."

"And then he can play?"

"I don't know," the doctor said, sounding disgusted at the question. "This has taken a tremendous toll on his body and mind. His eyesight is dulled. Before, he could rely on the drugs and alcohol to clear his head. That's gone now. Most addicts have a struggle just to wake up and go about their day. So I don't know about professional baseball. Keep him healthy, keep him on a routine. The woman too. You leave her to die and he'll join her in no time."

On the day after the invasion a gentle heat rose during the morning, carrying a feeling in the air stronger than a cup of black coffee. A brief rain hit in the night, so in the morning the city smelled fresh, as if the whole place had been hosed down.

Veeck beamed from his rooftop. People had already gathered on the sidewalk, lingering over the peanut vendors, the ticket sellers, strolling around the stadium while the Athletics practiced inside. There was that Mardi Gras feel he wanted, his band marching around and around the stadium, families strolling about, the police friendly and affable. The first ball game since D day—win one for the Allies, he thought. Veeck was hungry for action: the Senators in town, playing badly as of late; maybe his boys will even win a game. He had Jefferson on the mound, and the guy could pitch like he was blasting cannonballs when he wanted to, ripe for a breakout game.

At noon the ump cried, "Play ball!" By one o'clock, at the close of the fourth inning, the Athletics were already losing badly.

Veeck sat alone. By now the reporters who enjoyed gloating had long since grown tired of the fun—they'd rather watch in the confines of the press box. Veeck took off his shirt and lit another cigarette. From his perch he could hear the rumble of the crowd, the clang of the trolley below, the shrill of Adelis all the way from the depths of the stadium. Fans were throwing things at the A's. Little kids and their folks, sick of the losing, hurling their scorecards. Cute girls tossing the boxes of stockings on the field. He squinted. If you just look at the game, the green grass and that golden hue of the base paths, it all looks so innocent, so beautiful. There's no losing, nothing but baseball. I'm going to squint my way right out of the sport, he thought.

That afternoon Veeck watched the Athletics lose their fifth straight. He gathered up his empty cans, a crumpled pack of Luckies, and his binoculars. Down in his office he still took pains to maintain a spread of drinks. A calendar from the Keystone Franks Company hung on the wall, its bright red letters too garish for anything but a dank garage. Had it really been two weeks since a reporter bothered to show up after a game? He poured himself a short one, gulped it, then sat down at his desk to figure out which bank he would have to plead with to keep from calling their loan.

That night, a phone call. Veeck had fallen asleep at his desk, dreaming Shibe was overgrown with cacti, his wife and kids riding horses in the outfield. He fumbled for the phone. "Yes?" he said.

"Bill, it's Sam. Listen, you awake?"

"No, I'm not."

"Yeah, okay, I'm just calling to say that the system's down."

"Wait." Veeck stood, stretched, buckled over quickly to hammer at his thigh. Charley horse. He sat back down, rubbed his face, and picked up the phone.

"Start again, Sam. The system?"

"There's a strike. No buses, no trolleys, no subways. Today they were supposed to install five new motormen on the Philadelphia trolleys. Negroes. The Transit Employees Union fought with the government, and lost. The union must have told their drivers to call in sick. . . ."

"And nobody showed?"

"No, quite a few showed. But the leaders blocked the entrance to the trolley barns with their cars, told them to go home. And they did."

"Can't they get Negro drivers?"

"They've only got those five trained. And I guess those poor men are under police protection. They're terrified."

Veeck's thoughts jumbled together; he stood up, then fell back on the bed, a charley horse again. Roaring, he pounded at his leg, dropping the receiver.

"Bill, you okay—?"

Veeck hung up. The phone began to ring almost immediately. Slowly, and with burning deliberation, he took his leg off, massaged the stump, teeth gritted, and fastened the leg again. He stood and walked to the window. The phone rang. He stared out at the dark city.

A siren wailed in the distance. Sure, they're worried about riots, like Detroit. Who had warned him of something like this? Dozens had. "And how are they going to get to Shibe?" he said, almost a whisper. The phone kept ringing. The window was open, the cool breeze of early morning coming through. The smell of baking bread, the sound of bundled newspapers hitting the sidewalk at the corner. That siren, still wailing. Veeck's hands became fists. "How are they going to get to my ballpark?"

Down on the street he could see a kid, hurrying to get to his papers, running his hand along the outfield wall. The phone stopped ringing. As Veeck walked from the window to his desk, his artificial leg ground into his stump. He fell back onto his chair, gritting his teeth and flailing with the straps. The phone began to ring. "Shut up!" he hissed, and knocked the phone on its side. With a jerk, he pulled the leg off and hurled it at the wall.

The phone began to bray. He picked it up and slammed it down on the receiver. Every ten minutes it began to ring. Veeck tried to think of ways to get people to Shibe: maybe he could borrow a bus. He heard Spink: *So he can get people to his games but not to their jobs?* How could he make fun of this situation, how can you laugh at it? The phone rang. He yanked the cord out of the wall and knocked the phone on its side. He fumbled for the pack of cigarettes on his desk. Empty. He threw the pack at the bed, but it fluttered away and landed on the floor. Swiveling in his chair, head pounding, Veeck watched Shibe's features come to light as the sun rose. All he could do was wait. And he hated to wait.

By noon the mayor had shut down all drinking establishments, halted sales of any liquor, hoping to avoid riots. Police rushed into black neighborhoods to keep the peace. At NAACP headquarters the staff raced to make thousands of leaflets to distribute, urging black citizens to remain calm. They organized car pools. The city was in chaos: suddenly there were too many cars on the street, factories were operating at two-thirds capacity, and that much only because of the car pools. The sidewalks were jammed with pedestrians, sweating in the heat of the day.

Only twelve thousand showed up to watch the A's dispatch the Senators behind Verdell Mathis. Most of the players walked to the park, some drove together. It was a quiet contest: Buck scored three runs on a bases-loaded double and Jethroe cracked two hits, and they finally won—but the tiny balloon of hope was weighed down with worry about the city. The mayor halted Veeck's proposed mini-bat day ("They'd use those things like billy clubs," he warned), resulting in surly children who shouted at the A's despite the win. Adelis railed at the players, blaming them for the strike. The crowds around him seemed to agree, though they shut up long enough to cheer Buck's double. And the Lung kept getting personal, entreating Mathis to let his wife get some sleep once in a while.

In the locker room Artie sat down and rubbed his eyes. Campy noticed the fatigue on his friend's face, and sat next to him. "Nice try today, Artie," he said. "You'll get 'em tomorrow."

"I don't know," Artie said. "I'm hitting .195. Even Jethroe's startin' to pull some. And today's error . . ."

"Was just an error. Look: we won. Maybe this is the start, you know? It's a long season—we still got time to make a play for the pennant, and you got time to straighten your game out. Isn't Ray D.

helpin' you with your glovework?" Artie just nodded, not looking up. "You'll get your average up. Just like I think we'll turn it around."

"Roy," Artie said. "I used to hit near like Buck—not the homers, but the average. I could really hit. Push the ball here, drill it there. I thought I was going to be good, do something that would make people look at me, swell up with pride. But this, it hurts."

"Yeah, I understand."

"Do you? You know, Camp, I could make a good living elsewhere. Portland, Oregon . . . I know some people there. Damn, Roy, it's my people there. My uncle wants to help me get set up in a business. Selling automobiles. But Roy, maybe I ought to go now."

"What are you talking about? Listen, we need you more than ever. You'll come around."

Artie looked exhausted, with heavy eyes, a downward mope. "I'm tired, man. Goddam, I'm tired." He leaned toward Campy and whispered, "Look at Cool. Good-natured guy like him, he's dying. Kids are saying things to him. Dropping sodas on him. *Kids*, Campy. And that Pete fellow. I have dreams about him, banging that helmet, following me everywhere, even into the grave.

"It's making me think, man. This team, us, we'd be the best in the Negro Leagues. Shit, look at the lineup, man! Better than the Grays, better than the Monarchs ever used to be. And I don't know what's wrong. The people, the slump, every day, it's just . . . I'm tired, is all."

"I understand, Art. Listen, Portland, it's nice, huh?"

"Oh, hell yeah."

"And your uncle, he's excited to have you?"

Artie squirmed. "Well, you know, Roy, he's all thrilled about me playin' here, but . . ."

"Just like my momma. Oh, my poppa's happy too, but momma, she goes crazy every game."

They both sat and thought on this. Campy said, "Don't you think you ought to keep at it, give 'em something to believe in?"

"Roy, all they got to believe in now is that I'm not cut out for this," Artie sighed. "It kills me to think about my family. It kills me to think I'm responsible for . . . I don't know, for troubles. Every Negro in the world is looking at us, and we're sinking. Maybe I'm a reason for that."

"You're a part of this club. That's what's important, Artie. If Mr. Cochrane didn't believe in you, he wouldn't keep you with us."

"I guess, Roy." He began to dress.

"Artie," Campy said, "you gotta keep the faith."

"Well, that's not as easy for me as it is for you."

The conversation was over. Campy sighed and walked to the far corner of the clubhouse, dressed, and headed over to check on Josh and Grace.

Around nine, Benson, Serrell, and Jefferson decided to go out for a few beers and relax themselves. Benson was glad to leave Gibson for an evening, and he spent an hour convincing Campy to come along. Between baseball and Josh, it was a wonder Campy didn't have grey hair. "Listen, fellas," Benson said later, over drinks, "We need a real night out. This pal of mine, Jeke Washburn, from 'way back, is having a rent party. Has 'em all the time—looney bird holds money like it's sand." The basics of a rent party were simple: snag some drinks, convince someone either to play music or bring a record player, whip up some food, and charge everyone a buck or two or three to raise enough dough to keep the landlord at bay.

Jefferson said, "This sounds like a cool glass of water, and I been in the desert too long. These fucking crackers at the bus company make me want to—"

"We ain't talkin' about that, right?" Serrell said, punching Jefferson lightly on the shoulder. "Tonight, just skirts and liquor! Music?"

"Hell yes, boy!" Benson said. He put his forehead against Campy's, grabbed the scruff of his neck, and shook him playfully. "Brother, you and I deserve this!"

Campy shouted, "Well, let's go!"

Jeke's pad wasn't far from the stadium, a second-floor dive above a shoe store and a barbershop. The ballplayers walked the whole way, strolling in comfortable silence beneath a fat waning moon. The air was sharp and cool. From a block away they could see the evidence of the party, cars jammed fender to fender, some couples making out. Then they heard the music, drums at first, then some singing and guitars, then Benson cried, "Praise the lord, Jeke got a man with an axe!" He slapped Jefferson on the arm, and they jogged the rest of the way.

At the front door a portly man shouted, "Gene Benson, that you? It's me, Little Fred!"

They hugged each other. "Little" Fred towered a good foot over them, with a belly nearly as wide as a door frame. He frowned and said, "You guys ain't playin' so well."

"Man, stay back. You know it's nothin' a few stiff drinks won't take care of," Benson said.

"Hell," Fred stood to one side and waved them in with a flourish, "then by all means, heal thyself!"

As they climbed the brightly lit stairs, Serrell let out a whoop. Upstairs they pushed their way into the crowded apartment, filled to its four walls with people. In one corner Jeke had rigged a small stage and some bright lights. The band wailed, their faces shiny from sweat. Each musician writhed in place, converting his manic energy into sound: exploding jazz, pouring from each man through his instrument. The sax player, pausing for his turn, nodded to the beat and chewed his lips with the look of a prizefighter waiting for a starting bell. On the floor they were dancing like mad, twisting and twirling, without colliding, everyone in step. The place was thick with girls, and the players grabbed a couple of women loitering by the front door and pulled them into the mass. When the songs crashed to a stop, the crowd screamed and shouted, then began laughing and talking to themselves while the band took a few drinks and a smoke.

In the break between the music, Jeke jumped up on stage, pointed at Gene Benson and shouted, "Hey, everybody, we got the ballplayers here!" They cheered, and Benson shouted back, "Shut up, Jeke! Get that music playing, nigger!" Jeke laughed, jumped off the stage, and the band got under way. He elbowed his way through to his pal, but it was so loud they couldn't talk, so they just danced around each other.

It seemed like the floor would cave in beneath them. The place was so hot it'd boil your insides. Smoke filled the room, and it seemed like the air was gone. There was so little room it was amazing that no one got flattened. But it was a magic bag of an apartment, and everyone fit and fit comfortably. Best of all to the players, there was no baseball. Even the war vanished, the only traces being a pair of soldiers who wore their uniforms with the idea it would help them get laid. There were no strikes or Communists. Booze was passed around, and in the kitchen chili was bubbling on the stove—you grabbed a teacup and helped yourself. Campy wanted a drink, so he went into the kitchen for some beer and managed to find a wall-flower he could mumble to. She kept shouting, "What?" He mumbled something. "I'm sorry I can't hear you!" she said.

Campy yelled, "Why don't we go someplace quiet?" She liked that idea. They sneaked out the window and down the fire escape, and made their way back to her apartment.

Serrell came downstairs for a smoke and some fresh air, and maybe to see if there were girls who would do more than just dance with him. He wasn't the handsomest guy on the club and had foul breath. As he stared up at the stars, thoughtlessly, a man stumbled outside and shouted, "Stella! I thought you went home!" Serrell giggled to himself and then laughed at the sight: this Stella looked pretty comfortable with none other than his man George Jefferson. Jefferson whispered for Stella to stand aside. Serrell rubbed his hands together with glee. What would a party be without a fight?

Stella shouted something discouraging to her former beau. When he grabbed her by the wrist, Jefferson stepped in between and shoved the man into a parked car. Soon they were throwing each other around, barely able to land a decent punch but attracting a small crowd, hooting and hollering. Jefferson finally shoved his rival into the gutter. Stella's old flame stared at Jefferson, called him a motherfucker, and hurled a bottle at the pitcher. Jefferson ducked in time, and it smashed through the plateglass window of the shoe store.

"Well, Jesus Christ," Serrell heard himself say. It was as if they came from nowhere, right out of the air. Police, six of them, sticks out, grabbed these two and began beating on them. Jefferson knocked one cop to the ground and ran upstairs. A woman screamed. Two cars pulled up, lights flashing, then a paddy wagon, and Serrell crept into a doorway, cowering. Two dozen officers were now on the scene. The guy at the stairs collecting money ran away, two policemen after him, and then the battalion rushed in. From upstairs someone shouted "Police!" and the apartment emptied, people crushing to the windows and down the fire escape. Like water gushing up a pipe, the officers raced up the stairs, shoulder to shoulder, clubs up, a wall of blue. In the apartment they began whaling away mercilessly. There were more screams. A woman fell and others right on top of her. The bandleader, seeing his group trapped in a corner, shouted "Turn!", and they put their hands on the wall in surrender.

Jefferson wasn't about to stand for this. *These fuckers weren't going to barge in on our party*, he thought. Almost lifting a cop off the ground, he hurled the officer into a wall. Then he punched out another. He pulled out a switchblade.

By now Serrell was a good block down the alley, looking to save himself. He heard the pop of gunshots. There were more screams, this time hysterical. Serrell ran harder, desperate to get away, ashamed for feeling cowardly. Paddy wagons raced by him, lights flashing, then a fire truck and two ambulances.

At midnight Veeck shouted "Two killed?" and hobbled across the room to his desk. Sam Dailey stood there in the dim light of the desk lamp. Veeck's leg wasn't hooked on correctly, as one strap hung to the side. "My God. Any of our players?"

"No," Sam said, taking a seat. "But one was a woman. And the other was a soldier. There were fifty-three arrests. Benson's one of them, for loitering, but it's bad enough he's there. And Jefferson . . ."

"Yeah?"

"Stabbed a police officer. In the thigh, but stabbed him nonetheless. The DA wants attempted murder."

Veeck collapsed in the chair. "How? Oh, never mind. God, those poor people. A woman. An officer stabbed by one of my own men. And a soldier? Come home from the front and this is what you get." He took a deep puff from his cigarette. Finally he asked, "You've got Mitchell?" He was referring to a defense attorney they both knew, a former D.A. from Milwaukee.

"He's flying here first thing. But when I talked to him, he thought we should let Jefferson sink."

"Can't do that. If he's guilty that's one thing." Veeck lit a cigarette and pulled a bottle from a drawer in his desk. He took a long swig, then tossed it at Sam, who also drank. This late, Veeck thought, and he's still wearing a stiff suit and tie. "But if he's not . . . listen, call Keller at the *Inquirer*. And Burley, get Burley. The guy had Winchell's ear at one time, maybe he can get some good words. Ask him what he thinks."

"I already did. Both. Burley said this is going to be called a riot. He said with Roosevelt in Hawaii, the feds are slower to respond."

"Great. Keller?"

Next morning Keller's take was splashed across the front page for all to see: RIOTS IN GOOSETOWN. *Philadelphia Athletics Players Involved in Twin Killing of Woman and Soldier.* He suggested that someone had taken to looting a shoe store, and the police responded quickly. Tensions from the strike agitated an already volatile Negro neighborhood. A man, perhaps one of the Athletics, pulled a knife. One of the deceased was a soldier. This was mentioned only in passing, with a notice that, at the present moment, they could not verify if he was AWOL or not.

The next morning the streets were as still as they had been on D day. The mayor had his police force out in droves, wandering around the park in cars, on foot, even on horses, as early as five in the morning. The National Guard took people to their jobs in transport vehicles and began to drive the trolleys.

"Have the band wail, Sam, just wail," Veeck said on the phone that morning. "Spin that wheel. Baseball's important today."

The Guard patrolled the stands and the tops of buildings, rifles over their shoulders. Shibe was half empty. The fans settled in, quietly, and many were dressed up, as if they were in church. Adelis arrived early, fluffed up the pillow he always sat on, and began yammering about the strike and the riot.

Before the doubleheader, Veeck convinced a National Guardsman to spin the wheel that day, some kid who just about jumped out of his uniform he was so excited. He won a free dinner and drinks at a local establishment, and blushed when the bathing beauty kissed him on the cheek.

"Where will he play today?" the announcer cried, and the crowd roared like they were trying to make up for the empty seats.

The mood in the dugout was funereal. Each man just slapped his glove or stared ahead, chewing on tobacco or gum. Oscar burned inside—he'd make a speech, try to comfort and focus his players as a team, but probably Mickey would have him hauled out by security. The man was going crazy, Oscar thought, and he hoped that thought was based on actual observation and not just because he hated Cochrane and wanted to run the team. Oscar was a man who prided himself on being fair, and he thought he knew what was best for the team. Cochrane was in charge, that's how it went. But the manager was mumbling to himself, making odd decisions—like he tried to get Satchel Paige to pinch-hit for Josh Gibson. "The best for the best," Cochrane roared at the umpire, who found the decision so strange he came to the dugout to make certain Mickey knew what he was doing. It was only when Mack and Red subdued him that the game continued. Oscar shook his head—as it turned out, Satch wasn't even in the ballpark. And now Jefferson's out and Cochrane's holed up in his office. Oscar sighed, stood, and told himself there were worse places he could be. Like in jail or back in the Philippines. It could always be worse, he thought.

In the bullpen Jefferson's seat was conspicuous by being folded and set aside. Byrd draped Jefferson's uniform over the seat. Mack raced over and snatched it up.

"What the hell?" Byrd said, "We lost a great pitcher today!"

"Forget it!" Mack said, and scratched at the wire stuck to his chest. "And keep quiet. No talking in the bullpen, 'member?"

"I don't get it," McKinnis whispered to Jeep. "Mack's the chattiest bastard I ever seen, and now he's all silent treatment." Jeep just shrugged.

Behind Paige the A's won both ends of a double-header. With all the controversy, the A's brief winning streak—three games, and five of six—went virtually unnoticed in the papers, mere blips in a bad season, one reporter wondering why the A's seemed to play better when life was bleak.

After the game, Sam met Veeck on the roof to watch the sun go down behind Shibe. There was a mellowness to the evening that belied what was raging in town.

While Sam was going over the attendance reports, the bleacher phone rang. Veeck answered it. It was Cliff Webb, from the *Chicago Tribune*, an old friend. "Bill," he said, "it's over for Jefferson."

Veeck let out a heavy sigh. "Okay. Give me the worst."

"Landis banned him for the remainder of the year, for narcotics use and the pending criminal charges. If found guilty, he'll be banned for life, which is moot, of course, since he'd get sent away pretty much for his whole career. And Benson gets a ten-game suspension."

"Thank you, Cliff," Veeck said, and hung up. He stood, stretched in the dusky sunlight, and grabbed a beer from the cooler.

Sam closed his eyes. Returning to being a mortgage lawyer in Milwaukee was sounding more appealing with each passing day. "How long?" Sam said with a sigh.

Veeck told him. "Always good news up here," he said, forcing a smile on his face. "What do Elmer's reports say?" he asked, referring to Elmer Whitlow, the team's ticket manager. He had daily totals of advance ticket sales and reported the take after every game at home.

"Twelve-five," Sam said, wiping the sweat from his brow. "Twelve-five. Lowest total yet."

"You know, Sam, the one thing I just didn't count on was last place."

"People are buying bonds instead. Can you blame them?"

"No. But they'd do both if we sat in first. . . ." He tossed his cigarette away. ". . . Well, what difference does it make? You came here to make your weekly sourpuss report, so let's have it."

Sam ignored the barb. It seemed as if, in running this ball club, he was forgetting how much he enjoyed the sport itself. After a moment's reflection, trying to muster up the strength to cough up the bad news, he said, "Cleveland National called the loan, Bill. I don't know why, since we've not missed payments and our credit's still good. The voice in the back of my head tells me that the judge was involved—he's got powerful friends, Bill. And you're flaunting his edict . . ."

"I can't rent this place and watch games? I can't . . ."

"Please," Sam begged. "I'm not the press, you don't have to convince me. But you stirred up a hornet's nest. Listen, Bill, this means that if we can't keep Cleveland National at bay we'll have trouble raising payroll." He paused, waiting for Veeck's response, and continued when there was none. "We're not skating on thin ice, we've broken through and we're sitting at the bottom of the lake." He reached for one of Veeck's beers. "I did some figuring."

"Figuring, huh?" Whenever Sam did some figuring, not to mention drinking, there was bad news.

Sam took a gulp of the now-warm beer and made a face. "Oh, that's horrible. Listen, we need to sell out every game. And by that—"

"We'll sell out every game! Christ, it'll be just like Milwaukee, we'll fill Shibe right up to the top, add more seats if necessary! Once the strike's over and—"

Sam's voice rose. "Bill, we need to sell out *every* game. As in home *and* away. And *right now*, not after the strike. Even then, I'm not sure we can survive."

"Home and away?" Veeck rubbed his chin.

"We need every one of those seats filled. In Cleveland, Chicago, Washington—we have to have our half from a full house to break even."

"How close will we get just selling out at home?"

Sam gave a defeated laugh. "Even 75 percent attendance around the league means outright bankruptcy. It's impossible."

"Knowing what we know, we just have to put the machine in gear and figure out some way of promoting the games here and in other cities. Even without the help of the other owners."

"It also means we can't have any more episodes like the last few days," Sam said. "Expenses that pop out of nowhere. The strikes, Oscar's brawl back in May. Jefferson. The lawsuits. All these city violations, sanitation and structural problems that didn't seem to exist in April. That's more of Landis's work—he seems to know how to hit the pocketbook. And we've got people scared to come to the park because Negroes might act up. . . ." Veeck let him rant until eventually Sam calmed down. "Maybe if we told the players what was going on, the trouble we're in, some of them might defer their salary till next year."

"Forget it. They're baseball players, I don't want them distracted."

Sam folded his arms across his chest. "So what do we do?"

"I don't know."

"You don't know? Bill, I own this team too. You have to give me some ideas."

"I don't have any yet!"

Sam set his beer down on the bleacher and leaned toward Veeck. He sighed. "Bill, you don't have to believe me. I've talked with men who are sympathetic to our cause—Rickey, Stoneham—and they're convinced it's the judge. He's got a tremendous amount of sway with city governments. Rickey says that—"

"Landis wouldn't purposely—"

Sam made a face like his stomach was bothering him, belched, and then continued. "Listen to me! Landis makes mayors jump. He knows people in banking, government . . . the guy was one of the nation's top judges. Bill, what we've done, we've done, I grant you that. But payroll . . ."

"What about payroll?"

"We're not going to make payroll in two weeks!" Veeck was silent again as Sam continued. "If we can't make payroll, the commissioner could seize the club *now*, none of this wait-till-the-end-of-the-year stuff. Bill, look," he said, "it's June. *June.* We're in last place, so far behind that no club—you can look this up—has ever come from this far behind to win anything."

"No one's ever had a club like this before."

"My point is this: we're out of money. Okay, let's say we scrape up payroll. I suppose we can, somehow, we just have to figure out how, right? That's the Veeck way, fine. But if we can barely make payroll in June, how are we going to show a profit by October? The answer is, we won't. We'll show a loss and have to sell the club. But, Bill, we're sitting on money. And you know what I'm talking about." When Veeck didn't answer, Sam closed his eyes as if he were in great physical pain. Finally he said, "For the life of me, I can't figure out why you haven't pulled the trigger yourself."

Veeck lingered over the last of his cigarette. He shrugged. "You tell me: who would I sell?"

"Stop it. You know perfectly well. But if you need the details, I've got them. I've made some phone calls."

"And?"

"Rickey's interested, and so is Stoneham and Benswanger in Pittsburgh. And the beauty of it is they're all National League! Stay out of our way, know what I mean? Plus, Bill, I bet we can get a hundred grand for Buck Leonard."

Veeck laughed. "A hundred?"

"Sure. And that's just from one phone call, without haggling." Sam straightened himself up, thinking he'd plugged into Veeck's interest. "Listen, we can keep our draws—Satch and Dihigo—and sell off Buck, Ray, and Cool. You don't need a degree from Cornell to see that we can make a bundle off those players, still have roughly the same club—after all, we really can't get worse than last place—and still have decent players for the future. Irvin'll be back after the war's over. We have the makings of a great team . . . in two or three years."

Sam sat back, smiling, though he'd perspired through his coat. "It's what we should have done a month ago."

Veeck kept puffing away. "Sell Leonard?"

"Leonard and Dandridge and Bell. Maybe even Willie Wells. We could pull in over three hundred easily. Two for Buck, fifty for Dandridge and Bell and Wells. Probably more! These are old players, Bill, and the nucleus of our team would remain intact! Think about it! The Giants are so up and down, they could use the stability of Ray and Buck. Stoneham's all ears. He thinks those two will send them to the pennant. And Rickey *loves* Buck. We could get a bidding war on."

"You've done your homework."

Sam squinted in the light, now bright just above the dome behind home plate. He gazed at Veeck for a moment, trying to read his thoughts. Finally he shook his head. "You never struck me as overly sentimental."

"I'm telling you, we can still win."

"Are you out of your mind?" Sam shouted, and then lowered his voice when he noticed Veeck's neighbor looking up from her rooftop garden. "Look at the *standings* just like everyone else, would you?" Veeck didn't say anything. "So what about payroll next week?" he shouted.

Veeck lit another cigarette. "I sold the ranch."

Sam gaped. "You sold the ranch?"

"It's better property than I thought. A lot of land. It'll tide us over for a while. We can pay the Cleveland bank enough to satisfy them till year's end and still send out paychecks."

"Where's Eleanor going to live?"

Veeck winced. "Well, where do you think? She'll live *here*. She's on a train right now, with the kids." Veeck stared out at Shibe. "It'll be nice, having the family up here."

Sam slid off the bleacher. His shirt and coat were soaked with sweat, which happened each and every time he fell into an argument with Veeck. Even his shoes were filled with sweat. "Bill," he said, just before walking away, "coming back to the subject at hand, I want to remind you that I'm the president of the club and a major investor. And," he cleared his throat, "as president I might have to act in the best interests of the team. Do you understand?"

Veeck stared out at Shibe. "See you later, Sam."

Sam shook his head and walked away.

An hour later, a knocking came from his door below. Veeck was in no mood to meet a zealous fan, so he sat for a moment, smoking, waiting. The knocking continued.

Veeck leaned over the roof and shouted, "Who goes there?"

From under the porch awning came, "Mickey Cochrane, sir."

Veeck shouted at him to come up, then made his way downstairs to his office. As he entered, Cochrane was standing at the edge of Veeck's desk, hat in hand. "Sit down," Veeck said. "Something to drink?"

Cochrane didn't sit, nor answer the question. He seemed to wobble, back and forth, in nervousness. A single lamp lit the room from the side of the desk, making Veeck and Cochrane appear as if in a spotlight on a stage, deep black shadows surrounding a circle of white light.

"Mr. Veeck," he said, blinking rapidly. "I would like . . ." He took a breath. "Well, sir, I need . . ."

"Go ahead, Mickey. Maybe if you sat . . ."

Cochrane blurted, "I need to know under what capacity I run this ball club!"

"Pardon?" Veeck said. "Why you're—"

"No, no! Do *not* call me the manager! No, sir. For if I were the manager I would be allowed to make decisions such as who pitches in each game. If I were manager I would not get crossed signals and I would be able to discipline my players, as I have requested. If I were manager I would not have the feeling that the entire team is backing away from me. Except Roy. And a few others. Roy is a good young man, he—"

"Oh, now, Mickey—"

"Listen to me!" he shouted. "Did you know that Satchel Paige injured himself this afternoon, as I thought he would?"

"What!" Veeck shouted, surprising both of them. Lowering his voice, he asked, "How did he hurt himself?"

"He pitched two straight games today, that is how, Mr. Veeck. Mr. Paige claimed that it is in his contract that, with your approval, he may pitch both halves of a doubleheader." Cochrane was in a real froth, shouting every word and gesticulating like a politician in a park. "You sent Barnhill to Milwaukee without my consent. You force me to pitch Hilton Smith, who appears to be fighting constant pain. You have made them laugh behind my back. Every player comes crawling in here after I discipline them, and suddenly their fines, their suspensions, even their benchings have been reversed. What is to be done, sir? Do I need to resign?"

Veeck rubbed his forehead. Cochrane was about to speak when Veeck waved his hand. "Listen, listen! I hear you, okay? We'll compromise. I need Satch to pitch, but I'll let you make the calls . . . provided he's a starter. When he's healthy, of course. I won't fiddle around with your rotation. But I need Dihigo and Satch to play in doubleheaders . . ."

"Then I am *not* running this club. Every fourth day, just as it should be."

"Listen, Mickey—"

"Furthermore, I need Barnhill."

Veeck gave him a look of surprise. "Now you're trying to do *my* job. Barnhill, you can't have. He's—"

"Unfortunately I will have to tender my resignation," Cochrane said, and he pulled a folded piece of paper from his pocket and tossed it on the desk. "I am at the end of my rope. Even Mr. Filson is acting strange, paranoid, and he used to be the master of his pitching staff!"

Veeck grabbed the letter and tore it up. "Mickey . . . listen, this is a delicate situation. Barnhill's trouble, and he's not pitching well. And you know, with your record right now, last place and all, most owners would fire you right here, right on the spot."

Cochrane stiffened, trying to keep his legs from shaking. "You cannot fire me, as I have resigned."

"You're taking this all wrong . . ."

"I am not taking it any way! I am interested in making this a pennant-winning ball club, sir! *That* will never happen if I am not allowed to have the authority any manager needs. Are you listening to me? Stop staring at your hands, then! I cannot continue if I am not in complete control of my team." He stood up straighter and folded his arms. "You have my decision. When can I expect to hear from you?"

Veeck said, "Don't be so formal. Take a seat." When he didn't, Veeck shouted, "Take a seat, would you!" Cochrane sat reluctantly. "Mickey, listen—"

"Sir, I will get what I want or—"

"Or what? You'll go back to your farm and stare out the window?" Veeck sighed to calm himself, and reached for a cigarette. "You're right. I haven't been entirely square with you, and for that I'm sorry. I won't go back on any of your disciplinary decisions, beginning right now. You give a fine, it sticks. You sit a fellow, it sticks. But . . ." he said loudly, "there's going to be compromise. Like you asked, I won't tell you who to pitch, even Satchel. If you decide to sit him for the rest of the season, that's your decision. But if we're still losing and I see Satchel Paige loafing in the bullpen, we'll have another talk and it won't be about tendering your resignation. On the other hand, when it comes to Satch, I think we both know his numbers speak for themselves—he's won fifteen games, for God's sake."

Cochrane looked deeply relieved. "Thank you, Mr. Veeck. You are correct about Mr. Paige. I was just upset."

"Two things: first, the wheel stays. That's a promotion too many people love. On days the Cuban's not pitching, we use the wheel to determine where he plays."

Cochrane nodded. "Fine, sir, fine. I have to admit, I get a laugh out of it myself, and it allows me to use my bench and rest some of my regulars. But let us be reasonable . . . one game after Mr. Dihigo pitches, he has to rest, otherwise . . ."

"Got it. And you don't get Barnhill." Cochrane looked as if he were preparing a filibuster. "Don't start, Mickey! You get to run this club, but you don't get to run the whole corporation. Barnhill will be brought up eventually."

"Mr. Veeck, George Jefferson will not play again, and we both know that. You can waste money looking for someone with as much talent as Mr. Barnhill, or you can simply call him up."

Veeck sighed. "I would have thought you of all people would have been against Barnhill."

"He was having a rough time of it, as they all were."

Veeck said, "Barnhill's staying in the minors for a few more games, until I see he's ready and his lip's shut tight. For now, put a reliever in—all these guys used to be starters, especially McKinnis." He paused. "Do we have a deal?"

Cochrane thought about it for a moment before standing stiff as a soldier and offering his hand. "Mr. Veeck, I will remain your manager."

"Outstanding!" Veeck stood and shook hands. "Say, Mickey, I've been thinking of this for a while . . . what would you think about catching?"

Cochrane put his hat on his head. "I am too old to entertain such thoughts." He nodded, breathing a deep sigh of possible relief. "If that is all, then good day, sir." With that, he left.

Veeck wandered back upstairs to his rooftop bleachers, to drink a few more beers, smoke cigarettes, and watch the stars come out. Night had hit Philadelphia, lowering like a blanket. "What am I going to do?" Veeck said to no one.

It was chilly the next morning, but the sky was clear and the moon was deep in the west, pale against the new day. Campy stopped by Josh's flophouse, waiting to haul him and Grace to Newark. There they would spend the next seven days working out with the Newark Eagles, of the Negro Leagues, trying to get back in shape, trying to sharpen Josh's eye, trying to make him into the slugger he once was now that he was supposedly clean and sober from his time with the good doctor. Cochrane wanted to see Josh back in shape, how he took to decent pitching, and if he was ready to play again. He just didn't want to see this in the majors. Campy promised Cochrane that he would be honest, that he would score each game and bring back the results. It was a risk, not only because the A's would have to make do with a couple of cut-rate catchers while these two worked out in Newark, but because Campy could tell that Cochrane simply wanted Josh gone. He promised his manager that the old Josh would come back, and as he pulled up that morning, he made a wish on the pale moon that everything would work out.

Josh and Grace were eager to hit the road. They'd been up since four, packed and ready and chattering on about the promise of baseball. On the highway Josh kept staring out the window, craning his neck like a child who'd never seen the New Jersey countryside before. He rattled on the whole way, about the little strategies he'd learned from Biz Mackie, like fooling a runner by standing at the plate, arms down, as if there were no way the throw from the outfield would come in on time, making the runner think he could come in standing up, without the slide, and then, *boom!* Josh clapped his hands together. "You nail him while he's standing there like a goony bird!" Campy laughed. Josh said, "See that crow?"

"No, Josh, I'm driving, I—"

"All I'm sayin' is that my eyesight's sharp as a cat's claw. Right, baby?"

"I didn't see any crow, Joshy. You must be seein' real well."

Josh was high as a kite on his new sobriety. He flexed his muscles; they felt as strong and wiry as the cables that held up the Brooklyn Bridge. His brain was light, smart, unencumbered by all the crap that always bugged him first thing in the morning. The pain was gone, those headaches that felt as if someone had taken a hatchet to the grey matter. No more of the poison up there. And look outside! The world looked as shiny as a new toaster. His heart pounded fresh blood through his veins, and he swore he could feel it coursing through him. Josh's knees didn't ache. His back didn't ache. Christ, he was even regular. Had he known, he would have straightened out years ago. Years ago!

Grace rubbed Josh's shoulders. She was a nice lady, Campy told himself repeatedly. He wished he liked her more. But Grace had the unfortunate trait of being a real creep when she was strung out, and Campy couldn't forget the foul language, the sexual advances, or the insults. But she was a doll right now. Try to forgive her, just like momma said. It wasn't her fault.

Around noon they pulled into Ruppert Stadium, just a grandstand and a field that butted up against a garbage dump. No individual seats, just benches partitioned with a white line, the fences crammed with outdated advertisements. Crows and seagulls camped there to watch and cackle, stuffed on garbage.

Josh bounded out as Campy slowed the car. He ran to the diamond carrying his bat case. Campy shook his head and said to Grace, "Guess we better follow him."

"Guess so, honey."

The Newark Eagles were taking batting practice in front of a dismal crowd of exactly fourteen. The Eagles were one of the most storied franchises in the Negro Leagues, and had won the pennant just two years ago. But the war—and Bill Veeck's Great Experiment—had depleted their roster to a motley collection of has-beens and never-wases. Campy felt the sense of doom, as if he were in the company of a dying man. Maybe it was the deep, cloying reek of garbage, but it could certainly have been the crowd and the team itself, which practiced with a listlessness he'd never seen in a professional club. They looked moribund out there on the diamond. Even the sun-bleached advertisements forebode a certain decline.

Josh introduced himself, and the players gathered around to pay their respects. Campy walked to the dugout to meet Effa Manley, the Eagles' owner, who stood watching, arms crossed.

"Roy," she said, by way of a greeting.

He removed his hat. "Mrs. Manley, good to see you again."

She squinted at her players. "Good to see me," she said, doing nothing to hide her irritation. "You're lucky I'm allowing you to step foot on this field. The way Josh has been playing . . ."

"He's all straightened out now, ma'am," Campy said. Effa turned to Campy and looked him over, up and down. She always did that to the young men who came in her sight; it made him feel like a piece of meat. Effa was an attractive woman, sporting a sharp grey dress, jacket, perfectly applied cherry-red lipstick, and a baseball cap, which made her look cute. Right now she was angry, and Campy agreed with what he'd heard—that that's when she looked best.

"Your Mr. Veeck and his great experiment have done a swell number on our league, kid," she said. "He knows I can't squawk. I want integration as much as the next guy, but no one's interested in our humble team anymore. With any luck I'll be out of business in a couple years."

"Are our uniforms in the locker room?"

"You going to pay for them?"

"Pay—? C'mon, Mrs. Manley, listen here, I seen the fliers you got posted all over town. Josh and me, for the next six games. You're actin' like this doesn't help you out, two major leaguers playin' for free. But," he said, picking up the equipment bag, "if you want, we'll pack up and go to Harlem, play for the Cuban X club."

She gave him that look again. It was like she enjoyed arguing with him. "Go suit up. Tell the old man to do the same." Campy nodded and went to fetch Josh. "And hey!" she shouted after him. "That woman doesn't come into the clubhouse. In case you didn't know it, she's bad luck."

A crowd of just over seven hundred was on hand to see the Eagles play the New York Black Yankees, and most of them had crowded over the dugout, asking for Josh and Campy. "Five hundred more than usual," their manager said. It looked like it was going to rain, dark storm clouds gathering off in the distance, the humidity making the stench from the dump that much more oppressive.

Josh stood at the plate in the second inning. He rubbed some dirt in his hands, rolled his shoulders, and stepped into the box. Grace called out, "C'mon lover!" A couple of teenagers sarcastically yelled the same thing. Thunder rolled in the distance, and the coming storm threw some gusts their way, kicking up dust. The Yanks' pitcher nodded at the sign and fired his signature fastball.

It was a ball. Campy clapped like Josh had just torn the cover off. "Good eye, Josh!" he shouted.

Josh frowned and stepped back in. This time the pitcher nodded quickly, kicked, and fired.

Josh leaned back ever so slightly, the hands clenched, and West, his bat that day, cut through the air as quick as a sparrow. The ball shot into the darkening sky like a comet returning to space, a little white dot slicing against the wind. It was still rising as it cleared the center-field fence. Josh rounded the bases, clapping the whole way, drinking in the cheers from the feeble crowd. He raised his cap, hoping to make those few fans feel as if they were as great as the crowds at Shibe.

"Damn it all, boy, I saw that thing like it was the goddam fucking moon. And these," he pounded on his thighs, "they ain't achin' at all. Not at all!"

The Eagles won on two homers from Josh, and there might have been more if the skies hadn't opened up in the sixth. That night it was a celebration at Abel's Pharmacy for malteds. They ran through the slashing rain, slipped into the drugstore, Josh laughing all the way. He couldn't stop talking. "And my back son, it feels hard as timber! Firm, you know, and my knees! Didn't give out on me. Normally, rain like this—man, look at it!—I'd be feelin' like someone ground these knees into chuck. But, Roy, I saw that ball comin' in like it was rollin' on the ground. Two!" He shouted after the soda jerk. "Kid, I hit a pair of homers today!" He grabbed Grace by the waist and squeezed her. She gave a little squeal. Josh turned to Campy. "Okay, okay, now, son, listen." He leaned in. "I'm all thrilled and such, but I want to know, and truthfully, how was the moundsman? That lanky kid, he throwin' well?"

"Well, sure Josh, I'll be square with you. He wasn't as good as our starters, but good enough. And you hit one off his fastball and one off his curve, and I'd say the curve was quality."

"The curve was quality," Josh repeated, with a quiet reverence to his voice. "Damn, Roy, we're back. I mean, you been back the whole time, but between us, we're both back. Know what I mean? I mean, heck, we're going to tear it up, ain't we?"

Campy smiled. Just one game, he reminded himself. "Sure, Josh."

But it wasn't just one game. In fact, in the next game, against the Yanks' best pitcher, Josh hit five first pitches for five home runs. "I never seen anything like it!" the manager yelled, and even Effa Manley was hooting from her seat behind home.

On each pitch Josh's short swing cut through the air and knocked the ball so hard it seemed as if it had been made lopsided the way it spun in the air. Behind the plate he gunned down two runners and worked the pitchers well. And that morning it had been Josh who roused Campy from bed, and it had been Josh who worked with both Campy and the catcher for the Eagles.

Josh woke Campy each day, took batting practice, actually jogged—something Campy loathed—and worked out before and after each game. He ate ravenously and didn't even want a beer. The guy was emotional: at night he'd sometimes cry for all the time he'd lost, or cry because he read that the A's had lost (they split the Boston series, two games apiece). But the next day, in front of another capacity crowd, it was three homers and a double. "Moonballs, Roy. Things look like he plucked 'em out of the sky to throw at me. What can I do but try to stick 'em back where they belong?"

In the last game, Josh threw out the first pitch, was given a set of luggage and a silver cup for his performance. He cried again, tipped his cap, and promised them a real show. Campy never even had a chance to play, and he literally thanked God for that, praying every night with fervor that Josh would carry his performance back to Philadelphia.

They drove back to Philly, sipping milkshakes, all three in the front seat. The cheers were still ringing in Josh's ears. "If only I'd cleaned up earlier, son," he said. "Then you 'n' I'd be fighting for the All-Star spot."

"You'd be the All-Star. Besides, I'm not going anyway."

Josh sat up straight. "Nuts. Look, Roy, you going. Mark my words, it's you and Satch and Buck, prob'ly the Cuban. Son of a bitch is something else. But as for you, who's a better plateman? No one but the youth, right, babe?"

"Sure, baby, sure. But honey, you were all over that stadium! Hits, doubles, triples, how many homers? That's All-Star too."

Josh clenched and unclenched his left hand. "Seven. I think seven."

"No, no," Campy laughed. "Josh you hit *twelve*. Twelve in five games. And let's say you cut that in half up in Philly. Golly, Josh, I'd say that'd be pretty good."

They drove through the night. Josh and Grace fell asleep. Campy stared at the sunset, nothing but embers against the tops of the black silhouettes of the trees. He looked down at the dash. There was a little statuette of the Virgin Mary lit by the blue glow of the dashboard light. "Mary," Campy whispered, "I'd give up bein' in the All-Star Game you let Josh come back. I light a candle every day, though I guess you know that. On my knees every night too. Oh, and help Grace too." He thought he should add something more profound, but the drive dulled his thoughts. "Okay. Amen."

◇ **14** ◇

Sam, Wheeling and Dealing

"Bill," Eleanor said, "have you heard a word I said?"

The Veeck children fidgeted in the relentless sunlight on their father's rooftop bleachers. Bill Jr. and Peter, Veeck's nine- and four-year-old sons, climbed over their father as he squinted through a pair of binoculars at the ruckus on the field. There was a hot silence between the parents to match the heat of the day.

"What?" he said, letting the glasses fall to his chest. "Sorry, El, I missed that last part. Say, everyone having a good time?"

Bill Jr. squinted and placed his hand on his forehead for a visor. "Why couldn't I spin the wheel, Daddy? I wanted to pick where Deegee played."

The phone rang. Veeck patted Bill on the head. "Sorry, son, just one spin a game."

"Tomorrow?"

"Well, no . . . Eleanor?" he said to his wife, sitting with her arms crossed on the far end of the bleachers. "Can you explain why he can't?" He picked up the phone. "Yes? Yeah, Sam, I can see. Twenty-three-four isn't so bad. It's no sellout, but . . . What do you mean, no press? No one took a photo of the Wheel for tomorrow's paper? What do I have to do? Didn't you have a photographer there. . . . No, I'm not blaming you . . . well, okay, I *am* blaming you, don't take it so . . ." Veeck almost dropped the phone. "El! Pete's into the booze again!"

Eleanor scowled and wrestled a can of beer from Peter. "This is a wonderful idea, honey," she said, sarcastically. "I'm glad we're all one big happy family again."

"Sam, listen, I—Eleanor! Watch Bill Jr.! Listen, Sam, I'll call you in the seventh."

Eleanor pulled her son closer, whispered in his ear, and pointed to the diamond. Eleanor was a beautiful woman, athletic, freckled, looking every bit the professional horse rider that she was. Her muscles were bunched from use, she didn't look as good in dresses and silk, but in her trademark jeans and sport shirts she could take any man's breath away. Or, as with that afternoon, she could instill fear like no one else.

"So this is how it's going to be?" she said. "Us sitting up here on the roof, sniffing tar fumes and watching ants run around the bases."

"It's not that far away. Besides, El, you know this is how I live . . . I can't go into the ballpark."

"The kids would like to see the game without binoculars," she said. "And they would like to ride their horses and . . ."

"Oh, now! Pete!" he said, groaning as he pulled his son up to his lap. "Wouldn't you rather be up here, looking out over the whole city?"

"Where is everybody?" Bill Jr. said. "Momma told me there'd be lots of other kids."

"You said that? It's usually just reporters, El. When they show."

"Those lushes?" Eleanor said. "You didn't say *drunks*. You said *crowds*."

"They're not all drunks. And I just thought . . ."

Eleanor gestured to Bill Jr. to sit between her and Veeck. "You realize I still have Mercury in the stables?"

"We can ship her up here. Listen, El, would I have sent for you if I didn't feel we could work this out? You know I think about you day in and day—"

"Day in and day out, when the sun's up or the stars are shining, yes, Bill, I remember. I remember how you used to act. But I also remember Pete's birthday. Do you?"

"Well . . ."

"Oh, that's right, you had to go on the radio to plug the team."

"Well, we made—"

"Now here were are, homeless. The kids enjoyed their school. They had friends. They had room to play."

Pete squinted through the binoculars and said, "Who's that fat man with the helmet?"

"Why, that's a guy with your name!" Veeck shouted. "He's called Pete Adelis. If you listen carefully, you can hear his roaring."

Eleanor grimaced. "Why don't you stop him? I've read what he's saying! It's awful."

"He's paying a lot of money for that privilege. He's never actually *profane*. Oh, my!" Veeck slapped his forehead; one of the Browns had just knocked a double into the gap. Peter slapped his forehead like his father and said, "Ouch."

"Some game, hey, guys? You know, your old man used to work in a ballpark, Wrigley Field. When you're big enough, Bill, I'll have *you* working in Shibe. Would you like that?"

Eleanor asked, "You miss your horses, Bill?" Young Bill frowned and nodded quickly, as did Pete.

"Hey, son, watch this." Veeck set Pete down to his side, then pulled out a pocketknife, unfolded it, and held it up to his kids. "How many fathers can do this?" He plunged the knife into his wooden leg. The kids' eyes popped wide. Pete, stunned for a moment, began to wail.

"Good God, Bill!" she said, pulling Pete onto her other knee. "You're scaring the kids."

"Let me do that, Daddy!"

Veeck pulled the knife out, folded it, and put it back in his pocket. "Bill, your mom's right, we'd better take it easy."

"Can I use the knife?"

"No, son."

"Can I spin the wheel tomorrow?"

"Bill—"

The phone rang. Veeck sprang for it. "Hello? Sam, now's not the time . . ." Sam kept on. Veeck suddenly noticed his neighbor, pointing behind him. "What?" Veeck mouthed.

"Your wife's leaving."

He spun around. "Where are you going?"

"We're going to watch the game at the stadium," Eleanor said, rushing with her pile of kids to the door leading down to his apartment. "And then . . . I don't know. Maybe we'll go back to Tucson with my folks. Bill, I hoped that this would . . . never mind. C'mon kids."

"Wait . . ." Veeck yelled into the receiver, "Sam, I'm going to have to chase down my family. Have some more beer and watch the game and we'll start thinking about the money—" he looked at his watch "—in two hours." He hung up. Veeck hobbled as fast as he could down the stairs and out the front door. Twenty-first Street was packed with vendors and cars and people—his family had vanished into the crowd. As he stood among the children waiting for home-run balls, beneath the white-hot sun, Veeck felt tired, so physically exhausted in fact, he swore he could feel his artificial leg ache.

After the game—which the A's won on a screaming homer by Buck, and despite Josh's four strikeouts—an elderly woman, one of Veeck's many paying customers, chattered away while Veeck glanced down at the calendar. Sure enough, there had been a crisis each and every day since Monte Irvin had been drafted right after Opening Day. With El walking out on him, this one wasn't any different. He had suffered through a lot in Milwaukee—the lights blinking out, some vendor coming unglued when Veeck doubled an order, the team lush ending up in the clink—but as of late it seemed like the things you used to be able to count on were becoming wobbly, as if he'd look out the window to find that Shibe had suddenly warped and buckled in the summer heat. Food, drink, security, a good team winning . . . all of these had simply vanished. Veeck sat at his desk, trying to listen to the elderly woman sitting across from him. She was just some fan who came in with a beef about this or a suggestion about that: Veeck's door was always open and his phone number in the book like everyone else's. Unbelievably, he took fewer calls than one would think, maybe a dozen a day from the fans, one crackpot a week, if that. Racists never called, they just sent anonymous notes. This lady sitting across from him, she worked in a greengrocers, was a home-maker and proud of it, a jowly woman who looked like her clothes doubled as aprons. She was simply ringing in on the fact that the juggling vendors maybe ought to come to Section 151 more often, where she sat, with her little niece and nephew, eleven- and nine-year-olds, and those kids loved them, golly *she* loved them, why didn't they do that? Come up to 151 more often?

Veeck agreed that was a good idea and wrote it down. That's why he left the door open—you couldn't keep up on everything yourself, and the fan could tell you things you wouldn't think up in a million years. You oblige them, they come back. She kept on about all the great people who sat in 151, some of the best fans in the league. From a cardboard satchel she pulled out scorecards from every home game. Veeck looked down at his calendar, to a note he'd scribbled on that day's square, from another telephone call late the night before.

Veeck interrupted her soliloquy to say, "Let me ask you, uh . . ."

"Teagarten! Mrs. Lucy Teagarten," she said, with a respectful bow from her seat.

"Sorry. Mrs. Teagarten, who do you think ought to be in the All-Star Game?"

Wrong question. Ten minutes later Lucy concluded with her charged whisper, "There's absolutely no reason other than dad-blame politics that'll keep those boys—" meaning Roy Campanella, Ray Dandridge, and Martín Dihigo (she made sure to go in alphabetical order) "—from being starters. *Starters*, Mr. Veeck! Even if Ray's got a low average, he's got the RBIs and the fielding to be the star of any team! Just Buck and Satchel is an insult. To us fans and the players! I mean, gosh . . ."

Veeck nodded thoughtfully. "I agree. You make strong arguments."

"Why, they ought to let us fans decide! It's democracy! It was a crime they ever took the vote away . . . ," and Veeck listened patiently for another five minutes.

Finally he asked, "And what would you think if the commissioner canceled the All-Star Game?"

Lucy shook her head abruptly, as if she'd tasted something bitter that was supposed to be sweet. Her jowls quivered as she said, "No All-Star . . . ?"

"If it were canceled?"

"He wouldn't . . . ?"

"But *what if he did*. For argument's sake."

"Why would he?" she said, breathlessly.

Veeck stretched in his seat. "Let's say that he claimed it was to keep wartime travel to a minimum."

Lucy huffed. "Well, gosh darn it all. I mean . . . well, gol blame it all!"

"That'd bother you?"

"Gol blame it all!" Lucy gripped her chair, and her eyes bulged as if Veeck had just said a dirty word. "Travel . . . that's a bunch of, well, it's like what my boss always says, that's nothing but a bunch of bullhooey! Only he says it worse."

"Well, that's one way of putting it," Veeck said, standing. "Keep your chin up, Mrs. Teagarten. They just ended the blackout restrictions, so Landis won't cancel the All-Star Game. Nothing but a rumor, I'm sure."

She cursed the commissioner as she stood to leave, forgetting all that she'd come for. Veeck thanked her and escorted her out. Then he craned his neck out the front door. No one else was waiting.

A pal of his with the Pittsburgh Pirates had heard the news. The commissioner had spoken with Ralph Benswager, the owner of the Pirates, about canceling this year's All-Star Game, supposedly on account of the travel restrictions, even though it hadn't kept them from having All-Star Games in the past. It wasn't hard to figure out: why give the Negroes a national showcase to display their talents? Why show them mingling with the white players on the same team? Why give Bill Veeck any more money? Well, well, Veeck thought as he sat down, Landis is becoming quite the aggressor. It seemed to Veeck as if Landis were saying, "Your move . . ."

Veeck had a plan to force the game, but now he was beginning to think differently. Curiously enough, Colonel Jacob Ruppert, the crazy old man who owned the New York Yankees, and for whom Veeck felt a particular and nourishing hatred, had one weakness: the colonel thought that Sam Dailey was, in fact, a brilliant young man. He'd said that to a number of people, including Bill Veeck back when he was still a nobody in Milwaukee. Lately old man Ruppert was grumbling that young Dailey was being wasted with the Athletics, wasted in Philadelphia, and wasted in the company of Bill Veeck. Someday he should come work for the New York Yankees. When Veeck shared his plan with Sam the night before, it was one of the few times he'd heard Sam chuckle with glee: Sam loved the idea of working with Ruppert, as if on the sly, like a spy with the OSS. The idea was, before Landis could cancel the game, Sam would suggest to Ruppert that both teams donate their share of the All-Star gate to the war bond drive. Really hype the thing up. Ruppert himself could have the press conference, forcing the judge to hold the game. Sam was absolutely giddy. "Wow, Bill, we'll really stick Landis in the ribs for once. It's about time too. Even if we don't get the cash, the All-Star Game's worth it for the publicity."

Perhaps for the first time, however, Veeck didn't feel particularly joyous about the scheme. And it wasn't even the fact that he was handing over vast sums of money. It was a fact known to practically every baseball-loving American that the Athletics needed every drop of the green and then some. The Ruppert Plan would at least allow the All-Star Game to continue, and its publicity would allow the A's to reel in more fans, and maybe, just maybe, trigger more ideas for fun and profit. What those were, he didn't know.

But Mrs. Teagarten sent his thoughts down an entirely different path. The Ruppert Plan, like many of his other schemes, was reactive. Sure, they could surprise the commissioner, really stick it to him and force the game to go on (a noble cause), but then he would be fighting alone. The Ruppert Plan meant that Veeck and Ruppert came off as benevolent owners, and Landis, who would no doubt approve the whole affair, would emerge unscathed. But as Veeck's little discussion just now proved, the fans knew the commissioner was no pal of the Philadelphia Athletics. They knew he would do nearly anything to keep them from success. But they certainly didn't know everything. They didn't know about the beer, or the continued problems with the city sanitation department, neither of which was a problem for Connie Mack when he owned the A's . . . and when the park was a dump. Veeck believed the judge had his mitts in Irvin's drafting, probably in some troubles he didn't even know about. Spink was Landis's puppet, but the fans didn't know that. So might it not be better to drag the fans into the fight? If my last-place team can rile up Lucy Teagarten's gall, Veeck thought, imagine what keeping my All-Stars at home would do?

At that moment, through his open window, came the irritated honking of a car, a series of short, sharp blasts and the guttural cry "Come on, already!" Veeck's eyes thinned. This guy came to pick up his pal every day at this time, to head off to the factory. Carpooling due to that cursed transit strike. With every frustrated honk, it was as if Veeck were receiving a divine response to his questions. As the strike ground on, oddly enough it brought more fans out for the Athletics, nearly filling the park for the last game against the Tigers. While the A's were in Boston and New York, the rhetoric surrounding this transit strike grew worse and worse, and as people hoofed it to the factories, they began to do the math: it was the racists who were keeping them from work. The union kept on barking that they weren't going to let the Negroes drive, and that's that. Nobody shut those union drivers up. They spoke, and their big mouths were burying them. Maybe it was time he got the commissioner to do some yapping and dig his own hole.

Veeck called Sam, who answered the phone on the first ring. Sam was staring out the window of the Oval Office, which he'd occupied since Veeck's ban. At that moment he was watching Josh take batting practice and wondering why, now that the catcher was dried out, the hits weren't coming. According to Campanella, Gibson was clean and had torn up his five games in Newark. Now he was slumping. Gibson hadn't a hit since coming back. Before Sam could speak, Veeck got right to the point.

Forget their plan to force an All-Star Game, he said. They were just going to ride it out. "Why is that?" Sam asked, spinning around in his chair. "No, I understand. Bill, you're right. When you're right, you're right. I won't call Ruppert. Okay. Talk to you after the game."

Sam hung up, then turned and admired the sunny green of Shibe. The groundskeepers were busy prepping the field for that day's game. He leaned forward in his chair and looked down at the best seats in the house, right behind home. Adelis wasn't there yet. He was really making poor Wilson go crazy. They had to do something about that guy.

Fortunately that day Sam was looking at a near sellout. Unfortunately their last-place standing was hurting their ability to sell out the other ballparks. Unfortunately the strike would keep many of those fans from using their tickets, which also meant less money from concessions. Unfortunately, if the All-Star Game were canceled they'd lose all that good press. Sam sighed. He was lucky to have one "fortunate" for every three "unfortunates." All he could see were expenses. The clock in center with four bulbs out. Bill's fireworks were another arm-and-a-leg expense. Night baseball means the lights come on—electricity costs money, and that's more cash down the drain.

Sam ran his hand over his chin and readjusted the already tight knot on his perfectly straight tie. Bill Veeck really did a number in Milwaukee, but this was the major leagues. Bill was becoming sentimental, wasn't operating to the best of his capacity. Fun is good, but the team was in last, they weren't going anywhere. They might lose the ball club, and nothing Sam could say could convince him of that. For one year he and Bill would operate a last-place club and then throw it away. What difference would it make to keep every single one of these players? Sam reached for the phone, then paused. He stared at it. It seemed to loom large on his desk. Finally he picked it up and dialed Horace Stoneham, owner of the New York Giants.

Stoneham picked up after nine rings. It sounded as if he were juggling the receiver.

"Mr. Stoneham?" Sam asked.

"Sure! Yes, I mean. Who is it?"

"Sam Dailey with the Philadelphia Athletics."

"Of course, of course," he said, as if expecting the call. "So what the hell's the matter with you?"

Stoneham had run the Giants since 1936, and in that time had become known as one of the shrewdest judges of baseball talent as well as the game's most durable alcoholic. Each day he met the morning hung over, and proved he wasn't a fool by fervently sticking to his rule that you never touched a drop of liquor before 11 a.m., except holidays and early morning games.

"The matter?" Sam craned his neck and adjusted his tie again. He wished he had a glass of water. "Do you remember our conversation, Mr. Stoneham?"

"Do I remember? The hell's the matter with you, of course I remember. The Giants are still in the shit, you can read the papers. We win eight, then lose six. Right in the middle of the pack, jump up, then fall back down. Can't get people to come to the Polo Grounds if I paid 'em myself. Besides, what do you care? You fellows have some first-class ideas, but you're in the soup like I am. Your niggers fill your park, but they can't win. Some of your boys, though, I drink a toast to them."

Sam heard the sound of Horace doing just that. He glanced at his watch. 11:30. God, Stoneham didn't sound as if he remembered anything at all. "Mr. Stoneham, what about Buck Leonard?"

"What about him?"

"Think he might help the Giants? Like we discussed?"

Stoneham laughed, a wheezy, cigarette-and-booze laugh. "Are you crazy? No, Leonard wouldn't help me, just like Williams and DiMaggio don't help their teams. You must be drunk."

"Remember . . . we discussed your joining our little experiment?"

"Experiment? I don't like fireworks, the noise—"

"Mr. Stoneham, what about Buck Leonard?"

He roared, "What about him?"

"You could be the first in the National League to integrate."

"How would I do that?"

"You're weak at first base."

"Okay, so I'm weak at first. You just now figured that out?"

Sam blew out a hot, frustrated breath. "Mr. Stoneham, I want to trade Buck Leonard."

There was a long silence on the other end. "How's that?"

"We talked about this last week. As I said, you're weak at first. We've got the solution."

"Weak at first," Stoneham repeated. "You don't mean . . ."

"Buck Leonard, just like I said."

"Hold on." Sam could hear Stoneham pouring another drink. "You're giving me the pennant, you understand?"

"That's fine. It's not like we're anywhere near a pennant, Mr. Stoneham."

"With your talent, you ought to be closer to the top. Sure you want to do this?"

"If I don't, I lose this ball club." Sam was sweating buckets; his mind raced, the lapses had been too long, he had to talk more, calm the old boy down. As he grew more concerned, he kept adjusting his tie until he was almost choking. "Listen, Mr. Stoneham, Leonard could break Ruth's record, right there in the Polo Grounds. With those short foul lines of yours . . ."

"That sure would be a draw. What's your price?"

Sam just about jumped out of his seat. He could see why Bill loved dealing. "Mr. Stoneham, first let me tell you my vision. I see a white man playing on the A's and a Negro in the National League. One of each on both teams." Stoneham was silent, and Sam hoped it was from rapt attention. "Buck has the character to withstand the abuse all by himself. Furthermore, he's one of the greatest players in history."

"I agree, I agree."

"Frankly, I think you could make him a player/manager."

Sounding a great deal more sober, Stoneham said, "But I have a player/manager in Mel Ott."

"Not if you trade him to us. Plus cash."

"Ott's the soul of the Giants, and a great player himself."

"And Leonard's the soul of the A's. Only he's better. Mr. Stoneham, is Ott batting like Leonard?"

"No."

"Has he hit as many home runs?"

"But managing? Would my boys listen to a colored man?"

"They'd listen to Buck Leonard."

"But Ott . . ."

"I understand. You have to think it over. You need a day?"

"That would be great."

"Sounds fine by me." Then Sam summoned up a lie. "But call me by ten tomorrow, because Rickey's interested, and—"

"Rickey! He's looking into this?"

"Of course. We're thinking Dixie Walker and cash."

"Walker'd go insane playing with niggers! He's from the South, the deep South. He's on record saying—"

"I know, Horace, I know. You and I have a better fit."

Stoneham was quiet. "Fine. Ott and twenty grand."

Sam just about dropped the phone. "Uh, well . . . we'd mentioned nearly a hundred before. . . ."

"I would have remembered *that*. Thirty's my highest price."

Sam blinked. "I . . . maybe I ought to call Rickey. . . ."

Stoneham laughed. "Be my guest. Call Rickey and you'll give him Buck and pay fifty grand for the privilege. I'm giving you Ott and thirty. You gotta understand the risks I'm taking. See, with you, you got a team of coloreds. Me, I got a team of white men. That's extra security, tension, separate hotels, the works. I'm not paying a ton for an *experiment*." He said it like it was a dirty word.

"How about fifty?"

"Come to think about it, Ott's a calming influence. What if Leonard's a lousy manager? In fact, I wouldn't use him at all to lead. So I'd have to buy me another manager. I don't know."

Sam cleared his throat. "I'll go as low as forty."

"I'll give you thirty. Provided it's Ott and the cash for Leonard and Barnhill."

"Barnhill?"

"Why not? You don't really want him around. Kid's trouble. I'm willing to take all the trouble off your hands. You oughta give *me* thirty just for the privilege."

Sam thought on it. Barnhill *was* a problem. "Well . . . I suppose that sounds about right. Leonard and Barnhill and fifty," he said, glad that Stoneham wasn't there to see him, as his hands were shaking. "But it wouldn't take place until after the All-Star Game. If the game's canceled, we'll announce it in Washington, D.C., on the 14th.

The All-Star Game will be Buck's last glorious moment as an Athletic." Sam was even beginning to sound like Bill.

After a pause, which Sam thought was yet another drink, Stoneham said, "Bill won't give us any trouble, will he?"

"He'll be against it. But I'm president and the only one with authority. Landis might try to block it, but the way things are, I can't see how."

Stoneham whistled. "Well, Sam, this is just the kind of trade that makes this job so damned fun. Draw up the papers. Ott and thirty for Leonard and Barnhill. Call me tomorrow when it's all done."

"No, fifty . . ." But Stoneham had hung up. Sam stared at the phone. A lightheadedness filled him. Warm breezes brushed the back of his neck. Sam Dailey just about jumped out of his chair and out the window of the Oval Office. He should have been running this club from the get-go! It set his mind working: sell off the older players, keep the youngsters for the future. The A's weren't going anywhere but fourth, if they were lucky, and in three or four years, when the war was over, they'd be rich with talent. Monte Irvin and Campy'll be that much older and stars both. Heck, that's *if* the war lasted that long—maybe even next year! With the crowds this big for a losing team! "Whoa, ho-ho!" he yelled.

"Something wrong, Mr. Dailey?" Dot asked, stepping in.

"No way, Dottie. Say, take the afternoon off."

"Oh, thank you, Mr. Dailey."

He swirled around and watched batting practice. Buck Leonard. Ray Dandridge. Cool Papa Bell and Willie Wells. Outside of Buck, for those three, he could land a good hundred grand, enough to keep the team and then some. If things went from bad to worse, Satchel would have to bring in a quarter of million dollars, the most ever. Sam snapped his fingers. Satch was so good, Ruppert might even want him. If they kept Campy, Jethroe, Benson, all the kids, why, in three years get Irvin back from the war and they'd be the best team in the country. With profit to spare!

The plan folded open like a crisp road map in his head. Bill had it right at the start—sign these guys for a decent salary, the young guys for next to nothing. But if Bill thought to sell them later, he certainly forgot it. The old guys were hitting just well enough to beef up that almighty price tag. And, Sam told himself, he was integrating the National League as well, something to be proud about. He pulled his chair close to the window and watched the Athletics run to the field for jumping jacks, and he smiled. The stands were starting to fill. St. Louis in town, a good draw. More if there were buses and trolleys. Sam noticed that the strike hadn't kept Adelis from showing up; he was out there, already giving them grief. Buck and Ray were busy offering more pointers to Artie. They really knew how to help that kid. . . .

Sam stared out at center field. Cool was there, signing autographs with Sam Jethroe. Jethroe was finally hitting the pill and stealing bases, fast as lightning, "Faster than the word o' God," Cool bragged. Good thing Cool had been there. Too bad Artie was still struggling. For that matter, it was too bad Josh's time in Newark hadn't amounted to anything—the guy couldn't hit if his bat were three feet wide. He seemed sobered up, but that was it. Despite this, Sam chuckled at his ingenuity. Buck was already signing autographs for the kids straining over the wall by third base. "Ott'll be a good addition," Sam told himself. He watched Buck shout encouragement to Wilson, rallying his club. Sam pulled the blinds down. Why did he feel so moody all of a sudden? "All that money . . ." Sam turned abruptly and jerked the front of his suit straight. "Well, above all," he said, "I've saved this team."

That day it had been St. Louis. Boston, the Yankees, then the Indians and Tigers had come through, and the Athletics had split those four series, seven wins against seven losses. The day before, the A's lost the first game to the Browns, but that afternoon they pounded the Southerners in sweet revenge, to a full house. In the eighth, with the bases loaded, the fans watched with awe as Leonard stepped in, fouled off the first pitch, and then chopped a fastball clear across Twenty-first for home run number thirty-eight.

After the game, while the players showered and dressed, Pea Webber, the clubhouse attendant, walked in with the afternoon paper under his arm. "Sorry to tell you, boys," he said, though he loved being the bearer of news, "but the judge canned the All-Star Game. Gotta sacrifice, I guess. Let the soldiers have their travel." Then he tossed the paper on the bench in front of him and said, "And the army's takin' over the trolleys. Big news day."

The next morning Veeck had a breakfast meeting with the vendors' union, and on the way he rode the trolleys, listening. Grumblings about the commissioner and how he wasn't giving the A's a fair shake. Grumblings about the unions, how they weren't nothing but a bunch of idiots tryin' to ruin things at home. You couldn't hear the complaints about one without the other being mentioned. They were tangled together like the vines climbing the Shibe outfield. One guy was actually writing a letter to his senator, right there on the bus. He read it to Veeck: how Landis was out to get them, and what the hell, they hadn't canceled an All-Star Game yet. Just like the unions and those colored drivers. "Gee, Christ," said one fellow, who Veeck swore had been bullying his club from the bleachers just two weeks back. "Let's say our guys pull it out, that old bastard gonna cancel the World Series too?"

In two days' time the strike came crashing to a halt when the union finally grew sick of hearing not only the press but the citizenry howling at them night and day. Their drivers, who inexplicably wore their Transit Company jackets wherever they went, were spat upon, served lukewarm dinners at their favorite restaurants, ignored by bartenders, and generally loathed. The feds were on the verge of lowering the hammer and taking the system over entirely when it was announced that the Transit Company was back in operation with four new Negro drivers. When those trolleys hit the streets, the city celebrated like they'd just won the pennant.

The commissioner's announcement came as a complete surprise to J. G. Taylor Spink. That afternoon, in the sweltering news office in downtown St. Louis, as Spink was tapping away at the next issue's lead story, he heard a timid knock on his door. "Come in, Beth," he said.

His secretary Beth, a prim, elderly woman nearly six feet tall, wearing a look of indignation, entered. "I thought you should see this, sir." She handed him a telegram.

Spink read it, and as he did his face registered confusion. "When did the commissioner call?" he asked.

"He never called."

Spink didn't like that. When he'd asked Judge Landis a few days earlier if the rumors were true, to get him on the record, Landis claimed he had not heard the rumors himself. But, Spink recalled, he never said they *weren't true*. For the first time, Landis had kept *him* in the dark. "Thank you, Beth," he said. "Please be sure to have that memo I gave you typed up by the end of the day."

"It's in your box already, sir."

"Oh." Spink nodded, and she turned and walked out, closing the door quietly behind her. He folded his arms and tried to concentrate on his newest article, which argued that Buck Leonard, while talented, had to be measured against the players in the league, which, of course, had been decimated by the war. Leonard's home-run total, which might exceed Ruth's, was nonetheless tainted. . . .

Spink yanked it out of his Underwood, crumpled the piece, and threw it to the trash can, where it bounced off the rim and rolled slowly into a corner. Spink cleaned his glasses. He straightened up his desk. He turned and stared out the window at the Mississippi River crawling to the sea. He turned back to his pad, picked up his pencil, and licked it. The white page opened up before him, wide as the afternoon sky, an emptiness into which he was falling headfirst.

"Forget it," he said, rallying himself. Baseball was weak and everyone knew it. So why'd they need an All-Star Game? To display this weakness? Why, Landis should have canceled the games at the onset of the war. In fact Landis ought to make certain that the war years were somehow recorded differently, in a separate ledger perhaps, records marked with an asterisk to separate them from the legitimate numbers of the hallowed greats. The records were tainted. If Buck broke Ruth's record, well, it's easier with half the league fighting in Europe and the Pacific.

Nat Low's voice filled his head. Low had been arguing with him the week before, arguing this very point, questioning DiMaggio's fifty-six game streak. "Well," Low had said, "you might do the same for your boys. Think about it: if Joltin' Joe had met Satch during the streak, it might have ended, say, in the sixteenth game. Or Dihigo. Or Mathis, or Jefferson, or . . ."

It was a preposterous argument. Spink's jaw ached at the thought of it. No one could argue against the Streak! Or Williams batting .406 in the same year! True, true, if Satch had met Williams ten times, and if Ted had gone hitless, he'd have fallen below the magic number. But that hadn't happened.

Spink took a sip of lukewarm coffee and stared at the blank piece of paper. His thoughts turned to the A's last series against the Indians, just five days ago. He leaned back, opened the drawer, and pulled out the scorebook. He'd meticulously scored the game as he always did, and looking it over he found himself in a state of constant agitation. That game. It gave him thrills even then. Earlier, recounting the game over the phone to his wife, she had to yell, "Tom, Tom, you're shouting! What's the matter with you?"

Dihigo was the matter. That particular game the Wheel of Fortune had turned slowly, as if held back by a divine hand, and finally stuck for the first time on JACK OF ALL TRADES. "Ladies and gentlemen!" roared the MC, sweeping his free hand around the diamond. "Today Martín Dihigo will play every single position!"

"This ought to be good!" Low said, pulling up a chair between Spink and Burley. Spink shifted his seat a few inches away. In his excitement, Low had a tendency to spill things, and Spink didn't want his scorebook soiled.

Dihigo began behind the plate, catching, and he fared well, working the pitcher through a one-two-three inning. Then he moved on to first in the second inning, even scooped up one of Dandridge's throws in the dirt—no big deal. But in the third, playing second, Dihigo bounded over, dove, and snared what should have been a driving hit up the middle. He leaped up and fired to Buck, now at first. All three writers gave a start. Burley said, "Wells couldn't have made the play. Hell, there isn't a player in the league who could have, before the war *or* after!"

In the fourth, Dihigo turned his attentions to shortstop, and he worked a double play, fielding a bounding ball with ease. "Soft hands," Low said, and he elbowed Spink and made his pencil scratch across the page.

The Cuban played third base in the fifth, when Lou Boudreau smashed what should have been a triple down the left-field line. Except that Dihigo snared the curving shot in the web of his glove a good eight feet in foul territory, stopped, turned, and fired to first, the ball parallel to the ground the whole way, smashing into Buck's glove with a loud slap that could be heard in the upper deck. Boudreau, the speedy Boudreau, was out by five feet.

"That shut 'em up!" Low roared, slapping Spink on the back. Spink winced. Low was too loud. But he didn't say anything, pausing to admire the hieroglyphs on his scorecard. He ran his fingers across the front of the page.

Sixth inning, left field, just a fly ball to the Cuban, handled easily. After the seventh inning stretch, when Spike Jones played the most ear-grating rendition of "Take Me Out to the Ball Game," complete with cowbells, tubas, and a hot-water bottle that he'd manipulated to sound as flatulent as a cow, Dihigo worked center. First pitch was a lousy hanging curve that Indians third baseman Roy Cullenbine knocked into deep center. Dihigo froze, followed the ball against the sun, then turned and sprinted. He raced to the wall, looking back, then leapt, turning sideways as he reached up and caught the ball. He hit the wall feet first, ricocheted off, and backflipped to the ground standing up.

It took the crowd a split second to register what had just happened. The men in the press box were quiet, then jumped from their seats and scrambled to the phones and began shouting their stories to their editors far away. Spink didn't move but sat, pencil in hand, staring down at Dihigo, already crouched and waiting for the next pitch in center, as if he'd just caught a lazy pop up. Spink marked the play with a little star.

"Say, Tom," Burley said, "you okay? You're pale as a ghost."

Spink smiled, nervously. "Too much coffee."

And that was that. Right field didn't give Dihigo anything to do. In the ninth, on the mound, the Maestro shut down the Indians on seven pitches. "And the guy only went 3 for 5 with two doubles," Burley laughed.

Afterward Spink made his way to the Athletics dugout to talk with Dihigo. The Cuban spoke politely. More knowledgeable, Spink thought, than half the players I see every day, even back in peacetime.

Then there was Buck. Leonard was always a model of courtesy, Spink thought, one of the great spokesmen for the game. Buck asked him if Cleveland's Allie Reynolds still had the curve, if Spink thought they'd see it tomorrow. They spoke for about ten minutes and shook hands. Right then, it was like a switch had been flipped in Spink's head. He couldn't remember the last time he'd felt a grip so strong.

Staring at that scorebook back in his St. Louis office, he *could* finally remember. Babe Ruth. Immediately he shook the thought away. Leonard's no Ruth. He's a good ballplayer, Spink was content with that. He leaned over the page and began to type.

Commissioner Landis has rightly canceled the All-Star Game, but those players too good for the military have, as usual, a hundred complaints. . . .

Spink's emptiness returned, filling him up, swallowing any good feeling he'd summoned up that day.

He finished the article, which praised the commissioner's wisdom and berated his critics, though of course Spink hadn't actually heard one word of criticism. As he stepped out of his office, he handed the paper to Beth and said, "Take it down to Hal, see that it gets it into the next issue."

"Tomorrow's?"

"Absolutely. When you're done, you can go. It's a beautiful day, the Cardinals are playing."

Beth glanced at the page, and her face fell. "What a shame." She stood and turned off the reading lamp on her desk. "Maybe someday they'll get a chance. Are you going to the game?"

"I'll be taking a train to Philadelphia. To cover the Browns."

"The Browns," Beth said. "Funny how often your coverage coincides with the A's."

"Have a good afternoon, Beth," he replied. She walked briskly away, through the halls of the *Sporting News*. Spink didn't say anything. He watched her go. Glancing at his watch, he noticed there was still time to hop a train to Philadelphia.

◇ **15** ◇

Satchel vs. Josh

Satchel Paige loved to fly. He had bought himself a silver Budd Conestoga airplane, with a bulbous nose that made it look like some kind of sea mammal. The thing spelled class, he'd say, it spelled speed, and it set ol' Satch apart from the crowd. The Conestoga was fitted with a dozen rotating, reclining leather seats, a wet bar, a foldout bed, a phonograph, and plenty of space to cut a rug, should Satch have the right company. Little lamps with cherry-red shades made the mood just right.

Satchel's entourage was on its way from Philadelphia to New York City. Following an oval of bright light that slunk across the floor, Satch ignored the constant barrage of questions, leaned over in his seat, and stared out the window. It was a brilliantly sunny day. Little squares of farmland spread out beneath him. Damn those folks, he thought, workin' they tails off when there's so much more to life. 'Spose it had to be that way, the little people struggling, wrestling with life, scraping together their pennies to see Satch pitch. Or listen to old Satchel on the radio. He sighed. Satch wished he could pop a window and get some fresh breezes blowing through the plane. He felt stuffy, confined. Having just finished holding court with ten different reporters from across the nation, he was eager to settle down, relax, and then get to a ballpark. He looked at his watch. Only an hour to go. Far below, the farmland thickened into suburbs, the suburbs into city.

Wing Henry leaned in and said, "Satch, Satch, you've got to finish about Bismarck." Wing was, according to the business card he palmed off in every handshake, *The Personal Biographer of Leroy "Satchel" Paige.* Wing was a gruff, tiny, plump, bespectacled troll of a man who wheezed like a pug and seemed always to be on the verge of exploding in anger. Already he'd landed a hefty $5,000 advance for the authorized, tell-all biography of the King of Pitchers, and that made him act like no one had a right to talk to Satch but him. The reporters hated Wing. Satch was beginning to hate Wing. But Wing kept on: "You're getting everything all jumbled up, Satch, so you have to start from the beginning."

Satchel's stomach hurt, and he was tired. Frustration over the cancellation of the All-Star Game still ate at him, as he'd been dreaming of it all his life. He took some ice from his drink and crunched it. Wing waited, pencil paused over his pad like he was posing for a book jacket photo. The other reporters gathered around, eager for the drippings from Wing's questions. Okay, Satch thought, it's time to put on the show.

"Well, Ol' Satch was called to pitch to the folks what lived in the prairies of South Dakota one summer. Town called Bismarck. Some local promoter got it into his head to show off the greatest pitcher in the whole world! First colored man some of them folks ever seen! Satch had himself a hell of a team though, guys like, well, like Buck and Josh, and my pal Jeep here. Anyway, Satch personally whipped through a hunnerd an' fifty games one summer until the old arm felt like it was going to fall right off like a old apple from a tree. Didn't have a Jewbaby then.

"Got so people started to know about Satch, far and wide. Dizzy Dean took a notion to come and ply his trade against the great Satchel Paige, and that's one thing you gots to give Diz . . . the boy'll try his hand at anyone, black or white. Satch gets to playing game one and what happens? Ol' Satch tosses a perfect game. Over the long week, well, Satch don't just throw one no-hitter but four. Walked but two boys, and then on purpose to make things lively. And then . . .," he trailed off. "Then there was the Twenty-Seven."

"Four no-hitters," Wing said, his voice grating as if came off a metal washboard. "You'll need that many or more to beat the Cuban. He's already got—"

"Whadja say?" Satch said. A tense silence fell.

Jewbaby growled, "Wing, you know the rules. You *know* the rules, cat!"

The reporters crept back a foot or two as Satch stood. Wing sat calmly, waiting for Satch to relax. "Didn't mention the name," he said, hands up as if to defend himself. "That's what you said. Twenty-dollar fine and two days' suspension to mention the *name*."

Satch grumbled, gulped his fresh drink, and sat again. "Well, forgot the story . . ."

"The *no-hitters*. By golly, Satchel, you were about to tell us about the Twenty-Seven, against the Dean All-Stars."

"Twenty-Seven?" a reporter asked.

Wing beamed; he loved telling this story, it made him feel as if it were his alone. "Mr. Paige," he said with an elaborate nod, "once struck out twenty-seven men in a game against the Dizzy Dean All-Stars."

"Twenty-seven?!" There was a collective gasp, complete with whistles and the sound of a dozen pencils scratching away.

Satch rolled his ice in his drink for a moment as Wing pestered him some more about Bismarck, nothing but ancient history. They asked him about the Dean game. But Satch finally turned and stared out the window, ignoring them. After a moment, Jewbaby scattered the crowd and began to massage the hurler's arm. The number echoed in Satchel's head: *Twenty-Seven . . . Twenty-Seven . . . Twenty-Seven . . .*

As the plane descended into New York City, Satch kept his eye on the traffic shooting into Gotham. One day each and every one of them was going to say that Satchel Paige was the best baseball player the world had ever seen. Problem was, it seemed that for every superhuman feat, that damned Cuban matched it . . . and Dihigo was, Satch admitted, a whole lot more of a movie star than he was. Lanky doesn't ever beat tall, dark, and handsome, he reminded himself. And Satch was lanky defined.

Satch heard a gasp. It was his secretary. "There's smoke coming off the wing!" Sure enough, through the starboard side they could see a thick line of smoke trailing the engine, as if they were busy writing Satch's arrival in the sky.

Wing burst to the front of the plane and pounded on the door to the cockpit. After a minute of this, the co-pilot threw open the door and shouted, "Dick was right, you guys are probably pissing yourself to death. Well, we're almost down, the engine's still going, yes there's trouble but we're not going to crash. Unless you whale on the door like that again and scare the both of us right through the windshield. Got that?"

They got it. Everyone was silent. Any interest in baseball was replaced by the fragility of their lives. Satch stared out the window, watching the earth rising to greet him. Through a soup of humidity and smog, he gazed at the cars and houses and streets growing larger, their features becoming clearer, until at last he could make out the people and the makes of the autos they drove. When it seemed as if they were about to land safely, Paige returned to baseball: someday, he swore, his brush with death intensifying his resolve, you bastards will remember Satchel Paige.

As they stepped off the plane, Satchel noticed that the engine was making a sound like half its pieces had come undone. "Jesus," the mechanic said, "she's burned out."

"Meaning?" Satch barked.

"Meaning it's gonna take at least two weeks to fix this baby."

"Two weeks?" Wing shouted. "You have a full garage at your disposal!"

"For the passenger planes. There's a war on, baby, less'n you forgot." The mechanic wiped his greasy hands on his pants. "'Smatter? You guys got a luxury ride on the rails, anyway, dontcha?"

At one o'clock, in his suite at the Hotel Brigadoon, Satch had his post-lunch rubdown, then told Jewbaby to show up to Yankee Stadium at the usual time, around four, to work on his arm. He wandered downstairs, avoiding the rest of the club, and waved down a taxi that hauled him to the stadium. Satch wanted to get a feeling for the place again. In truth he had a hankering to get to the stadium early, throw some pitches, and just soak in the atmosphere. That, and to consider the magic number twenty-seven.

Paige was as excited as he had ever been, and feeling pretty damn great about that evening's contest, the first night game in New York City since the government had imposed blackout conditions after Pearl Harbor. Already a sellout, it was going to be the diamond of the season, especially since the All-Star Game had been canceled. According to Satch's publicist, every celebrity worth his fame would be there, from Sinatra to Toots Shor to Cab Calloway, the Duke, Veronica Lake, and many, many more. Some by the Yankees' dugout, some by the Athletics'.

In the clubhouse he breathed a deep sigh in the cool darkness. Sitting, he ran his hand over his uniforms, which Pea Webber hung up late the night before. There was the welcome aroma of leather shoes, gloves, the wool of the uniforms, dank concrete floors. A drip here and there from the showers and, far off, the sound of janitors hoofing it across the halls above. Satch stripped, slipped on the visitors grey. Then he headed to the equipment room to get a bucket of balls to throw into the backstop. Right then he needed to get his hands on a ball like he needed to breathe.

Satch flipped on the light. Josh was sitting on a bench, weeping, rubbing his hands together. Both men gave a start, and then Josh shouted, "Get the fuck out!"

Instead Satch stood, watching Josh hang his head, trying to keep the light from his eyes. He liked Gibson—they went back a long time. Mostly he liked to get the better of Josh, but right then he knew the slugger—or the "Phantom Slugger," as the *Inquirer* was calling him—was at his wit's end. The old boy had dried out, was sober and straight as an arrow. Satch could see it—despite his self-centeredness, he'd been in baseball long enough to know when a man was dried out or gassed on hooch or smack. Campy'd made a great deal about Josh in Newark, and Satch believed Josh had hit that pitching like it was church league softball. He heard how the great Gibson was back in form, and for a moment he believed it. But Satch could see that the years of hard living had taken their toll, and Josh wasn't equipped to handle that reality: it wasn't just the drugs that were keeping him from hitting, his body was falling apart. If anything, Josh was worse since Newark. His strikeouts rose, he couldn't hit for power, his knees were obviously shot, and though he was still sharp as a straight razor at calling pitches and rattling a batter, the guy couldn't throw a runner out for trying.

Noticing the bucket of balls, Satch flipped the light out and walked through the darkness and grabbed the handle. Both men were silent, Josh breathing heavily in an attempt to keep from crying some more. As Satch readied to leave, he turned and said, "When you're done, I need a catcher."

Satchel walked briskly through the tunnel and out to the edge of the dugout, halted, and took a quick peek around the ballpark. It was early afternoon, hot as hell, not a cloud in the sky.

Barely two o'clock, the groundskeepers were already busy, affixing the bases to their posts with straps, scrambling about the outfield repairing divots, scraping their rakes across the warning track, and picking the cobwebs off Babe Ruth's statue in center. Satch yelled at the head groundskeeper to bring the backstop out, he was ready to pitch.

Satchel groomed the mound, checked his glove, tightened the stitches with his teeth, stretched a bit, and checked the wind. Nothing. That was good. Humidity is good, though it can hurt a curveball. Better keep to the flaming pitches and the soft stuff. He stretched and took a jog of exactly fourteen feet. Then he blinked, opened his eyelids wide, and opened his mouth with a lion's yawn. Finally Satchel licked his finger, touched the dirt of the mound, and tasted it for luck. "Yes, sir," he said at last, not just to himself but to the hallowed grounds of Yankee Stadium, "today, ol' Satchel Paige is going to make history. One day they gonna have a monument to ol' Satch out there, even if he ain't no Yankee."

"Get your fucking head out of the clouds," Josh yelled as he hobbled to the plate, nearly tripping on the grass at the edge of the dirt. He righted himself and pulled down his face mask. "I can see you daydreamin' out there. Heck, if we could only buy you fer what you're really worth, sell you for whatcha you think you're worth, wouldn't have to sell a ticket all year." Despite the joke, his face was hard in anger. Josh was embarrassed: only Grace and Campy had seen him cry before.

Satch looked down at his feet. "Well, Josh, listen—"

"Fuck you. Get to the mound you prima . . . prima . . . prime rib, or whatever the fuck you are. Get up there and pitch."

Satch nodded and took a step back. "Jus' wanted to let you know. . ."

"Fuck you."

Satch grinned. All he wanted was to help, but seeing the slugger bent out of shape was even better. "Let's see if you can catch what ol' Satch got—"

"Throw the fucking ball. You lucky you can win today, the way your head's ballooned."

Satch fired a few pitches in, warming his arm up, really, but still throwing with the control and speed that a good four-dozen hurlers would kill for. Josh nabbed them, grunted, threw back, and shouted, "Better hit your corners better than that, you fuck, you ain't gonna win nothin'."

"Ain't lost yet."

"It's only a matter of time."

"Never."

"Only a matter a' time."

Satch kicked and threw another beautiful curve, breaking a good two feet. That impressed the pitcher: apparently the humidity wasn't taking as much off his curve as he thought. One of the groundskeepers whistled. Satchel nodded at Josh. "Today, in front of these millions, ol' Satch gonna perform the greatest feat that ever been done."

"Fuck that."

"Joshy, don't you go gettin' jealous 'n' all."

Finally the groundskeeper and his men lumbered out with the massive backstop. Josh stood and put his hands on his hips. "What in the livin' hell is that? You ask me to catch and you got the big net out? Wastin' my time?"

Satch shrugged. "A hitter'd make it all the better. So hit, then. If you can."

Josh stiffened. "How's that?"

"Go grab one o' them sticks a' kindlin' you got and see how royalty—that's right, you lookin' at the King—strikes out the little people."

Josh ran his tongue over his teeth. He glanced around. No crowds, no one but the dopes who took care of the field. Still a few hours to game time. Campy probably still thinking he's asleep. The kid was getting lazy; he'd sneaked out easily that morning, free from Grace and Campy, just to come to the ballpark to get the tears out. Maybe he'd get to hit in peace for once. "Fine, you cocksucker. I'll bury you right there."

The head groundskeeper was shaking with anticipation—his job kept him at the park for the Yankees and their Negro League tenants over the years, so he knew good baseball. "Hey," he said to one of his charges. "Knock off with the raking and watch. Boy, we're gonna see something no one else gonna see."

Josh opened his case on the dugout bench and ran his fingers over the bats. He picked up East and waved it as if he were trying to shake the bad luck from the grain. The dry wood made his palms tingle with pleasure. He gritted his teeth. Fuck 'em, he thought, eyes thinning. He spit and pulled his bat back and waited. Satch took his usual windmill spins, bent his body back, kicked his leg up into the clouds, knuckles almost scraping the ground, then fell back to earth and fired. His arm whipsawed the air and the pitch zipped in with a buzzing sound like an arrow from a crossbow. Josh swung, wrists snapping, slicing the bat through the thick air, and hit the ball square. It shot off the wood and sailed deep into center, ricocheting around the monuments to Ruth, Huggins, and Gehrig like a pinball.

Josh pointed his bat at Satch. "You motherfucker. Don't go shaving off no speed."

Satchel squinted. He *had* taken some off but didn't think the fat boy would have noticed. He said, "One of Satchel's practice pitches is as good as anything them Yanks could throw at you in a real game, anyway."

"Aw, shut up. Campy's right, you're only lookin' out for Satch. Throw a real pitch. One or two won't hurt you."

Satch stood there for a moment, as if unsure how to respond. Finally it occurred to him that Josh wasn't being anything but an ingrate. "Your funeral," he said at last. "We got what looks like fifty balls. Satch'll throw that many atchya, see what the ol' slugger can do."

Josh spit and ground his cleats into the dirt. "Quiet up and pitch!"

Back in the locker room, the players were just beginning to stroll in for their powwow with Mickey Cochrane. Dihigo entered, dapper as usual, with a Cuban reporter in tow. All the while the batboy was busy taping up Cool's legs, utility men Butts and Serrell oiled their gloves, and Ray and Wells argued about Buck's not joining the club for the trip to New York.

Ray was worried. Buck was missing, and he had always been first to the train. When the entire group had arrived at the station, and he hadn't shown, Ray made the train ten minutes late looking for him. "We're not waiting!" the conductor bellowed, and Sam pleaded with Ray to come on, they needed Ray at third if there wasn't Buck at first. On the way, Ray remembered that sinking feeling in his gut when he had popped by his pal's apartment, only to find it dark and empty. In New York, first thing, Ray had fed dimes and nickels into the pay phone trying to connect with Buck . . . nothing. Buck was the one guy on the club you could count on. Always early, never late, didn't complain. And now gone, just like that. Buck would have told him what was going on. Later that afternoon Cochrane posted the lineup. At first base: Archie Ware.

Cochrane gathered them around, looking fatigued like he never had before, his eye sockets hollowed, his face unshaven, his skin grey.

He didn't notice that Satch and Josh were missing; he wouldn't have noticed if half the club was missing. Cochrane paced up and down the rows of players, who followed him with wide eyes. Finally Mickey opened his mouth to speak, then clamped it shut, as if the thought had been cut off midspeak. He paused, then resumed pacing.

"This!" Cochrane shouted, "is a time of great change." He let that statement hang in the silence for a moment, before continuing. "A difficult time, a trying time." Cool was about to speak, but Cochrane held a hand out, as if silencing him magically from ten feet away. "I believe that the world has not yet seen the extent of the strange and wondrous changes about to be wrought from the greatest minds in the world. Incredible, when you stop to consider. The V-1 rocket, even if developed by our most hated enemies, a robot plane. The electric washer and dryer. B-17 Flying Fortresses. Why, Mr. Hourly gave me a copy of . . . what was that, Mr. Hourly?"

Red sat up, surprised at having been spoken to. "Ah, *Popular Mechanics*, Mickey."

"*Popular Mechanics*. And there, on the cover, it predicted that one day we will all own private airplanes to travel. A runway on your front lawn! Unbelievable." Cochrane stopped and gazed down at a catcher's glove lying at his feet. He stooped and picked it up. "Yes, even this mitt has evolved. Beautiful. The aches I used to have. My hands. See?" He held out his hands. The players stared at one another, baffled.

"Sir?" Oscar asked. "We were all wonderin'—"

"Ah, ah!" Cochrane shouted at Oscar and then gave him a glare that immediately silenced the coach. Patting the players on the shoulder as he walked by, Cochrane spoke quietly, firmly. "Machines. The promise of the future. Technological advancement. A few kinks in the prototype. The future . . . One day the future will shine on the Athletics. One day this will be a model team. One day . . ."

"Mickey!" Oscar shouted. "Please!"

Broken from his trance, Cochrane cleared his throat. "Yes, Mr. Charleston? Oh, yes, of course, Mr. Leonard. Mr. Leonard, Mr. Leonard. Gentlemen, Mr. Leonard will *not* be accompanying us here to New York. Nor will he accompany us to Washington, D.C., Cleveland, or Detroit. He will join us again in Philadelphia."

Hands went up, shouts were fired. Cochrane waved his arms. "Please! Mr. Leonard has volunteered with his draft board to perform essential war work while the team is on the road. To be precise, he will be a riveter with the Lindee Corporation. Because of this, he cannot leave Philadelphia for any extended length of time. And I commend him for that! You all should as well. Mr. Leonard has shown himself to be a patriot of the first order. His sacrifice will most assuredly mean that he will forfeit Babe Ruth's home-run record, among many others. Mr. Leonard might not accumulate enough at bats to qualify for the batting title, leaving it, perhaps, to Mr. Dihigo." Cochrane paused and seemed to size up Martín Dihigo. "Mr. Dihigo, someday . . ."

The men began to shout more questions at him, but Cochrane ignored them and retreated to the safety of his office and the bottle he kept in his desk drawer.

"What the hell do you make of that?" Wells grumbled to Oscar.

Oscar looked strained. "Nothing good."

Wells grinned, wickedly. "Maybe this means Veeck'll send him to the loony bin, where he belongs."

"Quiet! It ain't never a good thing when a manager cracks."

As the men finished dressing, Serrell looked over at the door. "Shoot," he said, shaking his head, "gonna be a rainout."

Campy said, "Rain? Are you crazy? The skies are as clear as water."

Serrell pointed to the door. "But I heard thunder." They paused, listening. It would be just their luck to have the first night game at Yankee Stadium rained out. "Didja hear that?" he said. "Told you it was thunder."

Serrell was going to add something when Cool shouted, "Quiet!"

Wells rolled his eyes. "Don't hear anything."

"Willie, shut up! Listen," Cool said, standing up abruptly. They were finally quiet. Nothing but a continuous drip from the showers.

Then it came, this time loud enough to break the silence. It was a sound like thunder splitting a prairie sky.

"Gosh," Campy said. "Didn't look like rain."

Cool shook his head. Then the boom again, echoing down the hall. "C'mon!"

They followed him down the runway, cleats clicking on the concrete floor. As they approached the broad swath of sunlight at the end, Cool held up a hand once more and said, "Wait." They waited.

"Shit, what was that buzzing?" Serrell said.

"You know that's Satch," Cool whispered. "C'mon."

They ran out to the dugout. Josh was pointing his bat at the stands, shouting, "Stupid motherfucker, you ain't getting' another a' those by me!"

"Fucking ingrate," Satch grumbled. He kicked and threw. And there it was again, that ferocious buzz as the ball spun in. Josh's weight shifted through his body from back to front as the bat connected and the crack and boom of bat hitting ball. It seemed to split the air. The ball shot up, lifting, lifting, until it clanged deep into the seats in the right-field upper deck, caroming with a mighty echo.

Campy was the last to step in. "Cripes, there's Josh!" He ran out and slapped his temple. "And Satch! Careful, you're gonna burn your arm out!"

"Kid," Josh said, "G'won. You been harpin' on me too long. Lemme hit a few, get this bat in shape."

"Double that! Quiet up and let ol' Satch send this shitkicker back to Pittsburgh."

"Forget it," Campy said, stepping right in front of the plate. "You throw that ball and you'll have to get it through this thick body. We got to win this game, fellows."

Both Satch and Josh looked as if they seriously considered allowing Campy to take a pitch in the head. The players in the dugout groaned and called Campy out, as did the growing number of fans who'd gathered. But finally Satch dropped the ball from his glove, nodded at Jewbaby, and appeared suddenly calm. He said, "That's fine, Campy, that's fine. I gots to put the ointment on anyhow." Then he turned to his teammates and announced, "Don't talk to me until the game starts. Cool, you got that?"

Cool watched him go. Benson shook his head. "What was that all about?"

"Not sure yet," Cool said. "But old Satch has something cooking on the back burner." Then he watched Satch and Jewbaby talking. At the top of the dugout he turned and said to Benson, "We might not need our gloves out there, dears."

Back in the locker room there was a knock at Cochrane's door. "Yes?" he said, wearily.

Satch poked his head into the dark room. "Cap'n?"

"What is it, Mr. Paige?"

"Well, sir, feelin' good today, 'n' all, wonderin' if I can't ask you to put Josh in behind the plate."

"Mr. Gibson? Why?"

Satch shrugged. "Don' know. Feel good about it, is all."

Cochrane stared down at the lineup card. What difference could it possibly make? They were headed for last, next to last at best. Leonard gone, that rock in the clubhouse, no doubt because he was tired of Cochrane's leadership. Cochrane had watched the men playing now for almost eighty games, knew what they were capable of, and as time ground on he realized that he could only blame himself. Old school versus new technology. What did he have to show for this amazing collection of talent? Barely out of last place, that's what. When Veeck had given him complete control of the club, he thought that would change everything. But that was a pipe dream.

"Fine," Cochrane said at last. He erased Dihigo's name, put Josh in at catcher, and handed the card to Satch. "Mr. Dihigo could use a rest anyway."

"Thanks, Cap," Satch said, and retreated.

Veeck was laughing. He was laughing hard, harder than he had in weeks. "Buck Leonard," he said through his tears, "Buck Leonard!" He couldn't stop.

"We needed the money, Bill," Sam said, not appreciating the joke. "This is truly unbelievable."

"What's unbelievable," Veeck said, "is the fact that Horace got you with his lush routine." Veeck shook with laughter now, he just couldn't believe the turn of events. "Buck and Barnhill for Ott. Oh, my! We would've felt that one for years!"

"And thirty grand!" Sam shouted. "We need that money!"

"Don't need it that bad." Veeck wiped his eyes. "Sam, count your blessings. Buck's volunteering to work saved us. Maybe he just wanted to stay in Philly. Or he legitimately wanted to help the war effort." He cleared his throat to show that he was about to become serious. "But this was a big mistake, Sam. There's a reason I haven't been interested in trading. Part of that reason is because no one would take these boys for what they're truly worth. The A's record's keeping the price low. Your trade would've hurt this club for five years, just on Barnhill alone." Sam looked ready to argue, so Veeck said, "Proof is in the pudding, pal. Barnhill and Leonard for Ott and peanuts is simple math."

"You tell me, then, Bill, how we're going to make money to show a profit?"

"I don't know!" Veeck shouted, tired of the same question. "I just don't know! Maybe we'll have some exhibition games, maybe we'll have contests, maybe . . . well, Sam, maybe we'll lose the team!" He ran his hand through his hair, which, to Sam, almost seemed a more fiery red when Bill was angry. "Sam, we have until the end of the season. Don't pull the trigger so quickly!"

"Hilarious," Sam said, reaching over to pull a cigarette from the case on Veeck's coffee table. He lit it and took a slow drag. "We can't wait any longer."

"You know what, I'm not just going to use these guys like they're scrap metal, ready to sell to the lowest bidder. We do that, we've ruined everything. Look at what's happening in the world— we're winning, we might be able to pull some sort of decent season out of our hats. We have a responsibility to these men, to the city." Veeck paused, then shrugged. "You know what, we have a responsibility to the cause."

"I never said they were scrap metal."

"Well, you were on the verge of making it appear that way." Veeck stood up and walked to the balcony of his hotel, looking out over Central Park. "Sam, we've been pals for a long time. It's important to me to have a friend like you. We balance one another."

"I suppose I should say thanks."

"Stop taking things the wrong way. I've made a decision today."

"Okay," Sam said, not really caring anymore.

"Yes, I have," Veeck said, and turned back to the room. "I'm going to the ballpark today."

Sam shrugged. "Fine. I doubt anyone'll tell."

"You don't understand: I'm running this team again. I'm moving back into the Oval Office while we're in Cleveland." Sam sat in his chair, unmoving. "Sam," Veeck continued, "all Landis can do is sue us. Take us all the way to the Supreme Court. That'll take time, probably longer than the season itself. I'm tired of trying to run this team from hotels and a mangy little apartment across the street." Veeck put his hand on Sam's shoulder. "Sam, I think you traded poor Buck away because I wasn't around to reason with you. And, I'll admit, I've made some bonehead plays myself, probably because I'm stewing by *myself*." Veeck handed him a smoke. "Don't worry. It'll be as fun as everything else this season."

Sam looked over the cigarette like it was something he hadn't seen before. He took a puff and sighed. "You're crazy."

Veeck laughed. "Isn't that why you dropped every dime on me back in Milwaukee?" Sam had to chuckle at that. Veeck stood, walked to the door, then turned. "Well, you coming? Satchel's pitching today!"

"Bill," Sam said. "By God, how is it I ever left law?"

"You didn't want to die bored," Veeck said. "Now let's go."

"Twenty-seven?!" Red bellowed, pacing the length of the dugout. "Some goal! Some goal, indeed. You're telling me he's going to strike out twenty-seven? What the living hell makes you say that?"

"The way that Satchel's pitching," Cool said. "I remember that time he K'd the whole of Dean's All-Stars. Up in Bismarck, me and Satch and . . . and Willie." He looked down the bench at Wells, who was busy boning his hickory bat. "Willie, old man, you remember, don't you?"

Wells just kept tapping the bone on his bat, ignoring Cool. So Cool continued, "It was a crazy day. Weird feel to the day, clouds on the horizon, sun right over you. Storms coming in, tornadoes gonna carve up the place. We're all worried about the weather, but Satchel, see, he went into a trance before the game. The darling was real nice to everyone, had a faraway look in his eyes, like today. Notice how he sittin' in the dark back in the locker room? Just like it happened that day. Wind pickin' up, and I swear he got that ball to ride on the gusts. Once the thing twisted like a corkscrew through the air. Lightning in the distance, you could hear doors slamming shut on the barns nearby. Everyone was scared, but they didn't leave, because they'd never seen a ball move like that. Never seen such talent swing and swing and swing—like they was trying to hit a ghost ball. Satch would just walk to the mound, walk back to the dugout, the whole time it was like he wasn't there. And when it was over, snap, he's back. Didn't say word one about the game—and you know Satchel, if he throws a gem, he makes sure the whole world sees its shine.

"Today's the same. Red, he's got that look. And I guarantee he won't be out 'till game time. And whether he really strikes out twenty-seven or not, well, you better keep both eyes open, because this is going to be a monument to the beauty of baseball."

Dusk had settled on the ballpark, and the shadows climbed the outfield fences. The lights burst on to the roar of the crowd. The stadium was packed to its paint-flaked rafters with shouting, sweating, hat-wearing, scoring, pencil-licking, popcorn-chewing, beer-drinking, carnation-wearing, cigar-smoking men, women, children, soldiers, priests, nurses, riveters, teachers, cabdrivers, cops and firemen, soldiers, sailors, and quite a few WACs, and even 132 cats that roamed the tunnels of the stadium, feeding off the mice that fed off the garbage created by the crowd. The artificial light shined onto the field and dribbled mock moonbeams through the neighborhoods and onto the bums, dirty children, and unfortunates who either couldn't afford a ticket or couldn't get one but were thrilled to be near the excitement. Determined to be heard, they put their lungs to the test and roared with all their might, banging trashcan lids and car horns to the radio piped outside.

Cutting through the piles of noise, the PA announced the starting lineups. Then the New York Yankees raised the league's largest flag over center field, and a girl warbled *The Star-Spangled Banner*. From high up in the nosebleed seats, craning their necks around the great dark girders, fans strained to see the lines of players shooting out in two directions from home plate. They elbowed one another in glee: the Yanks, as the cliché went, were "gonna moider 'em," and murder was most welcome, since the Bombers were in third, on the heels of the Tigers, and breathing down the necks of the Brownies. And the Browns and Tigers were battling each other in a four-game series. Adding it up, should the Yanks take three of four or sweep, New York's finest ball club would be looking good as the season stretched into August.

At the close of the anthem, the lines of players wobbled and broke, jogging into the dugout or onto the field. The stadium trembled with applause.

Veeck and Sam sat sweating in the bleachers, crowded shoulder to shoulder with the fans, Sam still in his suit and tie, mopping his forehead and doing his best to keep the sweat off his spectacles. He kept an eye out for the commissioner's operatives and asked Veeck to do the same. "Operatives?" Veeck said, laughing. "And what, pray tell, would they look like?" Sam couldn't answer that. Veeck felt elated, high as a kite being among the crowd and not sitting in a gloomy hotel listening on the radio. He gulped beer and chewed hot dogs, sucking mustard off his fingers. When he thought Sam looked too dour he would grab his friend by the shoulders and shout, "Enjoy it, man! Life's short!"

Each player in the dugout was suffering from butterflies and gooseflesh. "Whatever you do," Cool said, "don't mention Satch's goal to Mickey." Wells rolled his eyes. Was Cool crazy? Of course they didn't confide nothing to that crackpot anymore.

Artie was already sweating profusely. "Think he can do it?" he whispered.

Campy sat down and stared ahead. "*Satchel Paige.* Do you need to hear anything else?"

The A's did nothing in their first at bats. In the Yanks' half, Satchel strode to the mound, staring straight ahead. He hadn't spoken a word for the last hour. He held the ball in his hand and pondered it like Hamlet considering Yorick's skull, his eyes drowsy. The stitching seemed almost to smile at him. Kicking in the dirt, he watched the first Yankee, Frankie Crosetti, step to the plate. The applause began, as did the catcalls, the shouting, the cajoling, every slur and swear word and cheer and romp, the years of frustrating darkness rising and crashing in that instant.

Satchel checked Josh's signs. He nodded, remembering how earlier the ball seemed to gain some moisture from the air and drop like a damp sponge into a bathtub. Josh set himself for the pitch. All the crowd seemed tuned into this moment, their energy funneling from the stands and into Satchel's consciousness. He felt the lights burning. He felt the humid air swirling. He felt the moon, hidden by the lights, its mystic gravity whirring in his arms and head. Turning, Satchel wound up, raised his leg sky high, stretched his pitching hand as low as he could go, and his whole body fell as he threw.

Crosetti drilled the first pitch deep into the right-field corner.

Jethroe, fully expecting a strike, misplayed it, first staring in mounting disbelief as it shot from the plate, hugged the line, and dropped absolutely fair. Only then did he move, still unsure of what was happening. The ball ricocheted off the corner and bounced almost into center field, past his outstretched glove. Noise boomed from the stands as if blasting from the guns on the bow of a battleship as the Yankee batter burst from home, sped around first, around second, and then bounded into third, standing straight as a wooden Indian, panting, ninety feet from home plate.

Satchel's eyes looked like they were doing their level best to pull themselves out of his sockets. "That's one," Wells said, tossing the ball back to Paige. "Twenty-seven more and, man, we'll be in last place by nightfall."

In seventeen starts, resulting in a 15-0 won-lost total, Satchel Paige had not given up a hit on the game's first pitch. In fact, no one who opened a game against Satch had managed to reach first. He'd had but two hits in the first inning of all those starts. And Satchel knew all of that. His brain housed a twenty-story accounting firm of little Satchels, all of whom scribbled ledger after ledger of his statistics, feats, and—tucked in a black folder and filed away—his mistakes. The records spilled out across his brain: the fact that this was the very first triple he'd ever given up in the majors, that he'd never had a man on before two outs in the first three innings, that . . .

"Paige!" the ump screamed, trying to be heard over the din. "Throw the ball!"

Satch did. A slider, rolling through the heavy air like a bowling ball tossed by a third-grade child. The batter doubled, a rocket over Benson's head that smacked the statue of Lou Gehrig so hard the thing seemed to wobble. The following batter tripled him home, then Satch walked the next man, then watched in horror as the next batsman poked a full-count curveball for a Texas League blooper, sending in the man on third. A bunt to move the runners filled the bases as Satch bobbled the ball on the throw to first. Another triple—this time to the opposite corner—cleared the bases, a double sent that guy home, and a walk . . .

"Time!" Cochrane yelled from the dugout, marching toward the mound. He signaled Mack in the bullpen to send Gready McKinnis in.

"You ain't pullin' Satchel Paige. Not today! Look, Cap'n, that's one Cab Calloway sitting among such dubiousness as Mickey Rooney and the blue pipes, Sinatra! Why, La Guardia's in! It's Satchel's biggest night, Satchel's gonna . . ."

"Going to what? Mr. Paige, have you bothered to look at the score?" Cochrane pointed at the great black monolith with the score YANKEES 7, ATHLETICS 0 in bold white for the entire world to see. "Go sit down, everyone has an off-day."

Satchel refused. "You sit Satch, he's done . . . for the whole season!"

Cochrane stopped as if he'd been slapped. Then he began to laugh, right there on the mound in full view of the throng. Wells and Ray ran over.

"Sir," Ray asked, "do you need anything?"

"Do I need anything!" Cochrane guffawed. "You are damn well right I need something! I need you to haul this fool out of here. Mr. Paige, if you never pitch again, well, we will only lose *more* games. I cannot imagine that to be more painful than what we have already endured."

Satchel stared at the growing crowd of Athletics, at his manager who was busting a gut, and finally said, "Fine. You needs a committee to decide against Satchel? Fine, but Satch sits for good!"

Cochrane had no doubt that Satch meant what he said, and it made him feel light as a cloud. Josh had walked up slowly, first having hoped he could get away with sitting behind the plate, ignoring the meeting.

Cochrane turned to walk away, then stopped suddenly. He snapped his fingers. Turning to Mack, who was waiting at the mound for McKinnis, he said, "Forget McKinnis. Put in Jessup."

"Jessup?" Mack said, and then mumbled something unintelligible.

Cochrane roared, "Would you speak up? What's with you lately? You're talking into your chest."

Mack started. "I'm not talking into my chest. I'm not."

"Then get me Jessup."

"I was just sayin' that that kid's ERA is wider than the Hudson River."

"Mack," Cochrane said, draping an arm over his shoulder. Mack awkwardly tried to fold his arms to cover the bug strapped on his chest. "I am beginning to wonder if it is not commonplace in the bullpen to ignore the score of that day's game. Right now, with nobody out, we are facing a tremendous deficit. Jessup's earned run average might be approaching humorous proportions, but I ask you: does it matter?" He shouted the last part, though wearing a smile. Patting Mack on the shoulder, he said, "Indulge me."

Mack nodded, telling himself that Mickey was right, the game was lost, might as well use up a lousy arm instead of a good one.

But Cochrane was wrong. Mack was wrong. Armwise that is, for Jessup had been watching the score closely, and as the Yanks put up the runs he found himself as relaxed as if he'd been sedated. When Mack called him to the mound, he shrugged. Crowds didn't mean nothing now, right? Look at that fat score. Keep the lead or give up more runs, what did it matter except that he could throw a few? Confident, Jeep jogged to the mound, took a few warm-ups, and struck out the next two batters. Then, on four nice pitches, he induced an infield fly to end the inning.

As the Athletics pulled off their gloves and settled on the bench, Cochrane leaned on the dugout steps, clapped his hands and cried, "It is early in the game, men! Do not give up!"

Archie Ware opened the inning with a hard single, Jethroe and Benson each struck out, Cool bunted safely to first, sending Ware to third. Then Josh stepped to the plate and the outfield stepped in for the easy out.

Josh looked at East, gave his bat a couple of test swings, and muttered a prayer or a curse. He wiped his brow as he settled into the batter's box, rolling his shoulders before cocking the bat back. Behind him the catcher mumbled something, and the crowd shouted, cajoled, made fun of him. Josh the fatty, Josh the old man, Josh any number of weak swinging, impotent, homosexual invectives. It didn't appear to faze him. Josh kept his bat back, eyes forward, muscles tensed and waiting.

The first pitch came in and it seemed to roll through the air for Josh, nothing more than a sphere of cotton, soft and fluffy and easy to see. He rocked back, his weight gathering in his right foot before rolling across his body as he swung around and connected.

No one expected that sound. The pitcher dropped, and the catcher and the umpire both sprang back as if a bomb had exploded in their faces. At the crack, the crowds shot to their feet, gaping, pointing into the sky at what might have been, for all they knew, a magic act, a Japanese balloon bomb, something strange and unseen in these parts, namely a Josh Gibson home run. They barely had time to register the feat as it blew out of the park. Josh hadn't left the box when it clanged around in the right-field rafters before falling back onto the field, where a disgusted Yankee outfielder picked it up as if it were dog leavings and tossed it hastily back into the crowd.

"Some homer!" Oscar shouted as Josh descended into the dugout.

"Take it easy," Josh grumbled, but he couldn't suppress the smile that broke across his face.

Next inning Jeep still felt the iron rod of confidence; his arm was loose, and he kept the Yankees under wraps. In the fourth, with two outs, Josh snapped another home run, a line shot skipping off the outstretched hands of a dozen spectators. Both first-pitch swings, both acts of utter destruction. The kid who caught the second one held the ball aloft for all to see: it looked as if it'd been sandwiched beneath the wheels of a train.

The Yanks were flummoxed. They'd been unable to slap much off this lousy Jeep Jessup, who should have been tiring, should have been throwing the usual junk, and, was in fact tossing garbage, but it wasn't doing anything for the Yankee offense. While Jeep struck out only three, the Yankees couldn't do much but hit weak grounders around the infield, and two outfield flies caught for church-league outs. Polite applause trickled from the stands now and then, but soon this turned to savage boos. The Yanks were looking like bums.

With the A's down three in the ninth, Ware drilled a double into the gap, stood on second, and danced about as if he were about to steal. Jethroe laid down a sweet bunt that spun along the third-base line, threatening to roll out of bounds but finally settling quite fair on the infield grass. Benson, feeling ready to crack the game open, struck out instead against a new pitcher, a seventeen-year-old firebrand brought up to throw until the draft would take him to invade Japan, early next year. At Cool's turn, the kid revealed his speed and guts, throwing inside as if Cool weren't standing there. Cool, whose eyes had been sharpened by years of crackers like the one on the mound, worked the count full, fouled off five pitches, then drew a walk to load the bases.

Josh Gibson had been leaning on his bat, wondering if he'd get a chance to hit again. When Cool strolled to first, the chance was suddenly his, full of what amounted to the best drama of the baseball world. Fuck it, he said. Just fuck it. I'm washed up and worthless, but I'm here. He felt good, in his own way, head cleared of the junk. Even though his knees felt like they'd been broken by axe handles, he felt good. The crowd, though, was in a frenzy of nastiness for their goddam-Yankees-who-couldn't-hold-a-goddam-lead-if-it-had-a-goddam-handle-on-it, and the thrill of possibly seeing Gibson murder yet another one roused them. As he made his way to the plate, Josh rolled up his sleeves like John Henry coming to take on the machine. It was just a game of bat and ball, he thought. Gotta remember that. Gotta keep perspective. Groaning, he reached down to scoop up some loose dirt. He rubbed the bat handle and stepped in.

The young fireballer didn't give a rip about this guy, just some plump old Negro. The kid knew that Josh feasted on inside pitches, lunged at outside pitches, but his eyes—weak and old—betrayed him all the time, so you could fire one in there now and then, just to show off. Checking the runners, the kid went into his delivery and threw.

When Josh swung, a split second was all it took to know that the A's had taken the lead. The crowd rose in waves, pointing, shouting, until the cheers grew silent as they stared in awe and the ball rose, rose, rose. It grew smaller, barely discernible against the bright lights. Finally, still rising, it hit the upper roof of left field with a bang that silenced the last of the cheering masses, and bounced out of the stadium and into the darkness.

Bedlam. Outside the crowds, listening to the radio piped from speakers on the street, cried out in disbelief as the ball flew over their heads and fell with yet another bang on the hood of a police car parked across the street. From up in the radio booth, the announcer cried, "He hit it out of the stadium! He hit the ball out of the stadium! He hit the ball out of Yankee Stadium!" In the bleachers Veeck and Sam roared and rooted with the rest of the crowd.

Josh circled the bases, trying to weave his way through the fans who had burst past the police and onto the field. Even the Yankees applauded, and as he rounded third and headed for home, he was met by his teammates, hollering and jumping. It took six of them to do it, but they hoisted Josh up on their shoulders and carried him to the dugout, surrounded by half the team.

It was a five-hundred-foot haymaker, the knockout punch that sent the Yankees to their knees for a moment before falling face first into the canvas. For more than an hour the cops worked to gather the fans back into their seats. The A's added an insurance run on three more singles off the rattled boy pitcher, then Jeep, too caught up in Josh's homer to be nervous, dropped the Yankees one, two, three in the bottom half. The Athletics won 9-7.

"You going to the dugout to celebrate?" Sam said to Veeck, jazzed by the crowds and ready to have fun.

"Tomorrow," Veeck said as they sat watching the emptying ball field. "Let them have their time alone. I have a feeling there will be many more opportunities like this."

After the game, reporters crowded around Josh for the first time that season. Satchel sat, filing the crusted dirt out of his spikes and listened while Jewbaby rubbed ointment in his arm. He smiled slightly at the attention Josh was receiving. Even Cochrane was shouting and carrying on, nearly in tears at the feat, running around the room to talk about Josh with any unoccupied reporter.

On the train to D.C., Oscar had to laugh at the sight of Satchel Paige boarding sullenly. "Well, well, look who's humbled himself to join our little crew," he shouted. "Why, if it ain't Leroy Paige. Mingling with the common folk?"

Satch just grumbled. Sam, holding a clipboard, began to stammer. "Satch, where's your plane?"

"Busto."

"But . . ."

"Broken, man, what do you want ol' Satch to do, hitchhike?"

Veeck laughed. "Well, we don't have a berth for you, old man—"

Satchel gaped like he'd been told they were next playing on Mars. "No berth? So where Satchel going to sleep?"

Sam was about to offer his, but Veeck shouted, "Sorry, ace!" and pulled Sam back to the club car winking the whole way.

There wasn't a soul on that team that didn't have a guffaw sneaking a look at Satchel Paige trying to fold himself into the barely reclining seats in the coach car. Long legs stretched out, or knees jutting up, shifting, twisting. Once in a while the conductor would come along and shoo Satch's big feet out of the aisle. A baby screamed by his ear.

Around midnight Veeck couldn't take the joke any longer. He walked up to Satch, kicked him lightly on the foot, and said, "C'mon, ace, we have a bed for you."

Satch gaped at him. "You mean—"

Veeck chuckled, "That's right. We had one all along."

"Then to hell with you." Satch said, and curled up under the scratchy, tissue-thin blanket they'd given him. "Satch is livin' the life a' luxury right here, thank ya."

Veeck loved it. "It's your funeral."

Washington, D.C., Griffith Stadium. All day fans had spilled out from the neighborhoods surrounding the park to see the Athletics, still their heroes. Reporters, fans, the umps and ground crew, and every player would later speak of that game in hushed awe: it was as if the scene were in slow motion, the crowds on their feet, cheering and waving hats and handkerchiefs, the ball coming in and the great Josh Gibson swinging from the heels then, as if the air had suddenly gelled, that hollow, tree-splitting crack that telegraphed a home run deep into the right-field seats. Then another out of the stadium and into the dense foliage of the giant oak in right center, bouncing around the branches and shaking the tree as if it too were joining the applause.

It was a funny game: the A's lost and didn't care. Satch, his arm aching from using it as a pillow, gave up six runs. Clark Griffith, the wiry, grey-haired, irritable owner who publicly grumbled about Veeck but privately thanked his Lord and Savior for all the dough rolling into his vaults, tried to block the A's owner from entering his ballpark. But Veeck had a ticket to sit in the bleachers, which is just what he did. He roared like a lion with every play.

And they mopped up the rest, a four-game destruction in which the Senators were left begging for hits. Even aching Hilton Smith felt his arm harden from old noodle to iron rod and threw a shutout.

Just as suddenly, Josh returned to form. Between D.C. and Cleveland he hit a single homer in the games after he airmailed one out of Yankee Stadium. And he struck out thirteen times without a single hit. On the last game against the Tribe, Josh managed an infield fly and three strikeouts.

On the road the Athletics won thirteen and lost four, and leapfrogged over three clubs to land in fourth place, eleven games behind the Detroit Tigers, ten games behind second-place St. Louis, and now a mere five behind the reeling Yankees. As the Liberty Limited shot them around Toledo en route to Detroit for four, Dave Barnhill was on a bus for the same destination, called up to pitch there and in St. Louis, which would close out the road trip. Every man on the club hungered to play both teams, especially the Browns. All the while Bill Veeck was busy tidying up the Oval Office for his press conference the next morning, to announce officially his return to baseball.

◇ **16** ◇

Port Chicago

At the naval base in Port Chicago, California, sailors were busy unloading munitions from long rows of boxcars, hauling the weapons down trim docks and onto transport ships destined for war in the Pacific. The work was backbreaking, finger-smashing: first, the great heaving boxcars would roll in, rattling and shaking under their load while the men waited, sweating and impatient. Each car was stacked to within two feet of its ceiling with anything from 30mm shells to 500-pound bombs. Once the train settled to a stop and orders were given to unload, one sailor would have to scramble up inside the car, to the very top of the pile, and squeeze himself into that slim opening. Then, at another barked command, other sailors would lean a ramp up to him. Every eye was fixed on that ramp: the bomb would poke out, slowly, tilt, then fall onto the ramp and roll down. Anxious hands would ease the explosive into other hands, palms slick from the heat and anxiety. They would carry each shell, their backs hunched, muscles straining, fifty feet to the waiting ships. This process would repeat itself, over and over and over, all day and well into the night.

In the interest of increasing productivity, officers would have contests to see which division could load the fastest: if one group had filled a ship with twenty-six tons of ammo in a day, the next ought to load thirty. Men grew reckless, moving as quickly as possible, urged on by the promise of leave. On some occasions a bomb would roll off the ramp and down the pier, clanging into another pile, sending every man in sight to the ground. Despite assurances that they weren't equipped with detonators, every man in Port Chicago kept a tight fear at the front of his brain. Most barely slept. The tension drove some of them mad. One day a fellow marched in, buck naked, a necklace of dead seagulls around his neck. Another began speaking in tongues, and another, watching a pal drop a large shell onto a metal floor with a clang, tied a heavy bomb around his waist, said "Sayonara," jumped into the bay, and drowned.

Dave Barnhill's Uncle Hal knew the suicidal young man. Hal decided that he wasn't going to stand for any more of the abuses that drove his fellow sailors to killing themselves. A veteran of the navy for fifteen years—each and every one "a love affair," in his words— Hal was nonetheless ready for a fight. Because he loved the service, he would say, he had to mix it up. Like most enlisted men, he had a grudging respect for his officers: he knew all too well that among them were scores of dedicated men and equal numbers of scoundrels. Too often the scoundrels were in charge of operations like Port Chicago, men who lied (about things like detonators) simply to keep things moving. Hal knew, they all knew, that the bombs were deadly. Instinctively he sensed that this was why so few of the loaders were white—maybe 5 percent—and those were the lowest caliber of seamen, guys who pissed and moaned and were probably on the verge of being drummed out of the military. Criminals, even—Hal knew one cracker who claimed he'd raped Japanese girls throughout Hawaii, so they sent him to a place without women.

It was easier for Hal to gripe since he was, by his own admission, a rabble-rouser. He wouldn't stop questioning the safety of Port Chicago. He threatened to strike, threatened to go to the NAACP, to the Supreme Court. But this was the armed forces, not civilian life, and these threats were taken seriously and then seriously quashed: Hal was threatened with court-martial and hard labor in Leavenworth.

July 17th was an especially bad day. In the morning Hal had filed a complaint with his superior officer, mostly to keep a record that he could use in case there was an incident—exactly what, Hal couldn't predict. But he wanted a paper trail to prove he wasn't complicit. His superior was sick of the complaints, official and otherwise, and they fell into a raging argument. MPs were called, and Hal was placed under house arrest for trying to incite mutiny.

His guard was a baby-faced white kid with yellow hair, brand new, who'd enlisted to fight in the Pacific. He hated guarding Hal. When he listened to Hal tell about loading ammo, he couldn't believe the stories.

"Let's talk about something else," Hal said, seeing the boy's discomfort. "At least my nephew's coming back to the A's."

"Hard to believe you know a ballplayer. I mean, that you're an uncle. Of a ballplayer, I mean . . ."

"They're playing Detroit and St. Louie next," Hal said, ignoring the kid's stuttering. "First- and second-place teams. That'll be tough."

The boy set his rifle on the cot beside Hal. "Tough, yeah. But, but . . . I read the papers. Their pitchers are looking good, aren't they?"

He sighed. "I suppose you're right. After all, they won fourteen of their last seventeen."

"Yeah, yeah, that's the spirit, after all—"

The sky turned white. Windows shattered and the walls buckled. Every cot lifted from one end of the room and flew to the other side, Hal and the kid tumbling end over end through shards of glass, metal, and plaster. At the docks, a half-mile away, explosions lifted the transport ship *E.A. Bryan* seven feet out of the water, quartered it, and dropped its pieces back into the fiery water, to the bottom of the harbor. Another explosion lifted the *Quinault Victory,* nearly jackknifed it, and then it too sank almost immediately. Men standing too far away to die instantly were engulfed in flames. They dived into the black water, twisting into the depths like shooting stars. Eighteen docks, covering six city blocks, were torn from their pilings and thrown a good two hundred feet, or vanished altogether. Fires burned throughout the area, windows were shattered for seven miles around, and a subtle boom was heard in San Francisco, some seventy miles away.

Ray Dandridge was certain that Dave's uncle had been killed. Campy was equally certain that he emerged without a scratch. "That poor boy," Josh said, boning West, the bat that seemed to be helping him. "What are we going to do for him?"

"Worry about yourself, Josh," Campy said quietly, as if speaking loudly would curse them.

When Barnhill walked into the clubhouse before the game in Detroit, all eyes were upon him. Campy stood up, hand extended, and said, "Welcome back. I'll meet you in the bullpen."

Taken aback, Barnhill slowly shook Campy's hand and watched the kid bound on out the door. He fully expected the rest of the club to ignore him as before; instead they crowded around, welcomed him back, peppered him with questions while he dressed. Hal was shaken up, he told them.

"That's a piece of work," Wells said, again surprising Barnhill. "Sons of bitches, you mean they just had 'em slinging bombs around?"

"That's right," Barnhill said. "But the others—all five hundred of 'em—won't work unless they free Hal."

When Cochrane emerged from his office, the conversation stopped. "Are you ready to pitch today, Mr. Barnhill?" he asked.

"Yes, sir."

"You are certain?"

"Absolutely."

Cochrane nodded. He addressed the whole group. "Today we face Hal Newhouser. Look for those tipped pitches. Watch out for the change-up—remember to time yourself for those off-speeds." With that he clapped his hands, took a deep breath, and said, "Let us remind the Tigers that there is a lot of baseball left this season. Maybe by Friday they will not enjoy first place, right?" He allowed himself a rare grin.

While warming up in the bullpen, Barnhill caught up on the news and gossip, despite Mack's complaints to shut up and throw. Mack still wore the wire, but his baseball instincts were inflamed. He was beside himself with pleasure and gut-clenching terror: Barnhill's fastballs amazed him, but he was absolutely certain the kid was going to spout off about communism or some other treason and end up in the clutches of the FBI.

Every square foot of Tiger Stadium was packed with frenzied fans, standing where no seats could be had, with kids leaning and craning their necks to see around posts, with local press and photographers crowding the edges of the field. Barnhill didn't care. The place was integrated and he didn't care. Honestly, he thought, he didn't care if they won or lost. On the phone last evening, Hal sounded despondent. "Davey," he said, "some of my pals vanished. Not just dead. Gone completely. No body, nothing. And that kid I was talking to. I'm having nightmares. I see him. Couldn't a' been nineteen if he was a day."

Barnhill learned that the kid had been decapitated, and Hal had been the first to find him. Dave asked, "Anything I can do?"

There was silence. "No. Nothing."

"Tell me. Anything."

Another pause. "Dave, listen. I gotta fight. *I have to.* Once I get my head together, I'll be raising my fists every hour on the hour. Because I'm here in the navy. I love the navy, and I want to make it easier for the guys who come after me to love it too."

"I understand."

"Yeah. Well, it's like those guys who drive the buses in Philly. Probably love their work, just want the right to be able to do it."

"That's right, Hal."

Hal sighed. "You're a baseball player, Dave. Show me you love it. Tomorrow, just play baseball. That's all. Win or lose, I don't care, Dave." At this, Barnhill could hear Hal inhale on a cigarette, could imagine him leaning into the receiver. "Me and the guys, we love to hear about the A's. So just play." After a long silence. "You got that, Dave?"

Barnhill did. And today he was going to do just that: play the damned game. With his arm feeling great, he was firing his pitches across the bullpen plate with speed and precision. Mack sighed contentedly, peacefully. Barnhill hadn't said one word since he began to throw.

With the close of *The Star-Spangled Banner*, Artie hopped out on deck to wait his turn at leadoff. He dug into the box, butterflies floating around in great flocks in his stomach, and waited, stock-still. Newhouser had owned Artie to this point: nine strikeouts, nothing else. The pitcher checked the sign, turned, kicked, and fired.

Artie, usually a man who took the first pitch, stroked Newhouser's fastball down the left-field line, looking to go foul but kicking up chalk in fair territory. Huffing, Artie stood on second, barely able to believe his accomplishment. Wells doubled him in. Then Campy plastered a home run into the upper deck.

With a good lead, Barnhill struck out the first Tiger on four straight curves that left batter and ump bickering like an old married couple. Blood pounded through Dave's arms and chest, and he began to get a feeling for the batters, for what they were expecting, what would surprise them. He sniffed his glove; he'd had the thing for ten years, never noticed that it smelled like Hal's old glove, the one he used to use as a teenager, old leather mixed with sweat. Barnhill kicked at the dirt. The dirt smelled good, dry, that rosin bag, the grass. He turned to look at his players, edgy, waiting for his pitch. Squinting, he kicked and fired and struck out the next man. Then Campy called "Time!" and ran to the mound.

Barnhill asked, "What's up?"

"You're pitchin' pretty good."

"Thank you."

Campy sighed. "Golly, it's been a long season."

Barnhill began to laugh. "You came out here to tell me that?"

Campy chuckled. "Gosh, I don't know, just had to get that off my chest." He just started to chuckle, louder, and then he couldn't stop. "It's been one hell of a season."

"Okay," Barnhill said, still smiling.

Campy shook his head. "Look at Josh."

Josh was sitting in the dugout, staring intently at the left fielder, waving him over.

"So?"

"Bastard's trying to get him to the right position."

"And?"

Campy didn't say anything, the laughter was pouring out of him. "One hell of a season!"

Artie and Ray moved to the mound as the ump began his slow stroll to break up the conference.

Barnhill shook his head. "You okay, Camp?"

Campy was laughing so hard, tears were forming. "Would you ever have thought that we would be so damned bad?"

Barnhill stepped back, as if he'd been slapped. He should have taken offense at Campy. Should have been furious, or maybe he should have thought the kid was crazy. Instead he began to chuckle. Then he began to bellow.

Artie Wilson had to laugh himself. "What's so funny, Daddy?"

Barnhill could barely talk for his gasping. "What's so funny? Look around you!"

Everyone looked around, as if something utterly hilarious were just lying about, waiting to be seen. "What?" Artie asked, smiling in bewilderment.

Dandridge frowned. "Geez, you okay, Roy?"

Campy shook his head. "Look at us!" He began to laugh. "Who'd have thought, golly, who'd a' thought of all of this comin' down on us!" He began to double over with laughter. Barnhill couldn't stop either and leaned on Dandridge.

The ump shooed them back to playing, which only made them even more amused at the jocularity that had gripped them. Each man had something funny in mind: the thought of Buck made Dandridge tear up, the thought of that bastard drilling rivets, coming home, and finding out that the papers didn't write articles about riveters. Artie had to laugh about how he'd boasted that he'd always hit over .400 in the Negro Leagues, so damn, he oughta be able to hit well in the majors. Yesterday Jethroe pointed out that maybe his bat failures were a direct connection to his prowess in the bedroom, good or bad, and Campy found that particularly amusing right then.

The spell lingered in the dugout at the end of the inning: Cochrane guffawed about Adelis, about how he had to have knocked some screws loose with his billy club, and had you ever got close and *smelled* him? The guy stank like he bathed in sauerkraut and spoiled milk. And Jethroe thought back to those dopes in St. Louis who'd lugged all those watermelons in, and one or two of those crackers were down with hernias. And how all the A's pitchers got sore arms, except the ones that were in jail . . . or Communists like Barnhill. And what about those damn Reds? Nat Low scurrying about like a bug, and boy did Lester Rodney put away that roast beef.

Amidst all the humor, Barnhill allowed but four hits as the A's mopped up another.

Double plays, diving catches, even a triple play: for the next three games the A's could do no wrong defensively, either. Who would have been able to tell you they'd lost Monte Irvin, Buck Leonard, and George Jefferson over the course of a year? Who could argue that they fell apart under pressure? They crushed first-place Detroit as if the Tigers were nothing more than a bunch of gimpy sandlotters. The Tigers couldn't score, couldn't push a hit past the sweeping gloves of the infield or a liner past the diving arms of the outfielders.

The A's bats were back: Dandridge was belting liners all over the park, Wells's heavy bat was making mincemeat of the ball, Cool was laying down the bunts and hitting first by two strides. *And* stealing second. *And* stealing third. *And* finally stealing home. Once per game. Every game of the series.

"Darlings," Cool shouted after a particularly gruesome slaughter, "we're playing like this here's the East-West game!"

Best of all, Artie found his luck—blooper hits came to him at last, not just pop-outs; he and Wells were turning double plays as easy as passing the salt shaker at the dinner table. They suddenly seemed to be on the same page defensively, connecting with the cut-off men, perfect throws. Hilton Smith strong-armed his way through a second complete-game victory while Satchel and Dihigo closed out the four-game series with shutouts.

Only Josh Gibson was floundering—striking out, and with one feeble hit in fourteen tries. Opposing baserunners stole mercilessly as his throws were weak and off target.

Mack Filson wore a deep scowl on his face. He sat off by himself in the dining car on the train to St. Louis. He couldn't talk to anyone anymore—how could he betray his friends? Sometimes his neck ached from tilting his head ever so slightly for hours at a time—he swore he could hear the microphone squeak intermittently. Squinching his face into an even worse mask whenever anyone drew close, including his good friend Cochrane, Mack appeared unapproachable. Finally Gready McKinnis couldn't take it anymore. He elbowed Bill Byrd and said, "Something's eating that old buzzard. Let's go cheer him up."

Coming up from behind, McKinnis slapped Mack on the shoulder. "What's the matter with you, old salt? Can't stand it when we win? We're alone in fourth. Knocked these fuckers clear out of first. And next stop, those shitkickers in St. Louis."

"Leave me alone," he said, hunching over his coffee cup in an effort to mute the bug.

"Mackie!" Byrd said. "We're winning easy! Come on, Mack, it's like we paid the Tigers to lose!"

Mack stood like he was going to haul off and punch Byrd, knocking his coffee across the table. "Goddam it all," he said, "get the hell away from me, the both of you. I'm arsenic. Pure poison." With that he turned and walked out.

They rolled into St. Louis early the next day. At first the town was nearly the same deal as before, but with a few more supporters at the station, egged on by the A's movement up the standings. As usual, Sportsman's Park looked particularly grubby, like no one had bothered to sweep or clean the place since they'd last visited.

At the start of the game, Artie held his bat as if it were Excalibur. He used a Louisville Slugger that was white as cream and flashed in the bright sunlight. Digging in, Artie pointed it at the Browns hurler and waited for the pitch.

But as Artie waited he felt a chill run down his spine. His ear twitched, like a fly was buzzing around it. Gooseflesh rose on him. Calling time, he stepped out of the box, rolled his shoulders, and chopped at the air. A chill? It felt like it was a hundred degrees outside. Did he have a fever?

"Get in there, son," the ump said, gesturing to the box.

Artie nodded and stepped in. Then he heard it:

"*Artie.*" Nothing but a whisper. Over by the dugout, Wells was growling. Mickey was clapping, telling him to get a good pitch to hit. "*Artie,*" came the haunting murmur again. "*Artie.*"

Artie scratched his head and stepped back in. Now a sharp whistle, barely audible, fell into his ear like a drop of water, snaking through and into his brain. "D'ya hear that," he shouted, jumping out of the box.

"Hear what?" the ump cried. "Get in there and hit!"

Stepping in, he took a deep breath, pulled his bat back, and waited. "*Artie,*" came the whisper.

The whistle again. It attacked his skull, drove down through his bones like he was sitting on an electric chair. And then "*Artie,*" that ghostly whisper. He tried to shake it off, tried to focus. The pitcher kicked and delivered.

Adelis leapt onto his seat, screaming and whaling on his helmet. The wave of noise hit Artie like a torpedo into the side of a ship, and he swung at an awful pitch. His bat flew from his hands, spun end over end into the dugout, and clobbered Willie Wells right in the forehead, knocking him unconscious.

Artie sprang to the backstop, flailing at the webbing, trying to get at Adelis. Both the Browns' catcher and the ump struggled to restrain Artie, who was foaming at the mouth with rage. Adelis danced a little jig in the row, not two feet from Artie, and he chuckled, chortled, guffawed, waved his hand daintily, and then began to play a little tune on a concertina. The crowd loved it: the sight of a struggling ballplayer, gone insane with rage, caught in the backstop like some giant marlin, two—now three!—men doing their best to restrain him while this greasy giant of a man tormented the lot of them. To add to the fun, the fans tossed peanuts, popcorn, and hard-boiled eggs at poor Artie. One man pointed his stub of a cigar at Adelis and said, "Crikes, this oughter be some ball game!"

Wells was taken to the hospital where he was treated for a minor concussion. The rest of the game Adelis roared, cajoled, screeched; he played racist songs, farted, feigned snoring so loudly that he actually broke the crystal on a man's pocketwatch, and even played a wicked saw, which riled Gene Benson so much that he too swung and unleashed his bat ten feet into left field.

Cochrane shouted at his men, "Ignore him! He is nothing but bluster!" But Adelis had burrowed into their brains like a worm, and seemed even to have worked some hoodoo on their bats.

Campy knocked their only hit. The A's lost 1-0.

That evening Campanella pounded on Josh's door. Benson stood next to him, mumbling, "I'm tellin' ya, you'll see evidence of the hop. Ya see King Fat's face? Awful."

Josh opened the door and immediately broke into a sarcastic grin. He was bare-chested, dressed only in his shorts. "Surprise, surprise! Gracie, look who's come to visit! My star pupil!" Grace, sitting at a card table, wearing nothing but a slip, waved, her gaudy jewelry tinkling.

Campy rolled his eyes. Josh hadn't taught him much of anything lately, crowing over the home runs he was hitting with far less frequency. He grabbed Josh's arm and turned it to check the crook of his elbow. Josh frowned and said, "You are one suspicious bastard."

Benson said, "Check between the toes." Campy made a face.

"Go to hell," Josh said. "I'm clean."

Campy looked around the room. Clothes were scattered all over the floor. "What is going on?"

"My gal and I are playin' a little strip poker, if it's anything to you."

Benson stepped over next to Grace and scowled at her. He picked up her drink and tasted it without asking. "Ginger ale."

Grace shouted, "Christ, what you our lord high—you our judge 'n' jury?"

Campy kicked at Josh's shirt on the floor. "What the hell is the matter with you?" he shouted. "Gene and I, we been making promises about you, telling everybody . . . what in the hell's your problem?"

Josh held up his hand. "The mitt hurts a bit. Just an ache. I showed 'em in New York. You'll see."

"Oh, I'll see all right. I been waitin' all season to see. And what have I got? Nothin' to see but a has-been." Campy looked like he wanted to spit. "C'mon Gene. This place makes me sick."

They walked out. Josh stood in his doorway, fuming, and finally, as they reached the head of the stairs, shouted, "I been clean! You'll see! Josh Gibson's the greatest ballplayer on earth! Better'n Roy Campanella. Better'n Gene Benson! You'll see!"

Next day Josh bullied his way to the front of batting practice to take his swings. Wells fumed in the dugout, sitting out after his beaning the other day. Josh hit with decent power, scattered balls through the outfield, and even, to the shock of most, jogged with Cool and Jethroe on the warning track. But the whole time his teeth were gritted against the pain in his knees, and his stomach was in knots for the hell his body was putting him through.

Most of the gossip that day surrounded Veeck's announcement that he was returning to Shibe, the rightful owner of the team, and Landis would have to go to the highest court in the land to keep him from his office. "Now," Serrell read to Barnhill, from that day's paper, "the city's threatening that Shibe's gonna be condemned. How 'bout that. You can bet that's Landis. It's him all over."

Barnhill nodded. "Anything in there about Hal?"

Serrell shook his head. "White paper. Bet it's in the *Worker*."

"Yeah. Well, Rodney's working on it. So's the NAACP. I feel like—" Barnhill smiled. "Anyway, Josh's sure acting up."

"Old man's scared. I'd be too if I was hitting as bad as him, at that age."

Cochrane called them together, implored them not to give Adelis the satisfaction of being distracted, and emphasized a form of meditation in between innings. "Birdcalls, men," he said. "Focus on the birds. That was always my most effective defense against hecklers."

Wells was just about ready to kill the old man. Beaned by the worst hitting shortstop in all of baseball, and now birdcalls?

"Mickey doesn't understand," Artie complained to Butts. Butts listened and thought Artie was twice as skittish as before—terrified of Adelis and even more so of Wells, who refused to accept Artie's apology.

It was pandemonium in Sportsman's Park at two o'clock. Hot, heavy breezes were leaking through the old stadium, doing nothing to cool off the throng that had crammed themselves into every available space. The Browns' win the day before had left them three games in first with the best record the team had enjoyed in all its history. Never before had they come even close to second place in August. Every Browns fan in the city was at the ballpark—there really were that few—and Adelis meant to put on a show for each and every one. He made no attempt to hide himself this time, clanging, rubbing balloons, a chalkboard. In the fourth, in a blow that drove Artie almost literally crazy, he pulled a straight razor from his pocket, and when the kid stepped to the plate yelled, "Here's a suggestion!" and drew the razor across his throat, blood gushing.

"Pete!" Artie yelled, dropping his bat and racing to the backstop.

The crowd gasped. Adelis roared with laughter, pulled his hand across his neck, and suddenly no more blood.

Artie stood, trembling, bewildered, until the ump pulled him back to the plate. "Disgraceful," the umpire said. "Take it easy, son. Step in there and hit, that'll calm you." Artie seemed to agree, picked up his bat with a nearly lifeless hand, and stood in the box just as a hard-boiled egg struck him in the cheek.

He struck out five times that day.

As did Josh.

Waiting to bat in the eighth, Josh sat at the edge of the dugout, out of the view of the stands. "Gibson's next," he overheard someone mutter in the stands above. "Guy's got power like you wouldn't believe."

"Power. But that's all. Look at the rest of his numbers."

"Yeah, well, he knocked one out of the Bronx."

"So what? He can't even hit wartime pitching."

"Okay, so the guy strikes out a lot. But I heard he hit eighty dingers just a couple of years back."

"Against who? Negro Leagues worse than bushers, you ask me. Spite of the last few, guy's only got fourteen the whole season. Don't get me wrong, he's got some pop in that bat. But this is war pitchin'. Bring back the good guys, this guy'll be back to swinging against church leagues. Called him the Black Babe Ruth." There was a derisive laugh. "If this season's proved anything, this guy ain't any kind of Babe Ruth. And that league of theirs, nothin' but bush. Pure bush."

"'Spose you're right."

"Buck. That Cuban. Satch. Heck, most of 'em are major league, colored or otherwise. But Josh. That guy's nothing."

Cochrane shouted, "Josh? Are you going to hit, or do you want me to send Roy in?"

Josh stood and slowly walked to the plate. He took a couple of short swings with West and stepped in. Pulling his bat back, he waited for the next pitch. It came in, a darling curve that hung just right, and he clobbered it. The ball flew deep into the stands down the right-field line, foul. Next pitch came in, looming large as a pumpkin, a fastball straight down the heart of the plate. Josh's bat tore through the air, swinging so late the ball popped in the catcher's glove a split second before Josh even pivoted.

Sweat poured off him. Josh wanted to pluck his eyes out, buy new ones, anything. How had he missed that pitch? Shaking his head, he dug in, pulled West back, and again watched a perfect change-up float through his zone as if were being pulled in by a string. Josh swung with such force that he fell over on his bottom, in a cloud of dust. The crowd laughed.

Standing, he dusted himself off and walked rigidly back to the dugout, head hung low. "You'll get 'em next time," the batboy said. Josh was silent.

Strikeouts, weak flies, flabby grounders right at the Browns— and in one of their rare rallies, men on first and second, Artie to bat, a triple play against them. One by one, each of the A's wondered if all their luck over the past fifteen games had melted away. After the first two games with the Browns, the slurs intensified, their evenings were tense, sleep didn't come, and there were no more parties, just dinner, a few quiet drinks, and sleep.

They dropped all four games.

"At least we're going home," Serrell said from his bunk above Barnhill's. "And you're pitching well."

"We'll see," he said. "Hal would love a pennant."

"Season's not over yet."

Back in Philadelphia, around midnight, Veeck was mixing a hard drink before he headed to bed. Just as he was about to fall asleep, the telephone rang. He walked over to his desk, sat down, and lit a cigarette. The phone rang and rang. Sam could wait a moment for him to get the nicotine he needed. Finally he answered.

"Mr. Veeck, first of all, I'm not drunk."

"What? Who is this?" There was an unending clamor of machinery in the background.

"I'm at work. Third shift. Just got off break."

"Who is this?"

"Sorry. Name's Joe Early. I'm a big fan."

Veeck smiled. Okay, this I can handle. "Well, go ahead, Mr. Early."

"Call me Joe and I'll call you Bill, like I know you like. Listen, I been watching the A's all my life. This one, they're my favorite. Been havin' a great time at ol' Shibe too. Love them 'Nights.' Buck Leonard Night. Roy Campanella Night. Satchel Paige Night was the best. Thought the midgets were fun."

"Thank you," Veeck said, proud that someone appreciated Satchel's all-midget entourage.

"Thing is, Bill, ballplayers make pretty good dough. Me, I got kids, a mortgage, an old lady, no folks—they're dead, long time ago, influenza, I was lucky—but I got bills, you see? So, here's my idea. Why not have a Fan Night? You know, like, say, Joe Early Night?"

Veeck paused. "Joe Early Night?"

"Well, a Fan Night."

Veeck was sitting bolt upright. "Yes, yes, I understand."

"Okay," Early said, sounding utterly satisfied. "Just wanted to lay that one on ya. Gotta go!" He hung up.

Veeck laid the phone down on the receiver. He clicked off the light and sat in the dark, smoking. Shibe was barely discernible in the darkness. "Mr. Early," Veeck said. "I think you've got it."

◊ **17** ◊

Fan Appreciation Day

A manila envelope spun across Pete Adelis's linoleum with such velocity it seemed as if it had been thrust under the door by Satchel himself. Pete choked down the last bit of his cold cheesesteak hoagie as he ran to the door. He flung it open and checked the hallway. No one. He ran back to the front window and gaped down into the street. No one. Pete turned and stared at the envelope on the floor. For the last few months his breakfasts had been interrupted by these missives, which contained piles of private information on individual ballplayers. Inside were all the dirt on Artie Wilson's troubles, Ray Dandridge and his dog's various illnesses, Willie Wells's debts, Buck Leonard's real-estate problems, Roy Campanella's frustrations over Josh Gibson's various abuses. And all of it seemingly true, since whenever he worked it into his act it sure seemed to rattle everyone but Buck and Campy—though not for trying. Adelis scratched his jaw. Where did these reports come from? Some of the ones from the dugout, why, you'd have to have a spy down there. Then he shrugged to himself: did it matter? Paper-clipped to each report was a fifty-dollar bill. Adelis tore open the envelope with his teeth, slid the material out, pocketed the cash, and then, sucking bits of meat from his teeth, settled down on the davenport to do his homework.

Adelis fixed radios. His three-room apartment served as both home and office. Old radios were scattered throughout his living area and bedroom, even on top of the fridge. Quarts of paint, tubes, wires, tiny screws, pieces of replacement wood, manuals and newspapers were mingled among his personal belongings, mostly clothes he had piled on shelves (no dresser), his heckling getup, a picture of Franklin D. Roosevelt surrounded by reports from the war he couldn't fight in (chronic lumbago), and clippings of the Philadelphia Athletics, whom he'd followed religiously since he was a young boy. Every day he woke at dawn, worked until noon, ate, studied his reports, polished his kaiser helmet, digested his meal with a glass of Bromo Seltzer, practiced whistling, practiced his concertina, and finally arranged the whole works in a duffle bag before heading out to Shibe.

Before each game Adelis would steal out of his apartment through the alley, though there were usually a few people back there to give him grief or cheer him on. He walked briskly to the park, eager to get in and to his seat. As he drew nearer, the crowds thickened into great streams of fans. Adelis would never admit that he loved these crowds, neither would he admit that he sunk into a profound depression when the season ended. The rallyers; the cheap merchandisers, plugging their nickel wares from bushel baskets at their feet; the red-faced street preachers like moths to the great flames of sinners; the bums palming for spare change; and soldiers and sailors and sailors and soldiers, walking in hungry packs, or individually hanging onto some girl like she was the only thing in the world. Now and again, someone wanted *his* autograph, wanted to give the Iron Lung of Shibe Park some advice, or try to shout him down, making him feel like a gunfighter having to take on all comers. But the crowds also heightened his sense of loneliness: in truth, people didn't like Adelis and he didn't particularly like them, except for the folks on the radio, and the actress Gene Tierney.

"Keep 'em on their toes, Pete," the shrimp at the Lehigh Avenue stile said as he tore the Lung's ticket. Pete just nodded. Pushing through the great crowds, you would not be able to miss Pete Adelis, towering six foot seven with the shiny kaiser helmet, dressed in a white T-shirt, suspenders, and slacks, his big duffel bag and that belly that hung out over his waist like a prizewinning pumpkin. He didn't stop for hot dogs or beer. How could you shout with your mouth full of food? For Pete Adelis, plunging into the back of a broken Atwater radio or driving great spikes of noise into Artie Wilson's skull were both job and play. My work, he often thought, is more than what I do. I'm a performer, an artist, he would say.

At his seat behind home plate, he unpacked his tools: billy club, chalkboard, concertina, a dinged-up bugle this time, and a metronome hooked up to a small radio that he would amplify with the hope of messing with the players' timing. He sprayed his throat and blew a pitch pipe, then bellowed at the groundskeeper, who fell over his rake as a result.

The old fellow next to him winced. "Gah, Jesus, every game is it? Christ they warned me but . . . damn."

Already Adelis was soaked in sweat. Philadelphia felt as if it had been roasting in a Dutch oven for the past week. Out in the broiling sun, the humidity seemed to pour out of the white-hot sky, billowing down in thick clouds that made even sitting seem like a chore.

Seeing that Pete had quieted for a moment, the old fellow nodded toward right field, and said, "What do you think about Veeck's triumphant return?" Pete looked over to where the old fellow had gestured. Sure enough, there was Veeck in the right-field stands, surrounded by reporters who watched him drench himself with the new showers built to cool the fans off if they so desired. Boy, Pete thought, that sure looks good. But he was a professional, so he wiped the sweat off his forehead and hoped privately that a few girls would take a walk under those showers.

Adelis checked his stub: there, in bright blue and white and yellow, was Artie Wilson's face, printed on the ticket like a baseball card. Adelis smiled, exposing grey teeth. Oh, he'd give the kid the what-for today, just like in St. Louis. Snapped Wilson's little hitting streak like a dry twig. Adelis set the metronome at a slow speed. It ticked loudly, satisfactorily. He wet his lips. Where did he get these ideas? It was brilliance, sheer brilliance.

He sat back, watching over the old guy's shoulder as the man filled out his scorecard. Pete thought about that day's reports. Josh, it read, had been worrying excessively, barely sleeping. If he wasn't busy swinging his lumber early, boning them obsessively, or working on his crouch and throw, he would be sitting at dusk on the stoop of his house, trying to count the bats that flew crooked against the darkening sky. Pete could see Gibson though his binoculars, penciling some numbers on an old scorecard, now worn soft with folding and erasing. The reports told him that Josh would recalculate his average with each at bat. Pete noticed that should Gibson fail to play, he'd do the math again; if he failed to gather even one squibbler hit, he'd recalculate one more time. As the season shortened, the number of hits required to gain respectability increased.

Adelis's reports told him that Campy was little help to Josh. The kid would stop by Gibson's house with a casserole his mother baked, on the pretense of trying to get the slugger to sit and eat a decent dinner for a change. But he was obviously sniffing around for evidence that Josh and Grace had fallen back on the needle, all the while examining Josh's swings, trying to get to the bottom of why he struck out on such lousy pitches, berating Grace for being such a mess. Before games, Campy would burst into the bullpen, patronize Josh, obviously still skeptical of his sobriety. Campy sniffed his water, looking for booze. All this was good stuff, Adelis thought—maybe today I can get under the kid's skin as well.

In no time the stands were filled, the apartments across the street crawling with gawkers, and the Wheel was rolled to the mound to great applause. A little old lady was called in and almost fell over spinning it. It stopped on CENTER. Funny, Adelis thought, squinting, it never lands on the same spot two days in a row. A fix? Maybe he'd write a letter to the *Inquirer*. Then, to everyone's surprise, trumpets blared—from out in right field, a cherry-red '38 Plymouth convertible idled in, Veeck behind the wheel, flanked by a pair of bathing beauties that made Adelis's heart crinkle. A pack of photographers, from the major weeklies to the newsreels, stepped to the edge of the diamond, shooting away as the car pulled up beside the mound.

As Veeck climbed out, ushers in tuxedos began to roll out a variety of prizes. The cavalcade took a good fifteen minutes, with each treasure meeting a wave of thunderous applause. There were cases of Ballantine Ale and Moxie soda pop, six giant cans of Hershey's chocolate syrup, a box of Phillies blunt cigars, five robust hams, a midget bearing a gift certificate for forty gallons of gas, an Underwood typewriter, two bags of flour and one of beans, a hunting rifle, a set of pots and pans, a Schwinn bicycle with a shiny new horn, two pairs of suits and a dozen socks, and, topping this all off, pushed in a wheelbarrow by a circus strongman, a pile of five hundred silver dollars, which rolled up between the leggy women. Finally, another girl carried in a rose horseshoe with the words NUMBER ONE FAN emblazoned across it. Pete's eyes glowed: here were all the promises of wealth, nourishment, and sex.

Then his brow furrowed. This might be something, it might. Heckle the number one fan. Some poor schmuck wins, isn't expecting the treatment. Might just doom the whole series for these guys. He noticed the team lining up to greet the champion fan—they wouldn't expect old Pete to do anything but gawk.

Veeck held up his hands to silence the oohs and ahhs drifting from the stands. "Ladies and gentlemen," he announced, "let me tell you that it is my sincere pleasure to be here today, with you, in

Shibe." More applause. "Today, in spite of the best efforts of a certain unnamed judge who happens to hold a prominent place in major league baseball—" Heavy boos. "Now, now, the spirit of charity everyone, the spirit of charity!" he said, but caught himself laughing. "In spite of this individual's efforts, the Philadelphia Athletics baseball club is proud to announce that with today's crowd, we have just broken the all-time Philadelphia attendance record." This brought a standing ovation, even from Pete, as the men and women and children in the stands could now roar their delight at having participated in one of the many broken records of this Philadelphia ball club.

"Thank you, thank you," Veeck said, after allowing the noise to diminish on its own accord. "Today is our first annual Fan Appreciation Day, so in the seventh inning, during the stretch, there will be free beer and soda pop, one for every fan!" With this the crowd exploded in joy, throwing hats and scorecards in the air, and making the police fidget with the thought that these hooligans would be indulging in barrels of free beer in less than two hours. "Folks," Veeck said. "As I said, the Philadelphia Athletics couldn't have done it without you—"

Adelis couldn't resist, shouting into the small pause: "You coulda ended up in the basement without us!" he roared, to a smattering of laughter.

Ignoring that, Veeck continued, "In the past, our sponsors have generously supported a number of player nights. Some of you good people have taken collections to buy watches for many of our players, and we all thank you from the bottom of our heart. But that got me to thinking that it was time to thank the fans." Adelis sat coiled at the edge of his seat, club and bugle ready, ready to blow this unsuspecting sap right onto his bum. "And especially one fan, a fellow who's made playing here in Shibe a real treat. This fellow has attended every home game, and even quite a few on the road." Probably some old fart, Adelis thought, don't let that rattle you. Old, young, they all deserve it.

Veeck smiled, pointed behind the plate and shouted, "Please give a Shibe Park welcome to our number one fan: *Pete Adelis!*"

Adelis jumped up ready to blast his bugle when the words sank in. He stood with his mouth hanging open. The pair of gorgeous women sauntered up to the gate to the field, urging him on like a pair of sirens. Sweat began to trickle off his forehead, down his sides—he could feel every drop. His brain froze—this had to be a trick. Now it was his turn for utter public ridicule. But he was just one guy against a whole ball club! Run! Pete wiped his brow, felt a few hands patting him on the back, voices shouting at him, echoing through the confusion. He'd look like even more of a jerk if he ran away. Besides, look at all that ham. Summoning up his courage, Pete set his club and bugle on his seat, asked the old guy next to him to watch his stuff, and walked stiffly down to where the soft hands of the girls took him by the arms and led him to the gauntlet of players.

They were bigger up close. Darker, stronger, meaner, able to rip Pete's head right off its stump, scatter his brains across the diamond. They looked as if they could tear his limbs out to use for that day's bats.

Buck slapped him playfully on the shoulder. "Thanks, Pete, for whooping it up every day." Then Campy: "Boy, it's an honor to get the rib from you!" And so on down the line, Ray Dandridge tipping his cap and handing it over as a souvenir, while Satchel Paige stunned the crowd by pulling a fifty-dollar war bond from Pete's ear. By the time he reached the end of the line, Pete was drenched in goodwill, his mind racing. When he reached Artie Wilson, he paused, and Artie grinned politely, ready to shake his hand quickly. It was too much for Pete. The floodgates didn't open—the dam burst. Shaking with love for this team, he suddenly embraced the beleaguered shortstop, then turned to the mike, pulling Artie with him, and announced: "This one's my favorite!"

Pete Adelis was finally understood. In spite of the fact that he'd been fed personal information on the club each morning and had personally tried to sabotage the Athletics at every turn, in a matter of seconds Pete felt they finally understood that his heckling had always been for the benefit of the club. He'd even convinced himself of that fact. And now here he was, surrounded by a holy halo of ballplayers, beautiful girls like he'd normally scare away on the bus, and a cornucopia of prizes. *All for him.*

Veeck leaned in and, over the din, said into the mike, "Pete, you're one of us."

Still leaking tears, Pete turned to the microphone, and, summoning up a reminder of recent glory, said, "Today I consider myself the luckiest fan on the face of the earth!"

As the applause died down and the gifts were wheeled off the diamond, Pete returned to his seat, which was now adorned with gold and a plaque that officially deemed it "Pete's Throne." Then, at precisely 1:07 p.m., Eastern Daylight Time, August 4, 1944, for the first time all season, fueled by the love and admiration of the Philadelphia Athletics, Bill Veeck, and all 39,198 paid—who gave him a standing ovation as he returned to the stands—the Iron Lung of Shibe Park, setting his metronome, drawing his bugle to his lips, unleashed the full force and authority of his heckling on the New York Yankees. And every opponent that would cross the Athletics path from then on.

"We have captured the bear," Veeck said, settling into his seat. The Yankees couldn't have seen it coming. It wasn't fair. Pete was unmerciful, scraping his claws across a blackboard to the point where one of the Yankees was crying from the pain. When the third batter struck out, his bat flew out of his hands and hit his own base runner, as if lifted there by the wave of noise issuing from Adelis's lungs. "What's going on?" the next batter squealed, shaking and scratching himself all over. "That whistling, it makes me *itch*!"

The Yankees' skins crawled. They fought an acute tinnitus, battled nausea, and felt a sense of frustration and shame and anger they had never experienced before. The metronome, clicking away at a level that just tickled the inner ear, sent each batter swinging early or late. By the ninth, four players had been thrown out of the game for attempting to assault Pete.

Artie, cheered on by the Lung, opened the first with his second homer of the year, a Buck Leonard–like blast that smashed through the window of the now empty Devil's Island apartment. "Jesus," he thought, circling the bases, "it felt like my bat was charged with electricity." Wells doubled. The Yankee pitcher wiped his brow after each throw, adjusting himself, rattled by the tidal wave of sound Adelis was hurling at him. Odd, too, was the fact that, when directed at others, the Athletics did not notice the racket. "Seems just like plain old shouting," Cool noted.

And so with a big lead and no outs in the fifth, a new pitcher, and the bases loaded, Artie stepped up to bat again. Now it was like a ship emerging from the horse latitudes with a hurricane in its sails. His bat felt light, and the pitcher seemed as weak and brittle as spun glass, the ball dangling from an invisible tether in front of him. Artie Wilson, normally unnerved with the weight of three base runners in his path, cleared them like a reaper, slashing his bat and connecting with a slow curve that knocked out a different pane of glass in a different apartment. "The Athletics provided our local glass merchants with a run of new business," Low wrote in the *Daily Worker*.

Spink was himself unnerved by the ease with which the A's dispatched the Yanks. *Veeck continues to flout the commissioner's authority, and proceeds to deliver blow after low blow on the noble Yankees, who had to endure the abuse from one Mr. Pete Adelis, now in the Athletics' employ*, Spink wrote. *Mr. Veeck would have baseball ruin the war effort, would have the president himself berated, if only to make a morsel at the turnstiles. He is anathema to the war effort, playing in a dangerous park, flaunting the rules of rationing, building codes, and even labor and draft edicts*. Spink didn't believe half of what he wrote, which only raised his ire.

And Veeck, unlike the other owners Spink had ever encountered, acted as if the *Sporting News* didn't exist. He assailed Landis at every opportunity. Veeck spent the last week making himself visible at every bar and tavern and nightclub, promised a week's worth of fireworks every night at dusk, and let the fans have the run of the park after each contest. Lines gathered outside the Oval Office while he took more suggestions on running the club.

After his A's mauled the Yankees that day, Veeck laid out a spread, with prime rib and scotch, and the press ate up both his food and his words. Already he'd been followed all afternoon by a pack of ravenous photographers and hacks from the major weeklies. Immediately after the contest, Veeck held a press conference with ten of the most highly regarded building inspectors in town. They declared that Shibe Park was not only structurally sound but "in as fine a condition as any major league ballpark that we have seen, and as far from being condemned as a hundred buildings in the Philadelphia metropolitan area." The head inspector leaned in, and with a wry smile held up a document and crowed, "Even better than the City Hall, which, after a secret inspection conducted this very afternoon, I declare is in violation of over *two hundred* codes!"

Veeck beamed, wrapping his arms over the shoulders of the two closest inspectors, all of whom loved being the center of attention for once in their lives. "Gentlemen of the press," Veeck said, "if the commissioner's going to encourage the city of Philadelphia to condemn Shibe"—as had been threatened by the mayor the day after Veeck's announcement of his return—"then I urge him to do so. I will call the commissioner to the stand and force him to go on record for a change, instead of hiding behind city officials too scared to stand up for themselves."

"Gentlemen," Veeck said, "I have a good feeling about this ball club. You watch, the Philadelphia Athletics are going to make a run for the pennant." He laughed. "This year!"

"Eleven games back in August?" the *Record*'s Stan Keller remarked. "Let me have some of what you're drinking."

But the fans felt it too. After four months and just over a hundred games, it seemed as if the hoodoo was finally working. The amulets, the prayers, the talismans. Knuckles worn bare on wood. Balls tossed in the air thirteen times, caught each time. One fellow would walk from home without stepping on a single sidewalk crack, make his way delicately to Shibe, then hike around it three times before strolling up to gate seven, handing his ticket upside-down, and tapping the same beam twice before finding his seat. Paperboys would lob the *Philadelphia Record* just right, to land on the doormat without even an inch over the edge. "You do that," one explained to his younger brother, "and the pitcher gets a hit. Happens every time. Even Barnhill, who can't hit, I got it square in the center, and he drilled that homer in Washington, 'member?"

The kid remembered. He had his own shrine to Pee Wee Butts, and his brother had one to Sam Jethroe. Both players were on minor tears. And these kids and the men who turned their radios on four times and the women who brushed their teeth in just the right way felt, suddenly, the power of the ancient Greek gods—that victory was theirs to grant, that the A's opponents were nothing but dust.

Even the opposition players were going a little crazy: After Detroit was drubbed in four, one Tiger rattled on like a madman that Adelis ought to be caged, that Barnhill was throwing spitters, that Satch and Dihigo had done something illegal. Of course he didn't know what that would be—perhaps someone had put a plug of lead in his own bat, at which point, in front of a reporter with the *Free Press*, he proceeded to smash his favorite stick apart, looking for the lead. Inside there was nothing but wood.

Special reports rang out to the most tangled fighting in the Pacific and European theaters about the progress of the Athletics. How the five starters, Barnhill, Dihigo, Paige, Smith, and Verdell Mathis, were giving up an average of four hits and less than one run per game. How Smith nearly got a no-hitter, which would have been the fifth of the year for the team. Of Buck Leonard's tailing the Babe by a handful of homers and leaping high over the .400 mark. And Artie Wilson's bat finally coming alive. Soon the A's were just five behind the Brownies.

"Two weeks ago?" Veeck shouted, slapping the sports page.

"Eleven back," Sam said, dejectedly.

"And now?"

"Unprecedented, that's all I have to say."

"With just over forty to go, a pennant doesn't seem all that far-fetched. Or am I still dreaming?"

Sam and Veeck were sitting in the Oval Office, drinking and going over their debts late into the evening. "True," Sam admitted. "But we didn't count on half of our bills. Without extra income, we're doomed. And I can't find extra income—that's legal, anyway." Sam recalculated for the last time: "We cannot make a profit this season," he said, with a heavy sigh. "Pennant or no . . ."

"Wait," Veeck said, holding up his hand. "It just occurred to me: according to the contract, we have to show a profit by season's end. Including the World Series."

"So what!" Sam shouted. Then, just as suddenly, he clamped his mouth shut. "Bill . . ."

"Stop it, boy . . . you know I've got something. We're the hottest team in history, the team I knew they would be. They're finally having some fun. . . ."

"Bill, we can't guarantee a berth in the World Series. . . ."

"How much will we make if we go to the big show?"

"I can't say for sure. We might go to the Series and still lose the team."

"Indulge me."

Sam bit his tongue, closed his eyes, and began again. This was no easy task; in the World Series there were monies to be made from the league, from ticket sales, from broadcast rights, all of which were on record from the past. There were also concessions and souvenirs, which he could only speculate on. But Sam set to his work. After seventeen minutes he removed his glasses, rubbed his eyes, and sipped his flat beer. He held up a slip of paper. "Bill," he said, "using the best-case scenarios on food and so forth, we will, if we win the pennant and get a Series share . . . we will end up with a total profit of $160."

Veeck stared at Sam. On the wall over Veeck's shoulder a cuckoo burst out of its clock and announced six o'clock in the morning. When it finished, he said, quietly, "A hundred and sixty dollars, huh?"

"That's right. More if the Series goes to seven games, even more if we win."

Veeck stood and walked over to the kitchenette by the wall. He opened the refrigerator and pulled out some eggs. "Scrambled or fried?"

"Scrambled, fried, hard-boiled, I don't care," Sam said, joining Veeck and making some coffee. They cooked in silence for a moment, enjoying the task and the sound of the percolator and the eggs popping in the pan. They sat down Indian-style on the floor and watched the sun come up, drinking black coffee and chewing eggs.

Sam said, "It was a good run, Bill. Had we sold Leonard, we might not have made it, either, for all the people he brings in."

"Thanks for admitting that."

"I always liked Buck, and I just . . . I just wanted this again next year." Sam said. "That first year after Milwaukee, Bill, I thought I'd just die. Sitting in my dull office after a year of . . . well, a year like this."

Veeck nodded. "I know. It's impossible to go back." He stared out at the sky and sighed.

Sam finished his eggs and then gazed out at the stands, turning a gunmetal grey in the dawn. "I hope it's easier for the next guy."

Veeck nodded. "It's always easier for the next guy. Only," he added, "it isn't as much fun."

Chicago came to town with new bats and new pitchers: when the batters could manage to hit the ball (which wasn't often), their ground balls and line drives and shots to the gap were swallowed by a defense so light on its feet you could call it ballet. When Boston came to town, awful Boston, their pitchers might as well have been tossing the ball underhand.

The A's success could not keep Spink at bay: finally he had resorted to allowing that the Athletics were one of the "greatest wartime teams ever assembled, and surely a solid third-place team in the best of years." Jethroe cut the article out, tacked it to the bulletin board, and it became their war cry for the next week: "The greatest third-place team in history! Next week the greatest second-place team! One step at a time to the greatest!"

On the morning before their inaugural game against the first-place Browns, Grace woke to find Josh sitting in bed and staring out the window at the park across the street. A group of children had been hammering a ball around since they could see it in the dawn. It wasn't much more than a pitcher and a batter knocking the ball to a gaggle of five more kids out in center, who fought, kicked, and jumped for every fly.

Josh picked up a cup of coffee and offered it to Grace, who joined him at the window. "Did you see that?" he said, leaning toward the screen. "That kid made some catch."

She took a chance on touching him, stroking his head. His shoulders relaxed. "You're tired, hon," she said. "Tired, like me. Doc said we'd have these days, the upsies and slide-downs. You ought to tell them about your aches and pains—"

"No."

"Josh," she whispered. "You worry too much. Don't worry about this season. They'll still remember you." Josh watched the children play. "Whyn't you go over and play with them, Josh."

"Don't feel like it."

"*Honey.* You love playing ball."

"Children are cruel," he said, standing abruptly. "Get dressed. I got to get to the ballpark, can't wait on you."

Three hours before the game, the streets around Shibe were so crowded with people you could roll a baseball over their heads and it wouldn't fall to the ground. Children were everywhere, pretending to be Buck, who was now sitting just a homer shy of Ruth's record.

Mickey was sick that morning. He did not want to face the chore in front of him. The evening before he'd spoken with his coaches, even Oscar—especially Oscar. Josh was going down. To

Milwaukee. Then over the phone to Mr. Veeck, who kept clearing his throat even as he agreed. Milwaukee would be the lifeboat, just the thing to get Josh back in the game. Besides, the Brewers were a good team and Barnhill had softened everyone up for a Negro on the club. But Cochrane knew deep down that this wouldn't be the same for Josh as it was for Barnhill. Gibson's season was over. Maybe his career was over.

Sitting in his office, his anxiety once again brought out memories of his son. Over and over the kid with the yellow telegram and the purple tie. Gordon moving to California, Gordon doing his duty, doing his duty, doing his duty, that statement echoing in his head. Cochrane took a deep breath and walked out. In the dugout he surveyed the field. There was Josh, practicing his crouch and throws. Buck and Ray were already on the diamond, tossing the ball around. Campy and Gene were nowhere. Summoning up his courage, Cochrane jogged from the dugout to Josh.

"Josh," Cochrane said, and he put his hand on the catcher's shoulder to make sure there would be eye contact. "If we can take these games, I believe we will win the pennant."

"Oh, yes, absolutely."

Cochrane glanced around, as if confiding a secret. He sighed, and said, "Josh, you will not be playing in this series."

There was a brief moment of silence while the news sunk in. Then Josh nodded quickly. "Good, yes, good, let the boy play, he—"

"Josh," Cochrane added, "Mr. Veeck and I have had a discussion. We are sending you down to Milwaukee."

Josh chewed his lower lip and began massaging his glove.

"You only need a little seasoning. The Brewers worked wonders with Barnhill. Coach Ringer has agreed to play you each and every day. He is a fine hitting coach, and—"

Josh shook his head. "'Scuse me, but I . . . I can't do it."

Cochrane folded his arms. "And why is that?"

Josh looked up at last. "I'm old, Mickey. Older'n my thirty-three years. This is it for me. You take that pennant without Josh Gibson and . . .," he paused, looked out at the stands, filling with people, ". . . they won't understand." He pulled out a paper with his batting averages calculated. "Look, Mr. Cochrane, you can't send me down, 'cause I got it figured out. If I play and hit well in the last month, I can show 'em. I done it before, just last year in fact, so I can do it again. I'm Josh Gibson, don't you get it? Could have played 'longside Ruth, Gehrig, better than Dickey, better than you! You can't send me down, understand?"

Cochrane looked at that scrap of paper in Josh's hand. Then he kicked at the turf and said, "You can watch from the dugout and catch in the bullpen this series. And then you have a ticket for the ten o'clock train to Milwaukee on Thursday, when we leave for Boston. You *and* Miss Fournier, of course." He stared Josh in the eyes. "I am truly sorry, Josh." He extended his hand. Josh walked away.

Despite beating St. Louis in a squeaker, the mood in the dugout was sour. And it got worse: the Browns were relentless, walking Buck the whole series. He batted fifteen more times and received fifteen more intentional walks. Fans screamed, shouted, the press was adamant—there was even a comment by Eleanor Roosevelt in the *Saturday Evening Post* decrying the Browns for cowardice. Adelis roared, trumpeted, and drove the Browns to distraction, but they wouldn't budge. And so, when the Philadelphia Athletics took the first three games from the Browns, to sit but two games back in the standings with one left against them, Buck Leonard was still sitting at fifty-nine home runs.

That night Josh Gibson went for a walk. The few clouds had torn open as the sun set, igniting the sky with orange, and now the night seemed to exhale over the city. The weather reminded him of a May evening, just last year. Back when the *Pittsburgh Courier* had called him "unbelievable" and he had outhit everyone. Old Wendell Smith said he was the greatest catcher in history. Even a reporter from the *Sporting News* claimed he'd never seen a catcher like Josh Gibson, though he didn't print it.

Josh walked through the run-down neighborhoods of Nicetown, at the buildings that used to stand tall and proud and now looked like something big had knocked them askew. You wouldn't know to walk the neighborhood that it had once been beautiful, a place you could be proud of. Josh stood by an empty lot, broken glass and weeds and dog shit, and wondered what had been there before. He would never know.

Josh had wandered into the wrong neighborhood. He wanted to wander into the wrong neighborhood. He shuffled up a broken sidewalk to a run-down grey shack. Tick Jones sat on his front porch and flashed a few gold teeth and smiled as Josh approached. "Mr. Gibson," Tick said. "Haven't seen you in a coon's age."

Josh fidgeted. He nodded. "How you sittin'?"

"Fine, as always. Heard about Milwaukee. That's a crime. Why, Josh, you the greatest there ever was."

Josh scowled at this. "Shoulda taken better care of myself. No one's fault but my own."

Jones stood. "Don't blame yourself. Fuckin' nigger Campanella stole your job right out from under you."

"Shut up." Josh pulled some money from his pocket. "I've got twenty bucks."

"Shit, my friend," Tick said, grinning. "I'm just trying to cheer you up. But, hell with you, you come here sour. Shit, Josh, if you'd just stayed down in the leagues, you'd still be something today—"

"I told you to shut up," Josh said, grabbing Tick by the shirt. He lifted him off the ground, his fists curling around the loose skin on Tick's chest. "I told you to be quiet!"

Tick howled in pain. Josh smashed his fist in the thin man's face. He fell to the floor and didn't move. "That'll teach you," Josh said, standing over him. "Don't say nothin' about me, nothin' about Roy, you motherfucker." Josh checked Tick for a stash. Packet in hand, he crumpled the money into a ball and threw it on the body.

There was a groan. "Gibson," Tick croaked. "You paid. You paid, but you still gonna pay." Josh lit out for home.

Grace was in the living room, curled beside the radio. There were tears in her eyes. "Christ, honey bear, you ought to hear this soap story."

Josh scowled. "Shut that thing off, would you. You listen to that crap all day." He stormed out of the living room and headed out to the backyard, banging the screen door as he left.

After a moment, Grace followed him. Josh sat on a barrel, staring at the sky. "Baby?" she said. "It's gonna be—"

"Gracie, I'm not goin' to Milwaukee."

"Okay, baby."

"Can't do it. Understand?"

"Of course, baby."

"Times'll be rough." He gave her a thin smile. "But I thought we'd celebrate a little bit tonight." He held out the brown paper bag. She looked inside.

"Oh, my, Josh." A giggle escaped. "Oh, my."

"Can't all be angels," he said. His throat was rough as sandpaper. Glancing up at the sky, he noticed it was nothing but a slab of deep black. The city had devoured the stars. "There's nothing there," he mumbled. "Not a damn thing."

"Well, come on inside," Grace said, wrapping her arm around Josh's. "We got too much on our minds, baby. Too, too much."

Satchel Paige was on the mound the next day, firing his twin fastballs and that crazy, slow curve that seemed to vanish as it cut across the plate. The Browns couldn't do anything against him, and the A's mopped up the series.

Only Campy seemed depressed. Josh had never showed.

"Looks like Old Fat gave up on his last chance," Benson said. "That's gratitude for you."

"Quiet, Gene," Campy said, but he felt the same. Josh had let him down. Again, and in the worst way. Their last game together and he didn't come to the park?

Afterward Campy ran through a line of reporters to his car. He was an expert behind the wheel and managed, after twelve blocks, to shake the press with the ease of a seasoned taxi driver.

He pulled up in front of Josh's little grey shack, parked, and walked to the front porch. Weighing whether or not he should knock, he erred on the side of caution and pounded on the screen, which rattled. Nothing. After a moment, he knocked again, then didn't wait to let himself in.

The living room was dark and smelled stale. Dusk barely lit the place. Hamburger wrappers, apple cores, and peach pits lay all over the coffee table and couch. Campy reached down and picked up a brown paper bag. He looked inside. "Okay, Josh," he said with a sigh. In the kitchen he threw the bag with the syringe into the trash, closed the refrigerator door that had been left open, then walked down the hall and by the bedroom. He peeked in, careful to listen for the sounds of action he wasn't in any mood to see. There they were, crashed out in the bed. Campy turned, walked to the bathroom, and turned the shower on full blast. Making his way to the kitchen, he brewed a fresh pot of coffee. He checked his watch—still time to get Josh on the last train to Milwaukee. Sitting beneath the harsh light of the single bulb, still swinging a bit from being pulled on, Campy mused. Maybe, he thought, maybe Milwaukee would be the charm. Shit, who was he kidding? Campy pulled a mug off the top of the fridge, shook his head, and brought down a second. He had no desire to help Grace, none whatsoever. She probably got Josh back into trouble. But he remembered the doctor telling him they went hand in hand, his failures hers, and vice versa.

Carrying the steaming mugs into the bedroom, Campy set them down on the end table, opened the blinds to let in the sunset, reached over and flipped on the light. He blasted the radio to wake them. A riotous clatter of jazz came pouring out.

"Let's go!" he shouted. "You been sleeping all day?" Campy wished Gene were with him—Josh would be heavy. Standing over the bed, Campy shouted, "You're goin' to Milwaukee if it's the last thing I do!" Campy reached over and grabbed his arm. Josh was dead.

He recoiled, gasped, and stepped backwards, knocking over the radio. It crashed and the room fell silent. Campy stood frozen for a moment. Breathing hard, he leaned forward, carefully, and whispered, "Josh?" Campy reached close to caress Josh's cheek. Looking up, he noticed that Grace's eyes were open, unmoving. He closed them gently. "Josh?" he asked, his voice soft as a child's. Blinking rapidly, he leaned over and pulled the blanket up over them. He picked up the radio and set it in the center of the table. He walked into the bathroom and turned the shower off. The phone began to ring. He took the mugs from the bedroom to the kitchen, dumped out the coffee, and washed the dishes. Each time he stopped by the bedroom, he paused and stared at the two bodies, and said, "Josh?"

Finally, after the place was in order, after the phone had rung itself out, Campy stood in the doorway, staring at the bed. "Josh?" he said. He saw the case with Josh's bats. Those bats, he thought. Campy stepped inside and brought the case up to the table. He took out West and laid it between them. "There you go, Josh," he said. Then, carefully again, he switched off the light and walked out into the living room. He picked up the phone and called the police.

With his head in his hands, the bat case on his lap, Campy muttered "Josh" over and over. Soon red and blue lights flashed in through the curtains, the silence was broken by a clumping on the porch, and the police knocked loudly on the door. Campy closed his eyes. The pounding at the door grew louder, and it felt as if they were pounding on his head.

◇ **18** ◇

Season's End

Josh Gibson was dead. Even in Philadelphia the news sat in a corner of the front page, beneath the headlines of the liberation of Paris. Adelis, first hearing it on the Mutual Radio Network at dawn, dropped what he was doing, grabbed his bugle, and ran out the door. He didn't stop until ten blocks away, where he breathlessly pounded on the apartment door of the Shibe Park groundskeeper. Five minutes later the two of them were driving to the park. Then, while the yawning groundskeeper unfurled the flag to half-mast, Adelis stood on the damp grass before home plate and blew taps, which could be heard all the way outside the stadium, to the crowds of people who had already gathered on the sidewalk to pay their respects. Pete knew how to play taps—he was a lonely man and mourned nearly every day.

Someone stole Josh's uniforms, shoes, and catcher's glove from the locker room. A dignified man in a maroon cardigan circled the park, over and over, shouting, "What happened, Josh?" Some people scoffed: it was sad, yeah, but he wasn't anything more than a mediocre backup. A pair of kids with big Josh Gibson buttons stood outside the park, shivering in the early morning, bewildered, unsure how to act, trying not to cry or laugh nervously.

Red Hourly wondered aloud if the "whole fuckin' enterprise weren't cursed." Campy didn't show; neither did Cochrane. By noon, half the team boarded the Golden Triangle Limited to Boston to begin a three-game series against the Red Sox, with Mack Filson running the club. Most of the regulars, the men who'd played with Josh their entire careers, and Cochrane, would take the Fort Pitt Express to Pittsburgh for the funeral, then fly to Boston the following day.

Like Cartwheel, Josh's funeral brought baseball players of every skill level, using every available mode of transportation, from the thumb to the boxcar to the first-class Pullman. Nearly nine hundred people crammed into the Deliverance Evangelical Church, along with Campy, Oscar, Buck, Satchel, Willie, Ray, Cool, Hilton Smith, Verdell Mathis and Bill Byrd and Cochrane; more than two thousand more crowded the narrow lawn out front and into the street, necks craning to catch the words as they trickled through the slim transoms beneath the stained glass windows. They had come from playing baseball outside their factories and farms, men still toiling in the moribund Negro Leagues, in the worst little hovels and hamlets of the South, girls and women who also played for nothing but the sheer fun of it all. Many had followed Josh in his days in the Negro Leagues. Their dress clothes were wrinkled from being folded into cardboard valises, rutabaga sacks, or carried under their arms. Police stood watch, but there was no trouble. Later, Josh Gibson was buried along with his bat West in a small cemetery in Homestead. Grace was laid to rest next to him, holding a small photo of the two of them posed in Cartwheel.

The morning following the funeral, Veeck woke late in his hovel at the Sunnydale Cabins, around nine, his back aching and feeling stump-headed. He showered and dressed, eager to get to the ballpark and out of this crummy hole. Sipping coffee from a paper cup, he was surprised to hear a timid knock at the door.

"In!" he cried. Mack Filson stepped in. "Filson!" Veeck said, summoning up his last reserves of good cheer. "Good news from the pitching coach?"

Filson shook his head as he approached. He was dressed in slacks and a sport shirt. He wore his pride and joy—a warm-up jacket with the little elephant on the sleeves, bright white PHILADEL-PHIA emblazoned across the chest. "Mr. Veeck," he said, "I . . . I don't know how to say this, so I guess I'll have to come right out. I've been a traitor. I gotta resign." He ceremoniously pulled the jacket off and laid it out on the bed.

Veeck paused mid-sip. He took a deep breath. "I'm going to tell you something I want you to keep in confidence. Mickey tried to do the same thing earlier this season. I wouldn't let him. Just like I won't let you. But first tell me the whole drama, all four acts."

Mack screwed his mouth at Veeck's merriment. He held out a worn paper bag. Veeck took it and looked inside.

"The guts of a telephone . . . ?"

"Mr. Veeck, that's what I'm talking about, a traitor." He cleared his throat. "Mr. Veeck, a couple months ago I was called to the commissioner's office, and met him and Mr. Hoover . . ."

"Hoover?"

"J. Edgar Hoover, yessir, I met them and—" here his voice broke. He gathered himself and began again, but all he could say was "and—" before he had to clamp his mouth shut to keep the emotions from breaking loose. Veeck offered him a glass of water. Mack shook his head and began his tale. The whole story burst through his eyes and his mouth, tears and words and gusts of air that sometimes made him difficult to understand. Stories that should have made Veeck angry, furious, beside himself, except that he'd been bludgeoned so much already, another blow just didn't hurt.

"Well, maybe that's where Adelis got some of his dope," Veeck said. "Maybe the FBI was feeding him some reports. Continue." When Mack was through watering, Veeck slipped the jacket back on Mack's shoulders. He said, "Mackie, as long as I'm working in baseball, you'll have a job, you got that?" Mack did, and shook Veeck's hand so vigorously his leg almost came off.

At Fenway, scores of fans had gathered outside the park, some holding up placards with Josh's number 2 on them. Many wore black armbands. "Where were these guys when Josh was alive?" Jethroe wondered aloud. In spite of the chilly weather, in spite of the gloom and the mood, Boston was no competition for the full squad. The A's took two of three games and headed south, to Gotham.

Campy hadn't played since Josh's death, but he arrived in New York the evening before the series began. As the sun set that first night, he stole down the fire escape of his hotel, racing through the alley to the subway, hoping to avoid reporters and concerned teammates. One or two of the scribes from the big papers in New York had camped out by the garbage cans waiting for him—they chased after Campy, a rather easy feat, as the catcher's knees were rough and he could only waddle fast. Soon a crowd of reporters loped after him, following him into Harlem, desperate for stories about Josh.

Campy ducked into the Cathedral of St. John the Divine. He burst through the door just as the reporters scaled the steps. The first in their group reached to swing open the great wooden doors when a burly priest stepped in his way. "Get back!" he cried, shoving the reporter away. "Go away the lot of you! Leave this poor man alone."

"Hey, father, just comin' in for a quick prayer," the first reporter said.

"Quick prayer," he muttered. The priest began to roll up his sleeves. "I'll give you a quick prayer . . ." The reporters backed away, across the street, waiting for Campy like lions on the hunt.

Campy did not pray. He sat down and stared at the Virgin Mary and allowed the sweet, heavy silence to seep into him slowly, like stain into wood. He rubbed his hands and stared at the skin, admired his split fingernails, his calluses. They reminded him of Josh's hands. The priests were startled to hear a burst of laughter come from his direction. "Piss," he said quietly to himself, remembering Josh's elixir for keeping the calluses pliable. The laugh made Campy want to cry. But instead he genuflected, knelt, mumbled a quick prayer, and then stood up. He approached the pulpit and lit candles for Josh and Grace. Then he nodded his thanks at the priests and walked out the back way.

Outside, by the alley door, Campy stretched and shielded his eyes from the light of a streetlamp. Benson tossed a cigarette away and approached his friend.

Campy shook his head. "You follow me this whole way?"

"Wasn't hard."

Campy nodded at the canvas bag in Benson's left hand. "What are the baseballs for?"

"Watch." Benson pulled one from the bag, turned, and fired it square into the camera of a reporter hovering by the alley entrance. The guy stared in disbelief at the wreckage. Benson shrugged and turned to his friend. "Got me a date with a few lawyers, I'm afraid."

Campy nodded. "Yeah. But I want to be by myself a little bit, you understand?"

"Sorry. You're done with the solo gig, pal. I respect a man's privacy, but you go this long and you're catching a mental disease like old Cock. I'll walk with you. Hell, I'll walk *behind* you. Go where you want to go, Roy, but you ain't shakin' me."

Campy could see it was no use arguing. They wandered through the old neighborhoods with their weedy broken sidewalks, past the houses with the cracked windows and the foundation that made each place look like hitters leaning on their bats, past the decrepit neighborhoods and to an old empty lot, where a warehouse had burned down years ago and they'd cleared it. It was still full of bottles and broken glass and a tire or two. But there were also whole flocks of young kids beating the pill with sticks, squinting to catch the ball in the shine of streetlamps, diving in that treacherous gravel for grounders and line drives, tossing slop balls and shouting.

Campy leaned against a wall, arms crossed, watching. He said, "Josh used to come here. He used to play all day with these kids, until it was so dark you couldn't see the damn thing anymore." Then he gasped. "Gene . . ." he said.

Benson pulled out a flask. "Drink that," he said. Too tired to argue, Campy drank. The liquor was thick on his tongue and warmed his chest. "That's your blood, pal," Benson said, rubbing his friend's shoulders. "Now, we'll do this right." Lighting a pair of cigarettes, he placed one in Campy's mouth, and said, "Smoke that."

Campy smoked. After a few puffs, it woke his lungs. "Yeah," Benson said. "That's breath." He nodded to the kids. "And that's your soul, Roy. Grab a bat and go play." Staring for a moment at the game, Campy hesitated, then stepped up and asked to take a few cuts. The kids were glad to oblige. Benson watched, smoking. "Yeah, pal," he said to himself, "that's life right there."

They played until ten. When the game was over and the last kid went off to bed, the two friends ate burgers at a local greasy spoon. Around midnight, without speaking, Campy and Benson took the long way back to the hotel.

Next day Mack Filson strolled into Cochrane's office with Oscar Charleston. Mickey sat, hands in his lap, staring at the lineup card on the desk.

"Mr. Cochrane," Mack said, cheerfully. "We've been discussing it, and I don't believe that Hilt's unready for today. By that I mean he's fit as a fiddle. He's pitching dreams lately, strong as a bull, hey Oscar?"

"Mickey?" Oscar asked.

Cochrane looked up at them. His eyes were glassy. "I killed him," he said.

Oscar said, "Killed who, Chief?"

Cochrane looked away and mumbled, "Just like Gordon, I killed Josh. I killed them both, I killed them. . . ."

"Whoa, Mickey," Oscar said, running around the desk and beckoning Mack to do the same. "Say, listen, let's look at the scorecard, huh? What do you say, who's batting first?"

"Gone," Cochrane said. "Gone."

Twenty minutes later, Campy walked in, and at the sight of the crowds of nurses and attendants, he asked Gene, "What's going on?"

Benson whistled. "Looks like the skipper's lost it."

They didn't use the stretcher. His wife Mary was there; she walked out with Cochrane, his face ashen grey, his eyes staring into a faraway place, spittle on his lips. He was followed by two large men clad in white. Veeck stood at the doorway, tears in his eyes, clearing his throat over and over. As Cochrane passed Campy, he stopped, turned ever so slowly and said, "Forgive me, son, I just didn't know."

Afterward Sam followed Veeck into Cochrane's office. "Bill," he said, closing the door behind him, "when this hit him in Detroit, it was a good month before—"

"Yes," Veeck said, abruptly. "Call Oscar in here."

Every eye in the clubhouse was glued to the door of the manager's office, especially Wells's, who bit his lip in anticipation. Finally, all three men walked out, ashen-faced, nodding and mumbling their goodbyes. Oscar strode out, jiggling his hands behind his back, staring at his feet. Finally he noticed the team waiting on him, waiting for him to say something.

"Listen up," he said at last. "I'm guessing you know the bottom line. Mick's out, for some time I'm afraid, out from . . . well, he's out because he's . . ." Oscar pulled an unlit cigar stub from his pocket, shoved it in his mouth, and rolled it back and forth between his lips. He sighed. "Okay, you know what I'm talking about. So I'm in charge for a little while. So . . . that's all I have to say." With that, he retreated to the manager's office to make out the lineup.

Grinning, Wells approached the office door and knocked. "Yeah?" Oscar cried. Wells stepped in.

Oscar frowned. "Willie, I'm in the fucking worst mood I've been in since I first killed a man in the Philippines. Maybe worse, because I wasn't going to have to work in front of a stadium full a' people waitin' to laugh at my mistakes. So if you're lookin' to tell me how great this whole thing is, can it." Scratching away at the card, he said, "Get out in the field and throw. You're rusty."

Wells looked like he'd been slugged in the gut. He turned and walked away.

The five games against the Yankees brought five straight victories. The people of Philadelphia worked and sweated and would talk about the A's and how it looked like this year it was really going to happen. You wouldn't have thought it at first, but they were one hell of a ball club now. Walking through the crowded neighborhoods, past the identical brick homes whose porches stretched forever like images in a house of mirrors, a person would hear the sounds of baseball trickling out, of announcer By Saam's voice from a radio, and a shout of surprise. On the bus a pipefitter might bellow "Again!" and point to the article that showed how Dandridge's triple in the seventh pulled out another win.

But just as shocking to the baseball world was the fact that the St. Louis Browns were keeping pace. A race between the Athletics and anyone else would be surprising enough, but this was insane. The Browns had never been this close to a pennant—it was as if a unicorn had suddenly appeared, was discovered to have the ability to speak, and then began yammering away out the side of its mouth like Groucho Marx. The A's were one thing—this group of young and old Negroes from the Florida swamps who stumbled out of the gate and into the basement and then managed to put together the greatest August in baseball history, losing only one game, and still tearing up the league in September. But the Browns, in decades past, were worse than lousy, a team that never, not once in the last forty years, had scaled higher than second place in the standings, and hit that bridesmaid's position *only* once, twenty-two years earlier. But this summer, when the A's won, the Browns won. When the A's won two, the Browns won two. Then three, then four, then five. "Like a goddam tug a' war," the pipefitter grumbled. As the A's marched into the nation's capital, the Browns were still on top by a pair.

The pennant race had captured a nation desperate for distraction. In every movie house in the land there was action footage of Roy Campanella, Artie Wilson . . . and then shots of Buck Leonard, smiling and flashing the "V for victory" behind his rivet gun. It was three of four from Washington, and to no one's surprise anymore, the Browns stuck the Yanks for the same. Against the Indians, the A's continued their dominance, and Dihigo almost threw his fourth no-hitter there, a one-hit shutout with sixteen strikeouts. Veeck skipped the series in Cleveland and powered over to Philly, hammering out promotion after promotion for the World Series games. Red, white, and blue bunting now hung throughout the park, and little lights in the girders to look like the night sky. Series tickets went on sale, and

Veeck promised on the radio that the A's weren't going to get rid of the Wheel of Fortune. "Unless," he said, "we reach game seven, and then I guarantee you that Dihigo will play every position!"

St. Louis lost one game of their set against the lowly White Sox, which cut the lead to one.

Detroit proved troublesome and the A's split the series, two games apiece. In Black Bottom, Barnhill had to listen to the great debates boiling in Luke's front yard after the game, men and women entreating Barnhill to convince Wells to just "Choke up, man! Choke up!" as Lip put it. And when they heard the Browns taking two of three from the Red Sox, it sent the whole neighborhood into conniptions. Five left, two behind!

The Athletics arrived in Chicago early, around four o'clock, without a game to play until the next afternoon's doubleheader. At their hotel, Veeck did not climb into a suit. He ate a leisurely dinner of two steaks, a boiled potato with lots of salt, spinach, and two cups of strong black coffee spiked with chicory and a splash of Old Grand-Dad. He was in a jolly mood—two games out with five to play meant nothing to him, because his A's were going to take the next five. If he were a betting man, that's where his money would be. As he swallowed the last of his dinner, there was the usual phone call.

"What is it this time, Samuel?" Veeck said.

"This is Tom, Bill."

"*Mr. Spink!* To what or whom do I owe the pleasure?"

"Bill, the commissioner would like to speak with you this evening. How does seven o'clock sound?"

"Sounds awful. I have a number of social appointments," he said, thumbing one of his many books, "and won't be able to attend. I've got a question, though: do you get a stipend to be Landis's mouthpiece?"

"Bill, you had better be here tonight."

"I've heard that before."

"You paid opposing teams to throw baseball games."

Veeck was silent. "That's not funny even for you, Tom."

"Three no-hitters in Cleveland, Bill? Almost a fourth? The judge says he has evidence you threw those games. Paid the Indians. Paid Bradley."

Veeck took a deep breath. This whole season had been a war, sure, but to accuse him of throwing games . . . it violated his pact with the fan. He'd been accused of making a mockery of the sport, of starting riots, of insulting this hallowed tradition and that, and each time he could only laugh. Because the fan would know better, could make up his own mind. Call Veeck a traitor for integrating, for bringing Negroes into the sport at a delicate time, well, that had been rough, but eventually Joe Fan could see that these were great ballplayers. Call him an ingrate who ignored tradition with his bells and whistles and fireworks, and watch the fan cheer the new traditions and have fun besides. Tell his investors this guy was bad for the sport and they'd ask you how someone who packed houses could possibly hurt baseball. But to accuse him of throwing a game, anyone of throwing a game, called into question the very integrity of everything he did, and would stain his team worse than the 1919 Sox. It would ruin him, but worse, it would ruin the Athletics, and ruin integration. "Are you listening to yourself?" Veeck said, nearly pleading. "How could I . . ."

"The commissioner will explain at seven tonight." Spink hung up.

Veeck had never been so confused in all his life. Sweat broke off his forehead. Should he wear a tie? He didn't have a tie. He looked at his watch. An hour to go.

He picked up the phone and made a call.

"Hello?"

"Eleanor. It's Bill."

"The voice from the wilderness," she said. He waited. She took a deep breath. "Bill," she said. "Sorry. I'll be polite. Listen—I'm sorry about Josh. I remember when we drove to Kansas City to watch him and Satch. That was some game."

Veeck smiled at the thought. "It was, wasn't it? Josh certainly took a couple for a ride . . ." He sat up. "It's good to hear your voice."

"Whenever you say that, it means you're in trouble."

Veeck licked his lips. "I'm in trouble, El. Bad." He explained. Eleanor listened, then said, "So, Bill . . ."

"Yeah?"

"What are you going to do?"

He sighed. "What am I going to do . . .?"

"That's right."

"That's just it," he said, leaning back in his chair. "I don't have a clue. I think . . . I think this is it. Checkmate. Yeah, yeah, lawyers can help. The press could really help, but they'll only bury me. No one will touch this until a trial commences. And if that happens, well . . ."

"So, Bill," she said, a little firmer, "What are *you* going to do?"

"That's what I'm trying to tell you. There's nothing to be done. Nothing."

"So you're going to let your reputation go to seed. And Sam's. And, more important, your players. Buck and Roy and even Josh."

"El," he said, now irritable, "you don't get it. I'm fried. I fought Landis and I shouldn't have. He's got me in a place I can't fight from. Daddy was right . . ."

"Bill," she said, with a very audible sigh, "it's time for you to know that every once in a while your blessed daddy was wrong. And this is one of those cases." Veeck didn't answer. "Look. You've got the most exciting team that's come around since Babe Ruth was with the Yankees. People love them. I read that there are crowds of people camped outside your hotels."

"But, El, what if they found something from Mack's wire? Throwing games . . ."

"Did *you* throw games?"

"Never! You know me better than that."

"Right. And just because someone said you threw games doesn't make it so. Remember, they said Bill Veeck couldn't run a team in Milwaukee, right?"

"That's different—"

"And they said you couldn't run one in Philadelphia. When you were in last place they said this proved you weren't major league. Now that you're almost in first they're trying to peg something else on you. You didn't listen all those other times. Why now?" Nothing. "Bill?"

"Yeah?"

"Make him show you the evidence, and when he doesn't have it, go to the press. Lie to them if you have to. But don't go down without fighting. *That's* what your daddy would have done."

Veeck allowed himself a small laugh. "I suppose you're right."

"Why not call your friends in the press box and have them meet you outside the judge's office? A press conference right there in the street. Hit him right away."

Veeck was shocked. "That's a great idea."

"I have good ideas sometimes."

He could hear her smoking. She was probably lounging in bed, he thought. He wanted to ask her what she was wearing. "El?" he said.

"Yes, Bill?"

"Thanks. I owe you one."

"You owe me more than one. I have to go now. Pete's been acting up all afternoon. Let me know how it works out, okay?"

"Sure. Oh, El?" She'd hung up. He set the phone down, lit a cigarette, and watched the clouds stumble across the sky. They looked like baby elephants.

Standing on Michigan Avenue before the door that led up to the commissioner's office, Veeck paused, took his usual deep breath, and gathered himself. All the jokes and liquor in the world couldn't suppress the nervousness that always gripped him here. His palms started to dampen again. Inside, the secretary gave him the usual icy stare. He sat down and lit a cigarette, and waited.

Spink stepped out and greeted him. "Bill," he said, closing the door behind him.

Veeck looked at the secretary, then at Spink. "I'm having that curious feeling of déjà vu," he said.

"In case you're planning on calling your friends in the press, you should know that the commissioner won't be bullied, not on this issue. Not by Winchell, not by—"

"What about Hoover?" Veeck said. "Seemed to lead the judge around with a leash the last time he visited with my pitching coach."

Spink stiffened. "Hoover? If Mr. Landis was consulting with the Federal Bureau of Investigation, and he—"

"Very good, Tom," Veeck said, laughing. "Mouthpiece all the way. Well, I'll tell you, I have a right to see the rope they plan to hang me with. Since I never gamble, I'm curious as a cat how he plans to nail me for this one."

"You don't gamble, but you enjoy the company of gamblers."

"There's a big difference between that and throwing games. I enjoy the company of whomever I find interesting. If it's gamblers, so be it. Gamblers and rowdies and not a few bootleggers have helped Bill Veeck get to where he is today. Besides," he said, tapping Spink's lapel, "get rid of the gamblers and there goes half your readers."

"The commissioner and I don't see it that way."

"Are those Landis's eyes behind those goggles of yours?"

Before he could answer, the secretary asked the two men to enter. They bumped shoulders trying to walk in, and Spink graciously allowed Veeck to walk ahead of him. They approached Landis, who shook hands quickly and silently with Veeck, and sat.

"Mr. Veeck," the commissioner said, without a hint of friendliness, "how may I help you?"

Veeck couldn't help but chuckle. "You asked me here, remember? But since I get to talk, let me begin by saying that I would appreciate it if we all stop being so coy about everything. You know very well what I want. I want to see what evidence you think you have against me."

"Mr. Veeck, I don't have to show you anything. I am only alerting you to the fact that you are being investigated and are still banned from contact with your club."

"Until you give me proof, you'll have to have the army drag me out of baseball, Judge. I own this team. There's a contract that says as much, that also says I own the stadium, and no law in the land—save yours—could keep me out. I should've ignored you from the start."

"Quiet!" Landis said, banging his gavel. "You will be notified when I have made a decision regarding any measures to be taken against you or your club."

"Judge, you forget that in America a man is innocent until proven guilty."

"Not in baseball. The scoundrels who threw the World Series were all exonerated by a court of law. They never set foot on a diamond again thanks to my judgment. And no court would interfere."

"Since I haven't done anything, I'll get my day in court. And you *will* have to answer to someone."

"Mr. Veeck, I am a fair man. *You* are not a fair man. However, before you hear it in a press conference, beginning tomorrow, after my meeting with Alva Bradley, you will be barred from baseball for the rest of your life. Your team will be disgraced, and you will be disgraced."

Veeck turned red and squirmed. "I see."

"Furthermore, the Philadelphia Athletics have benefited from winning games unfairly. I don't think that other teams should be punished—"

"So you're going to cancel the whole season?"

"No. But the Athletics will not be allowed to participate in postseason play."

Both Veeck and Spink were taken aback by this statement. "You can't do that," Veeck said. "If my men take the flag, they have earned the right to play in the Series. So help me God, Judge, I will take you to the Supreme Court if I have to."

Landis did not look impressed. "Mr. Veeck," he said, "when you came into this office last April, you made it abundantly clear that you had no intention of respecting the Office of the Commissioner. For the past few weeks, you've been flouting my decisions. Let me tell you, Mr. Veeck, as soon as this office begins sorting through the evidence collected in Mr. Filson's wire, and as soon as we discover the truth behind this, you, your staff, and every one of the Athletics, the whole world will see why I made my decision."

Landis kept on. He admonished Veeck for every promotion, every spin of the wheel, every trinket and gag. Spink watched mutely, stunned. He opened his mouth slightly. Veeck began to shout at the commissioner, accusing him of being petty, shortsighted, a bad businessman, unpatriotic, racist. Landis banged his gavel once and shouted Veeck down. They both began to yell.

Spink said, "Commissioner, sir, you wiretapped a coach—?" But Landis and Veeck kept on shouting. Spink said, "Sir, you said, 'when you discover,' but you told me—" Only no one was listening to him. Veeck roared and Landis banged and roared right back, even threatened to call the police. Spink shut his mouth. He knew it was over. Veeck had the evidence he wanted—there was nothing. Nothing but the tapes from that pitching coach whose name Spink had already forgotten. But the FBI usually listened to the material as it came in, and they would have said something a long time ago. What was Alva Bradley going to say? Nothing. One witness, even if he did testify, he'd have to have a paper trail, anything. And he wouldn't. Spink could see that now. There wasn't any evidence because no one had done anything wrong but play some incredible baseball, and now they were going to pay for it. If the commissioner banned Veeck and the Athletics, that was all there was to it. Buck Leonard and his fifty-nine homers, his outrageous average. Gone. The Cuban and Satchel Paige and those magnificent duels. Gone. Spink's new favorite, Artie Wilson, he of the sharp liner and diving catches. Gone. Now and then, through the shouting, Spink would say, "Judge? Mr. Landis?" but he couldn't bring himself to raise his voice above the din.

Then, suddenly, it was over. Veeck turned to Spink and shouted, "And that goes for you too!" and stormed out. Spink watched Veeck go. He stood up. The commissioner wiped his brow and bent over a piece of legal pad and began scribbling. The silence was acute after the argument. Landis ripped a piece off the pad and began scribbling some more on another page. After a few lines, he tore off that sheet and held them both to Spink. "I've decided not to wait for Bradley's testimony. Here's my latest press release. See to it that it gets in the edition that comes out tomorrow and you will have an exclusive. Now if you'll excuse me, I have work to do."

Spink read the piece. There it was: Athletics banned. Veeck gone. Dailey gone. Bradley gone. Team to be returned to Connie Mack, its rightful owner. Alva Bradley and the Indians banned, including Lou Boudreau, permanently. In spite of this news, all Spink could think about was the National League, how the Cardinals had it wrapped up already, and his secret desire: Satch vs. Musial. The Cuban vs. Musial. Buck Leonard squaring off against . . .

"Mr. Spink," Landis said, with a definite note of impatience, "I have to ask your forgiveness in requesting your leave. I have a great deal of work to do."

Spink looked up and stared for a moment at the small man behind the desk. For the first time he noticed that Landis's teeth looked bad, rotten, as if his insides were unhealthy. Spink snapped out of his trance and walked out.

Veeck had emerged from the commissioner's office shaking with anger. Out on the sidewalk, the press corps was rabid for news. They could sense it was bad, smelled it like sharks detecting blood in the sea. The home front had not been kind to them, their stories nothing but patriotic tales of the men and women struggling at home, this political battle, FDR, and repeating the dispatches from the writers on the front who did little to hide their distaste for those not brave enough to work the trenches. Veeck was different—now their news was being fired across the oceans to hungry soldiers, eager to hear about the A's success, or their downfall.

Veeck growled at the press to wait a minute, let him compose himself before dropping the bomb. But, joy of joys, Dan Daniel had come to Chicago and was the first to ask a cockamamie question, shoving himself right in Veeck's face to do so. Unable to control himself, he decked Daniel. It had been coming to the writer for years, anyway, so when Veeck dropped him it was hard for most of the press to keep their cheers to themselves.

Problem was, the grapevine of Veeck's press conference had reached the fans as well. Alongside the reporters, crowds of people had also gathered to root on their favorite son, the kid of good ol' William Veeck Sr., who was doing his damnedest to let the common fellow have some fun and taking it on the chin from stiff-collars like Landis and Daniel and the rest of them bastards in the black-and-white trade. So when Veeck popped Daniel, a brawl exploded. Punches were thrown, jackets torn, a barstool—coming from who knows where—flew across the crowd, and the cops descended and began to haul away the combatants, one by one.

Low licked his lips. "You know," he said to Burley, the two of them standing in a doorway and watching the circus, "the real story's going to be in that holding cell that Veeck goes into."

Bradley grinned. "You're right. And I've always wanted to paste a cop. Let's go."

Low and Burley elbowed through the crowd and right up to a large policeman. "Hold it," the officer said, arms up. "Christ, you two, you couldn't be more obvious if you wore a sandwich board. Hop inside, I'll see to it you get the same cell. I got a family photo tomorrow, last thing I need's a black eye."

It looked like a party in the downtown city jail. Veeck's cell was filled with reporters who'd either tried to knock an officer down (missing in most cases, and taking a whack on the skull for their efforts) or, like Low and Burley, merely asked for the privilege. But there were some fans, some drunks, a shoplifter of ladies undergarments, and a fat kid who had slugged his recruiting officer for asking him about venereal disease in front of his mother. Veeck took time with them all, answering questions, pounding his fists like a populist reformer, climbing on his cot, vowing loudly never to quit.

When the clock struck five in the morning, Sam bailed Veeck out, leaving the rest behind. They hopped into a cab and shook the few reporters on their tails. Outside Comiskey Park they ate breakfast at an all-night diner and then walked the neighborhood as the sun rose. Veeck was supercharged, angry, grubby from his night in the slammer. "All I want to do today is sit in the bleachers and watch the ballgame," he said. "Fill out a scorecard, unbutton my shirt. The whole reason I got into baseball in the first place. I'm sick of all the fighting."

They walked for blocks in silence and decided to turn around and head back to the ballpark to watch batting practice. As they approached, fans would point at Veeck and Sam, nod and smile, raise a fist and yell, "You get 'em, Bill!"

Up in the bleachers, Veeck threw off his coat and unbuttoned his shirt down to the belly button. He loved Comiskey, with its crumbling concrete steps, weird angles, and great, eyelike windows that let the breeze in over the concourse and into the stands. It was hot and humid that day, a Chicago day, he liked to think, when the lake air came in fresh and mingled with the soup that passed for Chicago air, the exhaust and sweat of the city. As usual, the crowds began to gather around Veeck, asking for autographs. A kid who seemed made of elbows and knees pushed up and tugged on Veeck's shirt.

"Yes, son?"

"Mr. Veeck," he said, "would you sign this for me?"

"Sure kid." It was the *Chicago Tribune*, fresh from the newsstand. Veeck's picture was on the front page, along with a headline written by William Fay. "My God," Veeck said. He held out the paper and Sam's eyes bulged. There was the headline, calling for Landis's resignation in the face of fabricated evidence. J. G. Taylor Spink was not only the source but half the story as well. They both read the article while the kid fidgeted. Spink called on Congress. He told of the wire, wrote that he spent the night sorting through the best of the evidence that a friend of his on the FBI provided. There was nothing. Landis had lied. And his lies were a threat to any owner who wanted simply to run his team the best he could. Spink stated that Judge Landis was a threat to democracy, a despot, and that this would have been a *Sporting News* exclusive if it weren't so urgent. "Look at this," Veeck said, awed. "The guy is practically gushing. Begging Roosevelt to let Buck play in St. Louis. He even has Ruppert on record decrying the commissioner! That's a coup!" Veeck squinted at the press box clear across the diamond. "Come with me," he said, beaming. "I have to go give that guy a piece of my mind."

Veeck shoved the newly autographed paper back in the kid's arms and made his way through the crowds and to the press box. He pushed past the attendant and into the crowded little room, stuffed to the rafters with scribes. Smoke hung in the room. Veeck nodded and smiled at Daniel, now sporting a black eye, noticed Spink, and walked over.

"Tom," he said. "I came up here to thank you." Spink kept scratching away at his scorecard. "C'mon, Tom," he said. "Take a compliment. Even if it's from me."

Spink didn't look up. "Please leave me alone."

Veeck nodded and cleared his throat. "Okay, Tom. Let's go, Sam."

The A's seemed to respond to the news, trouncing the White Sox in both ends of the doubleheader. Later that evening, as the players loafed in the terminal bar before traveling south, the bartender rang a bell, climbed atop a stool, and announced that the Browns had beaten the Senators.

When they arrived in St. Louis the next morning, the crowds were thick and from every corner of the United States. *Stars and Stripes* had sent reporters to cable the news overseas. It took the team five hours to get out of the station, as every player had lined up to speak to radio announcers, the press, and their many thousands of fans.

That evening there was good news: Eleanor Roosevelt had managed to muscle in on the attention the two teams were generating. In conjunction with the draft board, she was seen signing a three-day leave for Buck Leonard, in the hope that he would break Babe Ruth's record in the last game of the season. Pictures of scowling Browns and a grinning first lady decorated the front page and sports sections, big bold lettering and angry commentary from the paper's editors ran beneath them.

After batting practice, Oscar spent an hour discussing strategy, going over the Browns lineup. "Willie," he said, "sharpen your spikes . . ."

"Sharpen my what?"

"You heard me. Sharpen them. Rocks in your glove. Get on any way you can, and when you do make them pay. But!" he paused for a second. "Only you, Willie. The rest of you, smile like you're waitin' on ol' massa. Mack—our fellows got hit how many times?"

He pulled out a sheaf of papers and yelled, "Nine out of ten so far!"

Oscar shook his head. "Nine times in ten games. And we ain't hit a one of them. But today . . . there's going to be pain." A happy murmuring came from the players. "Hold on, hold on! Here's the thing—the only fucker we crack is Vern Stephens."

"Vern Stephens?" Cool said. "He's nothing but a gentleman!"

"Damn right! And their best player! They love the guy. So, you tell every single one of them smug bastards who gets on, you tell 'em that for every pitch we take in the back, for every time we are hit in the brow with a weighted glove, for every mean glare, we'll tear into Mr. Stephens like he was Hitler sittin' by the road!" By now Oscar was shouting. "You go out there and take it to them! Now let's go!"

And so they began: Barnhill was masterful and dedicated his game-one victory to his uncle Hal, who was "rotting away for speaking his mind," as he explained to an eager press corps. Stephens got a ball in the back three times—once he was clocked on the crown of his head. The following day the heat was oppressive, as was the wind. A giant storm cell was chewing up Kansas and headed for eastern Missouri. Gusts of hot, damp air blew garbage and paper all over the field. Willie was a storm by himself, spiking the second baseman twice while the A's clunked Stephens three more times. It was amazing the guy could still stand. When it was over, they walked away with yet another win.

On October 1, 1944, on the 166th day of the season and after 153 games played with one remaining, the standings in the *St. Louis Globe-Democrat* read that the Browns and Athletics were tied for first.

The storm hit the city around midnight. It dropped the temperature twenty degrees, threatened tornadoes, rattled the old windowpanes, lashed against roofs, and sent lawn furniture tumbling end over end. The next morning it stopped raining, but St. Louis was drenched.

The outfield was slippery, the bases slick. After practice the A's watched the Browns take their cuts as the stands filled with people. The batboy climbed up on the bench and hung on the wall a new uniform of Josh's that Veeck had made for the occasion. The rest talked about Jack Kramer, the Browns pitcher, a strikeout artist whose curve, when thrown in between his fastballs, had managed to stymie them before.

Cool walked around the perimeter of the field, finally stopping in center field. He wanted to take a moment to record in his mind what was going on around him. As the men and women took their seats, he tried to imagine where they had come from. Just St. Louis? He remembered the people in Georgia waving as their train flew by, remembered the broadcasts in Chicago and New York and even the scratchy distant voices coming in from Nebraska and Kansas and Texas. All talking about the game. He waved to a little girl who displayed a pennant with his face painted on it—a homemade job, as Benson would say. Then he turned and ran back to the dugout.

Back in Philadelphia, an illness gripped the city, keeping scores of children and adults at home, a strange malady whose only cure was to soak up noise from the Silvertone radio. In Times Square, as on D day, thousands gathered to watch the news as it slid across the front of the Times Building. Lip's barbershop had the ham radio warmed up and tuned to St. Louis, and Lip was ready to lean out the window, ring a cowbell, and shout the score to the great crowds that gathered below.

Buck Leonard sat in the dugout listening to the broadcasters on the radio begin to address the game. As usual, Buck was signing a stack of photographs two inches thick and a pile of memorabilia—old balls, a hat, and many scraps of paper. And, as usual, he was surrounded by a pack of reporters, firing questions, taking photographs, shouting over one another. Buck smiled for the cameras as he opened his mail, which had arrived at the clubhouse in a pair of man-sized bags. He had paper cuts sliced across his fingers from all the letters.

Buck opened a letter. "Hold it up," one reporter demanded. "That's right, smile warmly at it, read it and smile, that's it, keep that smile!" Cameras whirred, flashbulbs popped. Buck stared down at the letter with a look of warmth and brotherhood. In block lettering it read:

BREAK THE BABE'S RECORD AND I'M GOING TO CUT YOUR WIFE'S BREASTS OFF, THEN HER HEAD, THEN BURN . . .

"Buck, you're losing the smile! Let's get this shot and then you can go!"

It was as if they knew this would bother him more than threats against himself. Stone-faced, Buck beckoned an officer over, asked again if he was certain his wife was being watched at all times, and received a curt nod for his concern.

A young corporal back from the war sung the National Anthem and followed this with "Dixie." Veeck stood at the anthem and even during "Dixie," staring at the boy, wondering. The kid was missing an arm. It seemed as if the war ate people, gobbled arms and legs and lives. When the kid finished, Veeck took a deep breath and applauded.

Then, as the Browns raced out to their positions, Pete Adelis—dressed in his kaiser helmet, a banjo across his back and a trumpet at his feet, his hands affixed with razor blades and a fresh chalkboard in front of him—stood and began to roar.

Wilson marched to the box, rolled his shoulders, and stared at the pitcher. The ump raised his fist and cried, "Play ball!" Artie stepped in. The game began.

Grinding his cleats into the wet dirt, Wilson took a couple of cuts with his bat and waited. Kramer glared at Artie and ignored the noise coming from behind home plate. He nodded at the first sign and sent a fastball inside, chin-high. Wilson hit the dirt, laughed, and stood up without brushing himself off. "Damn," he said to the catcher, "guess that's another beaner coming Stephens' way."

The catcher shouted "Time!" and stood. "That was a simple mistake! Why the hell don't you leave Vern alone!"

Oscar stood at the edge of the dugout, his left hand outstretched to keep the rest of his team on the bench—the last thing he needed was any of his players tossed for jumping into the fray—and waited to see if he needed to step in and separate his man from the catcher. He didn't—Wilson shut up and let the pitcher walk him with three more crazy pitches. Oscar's cigar rolled between his lips and his eyes darted about, surveying the game. There was blood on his cigar; he'd bitten his lip in concentration. When Willie Wells grounded into a double play, he almost bit the cigar in half. As he stood at the far end of the dugout, alone, waiting for the Browns to step to the plate, he wondered for a moment what Cochrane would have done. Then he cleared his throat and shouted at the opposing team.

By the fifth the fans were beside themselves with anxiety—shouting, drunk already, banging their seats, settling down only when the teams switched innings. A line of women by the A's dugout crossed their legs in unison for good luck to their Philly boys. Cops wandered the aisles, looks of malice chewing up their faces. And Pete Adelis carefully placed his metronome on the ledge behind home plate and blew a pennywhistle at the catcher, all the while squeezing out "Battle Hymn of the Republic" on his concertina.

Buck Leonard opened that inning to a volley of boos and a tidal wave of cheering. Those who hated him for daring to better the Babe tried to rattle him; they were shouted down by the many who wanted to see him knock in a pair. Again the nod came from the dugout: walk him. Furious, a hot dog vendor tossed a sausage into the Browns dugout. Buck was left stranded on base.

In Leavenworth Prison in Kansas, Dave's Uncle Hal had the news of the game reported to him by a friendly guard. "Last inning," the fellow said, reading off a slip of paper handed to him from the warden's office, "Stephens hit by pitch, sent to third on single. Two strikeouts by Paige and a groundout, 6 to 4, to end the inning. Six to four?"

"Shortstop to second base," Hal said. "Must've forced out the runner. That's good."

"Where's the lumber?" Oscar shouted in frustration after the A's failed to score, again, in the sixth. "Close this inning and come back with those bats burning! Kramer ain't but dog food!"

Satchel either acclimated himself to the humidity or the ball juiced itself up, for he struck out the side. His Whipsy-Dipsy-Do, Kentucky Charmer, Louisville Kamikaze, and Brand-Spanking-New-Son-of-a-Bitch-Bourbon-Lollipop, which was sort of a trailing fast-ball, were sizzling past every bewildered batsman. Kramer, for his part, wasn't doing anything but surviving on junk, striking out but one. But the A's sat on the bench, hands in their laps, watching in mute disbelief as dead grounders and weak flies popped off their normally supercharged bats and into the gloves of their rivals.

In the top of the eighth it began to drizzle. When the Browns' manager again signaled to walk Leonard, a hail of garbage rained onto the field. With that walk, everyone knew, Buck failed to qualify for the batting title. Adelis, jumping up and down on the Browns' dugout roof, cried "Coward!", farted and belched and spit a fountain of warm soda pop toward the Browns' bench. The game was halted for fifteen long minutes while order was restored and the field cleared of litter.

When it resumed, Campy stepped up and proceeded, on the third pitch, to drill a liner down the right-field line, sending Buck to third. Then Cool knocked a hard grounder to Stephens, who flipped it to Gutteridge, then to McQuinn at first for the double play. Meanwhile, Buck scooted home for the game's first run. With that the skies erupted in flame, and it sounded as if the stadium had been torn in half by lightning. The crowds, as if turned animal-like from the game and the electrical storm, nearly jumped onto the field for their excitement. When Dandridge walked and then Benson struck out to end the inning, the crowd seemed ready to burst onto the field to celebrate already.

Satchel didn't appreciate the rain. Game ought to be called, he thought, as he took the mound. Couldn't see to hit the thing, and the ball was slick and not to his liking. He wiped his brow, stepped on the rubber, and found that the noise kept him from announcing his pitches. So he fired his White-Bread—a simple fastball—at the first batter, Byrnes, who clocked it for a quick double.

Satch slapped his knee. He pouted and fumed as Dandridge tried to calm him. Paige stepped to the rubber, glared at Campy, and shook off the hesitation pitch. There was that tense stillness as he went into his windup. In came the Whippy Ball, a dancing fastball that should have risen just as it hit the front of the plate. It didn't—and Kreevich, a lousy-hitting centerfielder who seemed to be fuming with every at bat, blasted a line drive that caromed with a wet snap off Satchel's elbow. As the ball bounded down the third-base line, Byrnes raced for home. Dandridge finally gloved it and fired to Wells at second, but it was too late as Kreevich hustled in safe.

"Son of a bitch!" Satch howled to the gathering crowd. He was holding his arm and grimacing. "Don't just stand there! Put the fuckin' Maestro in!" he said.

No one liked what they saw: tie game, man on second, no outs, eighth inning, and the best pitcher in both leagues knocked out. But Dihigo ran in from his spot in right field, replaced by Sam Jethroe.

"That is it!" Cochrane yelled from behind his curtain at Bellevue. He almost dropped the receiver of the telephone. He had one of By Saam's assistants on the line, updating him from the broadcast booth at Sportsman's Park. A scorecard sat on Cochrane's lap. "Mary, Jethroe is just the man for us, a good hitter in tight situations. And Mr. Dihigo, well, he ought to shut these fellows down."

"Mr. Cochrane!" a nurse hissed as she ran in. "Please keep it down!"

Mary jumped up and shooed the nurse into the hallway to give him some privacy.

"Warming up," Cochrane whispered. "I tell you, the Cuban will shut them down. He will do it. I have faith in him. . . . " Cochrane sat for a minute, staring at his feet, lost in dreams of his son. How Gordon would have loved this season. Sitting up on his pillow,

Cochrane put the receiver against his chest to muffle the sound and stared out the window at the tops of the buildings of New York City. Would Gordon have thought differently of California if he'd seen me running this team? Maybe he wouldn't have been a pilot, maybe . . . For a moment he imagined himself in the dugout, pondering what he would have done differently if Gordon had been alive, given him strength. He gritted his teeth and closed his eyes. Finally he pulled the receiver back to his ear and listened quietly, staring at the white wall in front of him.

Dihigo struck out the first man he faced, then the Browns sent a pinch hitter in for Kramer. The Cuban walked around the mound, rolling his arm, squeezing the rosin bag, lost in thought. His arm ached. Diving for a ball in the fourth, he had felt a ping in the middle of his biceps that was troubling him now.

When he threw his fastball it had lost a good eight to ten miles per hour, and the batter, a young kid from Arkansas, sent it hanging deep into right field, over the head of the racing Sam Jethroe, and into the seats for a home run.

In Detroit a kid leaned out the upstairs window of Lip's and bellowed, "At the end of eight, 3-1, St. Louis!" The crowds of men and women around Lip's began to murmur, one or two gasped in surprise. A soldier yelled out, "Give 'em hell, you sons-of-bitches!"

"Lots of game left!" Oscar shouted, clapping. Rain had collected in dirty pools on the dugout floor and fell in long ropes from the roof.

By now it was coming down so hard you couldn't see anything outside the stadium, as if Sportsman's Park were now floating in a thunderhead high above the world. The ump, a sporting man who had the fever of high drama in his blood, would have called the game only if a tornado had touched down on the infield. He knew the world was listening. You don't call a game like that on account of rain. With every pitch the ball would send droplets spinning through the air like a whirlygig.

St. Louis brought in a new pitcher for the ninth, a hurler named Zoldak, a short, stocky player who had found a calling in wartime baseball. He was mediocre by any standard, but he'd pitched six good innings in tight games this season, and the manager wanted him in there. "The Coronary Kid," his teammates called him, for he couldn't pitch an inning without making the score close.

Sam Jethroe ran out to the box, as if by jogging he would some-how avoid getting wet. This Zoldak fellow didn't faze him: Jethroe hit a lousy curve for a solid single. But Jethroe was sharp. He rounded first as usual and, seeing the fielder jog in and the second baseman waiting casually for the routine play to finish, bolted to sec-ond before the Browns could do anything about it. He stood on the bag as the crowd sat momentarily stunned. The play brought the damp and irritable fans from their seats, brought the A's from their bench, fists up and cheering at the edge of the dugout.

Artie Wilson dug his spikes into the mud. Confident, he toyed with the Kid—as soon as he could see the little man ready to throw, Wilson would raise his hand and step out, take a few short cuts, and lean in so close it would appear as if a strike would club him right on the shoulder. Zoldak wiped his face, and Artie argued that he was doctoring the ball. The ump called for the ball, inspected it, wasting more time, bothering Zoldak's rhythm all the more. The ump tossed it back. Finally the first pitch came in: a ball in the dirt. Wilson re-peated the routine with every pitch. He worked the count full, fouled off a pitch, and watched ball four sail in. The Browns and their root-ers' collective jaws clenched and stomachs rolled. The Coronary Kid was back to working his particular brand of drama.

Willie Wells walked slowly, carefully, from the on-deck circle, carrying his hickory bat like a club. His uniform stuck to his back, and he ran a hand down the front of the bat, wiping away the water. Wells reached down for some mud to rough up the handle.

A fan yelled, "You're gonna send yourself back to Philly, nigger!"

Wells smiled at that. The fan tried to yell louder. Wells spit, took another deep breath, dug in, pulled his bat back, and waited. Zoldak threw a fastball right down the heart of the plate for strike one. One of Oscar's commandments: don't swing at the first pitch. Good idea, Wells told himself. Feeling overconfident, Zoldak shot the same pitch over the plate. Wells saw the pitch coming, big as a banana cream pie, and pounced on it.

The ball shot off his bat and right to the shortstop, who scooped it up in a fountain of mud and gravel and fired to second baseman Gutteridge, who stepped on the bag ahead of Artie and pivoted to throw. But Wilson didn't slide: he knew he was gone and leapt, spikes first, into the second baseman's thigh, collapsing his leg into the bag.

Gutteridge fell over clumsily, cut and bleeding, howling and trying to get up and maul Wilson. Wells stood on first, Jethroe at third, while the Browns screamed bloody murder and helped the new gimp off the field and onto the bench.

As Dihigo stepped in he surveyed the diamond, squinting against the driving rain. He crouched to shrink his strike zone and cocked his bat back. One out, two men on, a double play ends the season, a hit brings us that much closer. But the Cuban didn't give it a lick of thought, focusing his attention on the pitcher. Zoldak, for his part, had the situation heavy on his mind, and had completely, utterly forgot the book on Dihigo. Was he the guy who lit us up a couple of weeks ago in Philly? Christ, what had he done today? Inside, outside, where should I throw the damn ball? Zoldak couldn't remember, so he was overly cautious. Dihigo watched four awful pitches sail on by for a walk.

Despite the fact that virtually no one could keep score—as the scorecards had soaked to mush—every man, woman, child, every vendor, every sportswriter, every cop doing his best to watch the crowds and not the game, and particularly Bill Veeck and Sam Dailey drenched in the bleachers, knew the scene: the bases were loaded and Buck Leonard was up. He had three bats on his shoulder, tossed two to the side, and walked slowly to the plate.

Had Mother Nature understood the drama, there would have been a thunderclap, but the electricity didn't come on. Instead the wind picked up, shifting the currents of rain sideways, pelting the timid souls trying to see the game from the far concourse. The driving rain seemed to scratch at the eyes of the Browns, tensed for play. Water crawled up the noses and into the ears of the base runners. It trickled down the necks of the coaches and the umpires.

Buck waited while Zoldak turned to the dugout. The ump glared at the Browns' manager. The skipper was a gnarly man, angry, bent on finally dragging a pennant from this swampy game, a man who'd litter the base paths with land mines if he could stand the gore and get away with it. But he would also throw a pennant in the garbage if it meant keeping Buck Leonard, a man whom he loathed for being a Negro, from tying Ruth's record. Fully convinced that Buck would punish them, he stood at the edge of the dugout, baggy uniform soaked and hanging off him as if he were some bum in stolen clothes, nodded at Zoldak, and drew a finger across his chest. Zoldak, a mediocre pitcher right down to his bones, nonetheless spit into the downpour, and shook his head. It disgusted him too. But he would not cross his manager. So he nodded to the catcher who stood, arm out, and took four straight lobs as the crowd showered the field with trash, shouting furiously for Zoldak's head. With the walk, Leonard went to first, Jethroe came home, the others shifted, and the score was 3-2.

In the afternoons a generous square of white sunlight would move across Hal's cell at Leavenworth, a small gift that he took advantage of by shifting across the floor, book in hand, reading by natural light. But he hadn't noticed it move and vanish that day, and he couldn't help but realize that, as messages were relayed to him, with the delays the outcome had undoubtedly already occurred. No one told him it was raining. No one replicated the crowd noises or the wind or the crack of the bat, the smell of hot dogs that managed to ride the gusts now and then and fire the appetite of the fans who didn't dare move from their seats. But Hal sat, patiently, rocking back and forth on his cot by the bars of his cell, waiting. A guard walked over, rattled a cup on the bars, and, seeing Hal sit up eagerly, nodded and read from a slip of paper. He said, "Campanella strikes out. Bases remain full. Two outs. Bell at bat."

Cool Papa Bell stepped in. He twisted himself into position in the batter's box, gripping the bat tightly. He could hear a train rumbling in the distance, a hollow boxcar sound that at first he confused for thunder. Someone was still selling beer, a raincoat draped over the box of cups. Wells called time and stepped off base to tie his shoe. Adelis had found his concertina worthless in the damp and was blasting a charge on his trumpet. Cool drank it in. As his eye moved through the stands, he couldn't see a single empty seat. He leaned on his bat and smiled, almost imperceptibly. Then he closed his eyes. He laughed, just a slight chuckle, and stepped back in. Nodding to himself, he took a satisfying breath, turned to see Oscar furiously signaling, and waited for Zoldak's pitch.

The throw almost hit Cool in the head, spinning right out of Zoldak's slick palm. A sharp gasp popped from the crowd as Cool hadn't moved a muscle, hoping to get smacked and tie the thing.

"Holy fuck," the catcher said as he tossed the ball back. "I wished I'd had a Bromo right now. This guy's twisting my guts."

It was even worse when Zoldak fired another ball, this time in the dirt. The catcher looked over at the bench with an exasperated shrug, practically begging for a new pitcher. But the Browns' skipper leaned on the steps and spit into the rain.

Zoldak stuck out his tongue and tucked his shirt in deeper. He turned, sized up the runners, and threw a chest-high fastball.

The ump cried "Strike!"

"Ball three! Ball three!" Adelis yelled.

Zoldak's hands were caked with rosin. He wondered if he could doctor the ball up a bit with this white mud, toss it in with a good, sharp drop. Walking back to the top of the mound, he looked impressed with this idea, and shook off the curve. A fastball with all this goop would surely drop.

It didn't. Cool powered the ball down the left-field line, where the wind sent it bouncing foul into the stands. Zoldak looked pale. A grand slam would have shut the door on the season, that was for sure. But with two strikes, he thought, I can waste a lousy curve on this guy, and then lob my change-up.

Zoldak nodded at the first offering from his catcher, checked only Buck at first, pivoted and threw.

The curve barely dropped and Cool, bat cocked like he was going to swing for the depths, squared off and bunted perfectly down the line. Wells caught Oscar's signal and bolted for home as the pitch came in. Browns third baseman Mark Christman, normally a weak fielder, ran in as Willie bolted for home. Christman tried to barehand the slippery ball.

"Go!" Adelis roared, and the crowds roared with him.

Cochrane shouted the same, over and over as it was being replayed to him, and he was so excited he pulled the telephone onto the floor with a loud clatter.

Wells dived like a broken swan, slapping the tip of home plate. Christman threw the ball across the diamond and over the crouched Zoldak. Cool lunged and hit the bag a split second before the ball smacked the outstretched glove of McQuinn. Cool twisted and fell onto the foul line and skidded amidst a cloud of chalk and water.

The ump pointed to the bag, raised his fist and cried, "Out!"

McQuinn held his glove aloft and raced to the mound. The crowds shouted with glee and poured onto the field. Every possible scrap of paper was hurled from the upper decks like an avalanche, mixing with the rain to make an unholy mess. The Browns fell on one another in a great leaping pile in the center of the diamond. Reporters ran and slipped and shoved their way through the mass while cameras popped on the field as quick as lightning. Oscar tore out to first base, shouting and screaming and pushing the ump, Buck Leonard doing the same behind him, two giants trying to squeeze justice from him. Veeck and Sam stood and watched from the bleachers, soaked to the bone, ignoring the taunts of the fans around them. Without speaking, without looking around or acknowledging the fans trying to wave and say something, anything, the rest of the Philadelphia Athletics turned, heads down, and walked back to the locker room.

Monte Irvin sat by a radio in the barracks in London, where the game was being broadcast through a radio brought in by one of his superiors. All he could hear was the static of the fans and the broadcaster shouting, "What a game! What a game!" He was surrounded by men in uniform, men in their fatigues, each one quiet, some teary-eyed, all stunned, staring ahead and trying to come to grips with what they just heard. Monte just listened. He wished he had a ball to hold. Then he stood and, ignoring the concerned looks of the men around him, smiled wanly and said, "Some season."

In the hallway between the dugout and locker room, Oscar kept the reporters at bay, answering questions as best he could. Inside, Jethroe was bawling in front of his locker. Campy sat, half naked, and stared at his dirty, split fingernails. Cool mumbled to Dandridge, "I wished I could see it. I only heard it and I sounded safe, like I beat the throw." Buck showered and dressed, his mouth thin and short, and took a long time to adjust his tie. Wells took shots from a flask he refused to share with anyone else. The batboy didn't want to cry, wanted to look like he was a man like the rest of them, but his chest burned, and there was no one he wanted more than his mother. Artie went over and over every game in his mind, the one-run matches they could have won, all the times when he'd failed. He peeled at the tape on his hands, ripping his calluses, immersed in the pain. Benson plopped down next to Campy and offered his friend what would have been a victory cigar. He nodded; they smoked in silence. Martín Dihigo sat with his hand clamped over his open mouth, unmoving. Satch had carried Josh's uniform in with him. He tossed it in his locker, collapsed in his chair, and frowned bitterly.

Oscar stepped into the locker room backward, pushing out the swarm of reporters eager to shove cameras in the faces of his players. He shut the door behind him, making a sudden silence. Red-eyed, he started to speak but instead kicked a bucket with such force it sailed across the room and clattered into a corner. Mack Filson sucked on a cigarette and stared at the curling smoke, wondering if God had punished the team for his transgressions.

Red Hourly walked in from taking a piss, looked around the room, and said loudly, "Well, boys, there's always next year."

Gone

December. The kid woke at five, in pure darkness, the sunlight a mere morning promise behind the sky. Skipping out of his apartment and down to the curb, he paused to jump in place and stay warm, trying to make rings with his breath. After delivering the papers, he took the long way home, five blocks out of his way to Twenty-first Street, simply to run his hand along Shibe's right-field wall. As he slowed his walk to soak in the memories of the ballpark, he saw an old Packard idling across the street. A man stepped down off the brick front porch of one of the homes, struggling with a large box. The kid jumped behind the lightpole. He recognized the man right away—Bill Veeck. His pop was right: Veeck walks like anyone else, you couldn't tell he's missing a leg. Veeck fumbled with the heavy box as he tried to open the trunk, and for a moment the kid wondered if he should help, but he didn't want to insult a cripple, you should never do that, he thought. He watched as Veeck dumped the box into the trunk, leaned back against the car and caught his breath. Veeck didn't notice the kid, probably didn't notice much of anything.

But the kid kept staring—this was like seeing the Wizard of Oz, the man behind the curtain. Earlier in the season, the kid had waited outside the park, on Twenty-first, to catch one of Buck Leonard's towering home runs, and one of his pals elbowed him and, sure enough, he turned around to see Mr. Veeck watching the contest from the roof of his apartment, shouting into a walkie-talkie. The A's were his team and Shibe was his park, yet the commissioner banned him from his own place, tried every lousy trick in the book to ruin Veeck. Which, his pop said, the judge did—ruin him, that is. After all, Veeck had to sell the damn club, pardon his French. And when Landis died a couple of weeks ago, you'd think they would let him keep the A's, but no—a contract's a contract, the miser Connie Mack's in charge and the A's were gonna stink all over again. Besides, the kid's pop said that no one in baseball wanted a guy like Veeck around anyway.

The kid had clipped all the photos from the previous spring, the shots of Veeck standing with the Athletics. "The finest aggregate of Negro talent in the history of baseball!" the headlines read. He cut out the picture, the official team photo. There, surrounding Veeck, were Satchel Paige and Josh Gibson, Buck Leonard, Cool Papa Bell, and a host of young guys that white folks hadn't heard of, All-Stars in the Negro Leagues just one year before. Now look at 'em. Connie Mack sold half the players as soon as he had his claws back on the team, Buck and Ray D. to Brooklyn, Cool and Barnhill to the Giants (and his pop said it was all on account of Barnhill's mouth—the guy wouldn't shut up about Port Chicago, every day in the press!). Willie Wells retired to Texas and Mickey Cochrane to his farm in Ohio. Some of the players were working in liquor stores and haberdashers in the off-season; Campy helped his father sell vegetables. And Satchel was in the headlines every day, having signed a one-year contract with the White Sox. This after telling Connie Mack that the old fellow could essentially go to hell, old Satch was going to play for whoever paid the most, and that was the stinkin' Sox. It had seemed like the A's would be the only American League club without any Negroes. "But we're here now," his pop said. "Armed forces too. If we didn't have this season, would any of these guys have made it to other clubs?"

Watching Veeck almost made the kid forget it was December. Leaning against the same wall that used to throb with heat and energy in July, the kid watched as Veeck pulled a baseball from his jacket and admired it. They came that close, the kid thought, inches from the flag. *Everyone* talked about Veeck and the A's: his father called him a hero, but their neighbor spit in disgust and said Veeck was a dirty Communist. Later everyone would know that J. Edgar Hoover put spies in the bleachers, tapped the phones, and built a file so big three people wrote books from that source alone. The *Sporting News* accused Veeck of grandstanding, of making a mockery of the sport, bringing in lousy players, clowns they called them, but then the *News* suddenly rallied around them, named Buck Leonard the Most Valuable Player of the Year, Dihigo the Most Valuable

Pitcher. But they didn't support Veeck when he had to sell. The kid remembered his pop shouting at their neighbor, defending Veeck when the Philly papers claimed he started a race riot, said he was responsible for the transit strike that brought the city to its knees, and even argued that he might have brought on the court-martials in the Port Chicago incident.

And now he's leaving, the kid thought. Someone ought to say goodbye, ought to give him a parade like he gave us. The kid wanted to shout hello or thanks or can I have your autograph. Instead he just watched as Veeck lit a cigarette, climbed in the Packard, and closed the door. As the engine roared to life, Veeck scratched at the frost on the windshield inside the car. From down the block, a car backfired and the kid turned with a start. When he looked back, Veeck was gone.

The sun was coming up and the streetlights began to pop off. With the wind howling, the kid's eyes burned and watered. He turned his collar up to the cold, shoved his hands deep into his pockets, and walked home, taking his time. As he made his way down the street, he noticed one of Veeck's old banners, snapping in the cold wind. It was frayed but still a brilliant yellow and blue, with a picture of Martín Dihigo that asked, "Where will he play next?"

When you write a book of any kind, you quickly discover that it is not a solitary endeavor. It remains a source of profound amazement to me the number of people willing to usher this work along. Thanks to Josh Kendall, one of the earliest champions of the novel, who read the first chapter and offered his help. Josh steered me to my agent, Paul Bresnick, who took a chance on *The End of Baseball* and has navigated it through the stormy seas of publishing. Ivan Dee also recognized its potential, and I am grateful and honored to have a home with the distinguished writers under his wing. My friend Jeff Hess, whom I met at a writing conference in Hawaii, was one of the first to read the text, and made useful suggestions as did Pam Rosengard, another early reader. Barbara Burgess's sharp eye also helped me make this book so much better.

A number of fellow writers came to my aid. Jonathan Eig not only read the novel early on but was a rooter. Without his intervention, *The End of Baseball* might never have been published. Brad Snyder, Paul Dickson, Arnold Hano, Peter Golenbock, Jim Bouton, Lester Rodney, and Tim Wendel all read early manuscripts and offered advice. Brad Zellar, the greatest writer you've never heard of, read the book when it was still a pup.

My family and friends have never doubted that someday I'd have this novel published. Without their love and support, constant and unconditional, I would not have gone anywhere with this. They were all helpful: Mom, Dad, Jim, Dick and Jean, my brother John, Andy and Sherrod, John and Karin, Kristin and Heidi, Ally, Mike Haeg for his wonderful camera, and my pals at the St. Louis Park

Home Depot, where I put in seven years in order to pay the mortgage while working on this novel.

Finally, *The End of Baseball* is for my wife Janice, who has never rolled her eyes once at all my batty ideas, and the three women who helped nurture my love for the sport: my mother, Aunt Mary, and Grandmother Schilling. *The End of Baseball* is also respectfully dedicated to the men and women who inspired it, especially Bill Veeck and Josh Gibson.

A NOTE ON THE AUTHOR

Peter Schilling Jr. edits the online *Mudville Magazine* and has written about baseball in a variety of newspapers and magazines. He grew up in Michigan and now lives in St. Louis Park, Minnesota. *The End of Baseball* is his first novel.